ALSO BY ANDREW ELGIN

The Harmony Series

Finding Harmony, Novelette prequel

Songs Of Harmony, Book 1

Seeds Of Harmony, Book 2

AMBASSADORS OF HARMONY

A HARMONY NOVEL

ANDREW ELGIN

Cover by: Zoran Petrovic/on Fiverr as Visual Arts

Sixth Sense Books

150 Buck Run E

Dahlonega, GA 30533

Email address: andrewelginauthor@gmail.com

CONTENTS

PROLOGUE

Haven and Harmony: two planets circling the same sun. Neither were anywhere near a center of human civilization, even using astronomical measurements. They were far from any trade route when they were first, accidentally, discovered. They were essentially unknown and unnoticed in an unexplored, minor part of the galaxy.

A vast ship, a colony class ship, immense in size and aspiration, carrying everything needed to jump-start life on a new planet, had malfunctioned. Traveling at immense speed, its target planet long since lost, its systems saving the colonists for as long as possible until certain life-threatening parameters were breached, it finally tumbled out of the blackness into this isolated system. With nothing familiar in the skies or the stars to greet them, the colonists awoke to a new destination, a different system. Their observations and measurements at first confused them before they finally accepted that fate had decided they should live here, not be dead and desiccated, traveling without end in the vastness beyond. They blessed the luck they had had which had brought them to this system when they could so easily have come awake in emptiness and lived briefly in despair, dying one by one, alone.

They chose the inner of the two available planets. It was rich with everything they would need from the very start. The outer planet, with no easy accessible metals, was further out, traveling on a slower path than Haven. The choice was obvious. As was the name.

Seen from the edge of the system, Haven seemed to hurtle, where its sister glided. Yet, to the grateful, lucky, new inhabitants, the seasons seemed normal. All that they missed was a moon to light their nights. But they could live, were living, without one.

It was only after they had forged the beginnings of a fresh, world-spanning civilization that some, still amazed at the fate which had carried them to this system, wondered whether they had made the right choice. They wondered if they should be taming the planet, digging into it, carving it and sculpting it to meet their dreams and desires. It seemed, they said, to be disrespectful to their savior. Perhaps the other planet would have been the right choice. No metals would have meant a closer relationship with the planet. After all, they had left a planet behind them gouged deep and drained of everything it had to offer. It was why they had left. Did they have to repeat that here? It seemed this was a chance to live differently.

And so some of the people, looking for a new way of living; a way which seemed to have been offered them, took a ship to the outer, slower planet with its beckoning moon and named it what they dreamed of: Harmony.

But their new home was not easy, nor welcoming. There were trials which tested the resolve of them all. Some were found wanting and, sadly acknowledging their weakness, said farewell to their dream and traveled back to Haven. They left their companions and set off on the ship they had arrived in, determined to at least hold high their heads at having attempted to follow their dream. But they did not live to proclaim their pride. Not one survived the return journey. The cause was never established. Apart from the bodies, there were some samples of plants and some recorded stories of strange things that had been witnessed or perhaps experienced, tales which made little sense and soon became myth. The name of Harmony became a fable of a place where people lost their rational abilities or sank into something only slightly above a stone age. It was no longer a place to dream of.

The relatively small band left behind on Harmony, now completely isolated, took up the struggle to survive, as well as to understand the planet they now called home. They strove to listen to it, to become close to it in a way they could never have considered on Haven. And, slowly, very slowly at first, they spread and they learned. They learned of the planet, but they also learned of themselves, and the knowledge they gained brought them new understanding and began to change them in subtle ways that, because they were gradual, became accepted as normal. To them, Haven became a memory of a distant place of belching smoke and blinkered ignorance where people confused progress with wisdom.

As they grew slowly in different, yet still human, ways on Harmony, so those on Haven grew in the same way humanity always had done. Industry and government, education and politics, exploration and invention became more intricate and less personal and always expanding. And all around them, in the moonless night sky, the unknown stars shone and teased them with the need to find their own kind. But to do that required immense efforts, driving leadership and constant investment of energy and inspiration to a common goal. Whenever those elements existed at the same time, they were never harnessed effectively or for any length of time. And most of the time they did not coexist.

The original colony ship had been gutted, re-shaped as the basis of factories and mines and machinery, as it had been designed to do. Some small ships were used to dismantle and transfer the colony ship to the planet's surface, piece by piece. Those tiny offspring themselves broke down eventually. But, before the last of them disappeared, a new one was built. Better design. Better engines. But there was nothing for it to do. It served only one purpose; to provide a tangible connection with the stars in the night sky. When that began to fail, another was built. And then another when the second was failing. But none of them could travel into the endless space beyond the system. They represented the deep desire to find the rest of humankind, even if it could not, yet, be accomplished. The ships were the communal response to a shared dream.

Despite having the ability, there was hardly any contact made between Haven and Harmony, because Haven felt there was no need. No metals meant no progress to those on Haven. Harmony had been a failed experiment early in Haven's history. It was a planet for the curious only.

Not for anyone who wished for the stars. Once in every several generations, a ship had been sent, but there was no real purpose to it beyond the technicality of the voyage itself. After such fleeting visits, tales were told of a strange affliction, a curse whereby nobody could leave Harmony alive if they stayed too long, or ate any of the food or drank the water. Those on Harmony came to resent such contacts, seeing them as unwanted invasions of their privacy and as intimidatory displays. Whatever commonality might have existed eroded over time until those on Harmony believed Haven an unspecified but potent threat to their way of life, and those on Haven believed Harmony to be both uncivilized and stagnant in ambition. Not that that stopped them from using Harmony to exile the very occasional high profile 'irritant', when a visible, but expensive, 'mercy' was politically valuable. Plus, it was technically useful for testing new ship designs. In living memory, an armada had been sent to Harmony; supposedly to establish a base for deep space exploration. But it had failed in strange and unexplainable circumstances.

So the two planets, carrying the same human seeds at different rates around the same sun, nurtured and grew them in different mediums to have different aspirations. Harmony passed slowly and gently through the same seasons that Haven, by comparison, slid through with a seemingly headlong rush.

And there were the beginnings of a new idea germinating in the system. Nobody could say what started it or where it originated, but it had the potential to become larger. Whether it would grow into something worthwhile, something viable, remained to be seen. But the next stage of its progress was already unwinding. In only a few of Harmony's years, Haven was now beginning to nurture the new song she was hearing. How strong would it sound in time?

And the sun, as always, remained in the center, pulling the planets along. The children following their parent.

1

The unusual sound of raised voices nearby caught Myrella's attention. She put down the tedious report on projected harvests and tried to catch what was happening. There seemed to be some sort of argument going on in the outer office and then, suddenly, the doors to her office were flung open and there stood Mannert, her secretary, with a stunned look on his face. Pushing past him was an excited looking young man, who had obviously been running, as he was still panting hard.

"What is going on here?" she demanded. "Why all the excitement?"

Before she could speak further, the young man burst out, "We've been found!"

His obvious excitement along with Mannert's amazement meant that those words had a deeper meaning than was at first obvious to Myrella.

"What do you mean? Who has found us? Explain yourself."

The man was now standing directly in front of her desk. He had a look almost of ecstasy as he drew himself up, gave a small bow and in a more formal voice marred slightly by his attempts to control his breathing, said, "Madam President, it is my honor to report to you that we have been contacted from a deep-space ship which has recently arrived at the edge of our solar system, and that the occupants of that ship are human." Then his excitement broke through again and he exclaimed, "We're no longer alone! We've been found. There are others like us out there!"

Myrella felt a numbness, which another part of her mind translated as shock. "When did this happen? How do you know about it? Where are they?" The questions tumbled from her without her seeming to have anything to do with them. This moment was everything everyone had ever hoped for since the very first settlers had landed and looked at a sky they did not recognize on a planet they did not know.

"The message was received a few hours ago now," the man explained, still beaming in an almost inane fashion, his eyes wide and bright.

"I'm sorry," asked Myrella. "I don't know your name." She wanted a moment more to allow this news to become real.

"Brokka, Madam President," he said, bobbing his head as he did so but not losing the smile. "Assistant chief of the observatory. I was attending a conference here in Pannedon when I received the message --"

"Where's the chief?" she interrupted.

Brokka reined himself in a little, assuming something approaching a serious expression. "Essarin. His name's Essarin, ma'am. He was on vacation. But he has been notified and asked me to relay the news for him. He is hurrying back here but thought you should know first." Again the formality broke and he gave that huge, face-splitting grin again. "Isn't it the most wonderful thing ever to have happened? We can finally be with our own kind again!"

Mannert, normally the personification of self-restraint and gravitas, had by now given up any pretense of formality as well, sinking down into an armchair and shaking his head in disbelief.

Myrella was going to indicate a seat for Brokka, but realized she was shaking and clasped her hands together instead as she tried to control herself and inclined her head instead. "Please, Brokka, sit down and tell us what you know."

He perched on the very edge of the seat, leaning forward in his excitement. "It was early this morning. Very early." He paused a moment as he tried to gather his thoughts. "Are you aware of the sort of work we do, Madam President?"

"Looking at stars or something like that, I presume?"

"Actually that's only a very small part of what we do. Mostly we look at computer images and compare them. That's when we're not actively researching or... ." He caught the look on Myrella's face and hurried on. "The point is, what we found was that there was a swift moving point of light that hadn't been there several days before. We did some maths and realized it was small and close, relatively speaking. So we turned some other telescopes toward it and found it was transmitting signals. At first, we didn't hear very much, but then... well, what it boils down to is we heard them! They must have been hearing us from the first moment they entered our system and they have probably been broadcasting ever since. They were saying who they were and that they wanted to hear from anyone who could hear them."

"What did you do?"

"Nothing, Madam President. I called Essarin as soon as we knew. He said to tell you first and that we shouldn't do anything without your say so. That's why I came here so quickly."

Myrella sat back in her chair for a moment, her mind racing as she stared blankly at the ceiling. The shaking had stopped when she finally said, "Who else knows of this?"

"Only the two other astronomers who were there."

"And where are they now?"

Brokka shook his head. "I don't know. Gone home I assume."

Myrella snorted in exasperation. "Brilliant! So everyone's going to know far sooner than we'd like. That means we have to get organized here and quickly. We have to be in control of this." This was what she was used to; making decisions. And what she was used to made her feel less out of control. She snapped fingers at Mannert. "Wake up, man, and take some notes. We have so much to do. This is going to be a day to remember for certain."

Myrella had been blessed with clear, smooth skin which seemed wrinkle-free, meaning it was easier for her to appear younger than she looked. Not that she had spent much time worrying about appearing youthful. Her jaw-length hair had some grey strands at the temples but was straight and easy to maintain. She had a very direct gaze, with clear, brown eyes and her straight nose above thin lips meant that the first impression she made was invariably one of determination and focus with little time for irrelevance. She didn't mind people thinking that of her, as long as she could relax in private, laugh and generally let the weight of the day fall from her. But this news, she knew, was not going to give her much time to relax in the days ahead.

The next few hours were a frantic blur. There was an emergency session ordered where every representative was informed of the news. Along with that there were the press releases to prepare at the same time as various roles and tasks were assigned. That was the start of much discussion which occasionally became heated, especially when the content of the message which was to be sent in answer was discussed. Then there were all the arrangements to be made to welcome the newcomers. There was some confusion at first about this until Brokka informed them that it would take a long while to arrive from the edge of the system.

"They have to decelerate, lose a lot of speed as well as maneuver. Best guess would be about 30 to 40 days before they are here. That's assuming that they have technology we can understand. It could be very different, but we will be tracking them during that time, so there's no need to worry. The delay between our sending and their receiving will, of course, decrease as they approach."

"Looks like you'll have all the time you need," said Myrella to the small group assembled in her office. "Let's not panic over this, but go at it steadily. We want everything to be right when they arrive."

Corrivan was, despite Myrella's misgivings, actually helpful and contributed several intelligent suggestions. She wondered what he was up to and what advantage he thought he would gain from cooperating with her. Later, when all the tasks had been decided upon and allocated, everyone else had left and all that remained was to try to assimilate it everything, Myrella found herself and Corrivan alone together in her office. It felt good to have it almost to herself again. The wood-lined walls gave it a sense of formality and hinted at purpose and power enhanced by the carefully tended parkland visible through the windows. Inside there were, apart from her large desk and chair, two smaller desks, one of which could double as a table for informal meals, three sofas and several armchairs. Additionally there were two cabinets facing each other on opposite walls. With the soft carpet on the floor, it was, above all, a comfortable and accommodating space where she could work and think as well as relax when necessary. With the windows opaqued as they were now, it could feel secluded and very private. Right now, Corrivan was seated in one of the large and comfortable chairs near the wall furthest from her desk.

"A truly wonderful day," he said, with apparent sincerity.

"A busy one, certainly." She decided, just this once, to give him the benefit of the doubt. She went to one of the cabinets and poured two large drinks. "Momentous, for us all. To mark it, have a drink with me," she said, offering him one as she sat in the chair opposite.

He accepted with a slight inclination of his head. Normally, his sour expression seemed condescending to Myrella, but now, he looked merely tired. He cradled the drink in his long, thin fingers and there was a silence which, if not companionable, was lacking in the usual hostility.

"What do you think will happen because of this?" Corrivan asked finally. "I know others have asked the same thing, but, between the two of us, what do you really think will happen?"

Myrella squeezed her eyes shut and pinched the bridge of her nose, trying to lose the headache she could feel building. She felt tired and didn't want to have to think of what was going on outside. She was also reappraising her attitude toward Corrivan, who had been a long-time political thorn in her side. Why was he taking this cozy 'you and I' attitude now? It made her think more carefully before answering. "I don't know." She opened her eyes. "I suppose that everyone will go mad with excitement for a while, but I doubt that anyone is going to stay as excited right up until they land here. But beyond that? Who knows? We're assuming they're human like us, but what if they aren't?"

"Then how would they know our language?"

She shrugged. "It's just a thought, that's all." She picked up her drink and took a sip. "What do you think is going to happen?"

He looked directly at her. "I think this will see the end of the Revivalists. That's what I think."

She held his gaze for a moment, looking into his disturbingly pale blue eyes, trying to decide whether this was the time to get into a fight. It was the same agenda he was always bringing up. Was it worth countering him now? She decided against it, despite a deep desire. "Not that again, Corrivan. I don't see why you are so opposed to those people. And don't give me your usual speech about duty and progress and the like. Frankly, I'm too tired to listen to it. There's that rather large tree in the debating chamber to remind us that we cannot ignore the planet. I think the Revivalists are one of the reasons that tree is there. So, despite what you or I might think or want, that particular notion of yours is not up for discussion right now."

He merely gave the slightest shrug as if to say 'If that's the way you want it'.

"That aside for the moment, what else do you think will happen?" Myrella took another sip.

He finished his drink in one long gulp, put the glass down and laced his fingers over his stomach. Myrella wanted to slap the smug look off his face. Instead she waited.

"Quite obviously there will be significant technology available. That was pointed out earlier. Trading will take place, there will be some sort of diplomatic presence: those are to be expected. But having the universe opened to us will create entirely new tensions and factions within the people as a whole. What will happen because of that is hard to say, but there will be those opposed to the intervention of an outside power. Whether you want to label them Revivalists or not, it's going to happen. And, those in favor of these new explorers... well, they are going to be pushing for more and more of whatever they have to offer." He spread his hands. "That's just human nature, I'm afraid."

"And what if we are considered so -- what's a good word? -- backward," said Myrella, "that we are treated not as equals but as inferiors, not as trading partners but as a resource to be used up? Then what? I'll tell you," she said before he could intervene. "It will be a most difficult time indeed, more difficult than your assessment suggests. Dreams and hopes will be slowly whittled away to nothing. Everything will be hugely unsettling. In fact that's what's going to be happening whatever the end result is."

Corrivan nodded. "And that, of course, my dear woman," -- Myrella's jaw tightened -- "is why there must be a very strong leader at the head of a united group who will be ready to enforce law and order as necessary." He smiled, although Myrella thought it looked more like a sneer.

"And you, my dear Corrivan, are so in touch with what the workers want." Oh, yes, she could sink a dagger as well. He came from a factory worker's family. That, of itself, was nothing to be ashamed of. But he always preened as if he was some sort of nobility and never admitted his lowly beginnings. She hated those who were not true to themselves. And disregarding his roots, pretending they were not as they were, made him reprehensible in her eyes. She took pleasure in the barb, even as she reprimanded herself for doing it. "You would be President, I assume?"

He made a self-effacing gesture. "That's not for me to say, of course. But I do wonder why you and I are sitting here. Talking. It's not like you at all."

"Because, as a leader, as President," she let the word linger between them, "I have a duty to speak with everyone. Even those I disagree with. And, as you are one of the leading opponents of this government, I felt it right to see what your thoughts on the day's news would be. I had hoped to be surprised, but am not overly dismayed to find I wasn't."

"I thought, perhaps, we could be speaking of some sort of alliance, you and I," he said. "In light of the civil disorder which we both acknowledge will occur, it would make much sense."

Myrella allowed herself a genuine smile. "I think the word 'alliance' would be incorrect for what you had in mind. Until or unless there is a wish for a change, or a new government is put in place with a mandate to change this executive role I now occupy, I believe I will choose to stay on as President. After all, I am the first woman President in the history of our world. It would be such a shame if I were to step aside before my work was finished, wouldn't it?"

Corrivan's face was expressionless. "I wish you well, in that case Madam President. I have duties of my own to see to. If you'll excuse me?" He rose, gave a curt nod in her direction and left, the rigidity of his back reflecting the anger he was suppressing.

Myrella watched him leave, grateful for the heavy door which made slamming it an impossibility. She gulped the rest of her drink, swallowing her anger with it. "You can come in now, Mannert."

Her secretary opened the door, obviously having stationed himself nearby when he saw Corrivan leaving . "I did not think you would mind my overhearing. It seemed... prudent. I did hear most of it, and from what I heard I don't think there's anything new there, Madam President. He's going to make trouble out of this in some fashion. But that was always going to happen, wasn't it?"

In answer, Myrella poured another drink for herself and one for Mannert, indicating he should sit down in the chair lately occupied by Corrivan. "The only disappointing thing about it was that he couldn't be bothered to hide his intentions." She took a sip. "This day will go down in history, Mannert. It will probably be a holiday of some kind in the future. How many hundreds of years have we been on this planet? And we always wished that we weren't alone. But being alone, being apart from our own kind for that amount of time, that has to have changed us in some way. Maybe it's changed us so that it's not going to be such a celebration as we thought. Maybe we've changed enough so that we don't really want to have that connection any more. Perhaps we are so used to being alone that anything else just wouldn't feel right. Perhaps we'll resist it as an intrusion." She made a gesture of frustration. "I don't know what's going to happen. Not in the details anyway. But one thing's for certain, there's great change going to happen because of it. We're never going back to how were were, even yesterday. And all Corrivan can think of is stirring up trouble." She shook her head, more in sorrow than anything else. "Some people are beyond belief." She tapped a finger against her glass as she thought about the day's events. "Well, Mannert, that's what this tired woman thinks about it. What do you think? The people on this ship: what are they like? What will they do? What do you think's going to happen?"

Mannert looked at her with sympathetic eyes. He had been her secretary for many years, suffering the ups and downs of political life with her. Despite that, he was sitting upright in the chair, as if he could not really relax with her. His hands were clasped around the glass as if protecting it. "Whoever they are, they have the same basis as us, coming from the same stock, so to speak. We share, at some level, a common heritage. They are people just as we are. So, at their most basic I believe they are like us. Better technology of course, but essentially like us."

Myrella gazed blankly at the ceiling, wishing irrationally that it was all over and everything settled. "I'm afraid you're right. Very afraid."

2

It was a moist morning; damp air and dark, sweet-scented earth with tatters of clouds overhead running away before a cool breeze. The community of Bellwater lay behind them in the folds of the hills. The smoke from the hearths there drifted in the breeze, as did the sounds of the cows and sheep. The two people paused to look back before settling their packs and striding off into the countryside.

After walking most of the morning with the sun's warmth becoming stronger, they breasted a rise and saw on the path beneath them two other travelers coming their way. The woman, Carmeena, shaded her eyes as she studied them. Then she and the girl with her, Hanna, both closed their eyes and tilted their heads as if listening to something very faint. When they opened them, there were huge smiles on their faces. "Come on, Hanna! Let's go meet them!" And off they ran.

The two travelers toiling upwards had also stopped and were looking intently toward the two figures running toward them. After a moment, they both called out and waved excitedly until all four were together.

"This is a wonderful surprise," said Carmeena, grinning as she hugged the man. She stepped back to take a more critical look at him. "Farran, you look good. A little less weight, but that's no bad thing. Fit! You look very fit. Traveling obviously suits you well. And Endel? You have grown. So much! It's lovely to meet you both again. It's been so long."

Farran smiled gently and shook his head, but didn't let go of Carmeena's hand. "Endel and I here were heading this way to whatever the next community is." His voice was as deep and slow as Hanna remembered it. "There are only so many of them. We were bound to meet up with you or some of the others in time." His lined face rearranged itself into a smile.

"Have you heard news of any of the others?" asked Hanna, eyes sparkling as she smiled at Endel. He had been the first to work with her when they were both much younger and she had still been lacking in self-confidence about her new abilities as well as the strange new markings, called ribbons, they had recently acquired. She had not forgotten him. Not one bit. "You're the first we've seen since we left Newgrange, although we've felt them before, haven't we, Carmeena?"

"Yes, we have. But before we start swapping tales, let's find a place to sit and eat. One thing I've learned in my wanderings is that there's always time to relax and always time to eat and talk. And now you don't have to go where we've just come from. So that gives us more time together. And we have some fresh cheese, fresh bread, and some fruit courtesy of the village back there."

A little way off to one side there was a small stream trickling down the slope, splashing in small pools and over moss-covered rocks. Leaving the path, they made themselves comfortable by the side of the water, opened their packs and shared what they had.

"So who have you heard or felt lately?" asked Carmeena after a moment or two.

Farran thought a moment. He had definitely lost some weight, Hanna thought, but he still carried the impression of being a large man, and there was still some sadness in his eyes. The clothes he wore, like all of them, were simple, plain and functional, weary-looking from the traveling. "Isselta and Pol were together somewhere to the west of us. At least, they were the last time we listened for their songs. Not close enough to meet though."

Endel added, "And Pelle and Allegara are a long way distant. Much further away than Pol. I only heard them once a long time ago. I think

15

that's true of Bodren and Dennet. Knowing them, they'll be somewhere near a lot of water." He smiled and it looked natural now, and made Hanna feel warm. It also made her realize how much she had missed seeing him.

When Hanna first knew him, he had hardly ever smiled or spoken after arriving in her community alone, looking half-starved. He had probably been about her age, although no-one knew for sure. Whatever he had witnessed had isolated him from any friendship at first. With the help of Javin and Meldren, he, along with all the other wounded people, had begun to recover until he was able to speak without prompting and even begun to smile. In the years since she had last seen him he had grown into what she could only describe as handsome. His brown hair was longer and hanging loose. His eyes, also brown, but darker, finally looked as though they could see something other than pain in the past. There was genuine warmth in them as he grinned at her. As for the strange tattoo-like pattern under his skin, the same thing as she had on her cheek, it wasn't what caught her eye. She was reminded of what Javin had said about the sprites that Carmeena and Farran and the others from Harmony wore around their necks and how he didn't even notice it on Meldren. He had assured Hanna that it would be the same about the tattoo-like markings, or ribbons as they had called them. She realized, as she looked at Endel, Javin had been correct. She could see only Endel.

Carmeena smiled at the mention of Dennet and Bodren. "Bodren really did love looking at the ocean when we were on Harmony, didn't he?"

"How was it in the place you have just come from?" asked Farran. "Were you able to help many there develop talents?" The talents he was referring to were things like people moving objects with their minds, healing or applying heat with the hands, seeing the history of an object held in the hand, and many more. The four of them, together with the others they had been talking about, had been traveling around Haven for several years now, seeking out the small, Revivalist communities to try to teach the members what they could about the possibilities they had dormant in them as human beings. Everyone could do something that wasn't purely physical. But not everyone had a real talent. That was what they were seeking: people who could allow that unacknowledged place in their minds to be open enough to see things differently. Revivalists had turned their backs on technology and sought to live quiet and peaceful lives in small communities, working on the land. They were visiting such communities because, firstly, they were more likely to be welcomed there than anywhere else, and also because the people in those communities were already living more closely to the earth and were consequently more open to understanding and allowing such talents to happen. And, the more people who could do such things, the greater the chances that they would become close enough to the planet to be able to hear the songs; for the songs were the foundation of everything. To know the songs was to know the truth of everything. This truth wasn't something you were told. It was something you experienced.

Carmeena brushed her hands clean. "I suppose it's the same for you. We arrived in Bellwater -- that's the name of the place back there -- and did what we normally do; help out with the work in return for some food and shelter. You know, cleaning out stables, picking weeds, chopping wood. All the usual stuff." Farran and Endel both nodded at the familiarity of what she was saying. "Because we're new, they want to listen to what we can tell them. So we talk about other places and the things that we've seen people do. Find water, heal some simple cuts, move things around without touching them."

Endel laughed, "And, of course, they want to know if you can do any of those things."

"Absolutely," continued Carmeena, smiling. "So we show them some things and that gets them interested and the next thing, everybody wants to try. There's some new talents back there now. One girl was really good at healing, and a boy was showing some progress for moving things around. He could certainly do with your help, Farran."

"Oh, I think Endel's as good or better than me now. But do you think or feel that any of them were able to listen to Haven?"

"Maybe. Give it time. Who knows but one day one of them might wake up with ribbons on them?"

Haven, the planet, created everything in and on it using songs. Only some people were able to hear them and fewer still were able to hear them well enough to attempt to sing them for themselves. Those that could were able to create all manner of things; sing water to the surface, sing food when hungry, sing clothes, sing tools. Anything within reason and which Haven herself did not object to. Actually, they could only create them with the help of the ribbons which marked the faces of Endel and Hanna, or with the the sprites, the snake-like creatures coiled snugly around the necks of Carmeena and Farran. Sprites originated from Haven's sister planet, Harmony, which is where Carmeena and Farran were from originally.

"I haven't really listened to Haven for a while," admitted Hanna. "I mean, not <u>really</u> listened, just heard enough to do what needed doing." She felt a vague sense of guilt when she admitted that, as if she had been remiss in some way.

"I suppose that's true for us all," said Farran.

"Yes, but maybe we should be listening," Hanna continued. "After all, this is the first time we've met up with anyone from Newgrange. Doesn't that seem like something unusual?" Newgrange was the community where Hanna and Endel had grown up and which had been almost completely destroyed in one of many such raids on similar places. The government then had wanted to stop the drain of people leaving towns and cities and factories and had tried to intimidate or destroy those communities. Hanna and the others had rescued Newgrange, arriving after the attack, turning it from a desolate ruin with a few dispirited survivors back into a healthy and productive farming community.

"Maybe," said Endel. "Maybe we've met up for a reason? Is that what you're saying?"

"Yes. Perhaps we should be listening for something; a reason or a message or something like that." Hanna shrugged. "I can't believe that this is just an accident. Doesn't it feel like something more than that? I mean, I'm happy we're here together, but behind that happiness, isn't there something else going on?" Although she hadn't been aware of what she had been thinking, as with most things, when she spoke out loud, she could hear the truth in her words.

They closed their eyes and sank into sensing what was happening around them and within them. After a while they each opened their eyes again, but with thoughtful looks.

"I think you're right, Hanna," said Carmeena. "We've been lazy. There is a feeling of... I don't know how to describe it --,"

"Being pushed," interrupted Farran. "That's how it feels to me. Something big and pushy."

"Well, it would be big, wouldn't it?" said Endel, grinning. "It's a planet, after all. But, yes, I get that as well."

"Pushed to do what though?" asked Hanna. She had sensed something similar; an awareness that she wasn't in the right place and that she should be somewhere else. It didn't feel comfortable being here now, and she knew that the feeling would grow.

"I'm not so sure that it's about what to do, I get more that it's where to go," said Endel, confirming what she felt. That shared sense made her smile.

Carmeena pointed off to one side. "If it's anywhere, it's in that direction for me." The others agreed. "But," she continued, "what is in that direction? Does anyone know? Or how far in that direction we have to go?"

Farran thought a moment. "I'm trying to put together the bits and pieces we've heard from people. The only thing I can think of is that Pannedon, the capital, is that way. At least, that's what I think, unless I'm turned around."

"You're not the only one, Farran," said Endel, pointing at Hanna. "The ribbons don't move without a reason, do they?"

The three of them looked at Hanna's face. She was used to such scrutiny by now, and she, in turn stared at Endel's face. What she saw on his face was presumably the same as what they were seeing on hers. The ribbons, those strange tattoo-like markings, were sliding to rearrange themselves into a new pattern. Normally, they rested as a whorl on one cheek. But now, they were forming a circle between the eyebrows, and in the middle of the circle, a smaller one. Both shapes were moving; the outer one clockwise and the inner one counter-clockwise. As the circles were forming, so the sprites of Carmeena and Farran stretched outwards a little and uttered a low, throbbing note.

"Well, if that doesn't tell us something," said Hanna,"we're all stupid. We should get going," and she began to re-pack her satchel. The others did the same. Soon they were up and ready.

"I hope we don't have to actually get inside Pannedon," said Carmeena, with a shiver. "I don't like big cities. I prefer the countryside. I can breathe here."

"Have you been into any large towns or cities since you've been here?" asked Farran.

"Not into one, but close enough to know I don't like them."

"I guess we're going to find out then, aren't we?" said Hanna. She was about to start when Endel caught her by the hand and stood beside her. His touch felt wonderful to her, and she grinned and squeezed his hand. She looked at him, smiling, and said, "I'm looking forward to this journey."

Behind her, Carmeena nudged Farran and they shared a smile. "Let's find out what's in store for us, shall we?" she said. And off they set.

3

"Perhaps it would have been better not to have moved the stool away just as he was about to sit down." The speaker was a young, slim woman with long, light-brown hair, green eyes and an easy, wide smile. She was addressing her traveling companion, a younger girl with dirty blonde hair and a serious look to her grey eyes who was shaking her head in disagreement.

"I admit, it wasn't the cleverest thing to do. But... ," and here she paused as if savoring the memory, "it was worth it for the look on his face."

The elder of the two, Isselta, grinned in agreement. "I suppose he did deserve something like that. How many times did you say you didn't want to marry him?"

"More than enough. I'm not old enough to be anyone's wife and when I am, I still won't want to be. I think he was creepy and strange. He couldn't take his eyes off my ribbons." The girl, Pol, touched the tattoo-like pattern on her cheek as she spoke. "Seriously strange, he was. It was like he didn't want me, but my ribbons." She shuddered at the memory.

"Perhaps he thought that if he married you, you'd be able to make things for him, create things."

Pol snorted and adjusted her satchel to a more comfortable position.

The two marched on in silence through the countryside following a barely visible track pointing toward distant hills.

"Pol," said Isselta, "do you really never want to marry?"

"No." The response was swift and sure. "If I married someone, then I'd have to stay in one place, or at least not travel much. I want to see everything there is to see and do what I want, when I want."

Isselta nodded in understanding. "But," she added, "Javin and Meldren get to do all that and they are... well, there isn't the same sort of thing as being married on Harmony as there is here. But they're pretty much what you would call married. So, it can happen, is what I'm saying."

Javin and Meldren had taught others how to listen to the songs which made up the world. It was because of them that Isselta and Pol, as well as all the other gifted people, were traveling around helping others to realize what they were truly capable of. In a way, they were like missionaries, spreading the word and trying to change how people lived. They'd been doing this for years now since Javin and Meldren had returned to Harmony and Newgrange had finally become a viable community again.

"Maybe," said Pol, wrinkling her nose in thought. "But those two are rare, aren't they?"

"Doesn't mean it can't happen," countered Isselta.

They continued on, the only sounds around them were of birds and small, hidden creatures. The sun was warm and the stand of trees just ahead was inviting.

"Let's rest here for a while," said Isselta. "Maybe there's some herbs we can harvest for some trade at the next place."

"Wherever that is," said Pol, sliding down to rest against a tree trunk.

"Well, wherever it is, I hope it has cats in it." Isselta's face softened at the thought. "They are so cute and cuddly. They are completely adorable. I can't believe we don't have them on Harmony." Isselta, unlike Pol, had been born on Haven's sister planet but had chosen to stay on Haven. "Like starting a new life," was how she had put it. She had no intention of ever returning, not to face the memories of her father again and how she had, in self-defense, killed him. She was happy here.

"Cats sleep a lot," said Pol, trying to get comfortable.

"But, they're still cute, even asleep." Isselta was not about leave her daydream of cats. "I wish we had some with us."

Pol giggled. "You really don't know much about them, do you? Have you ever seen anyone traveling with one cat, let alone several? You won't. Because they do what they want when they want. I like the idea as well. But that's all it is. Just an idea. We had a few at Newgrange that I remember but they worked for their living, catching pests. I wouldn't want to travel with one though. Trust me on this one, Izzy," she said.

"Where are we going next?" asked Pol after a pause. "And is it far? I like sleeping under a roof. I've got used to it."

"Well, we could still be sleeping under one if it wasn't for your vanishing stool trick."

"Not my fault! He was creepy and deserved it. Plus, I think we'd helped anyone there who was going to have a talent. It was time to move on anyway."

Isselta gave a small start, then gazed off into the distance, a frown on her face. "Pol... "

"I felt it, too. Something just happened, didn't it?"

Isselta pointed. "Something that way. But what? Any ideas?"

Pol shook her head before slumping down a little more and closing her eyes. Isselta did the same, trying to find the source of what had just happened. It had felt, to Isselta at least, as though something had gently poked her in the head with strong, stubby fingers. There was nothing audible, but it had felt as though someone or something had been trying to say something.

As she shut out the immediate sounds around her and let silence fill her, she felt drawn to one direction and turned her head toward it, eyes still shut. As she did so, she felt a stronger tug, an urgency almost. Then she tried to feel what was behind that urgency. The only sense she could gain from tuning in to it was that there was a job or a task or some activity which was associated with that area. In other words, there was something she had to do.

She opened her eyes, squinting against the light and cocked her head at Pol in a wordless question.

Pol looked thoughtful. "Well, we know which way we should be traveling, at least. And there's something that we have to do when we get to wherever it is." She grimaced. "I remember the last time we got that feeling. We traveled from Harmony to here and that's when it all started." The 'all' she referred to was after they had learned how to listen to songs and what they could do on Harmony, they came back to Newgrange to find it in ruins. From then on, they had used their talents every day to help it regrow. And after that, they had set out to travel to as many other similar communities as possible to help others learn from them.

"It's the same thing I felt," agreed Isselta. "And I can't say I'm ecstatic about the feeling of having a job to do. I was quite happy wandering around from place to place." She stroked the sprite around her neck. "I don't suppose there's any point in not going, is there?"

Pol shook her head. "Not a chance. If we don't go, something else will happen and we'll end up where we're meant to be, kicking and screaming if necessary. But we'll end up there somehow." She looked around, as if seeing where they were for the first time. "It's a nice place here. Why not have something to eat while we think about it all?"

"Good idea." Isselta started to rummage in her satchel. "Wherever we end up," she said, putting some fruit on the ground in front of her, "I hope there are plenty of cats."

4

M eldren sat with her arms wrapped around her knees, hiding her head and trying not to laugh. She was perched on a rock above a clear pool of water fed by a stream coming from higher up in the hills. She and Javin, the object of her laughter, had found it by accident as they were traveling through the land in no particular hurry to get anywhere. They had decided to leave their previous home, the island known as The Sleeper, and travel wherever they wanted. They had lived on the island originally because being around people was simply too uncomfortable for them. Then they discovered that they could control how they were affected, so, after training others to do what they could do -- listen to the songs around them -- they had decided to leave. The idea was to see what they could see and enjoy the freedom to go wherever and whenever they wanted, after having had so much of their lives taken over by helping Harmony, the planet with whom they found they could communicate.

Right now, however, Javin was not enjoying himself. One of the benefits of leaving their island home, he thought, was that he would not have to go on a boat again. He had always hated being taken to the mainland and back again. The sailor, Amleek, had been excellent and his boat well constructed. But Javin had never taken to it and had spent each journey in misery, waiting only to jump off at the end. He had voiced all of that to Meldren.

In return, she had said, "But you shouldn't have to fear the water, Javin."

"It's not that I fear it," he had replied, his pride somewhat dented by the accusation. "It's having so much of it and it moving in strange ways when I'm on it in a boat."

Meldren had nodded and that had appeared to be the end of it. Until this pool had showed up. They had been traveling following half-hidden game trails through a countryside made up of rocky outcrops amidst smooth hills covered in small stands of bushy, tree-like plants. They had been drawn to the sound of water and had looked down on this bowl-shaped pool of clear water. Upon seeing it, Meldren had exclaimed, "Perfect! This will be perfect for you, Javin."

"In what way?"

"You can conquer your fear of water once and for all."

"But," he had argued, "there's not enough room for a boat and I'm no good at making one, or singing one."

Meldren had looked at him with a mischievous twinkle in her eyes. "It's not about floating on it. It's about swimming in it, being at ease in it."

Javin had looked at her with astonishment. "Me? Swim? Here?"

"If I did not know you better, my sweet man, I would say that you cannot swim. Can you?"

And that was how he had ended up in a clear, ice-cold, rock-lined pool of water, just too deep to stand up in and just too wide to push off from one side and reach the other in one or two strokes. He assumed he had entered the water to show he was not afraid. But the memory wasn't clear at the moment, as he was very busy trying not to swallow water.

"You're doing so much better," Meldren said, failing to hide her amusement at his predicament. He was splashing wildly a bare arm's length from the edge and making very little headway. "A little less arm-splashing and a little more useful leg-kicking. You're really getting the hang of it."

Somehow he made it to the side and gulped in air gratefully, shivering. "I think I am freezing to death in here. And I also think I've made my point that it's not the water I'm afraid of, thank you very much." He pushed his hair back and hauled himself out. "And I have to say that you, Meldren, normally the love of my life, were of absolutely no help whatsoever and also took far too much enjoyment in my suffering." He pulled his clothes on, waited briefly for his sprite to slide up his arm from the ground and resume its place around his neck, and then clambered up to sit beside her on the sun-warmed rock and let that and the sunshine ease his sense of wounded pride.

"I mean, you could have held out a branch or something for me to grab on to, couldn't you?"

Meldren, still smiling broadly, shook her head. "Oh, no. That would have been too dangerous."

"Dangerous? How?"

"I might have fallen in myself."

A silence extended itself between them. Finally, Javin said, "You can't swim either, can you?"

"True. I can't."

"But you said --,"

"--Absolutely nothing at all. It was all in your head. And I'm not the one with the problem of being in a boat." She leaned in and kissed him. "Besides, you should be grateful I care enough about you to teach you these things."

They sat close together gazing at the pond.

"It is fun, though, isn't it, doing this traveling?" he said at last. "We've seen a lot, and mostly it's been enjoyable."

"I don't think I could ever go back to living in one place for a long time," agreed Meldren. "I've completely forgotten about how we felt when Harmony was getting us to do things. How we used to moan!" She shook her head and smiled at the memory.

"Here's to never having that problem again," said Javin and he stretched himself on the rock enjoying the warmth it gave off.

Meldren stretched out beside him. "Now that's a brave statement to make, if ever I heard one."

"Oh, surely we're safe now? We've been left alone for so long, there's no chance that Harmony is going to ask anything more of us." He smiled. "It's all been done long since and all those people we left on Haven, they're the ones who are going to be called on and pushed and pulled. Not us. I'm certain of it."

The sun slowly sank and they finally left the rock to go back to the nearest stand of vegetation on the slope above them, where they had left their few possessions.

"I know we said not to," began Javin, "but I am really hungry and, just this once, I'm going to sing up some food. Something that is not dried fruit, dried meat, old bread or stale cheese. I'd like a change for once. What do you say?"

Meldren smiled. "Why not? It's been such a long time since we have sung any food or found any fruit to pick. Remember that time when we were by that lake? Damp, soggy ground, no shelter, no clean water." She shivered at the memory. "We didn't sing then, so I say we're owed a good meal."

Javin rubbed his hands in anticipation. "Excellent! What shall we eat today?"

Meldren closed her eyes as she thought. Opening them, she said, "Something warm. Something we used to eat when we lived on The Sleeper, or something we ate in Littlehaven. Something with memories of those places. Because they are good memories."

"For me, that would be something with fish," said Javin. "But you used to cook that, so you should be the one who sings it to make sure it turns out right." He made a quick gesture with his hand, touching his chest and forehead, greeting and respect combined, before ending with a flourish in Meldren's direction. "It's all yours, my love. But don't forget to sing something to eat them with!"

"Remember what I told that young boy, Endel, when he asked about doing everything with song?" asked Meldren. "I said that it was important to be able to do things yourself, without help. And look at what we're doing now." She smiled and shook her head in gentle self-recrimination. "Fine guides we are."

Javin grinned. "But as long as he's not here, I'm not going to tell on you. Now, get to it, because I'm hungry." He settled himself and watched as Meldren closed her eyes. She was silent a moment before nodding gently to herself as if to say, '*yes, that's it, that's the sound I need to hear*', and then she began to sing. It was no ordinary song, not any ordinary rhythm or sound, but something which seemed to twist the air in front of her into vague translucent shapes which coiled and moved, gaining substance as they did so. Her sprite added its own voice to hers, deepening it, adding a subtle complexity to it which her human voice could not have done. What he was watching was the result of both of them knowing that everything in the world was created from sounds and songs, and that by singing in the right way, making the right sounds, it was possible to create what you could hear. For that was the gift they had been given by Harmony, the planet. It was a rare gift and one they had shared with those few others which Harmony had brought to them and who were now on Her sister planet, Haven.

Slowly the shapes became more certain, less blurred, and an inviting scent wafted his way. The song came to a conclusion and there, on the ground between them, were two clay platters filled with steaming hot, fragrant fish with vegetables and some bone forks and spoons to eat with.

He breathed in appreciatively and nodded his thanks as Meldren opened her eyes. "You're right. This does take me back to Orland's place. He fed us well and taught you cooking. Good choice!" And he picked up the utensils and attacked the food, making small, happy noises between bites.

Soon, the platters were emptied and they sat in companionable silence watching the moon rising for a while before lighting a fire. For this they always used a song, as it was the most reliable and quickest method. Generally, however, they sang only when they really needed to, preferring to live as normally as possible as they satisfied their wanderlust.

Tonight, they appreciated the warmth of the fire and fed it occasionally with sticks they had gathered earlier on their arrival. It was always a quiet, contemplative time for them both, and they enjoyed seeing shapes in the flames and the smoke, talking quietly about where they had been, what they had seen, and where they would be heading before eventually falling asleep.

But this night, as they watched the flames, they became aware that the smoke wasn't drifting up and away, but seemed to be gathering and remaining in one place. As they watched it, so their sprites began to hum a bass note, startling them and making them look to each other. The smoke continued to thicken around the fire, hovering above head height. As it did so, their sprites hummed louder.

There, above them, a shape was forming, made of smoke. It finally resolved itself into a face. It was of a woman, smiling. The shoulder-length hair was moving as if in a breeze and a lazy, wide smile appeared. The face seemed familiar but neither could give it a name. Then the smoke flowed and made a different face, a male face this time. Again, it seemed vaguely familiar, but, again, neither could name it. A broad brow, quite serious-looking. It, too, faded back into the smoke much more quickly, and the smoke seemed more agitated, as if it were being stirred vigorously by unseen hands. It took a moment before another face formed. This time, the face was younger and this time there was instant recognition.

"That's Pol!" exclaimed Meldren. "Nobody else can look as serious and as happy at the same time."

"But who were the others?" asked Javin.

As he spoke, Pol's face morphed to become older but still definitely Pol. Then the first face appeared again, and it too morphed. But instead of aging, it became younger.

"Isselta! That's Isselta," said Meldren. "The first face must be how she looks now."

"Well, in that case," said Javin, "the other one must be Endel. He always had that serious look." As if in response, the other face appeared and became younger, proving Javin right.

Then, in swift succession, all the others they had taught and who were now on Haven appeared in the smoke before them. Timoss, Perray, Carmeena, Hanna, Farran, Dennet, Bodren, Enrick, Allegara and Pelle. They all appeared one by one in the smoke.

"But why are we being shown them?" asked Meldren. "Are they in trouble?"

"I think we're about to find out," Javin replied quietly.

Abruptly the smoke vanished and the sprites stopped their humming, leaving only the small, crackling sounds of the fire. There was still tension in the air and Javin and Meldren held their breath, waiting for it to ease. Finally a breeze flicked the flames higher for a moment and, as they died back down, so the two of them heard the word 'Soon', as if whispered in their ears. As the breeze departed, it left behind the words 'Leave soon', fading into the night.

Neither Javin nor Meldren spoke for a while, too amazed by what had happened, trying to make sense of it.

"That hasn't happened for a long while," said Javin finally.

Meldren poked at the fire, sending sparks spiraling up. "*Oh, we'll never have that problem again*, he said. *Harmony's finished with us*, he said. *She'll never bother us any more*, he said." She turned to look at him. "I told you it was a brave thing to say. But I really should have said it was a stupid thing to say."

"I'm sorry," he said, but not really feeling it. In fact, there was a part of him which was excited by this call to the unknown. Not that he would share that with Meldren. Not yet.

"So you should be. Now we've been given warning that we're leaving. But, as always, we have no idea why or where."

"Haven. That's where. Otherwise why show us their faces?"

"I hope they're safe," she said.

"We're going to find out, aren't we?"

"That and much, much more, I think." Meldren tossed the stick into the fire and scooted back beside Javin. "I doubt that you really are to blame for Her contacting us again."

"Thanks."

"But you have to admit that the timing stinks."

"I do admit that." He paused. "At least I won't be swimming any more."

"That wasn't really swimming. It was splashing."

"Huh. Like you'd know the difference... But what happens now?"

"Now?" Meldren gave a puff of laughter. "Like it always was. We get to find out when Harmony wants to tell us. That's what happens now. And we wait."

5

B y now the atmosphere aboard *Lightning*, the crew's nickname for Deep Range scout ship DR16, had calmed down somewhat. They had been on the last long leg of a speculative sweep across an uncharted section of the galaxy.

They had been out surveying a long time making a few finds, mostly small and of little value, with none of them looking impressive enough to warrant a mining fleet. An asteroid or two, one planet with only a mildly corrosive atmosphere, but nothing really stunning. At best, there would only be the odd mining camp set up and perhaps there would never be enough to merit more than some smaller franchises over the long term. Sure, they would provide an income, but it would take years to realize. Everything else was either too small in terms of accessible deposits or buried within hostile environments which would make any extraction too expensive.

Feeling frustrated, they had swung by this supposedly unexplored system before heading home. And that's when they had picked up signals. Signals! Understandable signals from a planet in the system they were to explore, when there should have been nobody there. That was the shock. There were no records of any exploratory expeditions, no records of any colonization, not even any whispers or hints of illegal activity in the area. That's why they were here. It was uncharted, unknown, a blank spot. At most they had hoped for a small find; some gold, some platinum perhaps. Something which would cheer them up, make them feel that the trip had been worthwhile.

None of them had even contemplated anything other than mild disappointment. And yet, the electronic chatter they had picked up was real and, even more surprisingly, it was recognizably human. Certainly there were strange accents, but it didn't take much effort to understand.

What else could they do but say 'Hello'? That's what worried Captain Kellerman-Stobbant, or simply Stobbant as she wished to be known amongst her crew when in space, but not on the ground. There were standards and formalities to be observed and such familiarity could, if discovered, be fatal to advancement. But she was ever the rebel in space. She gnawed at her lip as she thought through the possibilities which this contact had opened up.

First, she had had to send a communication. After all, she had no idea when her ship might be spotted, or even if it had already been. Delaying a message could look suspicious. The people there might be warlike, and DR ships were not equipped for any such encounter. Should she have sent anything more than an ident? But that would have made no sense. Probably. And it might have alerted the people to who and what she was. Assuming they could or would do anything about that. Too many unknown variables to know if she had chosen the correct path here.

Secondly, what were these people doing there? Were they mining illegally? A rogue franchise trying to buy its way back to civilization? Perhaps a backdoor trade route for drugs and they had stumbled upon it? She shook her head. It was all too banal, the signals they had picked up. If she had to put an alliance up for surety, she would have wagered that some of the signals sounded like entertainment and others sounded like serious discussions. Some of it she could not understand. But overall, it sounded like an entire civilization, not a temporary mining or trading post. It was too complex, too much information for something small and short-term.

She was not equipped for this. That she was certain about. She was not trained for this, which she was also positive about. She didn't like the idea of having to deal with people. That's why she liked her command: a small ship, a small crew and as much space as she could travel through. All she had to do, normally, was mark planets or asteroids as potential mining sites. A survey from a distance, a short surface stop if conditions allowed and some more detailed surveying, collate the reports, mark them as belonging to this ship, and that was it. Then back home to register the finds and work out dividends to be shared. It was a living and there was always the hope that one day there would be the big find, the one that would grant them enough income to give them their dreams, maybe even make them a valuable alliance partner.

She and her four crew were all of a mind. They liked deep space more than people and their ship more than cities. They were loners and happy to admit it. Being in control of their lives; that was important. Able to make decisions for themselves, as long as they were in space. She had some measure of independence and had planned her alliances well so far, but she wasn't looking to them for her long-term sanity. With one good find, a quick return, or selling shares on, she could break alliances and do what she wanted. She wanted only her own space and only her own terms. But now... .

She gave a frustrated sigh. "Why couldn't they be somewhere else?" she asked for the hundredth time, voicing what the rest were thinking.

"There is the other planet. It's further out. Perhaps we should look there first?" asked Norall-Severent, the navigator.

"We can't," replied the captain. "We have to assume they already know we're here. We can't stop off along the way and look at something else first. Who knows how they'll take that? Could be a breach of good manners demanding a strike for all we know."

"Well," said Lessterenman, the comms officer, "if we assume that there are minerals worth mining on either planet, and we can guess that's true to some extent from the fact that people are living on one of them, then we should follow protocol and launch a beacon."

Stobbant nodded. "Hopshan," she said, "is there anything in your analysis that would suggest that these people have anything like our level of tech or that they could track a beacon? For all we know they might be armed and dangerous and willing to fire on us if they think we've done something... underhand. I want to know before we approach much closer, because they might be able to spot the launch."

Parra-Hopshan smiled, not in the least upset that the captain had used the familiar form of her name. The crew tended to be relaxed, at least among themselves, when aboard. Being too uptight about formal names was a recipe for disaster in the confines of the ship. Her job was data analysis. But usually it did not involve other civilizations. "It's all low level stuff that I can see. No long range sweeps of anything that I can find, not that we're well-equipped to spot those sorts of things. I'd say either they are way beyond our level of tech, or way below it. My assessment is way below. They won't spot anything this far out unless it's by pure chance. And even if they did spot it, that doesn't mean they'd know what it was. We sent the signal out using their frequencies which means it will be very slow in reaching them. I've not found anything which suggests they have our sub-space transmission capabilities. That's another reason for thinking they are behind us."

"Good. Then see to it. Get that beacon launched with the outbound pointing away and back home or to the nearest relay so they can't pick it up. And make sure we tell base what we have found. Use the narrow beam to make it harder for them to spot. It's up to them what happens next. Thank all the stars that's not something I have to worry about. We'll get in, visit, and get out. And when we get out, we'll be taking one of theirs with us. Finding this is annoying, sure, but it is a new find. Something that's not on the charts anywhere? That's got to be valuable. New civilization, new source of minerals; there's bound to be plenty otherwise they wouldn't be there... . This could be the big one. We'll take someone back with us as proof get it registered and the rest is up to everyone else as far as I'm concerned."

For a while after, there was a contemplative silence throughout the ship with each crew member seemingly lost in their own thoughts. Would this really be the big one? Would this be the one that would make them rich? The one every DR crew dreamed of? How to get in and out as fast as possible yet make the claim stick? And, more importantly, which of them was going to be unlucky enough to wait out the journey land-bound while the rest of the crew raced back to register the find? Their presence on the planet would ensure their claim was valid in case any other ship happened to enter the system. Who would the captain pick? Someone she trusted more or someone who might be better positioned to form a stronger alliance against her if they returned with her? There was much to think about.

Some time later the co-pilot, known as Evan, but whose full name of E-VANT4 indicated that he was a clone, leaned back in his seat staring at the bulkhead, put the remains of his meal down and said, "What's going to happen to them now? They have no idea how their lives are going to change. And we're the ones to have started it."

Parra-Hopshan shook her head. "That's not for us to decide, is it? We're just surveying. For all we know there's not enough of anything for them to be worried about. And if there is enough, then think of the bonus we'll all get. Plus, there's the other planets as well. This could be the richest system we've encountered. I could buy my own ship and go where I want to go when I want to. Maybe find a planet I want to settle on. That's worth thinking about."

"Really? Settle down in one place, one planet?" Evan was obviously surprised by the idea.

Parra-Hopshan made a '*why not?*' face. "Who knows? It might be fun. If it was the right place."

"The right place? You mean with food supplied and a smart building? No travel? Doesn't sound that great to me. No tech and everything that goes with it? Living in raw nature?"

Parra-Hopshan shrugged. "It might be interesting to find out."

Evan was silent. *Lightning* continued to decelerate, sliding down through the system, inwards to the sun, toward the planet they had heard.

6

As the scout ship gradually approached from the outer limits of the system, so the group of Carmeena, Farran, Hanna and Endel steadily made their way towards Pannedon. Approaching the city from the other side were Isselta and Pol for the same reason; they felt they were being pulled toward the city.

The problem for them all was how to avoid being noticed as well as how to find places to sleep. Their clothes, their bare feet, but above all the sprites and ribbons gave them away as being outsiders. They knew from experience that Revivalists, people they usually stayed and worked with, dressed similarly. They also knew that Revivalists were unpopular in the cities for their lifestyle and beliefs and many communities had been attacked because of that. So they traveled through the suburbs as cautiously as they could, moving mainly by night, and either singing food or taking produce from gardens; whichever exposed them the least.

"I wish I had learned to read," moaned Pol quietly one evening, as they made their way cautiously through a series of hedges, avoiding the well-lit road nearby. "I could at least read some of the signs they have here."

"I'm not much better," admitted Isselta just as quietly, wincing as she untangled herself from a branch. "I can write my own name, but not much more. But I don't know that it would help us much. It's not as if anyone is going to be hanging out signs to let us know why we are here."

"How much further do we need to go, do you think?" asked Pol. "Do we need to go right into the center or what? And what is this all about really?"

Isselta didn't answer for a moment, concentrating instead on finding her way. When she was standing next to Pol and pulling leaves from her hair, she said, "Why don't we see if we can find out? I'm tired of this method of traveling. It's embarrassing for one thing. Give me the open countryside any day! We're moving so slowly it's going to take ages to get anywhere."

So the two of them, after checking as best they could to see if there was anyone nearby, hunkered down and let themselves sink into the quieter world inside them. There they could sense the flow of the world and where they were in it. There were songs all around them, but they were only telling them what was here and now. It was of no help to hear that background of sound. They tried instead to find if something in the future tugged at them more, or came from a new direction. They were open to anything at all which might help them decide what to do. It was like being a leaf and trying to understand where wind might take them when they could not see it nor comprehend what wind was, only know that it held their future in it.

When they opened their eyes and let the present intrude again, they sat for a while trying to interpret what they had felt.

"To me," whispered Isselta, "it felt more like being part of it all. I can't really explain it, but it felt like we were welcome right in the heart of things in Pannedon."

Pol nodded. "That feels right. But there was something else. At least, for me there was. It was as though getting there was easy. Don't ask me how. But I do know that pushing through hedges and stealing food isn't easy or fun or anything at all except hard. Which means we should be traveling differently. But how?"

It was Isselta's turn to agree. "Yes, the getting there was different. But didn't you also feel like it wasn't the right time to be wherever exactly we're meant to be?"

Pol re-examined her memories. "Hmmm. That's right. Have we been traveling too fast? Hardly seems a possibility. But... ," and she shrugged. "So, what's next? What do we do now?"

There was silence as both considered their immediate future. "Shouldn't we find out about the traveling thing first?" asked Isselta.

"What other ways are there of traveling?" asked Pol.

Silence again.

"Well," began Isselta slowly, "the only other type of traveling I know of is when we went between Harmony and here. But that was done with the planet singing us, or keeping us inside the song." She shook her head. "I've no idea how it worked, but it did."

"I remember it, but I wouldn't know how to do it," said Pol. "But, it might be something like that, mightn't it?"

"But we don't know where we're going or when we are supposed to be there, so I don't see how we can do anything like that." Isselta frowned.

"But let's try anyway," said Pol. "I hate this as much as you do. So why not experiment instead?"

Isselta was cautious. "How?"

"Seems to me," said Pol, "that if we can hear a song of a place, we should be able to go there, shouldn't we?" Accepting Isselta's grudging nod as an indication to continue, she added, "So why don't we sing ourselves back to that lovely place we stayed a while back? The one with the trees overhanging the river and lots of soft grass instead of this gravel and hard surfaces we have to walk on. What do you say?"

"Possibly," said Isselta. "But I want to be able to come back here if anything goes wrong. So we should know what this place sounds like. Right?" Then she stopped and thought. "But we never listened to that place by the river. So how can we know what the song is?"

"We don't," admitted Pol. "But we do know what it felt like and how much we enjoyed it, don't we? I can still remember the cool water, the shade, the smell of the grass, the peace. That should be enough, shouldn't it?"

Isselta shrugged. She didn't know how she felt about the suggestion and she also didn't want to say that their memories might be different and that that could cause problems. But Pol's enthusiasm was always beguiling and she felt herself being nudged, as ever, toward agreeing with her.

"Why not?" she said at last. "We've nothing to lose and staying here is not something I want to do."

Pol was ready for this and had obviously given it some thought, given the speed with which she spoke. "We need to be together, of course. And we need to listen to it and to each other and be able to sing it together. I hope it won't be too loud though and attract anyone. But singing together there's more chance we can do this. Ready?"

The two sat back to back and focused on the campsite by the river they both recalled. As they let the details build, so they tried to hear the song which made that place what it was. It came in parts and in stuttering sounds at first but gradually became clearer and easier to hear. They each began to sing very softly as they sought to isolate the sounds they wanted from the songs all around them. As they gained focus, so Isselta's sprite began to help by adding the sounds and harmonics only it could produce and Pol's ribbons swirled from her cheek to her forehead, forming a star-shape as they did so. The sounds began to swell in intensity and then Isselta could feel a subtle change in the way the ground felt beneath her. She kept her eyes shut and concentrated on singing the right sounds. As the song became clearer and stronger, so she felt as if she were sliding in some strange fashion, or the world was moving beneath her. Whatever the truth of it was, she knew instinctively that the song was working. She listened to Pol and adjusted her contribution automatically, following some deep inner sense of what was effective.

Suddenly she knew it was complete. Her voice tailed off and she allowed herself to sense the world around her again. Even before opening her eyes, she knew they had achieved it. The grass she touched with her hands, the scent and sound of the water nearby; they were where they had wanted to be.

It was still nighttime. And here, there were no artificial lights to take the place of a moon. It was the deep darkness of a normal night, but she turned round anyway to Pol, happy and surprised and amazed all at the same time. She couldn't see Pol's face clearly but the girl radiated excitement so strongly that Isselta felt it washing over her.

"We did it, we did it, we did it!" said Pol. "We sang ourselves here. We can do it!"

They spent the next several minutes congratulating each other and generally basking in their achievement before Isselta said, "Now all we have to do is find out where we are going and when we have to leave and hope that we can sing ourselves there like we sang ourselves here."

"We'll be fine," said Pol with her usual assurance. "We're not going anywhere right away. We both sensed that. All we have to do is listen more carefully than usual. If we can do this and we know that Pannedon is the target, I'm sure we'll be told somehow precisely where and when to go."

"Maybe you're right," said Isselta.

Pol chuckled. "Of course I'm right and, deep down, you know it too."

And Isselta had to agree about that.

7

The group on the other side of Pannedon; Farran, Carmeena, Hanna and Endel, had given up trying to hide from everyone and were walking towards where they felt pulled. It made for an easier journey physically, but they got many strange looks and people muttered at them as they passed. There was nothing that could be classed as a threat, but there was an air of growing uneasiness which seemed to thicken around and settle into them as they traveled.

One night, after having slipped into some sort of open space, a park of some kind Carmeena thought, to sleep, they felt too uneasy to relax sufficiently.

"I feel too nervous about being here," said Carmeena. "I'll sit and stay awake for a while, then I can wake someone else and they can take over. If that's something that might help."

"What if we get arrested?" asked Endel. "What do we do then?"

Carmeena didn't recognize the word. "Arrested?"

"We are probably breaking some law or other being here or doing what we're doing," explained Endel. "And if laws get broken, then people come along and arrest you for it and take you away and put you in a prison or something like that."

"But if I don't know what the law is, how can I be arrested for breaking it?" asked Farran looking confused. "That's not fair."

"We haven't been in big enough places to meet policemen -- the ones who do the arresting," said Endel. "I only know of it because one of the adults in Newgrange, the place you found us, used to be a policeman. I used to hear him talking."

"So you're saying that the longer we stay here and keep walking, the more likely it is that we get arrested?" asked Carmeena.

Endel nodded.

Farran said, "Some of those places we've stayed at have had people taken away --,"

"-- or killed," put in Carmeena.

"Is that what you mean?" continued Farran.

"Something like that, except the ones who were taken away, I don't think they were policemen who did that."

"Where do you go when you're arrested?" asked Carmeena.

"Prison," said Endel. "It's a place you're not allowed to leave. It's a place none of us want to be in, put it that way."

"We could always sing ourselves away from a prison, couldn't we?" said Carmeena.

Endel sighed and shook his head in reply. "It would probably make matters worse if we did."

"In that case," said Hanna after a moment or two, "I think we should see if we can find out in more detail what we should be doing."

"What do you suggest?" asked Farran.

"I think we should tune in to everything, everything around us, and see what we get. After all, we're much closer now than when we set out, so we might be able to get more detail." She patted her stomach. "And let's not forget that we're running out of food and I don't think we anybody here wants to trade with us. Singing it could become more difficult, the more people there are around."

That brought some grunts of agreement. Just as Isselta and Pol had done, the four of them became still and reached inside themselves for some guidance, some sense of what to do next.

After a short while they looked at each other, ready to share. Farran began. "I had a feeling that we're meant to be waiting. Waiting for something, but not here. Something like waiting for someone."

"That's something like I got," said Carmeena. "For me, it was a feeling of tension, of holding back, but waiting would be a good way of describing it."

Endel added, "And you're right about it not being here, whatever it is. I think it's somewhere further out. Or, maybe not. It feels like I'm being attracted further in toward this city, but at the same time I feel a drag on me to go outside of it as well. I don't really know how to describe it."

"What if," began Hanna more slowly, "what if the things we're feeling are all correct and that we have to go through the city to the other side? That would account for the draw for us to go in to the city as well as for something outside of it, wouldn't it?"

"But why have us go into the city instead of going around?" asked Farran.

"Speed, probably," said Carmeena. "It's going to be quicker going through than around."

"Yes, but what about the police and the arrest thing, as well as the food?" continued Farran.

This was followed by a silence.

"We don't know where it is we are headed, do we?" asked Endel.

"Only that it is on the other side," said Carmeena.

"How long do you think it will take for us to get there?" he continued. Carmeena shrugged.

"Can't there be a quicker way? I mean, instead of walking?"

"I'm not running, if that's what you mean," grunted Farran.

"You mean sing ourselves to wherever we are meant to be?" Hanna said.

"Exactly," said Endel. "Why can't we travel to wherever it is the same way we went to and from Harmony?"

"But we don't know where it is we're going to," said Carmeena.

"*We* don't," said Hanna, "but someone does or we wouldn't have been sent here in the first place."

"Makes sense to me," said Endel, smiling at Hanna in the gloom.

Farran still wasn't pleased. "But why get us to walk all this way into a place where nobody really likes or trusts us if we could have sung ourselves to a different place."

It was Endel's turn to shrug. "Maybe it was to test us to see if we really were willing to go anywhere. And then another test to see if we could figure out a solution. For all we know, this is something that Haven finds really amusing. But it's worth a try, isn't it?"

"The problem remains," said Carmeena. "We don't know where we're meant to be going, so how do we get there?"

"You're missing the point," said Hanna. "We don't have to know. All we have to do is listen for the song which will take us. And if we can't hear it, then we were wrong and we'll have to walk. It won't make much difference. Sing or walk, we'll get there."

It took a few more minutes before Farran was truly convinced and for Carmeena to accept that Hanna and Endel could be right.

"Let's just focus on the fact that we know we're meant to be somewhere else and let that thought guide our hearing," said Endel. "We'll give it a few moments and if nothing happens... ," he made a dismissive gesture.

With that, the four of them sat in a circle and bowed their heads in concentration. Letting their senses tune out the surface sounds around them, the sounds of the world, they felt their way toward the deeper, hidden sounds, the sounds which were inaudible if you did not know they existed. These were the true sounds of the world, the sounds which formed it and shaped it. In amongst those sounds they strained to hear the sequence they sought, the tune which would lead them metaphorically and literally to its destination and, in the hearing of it, take them with it.

Each of them could hear these world songs, and they also instinctively knew when they were all hearing the same song. It was as though the song became stronger as each one tuned in to it. As they listened, so they heard a more liquid sound growing, as though an unseen river was moving toward them. The sound, the song, swelled until all other sounds withdrew and they were held within it. They felt it enfold them and, as that happened, so they lost all sense of where they were. They surrendered themselves to the force within the sounds and couldn't even tell if they were breathing.

This lasted for an unknown amount of time before the song holding them began to fade, peeling away note by note to leave them, still seated in a circle.

The sounds of the surface world, the noises which everyone could hear, formed a gentle background until it was broken by a voice.

"I hope you've brought some food with you."

They opened their eyes and, in the dim starlight they saw the dark presence of two figures.

"Don't just sit there, get up and introduce yourselves. We've been waiting for you. I'm Pol and this is Isselta."

8

Myrella's headache was now a throbbing lump in her head. She had no need to look at the large calendar on her wall to know that The Landing (it always had capital letters in her mind) was only ten days away. The last twenty-five days had been a blur and she couldn't remember when she had last slept a full night through.

Everything on Haven was about the ship, it's projected course and orbit, ideas about how it was decelerating and what it would bring. From idle speculation about the possible make up and sexual preferences of the crew to more serious discussions about the technology and the society which had made such a voyage possible. Mixed in with these were arguments about what would happen here on Haven. Discussions sometimes turned into arguments and sides were taken. Society seemed to be changing daily and ideas became arguments. The Steady Staters were those who believed that, after the initial flurry of interest and excitement had died away, everything on Haven would remain very much the same as it had always had been, albeit with some useful new technology. The opposite view was held by those known as the NT's or NewTechs who envisioned a wonderful new society energized by the influx of new ideas and technology which would flow unceasingly to Haven. These saw everything being changed for the better; a whole new way of life for everyone. Both sides were based solely on speculation and, often, anger at what they perceived as being weaknesses in society.

Those were the two main groups, but there were also the Revivalists. The little information they gathered about the ship made them see its arrival as yet another threat to their way of life and feared that what had, up to now, been sullen antipathy interspersed with acts of violence toward them, would change into more persistent active aggression. Mostly, they kept to themselves and continued living as they had always done, hoping for the best.

Trying to balance these major factors as well as other minor ones, was proving a nightmare and was the chief cause of Myrella's headache.

"I am sorry you are feeling so tired," said Mannert in his quiet way, "but... ," and here he slid a folder across the desk, "this is something which does require your attention now." He also placed a couple of pills on the desk and poured some water. He stood and waited.

Myrella pinched the bridge of her nose, squeezing her eyes shut to try to block out the thudding pain behind them. She gulped the pills down and nodded in appreciation. "What is it, Mannert?" she said when she opened the folder. "What's so urgent?"

Her secretary inclined his head toward the folder. "This is a report and assessment of certain interests in the NT faction which might prove useful to know."

"Mannert," she said, squinting up at him, "I've been reading this stuff for days. I know that the NT's hate the Revivalists, and that some of them want me out of office so they can negotiate better deals with whoever has sent the ship. This isn't news."

Mannert remained standing quietly with hands folded.

Myrella sighed loudly, mainly for effect. "All right, I give in. But, as you obviously know what is in the report, you can tell me. But only after you have poured us both a drink. Make yours as large as you like, but make mine larger. If I can't have any peace, at least I can be civilized about it."

When they were both seated in the armchairs to the side of her office, Myrella took a large swallow and let her shoulders slump. "Tell me the worst, Mannert, but keep it short."

Mannert placed his small drink carefully on the side table and leaned forward. "The report speaks of the NT faction and how it is growing. It also speaks to the idea that a number of Revivalist groups have been attacked by probable members of this faction." Myrella made a hurry-up gesture. "The heart of the report is that Corrivan is building a private army within the NT group, although nothing can be directly linked to him. Estimates put the size of the militia as soon being large enough to pose a direct threat to the existing police force."

"And the purpose of this militia is... ?"

"The report suggests that the militia could be used to cause sufficient disruption to law and order to force your resignation, or to directly attack the Revivalist movement and all their sympathizers in a concerted attempt to remove all such people from having any say or influence at all in any negotiations which will occur after the landing."

Myrella nodded her thanks and then took another sip. "The report is trustworthy?" Mannert's raised brows and slight inclination of his head were answer enough. She tapped her fingers on the glass. "It amazes me that anyone can really be so stupid, so naive." She gulped down the rest and played with the glass, twirling it in her hands, watching the gleams of light spilling from it, aware that her headache was already reduced a little. "First, and most important, we have no idea what these people will do when they get here. We could, according to some, end up as slaves with no input as to our fate. Or, we could simply be overwhelmed by technology in such a way as to make it impossible for us to resist whatever their intentions might be. I'm not going so much for those scenarios, but as they undoubtedly have the technology to travel across space, it would seem unlikely that they would want to talk to us if their intention was to wipe us out or enslave us. Maybe we have something here which we take for granted but is valuable for them and all they want is a way to pay us to allow them to take it back." She shrugged. "What makes Corrivan think that he has the ability to negotiate anything at all with them? But it's more stupid than that even, isn't it?"

She placed her glass on the side table and used her now empty hands to add emphasis to her words. "Has everyone forgotten about the damn' tree in the middle of this building and how it appeared? Has everyone actually chosen to ignore that there is another presence here, another power here, however symbolic, that has some sort of say over what is going on? What is Corrivan *thinking*? Is he even remembering that we have a tree there? And doesn't he actually recall that it was there because it wanted to ensure that Revivalists were not to be harmed? I don't understand what exactly that tree is. I don't think anyone really knows what it is. If half of the stories about it are true then it does have some sort of role to play, although what that might be is not anything I can think of. All I know is that it looks like a tree and that it is important that we don't harm it. Beyond that... ?" she shrugged eloquently.

"Perhaps," murmured Mannert, "people do think of the tree as merely symbolic. Perhaps they think it is without power and it is merely a show. After all, nothing has happened to it or there has been no activity or response from it even though there have been attacks on Revivalist communities. Maybe Corrivan has decided that it is not an actual threat."

"All I know is that there are times when I look at it and I wonder about it. I can't in all honesty say that I believe in everything we've been told about it, but the fact is it's there and there's no good explanation for it," she said. "Do you believe that tree is symbolic and without power?"

"No, ma'am, I do not. I share your views and would prefer to err on the side of overestimating it. Perhaps there needs to be a certain level of violence or a certain number of places need to be attacked before anything happens. I do not know, but I do feel there is nothing purely symbolic about that tree."

"But in that case, as you pointed out, why hasn't anything happened after attacks on communities it said it was protecting?"

"Perhaps it's giving us a chance to stop the attacks. Perhaps it's watching us and judging us."

Myrella, after a pause for thought, said, "Being judged by a tree? How would that sound if we made it public?" She made a wry smile. "It's waiting, then. That would make some sort of sense I suppose. Watching and waiting. But we don't know what for, do we?"

Mannert shook his head. "Perhaps it's not a 'what' but a 'who'. Perhaps it's not an action it's waiting for, but a person."

"What do you mean?"

"Maybe there's one key person in all this and if that person dies or does something pivotal, then that's the signal."

Myrella shrugged. "That's something we can't do anything about though, is it? Not if it's a person we cannot identify."

Mannert shifted uncomfortably in his seat. "Or, maybe, ma'am, it's waiting for you to act."

"We're talking about a tree, aren't we? As if it's a person. What if it is waiting? What do I do? Imprison Corrivan? Beef up the police force? Call in the army? Send a bodyguard to each Revivalist community? None of them are the answer, Mannert. None of them. All I can do is work to keep as many of the factions from fighting each other and be seen as a calm spot in the storm. I can't be worried about what that tree might be thinking, assuming it can think. I've got too much else to worry about. Every bit of what happens as soon as they arrive will be absolutely new to us as a society. And my job is to stop us all from reacting in the same tired old ways we have always acted. I want peace, Mannert. But not at any price. I want us all to look as if we are united, even if we are not. But I cannot force that upon anyone either. All I can do is work and hope that the shock of it all makes everyone take a step back and think."

"And if they don't, ma'am?"

She held out her glass to him. "That's going to take the rest of that bottle to figure out."

9

The landing, ten days later, from the point of view of everyone on Haven, was both amazing and deflating at the same time. It was amazing because here was a ship from some unimaginable distance, from some unimaginable society, touching down on Haven. The strangeness of every aspect of it, the break it signaled from all of their previous history, was too much and too big to contemplate. It would only be slowly assimilated for many, many days.

But it was also deflating, because after the silence fell around them as the engines were shut off, and the hatch opened, only people appeared in the doorway. There were no monsters, no strange-looking new species, only humans looking very much like everyone else; dressed somewhat differently, but people nonetheless, apparently without any sort of superpowers. They looked and acted like every other person. To see the ship, to understand what it meant to everyone on the planet, and then to see only people coming from it; there was a disconnect somehow. The two did not feel as if they should be together. And yet they were.

In the period immediately before the landing, there had been many communications arranging the where, the how and the when of it all. The strangeness of the language, the unexpected lilts and phrasings, the new words; they had become easier to understand and accept during these exchanges. So when the crew finally appeared, everyone knew what to expect, what speeches were to be made and what introductions were to happen when.

The stately ride into the capital, the meals (carefully vetted for the strangers' tastes, as far as could be ascertained), the lodgings and the security to give them privacy had all been arranged. The interviews, the questions, the holidays and the entertainments had all been meticulously prepared and organized. It was still all new, still all wondrous.

For the crew of *Lightning*, their arrival was more of a unending barrage of new sights, sounds and smells and the constant necessity to smile and keep clean. Kellerman-Stobbant had made each crew member check their fleet uniforms and make them as neat as they could. While they were on public view, they were not allowed to wear their normal, dirty, creased clothes.

"For as long as we are here," she had said on the descent, "you will look like you all are wonderfully wealthy, incredibly well-mannered, very healthy, and, above all, polite. Anyone who is not any of those things I will personally make sure that they lose their claims to profit sharing. Is that clear?" She had glared at them one by one, willing them to disobey her and make her even richer. "And Evan? That's your name while we are here. You will not call yourself E-VANT-4, you will be called Evan. Nobody mentions clones or cloning, as we have no idea what they think of that. Remember, our prime purpose here is to make a complete and detailed survey, keep them interested but without giving any real details. We keep them happy. Also remember this. No small mining camp here! When the mining ship arrives, we'll be leaving. Earlier if we can. But we'll be taking the survey reports with us to ensure the payout. What happens here after the mining ship arrives is none of our business and never has been. Clear?"

Parra-Hopshan had been picking at a thread on the cuff of her uniform. She looked up and asked, "So what *do* we tell them when they ask what's going to happen?"

"We tell them what we agreed on. We tell them that the Empire will look after them and that there will be great things for them once they are within the Empire."

Norall-Severent then asked, "What if they can tell we're lying to them? What then?"

"Well, we'll worry about that if it happens. Plus, great things will certainly happen. That's not a lie. Any other questions?"

"How long before we take the witnesses back?" This was from Evan.

"As soon as we get permission to survey the planet, we're off. And remember we're calling them ambassadors, not witnesses. Lessterenman and you, Parra-Hopshan, you're staying. It's been arranged -- stop moaning, it's standard due to your roles on board -- so make sure you have some other clean clothes. Do the job well and accurately and we all make a lot of money. And, when we do, you two each get an extra share for being planet-bound while the rest of us leave you here."

"Have they got an ambassador for us?" Evan asked. The way he said it, you could hear quotation marks around the word.

"Not that I know of. But they wouldn't tell us anyway, would they? There's going to be a whole lot of talking and smiling and meeting people which, we all know, is not what we signed up for. But we're here, so we have to do it."

They were all tested in these areas over the next two days. The endless parades and speeches and strange food took their toll. Evan, of course, remained quite calm and reasonable all through it, but Norall-Severent was mightily sick the first night and Parra-Hopshan punched the wall of her room in to relieve the stress. Kellerman-Stobbant's reaction was to take stimulants as often as possible to maintain a show of interest and concern. She wished she had thought to nominate Evan as acting captain so that he would be the one to be first to speak and give answers to the ceaseless questioning. He wouldn't have mentioned it later, so her rank would have been safe. But it was too late for that now. Lessternman kept quiet mainly, letting the ranking officers do the heavy work, speaking only occasionally, and then in short sentences, and when there was no other option.

"When do we get started, captain?" asked Evan, the second night. They had decided to eat together in Kellerman-Stobbant's room. They had been allocated the entire top floor of the best hotel in order to provide some sort of privacy. The two floors immediately beneath were empty. The rest of the hotel was occupied by their guards, some few government officials, and the many, many media. Their food preferences had gelled a little and they were by now reasonably sure that what was in front of them would have no unpleasant surprises. At least it wasn't space rations.

"Tomorrow," said the captain with a mouthful of food. "We're going to get serious about negotiating to start surveying as well. We're meeting again with that woman, Mycell or something like that."

"Myrella," said Lessterenman.

The captain poked a finger at him in acknowledgment as she swallowed with a grimace. "Her. We're meeting with all the main people and they're going to sort out who comes back with us and who's going to stay with you two surveyors. I've got to go, but some of you can stay here. Evan and Norall-Severent, you get tomorrow off. You other two, you're with me. The two of you staying here, sleep or do something which doesn't attract attention. Stay inside if you like, but if you go out, go together and be nice. We'll be back as soon as we can." She prodded at one of the side dishes. "Does anyone else want this, whatever it is? It doesn't look right to me."

10

Kellerman-Stobbant was grateful for her medication the next day. After preliminary talks in Myrella's office, she and her two crew were invited to address the assembly. This had been arranged so that she could answer questions about the Empire as well as explain what they were planning on doing here.

Walking toward the chamber, Myrella had placed a hand on the captain's arm and said, "When you enter, you might well think that we, as a people, are somewhat unusual. But I assure you, what you are about to see is something which we all consider to be very important to us all." Kellerman-Stobbant didn't know how to react to that but shared a puzzled glance at her crew members. Squaring her shoulders, she took a deep breath and waited until the doors were swung wide and she felt Myrella's hand on her elbow. Once more she cursed the fact that there were people here and that they wanted to see and speak to her. Why couldn't it have been a bare planet?

Forcing her smile to stay in place, she took a couple of steps and stopped short at the sight of the vast tree which dominated the chamber. Her mouth dropped open and she looked up and up to where it brushed the ceiling. She was oblivious to the clapping and cheering which had burst forth until Myrella took her elbow again and managed to get her walking to the large desk and lectern.

"Why do you have a tree in here and why is it so big?" She could not take her eyes off it.

Myrella merely shook her head and said, "That's not really important right now, is it? We can talk about it later. Don't worry about it. Let's get started, shall we?"

When the applause had finished, the three shipmates found themselves seated in front of the large desk as Myrella introduced them one by one and then gestured for the captain to speak.

By now, she had regained her composure somewhat and was able to deliver the speech the crew had worked on. It gave little away. Then she introduced her two companions.

"These two will remain here on Haven as a sign of good faith while we ferry your ambassador back to The Prime at the heart of the Benevolence to meet our Emperor and negotiate the details of how you wish to become a part of the Empire. While my crew-members are here, they would, obviously, like to see as much of the planet as possible and, if possible, they would like to offer their skills in helping you understand more about the planet using our technology."

"What does that mean?" called out one of the representatives. "How does that work, understanding more about Haven?"

"It means," said Kellerman-Stobbant, "that we have technology which will allow us to explore deep underground and in the oceans to a level of detail which, currently, I doubt you are capable of. That is all."

Another voice called out, "So your ship is going back where it came from. Does that include the craft you used to land here?"

"No. The landing craft will remain here. It is incapable of deep space flight but does have long-range communication abilities, allowing us to notify you of our arrival earlier than your instruments could."

"We know you want minerals from us, and probably other things as well." The speaker was an older man who had stood up to be more easily seen. "You say you will pay us for such things but, if I read this correctly, such payments would only have value within your Empire. Which would mean that, unless we become part of this Empire the payments would amount to very little of worth indeed. What would you say, from your experience, could we expect to gain from membership apart from such payments? What changes might we expect? Your speech was long on platitudes but short on details. I'd like to hear some details and I'm sure I speak for the majority of us here." He sat down amidst a shower of polite applause.

Kellerman-Stobbant made sure her smile didn't falter as she took a deep breath. This was the bit she wasn't looking forward to. "Obviously I can only sketch out the possibilities of some of the things you might expect to have as a result of joining the Empire. The precise details will, of course, be negotiated by your ambassador. However, having said that, I can suggest that you could look forward to a significantly higher level of technology; technology which is an improvement on what you have; technology which will make significant and lasting changes to your quality of life. Entertainment, new industries, new foods, new materials; all these are fairly certain to happen. But perhaps the biggest change of all will be that the stars will be open to you. You will be able to travel beyond this system, see fantastic places, even choose to live elsewhere in the galaxy. There are many planets in the Empire, each of which has its own interesting features. There are many, many worlds waiting for you to explore. Of all of the benefits of joining, this is perhaps the one which is the strangest of all. Strange and yet wonderful."

A tall, thin man who looked as if he was going bald then stood up. Kellerman-Stobbant could not help but notice out of the corner of her eye how Myrella flinched as he did so.

"Captain," he began in a voice which made her think, and not in a good way, of her first commander; a man several ranks above her socially who could not keep the condescension from his voice. "Captain, my name is Corrivan. I'm pleased to be able to introduce myself to you instead of launching directly into questions. I wouldn't like you to think that we have no manners, no sense of civility, here on this technologically backward planet. Captain, if I may, I would like to know what is the Empire's policy where the majority of a planet's population is eager to join but a backward and ignorant section is resolute in ignoring or opposing such membership. What, do you suppose, would be the policy of the Empire toward such people?"

Kellerman-Stobbant was about to answer when Myrella leapt to her feet. "Corrivan! This is not the place to air your personal vendettas. You should resume your seat!"

"I shall certainly do no such thing, Madam President. This is an open session of the assembly and, as such, has no rules on what can and cannot be discussed. It was, in fact, yourself who suggested just such a protocol if I recall. So, with the deepest respect," and here he bowed, "I leave my question open and am hopeful of an answer from the captain."

Seeing these two antagonists, Kellerman-Stobbant reconsidered what she had been about to say. 'Be nice' was what she had told her crew, and it was what she was determined to be herself. Making sure her smile was still there she turned to this Corrivan person and said, "I am sure that such problems as you describe should be settled on the planet in question. The Empire does not seek to impose one faith, one perspective on all its planets. That would be impossible. The Empire is not known as the Benevolence for nothing. It is an alliance, not a dictatorship. I hope I have answered to your satisfaction."

The meeting dragged on a little while longer before Myrella brought it to an end and the crew were able to leave. As she left the chamber, the captain still wondered about the tree and whether she would even understand what it was doing there.

Seated once more in Myrella's chamber, she wondered if any of them here could guess she was anything but a diplomat and how her family would react to the news that she had spoken on behalf of the Emperor himself. The social implications were most interesting.

11

Myrella said, "I should have warned you about the tree. I'm sorry
about that. It's something we have become accustomed to here,
but I can see that it could be a shock the first time of seeing it." She had
decided to head off any questions about the tree by mentioning it first.
Secretly, she had quite liked the look on the captain's face. It had been a
genuine response, not a carefully prepared one. And that had made it far
more interesting. It showed the captain was able to be shocked and
surprised. What else would be a surprise, she wondered? The memory of
that helped quell her irritation at Corrivan's question. She wondered
what, if anything, the captain or her crew had made of him and whether
they saw him as she did; an irritating man with ambitions of power at
any cost.

"Yes," replied the captain. "It was certainly... unusual." Myrella noted
how the smile appeared to be fixed on the captain's face and wondered if
it was not something she did often. The two crew members sitting with
her flicked a smile on and off whenever they were being noticed, but
otherwise, they spent the time gazing around them as if trying to catalog
their surroundings. "There must be a reason for such a thing. Did you
build this place around it or... ?" asked the captain.

"Not really. It has a somewhat long and complicated history attached to it , but it is something we rather treasure as a result. There are many stories associated with it. It would take too long to explain it all here." Myrella thought that was the simplest way round the issue. Make it sound like a custom and nobody will question it.

"Oh. I see."

Apparently, it had worked. Myrella hastened to change the subject. She inclined her head toward the two crew members. "This would be a good time to finalize the details of your crew's stay here while we finalize who our ambassador is to be."

"This has not been arranged yet?" The captain seemed genuinely surprised.

"You are probably aware that there are many factions on Haven. It was, after all, brought to your attention just now; for which I apologize. Many people wanting slightly different things. It is not necessarily simple to please everyone. Of course, we have various people in mind, but we really wanted to meet you first, hear a little about where you come from, before we decide on who would be most fit to represent us. But please don't be concerned, as we will have our ambassador to you shortly." Myrella hoped the lie would be unnoticed. The amount of arguments and the numerous claims to seniority which the subject had aroused had left her feeling that the role was impossible to fill and that anyone who wanted to do it was, quite frankly, too irresponsible to be trusted with it. She planned on making her final choice after this meeting and after consulting with Mannert who had a calmly dispassionate outlook on such things. There were one or two who seemed at least able to fulfill the ceremonial duties and present Haven in a favorable light to the Empire.

There then began the negotiations about what would happen to the two crew who would be left behind. The man and the woman seemed not particularly concerned with this, answering questions when they could but leaving most of the details to their captain.

"Forgive me for saying this," said Myrella at one point, "but it does feel very much as if they are hostages and that, should anything untoward happen to our ambassador, they would be expected to pay dearly for it."

"I can see how it might appear," replied the captain. "However, it is merely a politeness on our part. We arrive from a large Empire you know nothing about and take one of yours back with us to face who knows what. So we leave some of our crew here as a way of reassuring you of our good intentions. After all, we will be gone quite some time. There is the journey to our home of course followed by the negotiations and the journey back." She spread her hands. "Who knows how long that will take? Yet we leave our representatives with you for all that time. All we ask is that you treat them well and, maybe, allow them to see as much of the planet as you wish. Do not think of it in terms of hostages but as new friends."

"I'll certainly try," said Myrella, and she beamed at the crew despite feeling a sense of vague unease about the situation.

After a lengthy discussion about what these two 'friends' would or would not be doing, could or could not do, it was agreed that their ship would have unlimited access to anywhere they wished to go on Haven provided they were escorted by at least two representatives. These representatives would be there to smooth over any local difficulties which might arise, and also gain an understanding of what information they might be able to provide about Haven. Plus, it would allow Haven's scientific community to gain some insight into the new technology.

When the captain and crew had left, Myrella felt exhausted and gratefully accepted a stiff drink from Mannert. "I suppose we can't put off appointing an ambassador any longer, Mannert."

"No, ma'am, we cannot. Who are your top choices, if I may ask?"

Myrella gave a toothy grin. "You know all of them as well as I do, Mannert, so stop acting as if you have no idea."

He received the mild reproof with a gentle inclination of his head.

"I would love to send Corrivan, but I rather think he would consider it as a means of getting him out of the way here... which, of course, it would be. And who knows what he would get up to in the heart of an Empire? Oh, no. Doesn't bear thinking about. He's my top contender but out of the running. After him I am leaning toward Perrani and Shooltan. Both of them have good negotiating skills and are old enough to have seen most of the tricks which will probably come their way. I have only dangled the possibility of them being considered to see which way they would jump and neither of them ducked away. Of the two of them,

Perrani is probably ahead a little by virtue of his coming from a very wealthy family so that he would, I hope, be less likely to be swayed by what is bound to be a huge display of wealth and power. At least, he's never seemed to want for more than he has."

She held up her glass and swirled the liquid around, studying the play of light. When she next spoke, there was an air of abstraction. "I do wonder, Mannert, whether there's any difference in who we send. When I'm with those people, I can't help but get the feeling that we're being played in some fashion. They're altogether too nice. And they're not really your typical diplomats. There's few flowery words and phrases. But then again, perhaps that's how diplomacy is in the Empire."

"Forgive me, ma'am," interrupted Mannert, "but if it is an Empire, then diplomacy is going to be the same there as here; people not asking directly for what they want and going behind everyone's back to obtain it without being seen to be greedy, or having lied."

Myrella laughed. "Perhaps you, my cynical secretary, are the perfect ambassador."

Mannert waved away the idea. "No. Thank you, but no. I prefer being among the diplomats here. At least I know who they are and what they want."

Before they could continue their discussion, there was a knock on the door and one of Myrella's staff entered looking distinctly uneasy.

"What is it, Burnam? Is something wrong with our visitors?"

Burnam was a solid-looking man with a very conservative taste in clothing and a permanent frown on his face. He shook his head. "It's something else entirely, ma'am." He gestured vaguely behind him. "It's in the assembly chamber. It's the tree, ma'am. It's... well, it's holding some people."

At the mention of the tree, Myrella handed the glass to Mannert and rushed out, trailing Burnam behind her, calling out, "Is anyone hurt?" Arriving at the doors of the chamber, she steadied herself and, reassured by Burnam's insistence that everyone was well, she slowly opened them and peered inside. Normally at nighttime, there would only be some small wall sconces glowing. But now all the lights were full on, making it easy to spot two pairs of feet off the ground, the bodies presumably being held in some fashion by the branches of the tree. The feet were not moving, giving Myrella cause for concern. But then a voice, distinctly recognizable as that of Perrani, called out, "Is someone there? This damnable tree has got me round the waist and will not let go. Get an axe or something!"

Another voice with the more cultured tones of Shooltan chimed in. "I can't see a thing. There's leaves and twigs and branches all round me."

"Are you injured at all?" asked Myrella.

"No," said Shooltan. "My dignity is severely bruised, but apart from that, I appear to be unharmed."

"Me, too," added Perrani.

Myrella turned to Burnam. "Who found them?"

"The cleaners found them. They heard them and rushed to tell me. And I told you."

Turning back to the tree, Myrella asked, "How long have you been there?"

"Since the end of the assembly," said Perrani. "Everyone else left and I found myself blocked by branches I hadn't noticed before. Then, before I knew it, I was scooped up and, well, here I am."

"Same for me," complained Shooltan. "Can you please do something and ask it to let us go or give it whatever it wants? We've both tried asking nicely. We've also shouted at it and offered it anything at all, but perhaps you might have the golden touch, Madam President? It is very embarrassing and not something I would wish others to know about."

Myrella almost grinned at that, but before she could respond, Mannert leaned forward and whispered, "Both Perrani and Shooltan held by the tree? Nobody else out of the whole assembly? Considering our earlier conversation, might there not be a message in that, ma'am?"

Myrella turned to him, a look of surprise on her face. She nodded thoughtfully.

"Madam President? Please?" asked Shooltan, a definite note of pleading in his voice.

"My apologies, Shooltan. I was considering what to do. I think that I may have the answer to your predicament." *But not to mine*, she thought. She considered her next words carefully. Finally satisfied, she moved closer to the tree and held the nearest branch she could reach. "I understand what it is you are saying and I want you to know that I

respect your wishes and will act upon them to the best of my ability."
Except I have no idea what to do next.

There was a rustling and an unfurling and two bedraggled men were eased onto the floor by branches which curled back.

Perrani, seated on the floor, brushed himself vigorously. "I don't suppose you are going to tell us what that meant?"

"Sadly, I am not, gentlemen. At least, not now. There may come a day when I can, but for now please accept the idea that this tree might well have saved one of you from something you would not have liked."

That caused both of them to look sharply at her, as if weighing the truth of her words. Neither man looked pleased but, being politicians, they were able to accept that it was better than no answer at all and acknowledged Myrella with brief nods before leaving. Burnam accompanied them to the door and looked back as to whether he should wait for Myrella and Mannert. Myrella waved him on saying, "Look after them and make sure they are uninjured. You can shut the doors as you go."

When the two of them were alone, Myrella slumped down into the chair behind the large desk, her normal place during sessions. Mannert sat on the edge of the desk. Both of them stared at the tree. Neither spoke for a while. Myrella hoped that, somehow, the tree would utter words, understandable words, words which would make sense of what had just happened. She felt that she was being stared at in return and didn't like the idea. To break that thought, she said, "So the tree *can* do things. One of things it does, apparently, is listen in on what I'm thinking." That didn't seem to help. In fact, she didn't want to think about that at all. She forced herself to focus on what to do next, not dwell on the things which might be true but disconcerting.

"Yes, it would seem that way, ma'am. Both of your top candidates held prisoner? I think that shows that neither would be acceptable."

"I agree with you. I do. I don't see how else to interpret it. But, damn it all, Mannert, we've had attacks on Revivalist communities and nothing's happened, and now, just because I had an idea for an ambassador, it makes its attitude known. It makes no sense." Mannert nodded gloomily in agreement.

"But what do we do now? I have no idea who else I might consider and I can hardly call all possible candidates in here and say, 'Just stand in front of the tree, would you, and see if it likes you'?"

"I am just as empty of ideas as you are, ma'am."

The two of them returned to staring at the tree as if a message would appear on its leaves for them to read. After a while, the silence of the large chamber was disturbed by a sound which seemed to come from far away, as if it was being sounded down a large, hollow tube. It was no tune either of them knew, yet it seemed almost familiar. It grew louder and louder until Mannert stood up in front of the desk while Myrella seriously considered running for the door. She was too late, however. As the crescendo approached, so a swirling mist began to form between them and the tree. It solidified and, as the last note dropped away, it too vanished.

Where it had been, there were now six people, each one of whom looked as stunned as she felt.

12

There was a silence born of amazement which stretched out before it was finally banished by one of the new arrivals, a young woman dressed in, from what Myrella could tell, old, stained cloth of no particular shape, who, after stopping and looking around, pointed at Myrella and said, "Who are you and why are we here?"

Myrella was immensely impressed by Mannert's response, which came back so quickly as to seem prepared. "I think those are questions we might ask as well, as this is a secure building you have entered in some fashion."

Speaking seemed to break the spell and suddenly everyone was talking at once. Myrella tried to wave them all into silence. Her frustration of recent times led her to take her shoe off and bang it on the table. It worked and there was silence. As they quietened, so she noticed that the adults seemed to have strange necklaces and the others all appeared to have tattoos on their faces. She wondered if it was some sort of tribal markings. But what possible tribe could they be from? There were no such tribes. She was sure of it.

"Thank you!" she said, putting the shoe back on. "Obviously this is a very strange thing indeed. Everyone here is in the same state of shock I would imagine, so let me try to start making things a little clearer. My name is Myrella and I am President of Haven. This here is Mannert, my secretary, and we are standing in the main Assembly Room. Behind you is the tree which appeared in this chamber some years ago, although nobody really knows how. You have obviously come from somewhere else. The how or why of that we will get to later. Now, it would be easier I think if you were to introduce yourselves, starting with the young lady who first spoke."

"My name is Pol and we came -- ,"

"Not yet, Pol," interrupted Myrella, making a slight bow as she did so. "One thing at a time would be best."

Pol frowned slightly but then shrugged in acquiescence.

The woman next to her spoke next. "I am Carmeena." Myrella acknowledged her with a small bow of her head.

"Hanna," said the other young girl. Another bow.

"Isselta." The young woman examined Myrella with a steady gaze, who returned it with another small bow.

"Endel," said the teenage boy. Again, she bowed.

"Farran," added the last man who bowed before Myrella could.

"Excellent," said Myrella. "I hate talking with people I do not know. Now, I suspect that you have a tale to tell, and I for one would very much like to hear it." She put her hand up as several of the newcomers opened their mouths to speak. "I would like to hear it, but not here. Mannert," she said, turning to her secretary, "please arrange for some food, enough for all of us, to be brought to my office so that we might get to the bottom of this." Mannert bowed and moved off swiftly.

"Before we leave the chamber here, are you all familiar with this tree?" She felt instinctively that there had to be some link between these strange people arriving and the tree's treatment of her two possible ambassadors. Plus it would give her time to assess them a little more and prove to them that she was not a threat. They did not feel threatening at all to her. If anything, they felt, not out of place so much, as to give the impression they saw things differently. But definitely not a threat. They all looked as if a good bath would be welcome news, but none of them seemed undernourished in any way. Indeed, beneath the grime they appeared to be very healthy. Also, none of them was wearing any shoes. Most strange.

The six of them turned to look at the tree. The older woman, Carmeena?, reached out to the nearest leaves which seemed, to Myrella's eye, to respond, the branch moving slightly toward the woman. Of the others, she noted that the two youngest looking girls, Pol and Hanna was it?, had closed their eyes and bent their heads almost as if they were listening to something Myrella could not sense. She could have sworn that the tattoos on their faces moved and formed a new pattern, but that was obviously impossible. She must be more overwrought than she realized.

Their actions weren't what she was expecting at all. A simple answer of yes or no was what she *was* expecting. Farran and Endel and Isselta were looking at the tree very carefully. None of them spoke for a moment.

Just as Myrella felt like giving a cough to regain their attention, Carmeena turned back to Myrella with a smile on her face. "It certainly is a wonderful tree. Very beautiful indeed. Very powerful as well."

Farran added, "It's not a usual tree, is it? There's something special about it, although I'm not quite sure what that might be. But as Carmeena said, very powerful. Very powerful indeed." And then the woman did a strange thing. She reached up to her necklace and stroked it as though it were alive. Perhaps it was a nervous habit, Myrella thought.

Endel nudged Hanna. "What did you get?"

By this point Myrella felt more like an observer, not the person in control of this situation. But what she heard next made her feel most definitely like an outsider.

"It's a strong song, certainly," said the young girl. "The song is woven all around and inside this building. It's not just a tree. That's the way the song wants to be seen. But it's not really only a tree."

"Yes," added Pol, as if Myrella was invisible. "It's like if you listen to it, it's where you can hear everything through it. Everything on Haven comes through it and everything from here goes through it to Haven. It's like a... like a... " she struggled to find the right words. "It's like a doorway. That's the best I can think of."

The six of them were all talking to each other, ignorant of Myrella until she did finally clear her throat. She had wanted to explain to them how it had appeared and that nobody seemed to know exactly what it was doing or what it was for and then these ragged people came in and effortlessly seemed to know a great deal more about it than anyone had ever dreamed of. Not for the first time that day, Myrella felt off balance at the way things were turning out.

"Well," she said in what she hoped sounded a bright and lively voice with no hint of uncertainty, "that's most interesting." Saying it, she was aware how lame it sounded. "Perhaps we could go and have something to eat and continue this discussion?" Her natural political instincts kicked in, and, although she knew she was out of her depth right now, she set off for the exit knowing they would follow. It was important to be seen as a leader, especially at times when she had little idea what was happening.

By the time she had arrived at her rooms, Mannert had once again proven his organizational abilities, for there was plenty of food, some of it hot, and enough water, juice or alcohol for everyone. Also, the short journey had give her time to collect herself and to think about what was next. What she had just witnessed was to be mulled over later. Pushing it to the back of her mind was a struggle, but a necessary one, if she was to finish this interminable day and find some peace in her mind. At least her headache was gone. Or had it simply been overwhelmed? What was of greatest importance now was to uncover what they were all doing here.

After allowing them to eat undisturbed for a while, during which she noted that none of them seemed in the least put out anymore, she began to ask her questions.

"Where have you all come from? I assume you were all together and weren't living separately when whatever it was that happened happened?"

For the first time, Myrella noted some caution amongst them as they looked from one to another to see who would answer. Finally, the young man, Endel, sitting next to Hanna, said, "Have any of us heard anything here which seems wrong or out of tune? If not, then I say we go ahead and tell her." That seemed a strange way to start answering her question. He peered around and everyone else gave shrugs or nods of agreement.

Apparently it fell to Carmeena to be the spokeswoman. "We were living together in a place outside of the city. We found a pleasant place to stay and... we were waiting there."

"Waiting? For what?"

Carmeena, like Pol earlier, tried to find the right words. "We were not really sure. All we knew was that there was something we were needed for here in Pannedon, something we needed to do perhaps, but we didn't know what. All we knew was that the time was getting closer."

"Are you Revivalists?"

"No. Although we know some of them and we have been living with them on and off. But we're not exactly the same as them."

That didn't help her much. "I accept that you might not be able to give all the details I would like, but perhaps you can tell me *how* you got here, because that was very strange indeed." And that was putting it very mildly. "I know what I think I saw, but I suspect that's not the truth of it. And, besides, where you arrived is normally a very secure place. I'd like to know more about it. Is security something I need to be concerned about?"

Carmeena responded by asking, "What did you see when we arrived? What was it like?"

Myrella tried her best to answer. Whatever had happened was not something which was easily put into words. As she realized that, she realized also that it was that unsayable aspect of it which made it almost less threatening. She should have been frightened, called for guards, and yet neither she nor Mannert had reacted like that. Perhaps there was something else going on, something which, for this day at least, joined them all and made them... not enemies, not friends, but allies perhaps. "I first heard something, like a tune, a song perhaps. But it got louder and I couldn't tell where it came from. And then there was a sort of mist which appeared and as the song or tune or whatever it was got louder, so the mist seemed to become thicker. But as the sounds died away, the mist did as well and, well, there you all were. At least, that's how I recall it. Mannert, can you add anything?"

He shook his head, his expression showing that his usual self-control was liable to break if he was not careful.

Carmeena had listened carefully to Myrella and nodded along as she spoke, occasionally stroking at her necklace in an absentminded fashion.

"Yes. That sounds about right," she had said at the end of it. "We got sung here and that's what it looks like. Not that we were expecting it at all, were we?" she asked, looking around her at the others. They all shook their heads. "We were about to eat -- which is why this food was very welcome, thank you -- and then we felt a song build up around us and, whoosh! we arrived."

Myrella was trying hard to understand, but this was beyond anything she was prepared for. It must have been obvious in her face because one of the other women -- Pol, was it? -- got up to place a reassuring hand on her shoulder. And that in itself was one more thing she was not expecting.

"It probably seems a little strange to you," she said, looking down at Myrella. "It would take far too long to explain everything." Pol now squatted down to be at Myrella's level. "The point is not how did we get here but why are we here at all? Isn't that what's important now? Because none of us know." She held Myrella's gaze a moment before returning to her seat.

Myrella was enough of a politician to recognize that some things do not have easy explanations, but that other things, no matter how strange the surroundings, are important to focus on. She was grateful to Pol for making her look at what was important. She took a deep breath. "It is obvious," she began, "that you all have certain abilities or senses, or something which allows you to do what you do. But as the young lady here, Pol, said, why are we all together now? I confess that I am unsure, at the very least, what that answer could be, but I hope that between us we can begin to make some headway. Perhaps you can enlighten me as to how you got here later on. Maybe I'll be able to understand it or not, but I would like to hear it nevertheless. Now, let's get back to what happens now you are here. And I'm assuming from what you've said, how you are acting and how I feel, that you are not a threat. Please don't prove me wrong, as I'm sure Mannert here has put somebody on alert?" The slightest of nods from her secretary reassured her. "You said that you had been waiting for some sort of sign, but you were unsure what. Is that correct?"

The young man, Endel, answered first. "More or less. We knew we were waiting to come to the heart of Pannedon and that it would be some time soon."

"Waving aside the 'how' of it again, you're saying that nothing happened where you were which might be thought of as a trigger in some fashion?" asked Myrella hopefully.

There was a general shaking of heads and then Pol said, "Well if it wasn't there, then it has to be here, doesn't it? What happened here before we arrived?"

Myrella considered what to say. After all, she did not know anything about these people and what or who they might represent. To provide details of government business to unknown people was hardly good politics. She chose her words very carefully. "Prior to your arrival, that tree which interested you so much began to move unexpectedly. Branches waved around. It was the first time such a thing has happened." She hoped they would accept the severely abbreviated version of the truth as she had no intention of revealing what had actually occurred.

The newcomers were silent until Hanna said, quietly, "I wish Meldren was here. She'd know if it was a lie."

Farran nodded and his deep voice rumbled around the room. "Doesn't matter. If the tree moved, no matter what it was doing, it is important to Haven."

"Good point, Farran," said Carmeena, pushing her long, brown hair back over her shoulders and reaching into a pocket for a strip of leather to tie it back. As she did so, Myrella could have sworn that her necklace looked directly at her with tiny, sparkling eyes. But they must be jewels, she reassured herself. Jewels set in a piece of fancily carved wood. The alternative was too much to accept. Not on top of everything else. "And, as this is the place where decisions are made about Haven," Carmeena continued, "I would think that the tree has an interest in one decision in particular. A decision never made before." She turned to look at Myrella. "Would that be right?"

Myrella felt that these strange, dirty people could see inside her. She was reluctant to give anything away that she could keep to herself, but she was equally certain that it would prove to be difficult. "You must be aware of the arrival of the spaceship?"

She was met with blank stares.

"Surely you must have heard about the fact that we've been contacted by another human civilization? There's been nothing but news about it everywhere!" Again, the blank stares.

"You must be joking with me. Everyone has an opinion about what's going to happen when it arrives."

"Remember, we've been living with Revivalists and we've been living out in the country for a while now," said Carmeena. "We have neither heard nor seen any news about this spaceship. I did hear something once but I didn't pay much attention." She shrugged as if it was so evident that she should not have been called upon to provide an explanation.

Pol looked thoughtful, "I'm fairly certain now that the tree's movements, whatever they were, had something to do with a decision you were making, or had made about this spaceship. And, if it was the first time it had done anything like that, my next guess is that whatever you were thinking of doing, it did not agree with? Am I right?"

Myrella, feeling beleaguered, nodded.

"But we're not the answer to your problem," said Hanna, "or we'd know what we had to do right away. Which means you need us and our abilities to help you with the decision."

"What was the decision?" asked Endel.

Myrella looked to Mannert to see what he thought or if he could provide some support. Instead he spread his hands palms up and made a face as if to say, *'You've no choice but to tell them.'*

Myrella looked at Carmeena. "I was debating about who to appoint as ambassador."

"Ambassador?" The word obviously meant nothing to Carmeena. Another example of the strangeness emanating from these people.

"The person who will have to go back in the spaceship to negotiate a fair arrangement between the Empire and Haven. They will have a difficult time, I am sure, and I wanted to find the best person for this task."

"And the tree didn't like who you were thinking about?" asked Pol.

Myrella paled slightly. "That tree can understand what I'm thinking?" Although it had been mentioned before, the thought of it still shocked her. Hearing someone else say it out loud made it more real. Her voice rose. "That's... that's not possible. Not possible."

"Actually, it's more than possible." Pol sat back and waited for Myrella to regain her composure. Jerking her thumb over her shoulder, she said, "That's no ordinary tree in there. It is, in one way, the whole of Haven. Or, at least, as much of Haven as can fit into it. That's what we think it is." She looked around at her friends. "We've not seen or sensed anything like this before, have we?" There was a general shaking of heads. "It doesn't look it, but that tree is as big in some ways as the whole planet. Something as big as a planet can do many things. I would guess hearing what you think would be easy for it." More nods.

Hanna continued. "The tree didn't like your choice for ambassador, and it wants none of us here, otherwise we'd all have felt something. But, if it's someone who should go, then it's nothing to do with our talents that I can think of. Perhaps we'd be better off asking it ourselves." She turned to the others and said, "What do you think?" and once again Myrella felt like an outsider in her own office.

There seemed to be general agreement. "So," said Hanna, "We'll go and ask it who should be this embassadin or whatever you call it." She was half out of her seat when Isselta, who had been quiet up to now, put her hand up to stop her.

"There's no need to go," she said as Hanna sat back down. Endel, she noticed, patted Hanna's hand as if to reassure her. "Think about it. If it's none of us, and she," gesturing at Myrella, "has had her guesses turned down, then it's someone we know and she doesn't." Isselta grinned. "I'll give you three guesses who it is, and neither of them is going to be happy about it."

Pol added, "Oh, but it will be good to see them again, won't it." She was grinning as well.

Myrella, more confused than ever, suddenly felt the room filled with what she would later say was a presence. For a long moment, she felt she was in the depths of a forest, to the point of dimly seeing trees all around her and hearing its sounds, smelling it even. It was utterly peaceful and she immediately felt totally at ease. All her concerns, all her tiredness, were leached away by something huge and soothing and caring. The moment passed and she looked at everyone there, and they were all smiling.

Hanna, laughing happily, looked at her and said, "It shouldn't be too long now, if we're right."

13

E ver since Harmony had shown them their friend's faces, Javin and Meldren had been unable to truly enjoy the days. The waiting for whatever was to happen dragged at them, sucking away their ease and contentment. They could get no clear picture of why they had been contacted again or what their role would be. They only knew that they weren't going to have to wait very long. But the lack of clear knowledge chafed at them.

Instead of wandering from place to place as they had been doing, they had decided to make a more permanent camp by a river. There was food to be caught in the river and with what they already had with them, they had enough food to last a while. The low, spreading bushes nearby acted as perfect covers for sleeping at night and provided shade during the day. All in all it was a most pleasant spot, but knowing that they would be going somewhere else at some time for some as yet unknown reason made them listless and quiet.

Sitting on the banks as the moon rose, dangling their feet in the cool, fast-flowing waters, Meldren let out a long, slow sigh. "I really want this waiting to be over. It's almost worse knowing that something's going to happen than it is to be taken unawares. I cannot settle to anything." She kicked her feet, the splashing sounds seeming loud in the twilight.

"I agree. Waiting is worse," replied Javin. "But, I have to say that there is one bright spot in this."

"What's that?"

"I don't have to learn to swim."

Meldren made a grudging grunt of laughter. "You're still worried about that? Don't for one moment think that this means you will get out of learning to swim. It only means that it's postponed."

Javin gave a melodramatic sigh. "Now I know you truly hate me."

"If you only knew how much it hurts me to watch you as you suffer and struggle. But it has to be done for your own good."

"Pah!"

Meldren's feet continued to splash in the river. "Do you feel that whatever is going to happen is really close?" she asked eventually. "For me, I can't tell anymore. I'm too close to it. I can't stand back and sense it."

"Same for me," he replied. "It's felt like it's been really close for so long now."

More splashes.

"Javin?"

"What?"

"Do you think we should have nice clean clothes on when we go?"

"I hadn't thought about it."

"We might have to make a good impression."

"I would think that arriving out of thin air would make a pretty good impression all by itself."

"But shouldn't we look, I don't know, not... "

"Not as dirty-looking as we do now?"

"Yes. But I wouldn't have said we were dirty."

"No, you only thought it."

"We could make our clothes cleaner. We could sing them clean, couldn't we? And, we will probably look strange to whoever it is we're going to meet, because I can't think it's going to be only our old friends."

Javin sighed. "Oh, why not? After all, it will give us something to do, won't it?"

"Then I'm going to wash and braid my hair first." Meldren was suddenly more lively. "While I'm doing that, you can sing our clothes clean and make sure you get rid of any holes or tears. Plus, if you think we'll need any satchels or things like that, you can sing those for us as well."

"Yes, dear."

"Did you really just say that? Did you really just say 'Yes, dear' to me? You are in so much trouble now. So much."

The next few moments were filled with squeals, shrieks, pleas for mercy and the sound of Javin crying out from being drenched as Meldren stood in the shallows, scooping and throwing water at him.

"Well, that feels a whole lot better," said Meldren as she lay on her back on the bank suppressing her laughter.

"And I feel a whole lot wetter."

"Serves you right. I have no sympathy at all."

Whatever either of them was going to say or do next was made redundant as a single, impossibly clear and resonant note sounded. It was long and low, and everything became still. The river slowed, the clouds stopped moving and even Javin's hair stopped in mid-shake, water droplets held in suspension. Their sprites however, uncoiled from their throats and slid to encircle their heads at their temples, echoing the note as they did so. As the two creatures held the note, so the original sound developed complexity and became first one chord, then a series of chords building and building into a symphonic blanket which enfolded the two startled people. To Meldren's eyes, everything still seemed in slow motion, although she knew she was breathing normally. At least, it felt as if she was.

As the sound built, so she saw the old, yet familiar wall build around them, blurring their view of the river and the moon, thickening until it was completely opaque. Then, although there was no way she could see, she knew that they were moving, more and more swiftly. It was something she could only feel. She reached out for Javin, but her hand moved more slowly than she was used to. She could see him reaching for her. Their fingertips touched and she grasped his hand, feeling better for the contact.

She did not know how much time passed, but she began to be aware that the wall around them was softening in some fashion. There was now a sensation of movement again, she could flex her fingers and they responded as normal. Aware that their journey was about to end, she sought to compose herself, all the while silently cursing that she looked like a wet rag.

Abruptly, the sound ceased, the wall disappeared and she and Javin found themselves standing on something very soft in a room which felt quite warm and that there were a number of people there as well. She felt her sprite slide down to her neck again. She felt certain there were two people here she did not yet know. How she knew that, she couldn't tell.

Before she could look round, a voice rich with laughter spoke. "Javin and Meldren! We knew you were coming but we didn't think it would be this quick!"

And then she recognized the faces, well, nearly all the faces. "Isselta! Is that you? Oh, you look well! And Pol? Surely not! I recognize the face, but you've grown so much, both of you." She waved her hands around at a loss as to how to express what she felt. "Carmeena! I'd recognize you anywhere." She grabbed at Javin, pointing at the smiling woman. "It's Carmeena. And Farran. Oh, but you two look wonderful. And that surely can't be you, Endel, can it? Really? You look so happy now. And you're, I'm not sure, but I think you're Hanna. Is that right?" She looked back at Javin. "They really are here, and they look so good."

Javin was beaming and hugging and exclaiming as well. "This is so good. So good to see you all again. But where are the others?

"They're well as far as we know," rumbled Farran, smiling hugely. He gestured at the others. "But it seems that we here are the ones who have been called on for this, whatever it is."

Meldren gestured at herself taking in her damp clothes and wet hair. "We hadn't planned to arrive looking like this, but... ," and she shrugged helplessly.

The strange woman could no longer contain herself. "Excuse me, but is that some sort of snake around your neck?"

Meldren reached up to her sprite and stroked its head with a finger, smiling as she did so. "Oh. Hello. We call them sprites but as I've never seen a snake I don't know if it looks like one or not."

"But it's alive!"

"Well, yes. Of course. They help us in what we do," said Meldren pointing at Carmeena and Farran. "And the others have their ribbons on their faces."

The woman appeared to have no idea how to react to this information apart from shaking her head. Mannert put a steadying hand on her shoulder and, with the other, offered her a large glass which she took and gulped at, before coughing and making a face.

"I'm really sorry about the mess. We had planned to have clean clothes and I was going to braid my hair but... ." Meldren's voice tailed off as she realized that this was going to be much too much information. She changed direction. "I'm also sorry that we haven't been properly introduced yet. Javin and I were so glad to see our old friends." Here she stood erect and made a formal, flowing movement with her right hand, touching her forehead with two fingers before ending with her palm facing outwards and a gentle bow of her head. "My name is Meldren and I came here with Javin." She waited expectantly.

The woman put her glass down, took a deep breath and stood up straight. "My name is Myrella and I am the President of Haven." Here she extended her hand.

Meldren didn't know how to respond. Javin leaned in and whispered, "I told you. We shake hands here. Remember?" Meldren grasped the offered hand and waggled it from side to side. Myrella's face was a picture of surprise. Meldren then turned to the other stranger, the man who had said nothing so far. Again she repeated her salutation but was pleasantly surprised when Mannert responded by echoing her movements fairly accurately as he introduced himself to her. She grinned at the compliment.

The formality appeared to have produced a more balanced and congenial atmosphere, and there were smiles all round as they all were seated again, Mannert having found two more chairs from somewhere.

"I really do want to apologize for arriving looking like this," began Meldren. "We are not usually this... this... , what's a good word for how we are?" she asked Javin.

"Messy. We're not usually this messy." Javin gave an apologetic shrug. "But it is warm in here and we're almost dry and I see there's some food. Would you mind?"

Myrella waved him on. To Meldren's eyes Myrella looked as if there was nothing normal for her to hold on to right now, so anything which happened was something she would try to understand later. Meldren doubted Myrella would ever understand. Not completely. Myrella waited, along with the others, sipping on her drink. Meldren and Javin found some fruit and munched on it.

"This has been a most unusual day. Most unusual indeed," said Myrella looking distinctly shell-shocked. She proceeded to fill in the details, aided every so often by one or the other of their friends. "And so, you see, it appears that you are here as an answer to a problem we have on Haven."

Meldren had been listening hard as she ate, and had been watching the colors around Myrella but could find nothing which seemed substantially false in what she had been saying. She knew, from the way Javin held his head, that he had also been listening for any lies in what was being said. "You do know that we're not from Haven, don't you?" began Meldren. "Strictly speaking, Javin was born here, but we came from Harmony just now. We did not know about the ship or anything until you told us." She saw Myrella's expression. "Ah. Sorry. Perhaps that's a big jump for you, us coming from Harmony. But it's true." Before Myrella could react, Meldren hurried on. "You should also know that the tree in the big room was because of something that happened with Javin and myself. We were there when it arrived. You could say that we helped it be there in a way."

She clasped her hands together and leaned in to Myrella, a look of concern on her face. "I'm sorry that everything is happening so fast for you. It must be difficult to take in all of what we are saying. Maybe, someday, we'll all be able to sit down and really help you to understand everything. But, for right now, I think it is probably better if we get on with the reason for us being here. So would anyone like to explain, please?"

Hanna volunteered. "I think that Haven wants you to be an embassin or whatever the word is."

Mannert corrected her. "Ambassador. She means ambassador."

Meldren felt and looked puzzled. She turned to Javin. "What is that? What does it mean?"

"I think," he said, "it means someone who represents the government and talks on their behalf."

"Why would anyone do that? Why can't any government speak for itself?"

Javin shrugged. "That's all I can think of."

Meldren turned back to Mannert. "Why can't you speak for yourself? Why have anyone else speaking for you?"

It was Myrella who answered, having finally regained some composure. "That is because the people our ambassador has to speak with are a very, very long way away from us. People from another civilization, a civilization on planets in another part of the galaxy have come here and we need someone who will go back with them and make sure that Haven is treated well by them. That's what we need an ambassador for. And, apparently after the events of the day, one or the other of you has been chosen... by a tree" -- her expression made it clear she could not believe she had said that --, "to be our ambassador."

"No," said Meldren. "Absolutely not. You're not asking us to decide whether Javin goes or I go. That is not a choice we shall make." Myrella looked at her in confusion. "Either we both go or neither of us goes. It's that simple." Meldren shook her. "I cannot believe that you would ask someone to go on their own like that."

"I only meant that one person would be the ambassador. I certainly didn't mean going alone. That would be uncivilized."

"Then why can't we both be ambassadors?"

Myrella looked at Mannert for help and he returned her look with a stony face.

Isselta, sensing a gap in the conversation, said, "So you are actually agreeing to do this then? No questions? No arguments? Nothing like that? I thought, we all thought, that you would be angry and upset and refuse."

Meldren smiled at her and said, "I suppose you might have forgotten who it was that asked us here, and who helped us get here from Harmony? It's not like either Javin or myself have had any luck at all at going against what a planet wants. It's easier if we just say yes at the start and get it over with. At least, that's been our experience." She wrinkled her nose as she thought. "Besides, it can't be that bad if Haven picked us. Whenever anything like this happens, we are always looked after, aren't we, Javin?"

He reached for her hand. "It's true what she says. We knew something was going to happen but not what," here he shrugged, "which is standard. But I'm with Meldren. If we've been chosen, it means we're going to be looked after, and it's going to be impossible to fight it." Addressing Myrella, he asked, "What is it that we have to do and when do we have to do it by?"

Myrella's arched brows revealed her surprise at this no-nonsense approach. "We would need to discuss a lot of things and we would need to start as soon as possible. There are many, many things to consider, which, as you don't live here on Haven, you might find difficult to understand or appreciate. Perhaps we could begin tomorrow morning, early? It has been a very difficult day indeed, for me at least. I would greatly appreciate some sleep. If you would not mind? I'm sure Mannert here can find you both a place to sleep as well." He nodded.

"We'll all need a place to sleep," said Endel. "Do not think for one moment that any of us are going to leave here without knowing what is going on." The others all nodded in agreement, most of them with looks of amusement on their faces.

Myrella stood up and spread her hands. "This is beyond me now. Mannert, if you please, can you provide some sleeping arrangements for them all? It's probably for the best if they stay close rather than in hotels. It would spark too many rumors. I am going to my apartment, and I am going to try to sleep. If you are all still here in the morning, I will know that this has not been a strange dream. Excuse me and goodnight."

14

The following morning, early as promised, Myrella left her apartment in an annex to the main building, making her way to her office. All was quiet as she entered the corridor leading to the office complex. However, she heard a disturbance as she came nearer to her suite of rooms. The sounds of raised voices was plain. In particular she could make out the distinct tones of Corrivan demanding something or other. Silently, she paused and put her hand to her head. How could she have forgotten? Virtually nothing happened in this building without someone noticing it. Of course, the cleaners would have talked about what had happened and then someone somewhere at some time must have overheard the strangers. The strange events of the day before had thrown all thoughts of the swift spread of rumor and hearsay from her mind. This was not the start to the day that she would have wanted, but, nevertheless, here it was and she had to do something about it. Squaring her shoulders and sucking in a deep breath, she decided on a course of action and marched round the corner where she saw a group of about nine or ten people, councillors she thought, with Corrivan in the middle of them, all shouting and gesticulating at poor Mannert, who was resolute in keeping them out of her office.

"Thank you, Mannert," she said in a tone loud enough to carry. "I'll take it from here." Mannert gave a very brief, tense nod but remained in front of the doors.

Corrivan whipped around and pointed at her. "Hah! So here is our supposed leader who is making deals behind our backs with our friends from the Empire. What treachery are you involved in now?"

Myrella's face was as a stone; hard, expressionless and cold. She stared at Corrivan and continued walking in such a determined fashion that the other councillors opened a way before her as prey peels away before a predator. Reaching the doors, she turned and a part of her was delighted to see one or two flinch slightly. "Before you make yourselves look any more foolish and childish than you do now, you have some interesting discoveries awaiting you. I suggest you decide who shall represent you and then the rest of you disperse." There was barely a pause. "Corrivan, you can come in, and the rest may wait elsewhere. You will not wait outside here, or I shall have you removed. And, before anyone says that I can't, or that it's unconstitutional, I really do not think you will want to challenge me in any way until you are aware of some new events." She turned back, threw open the doors and marched in to her outer office calling on Corrivan to follow her as she did.

Inside, Mannert shut the doors and Myrella turned again to confront Corrivan, still angry, not to be argued with. "I am not in a good mood, councillor. I have had little sleep and before that, many strange surprises. I'm not even sure what I believe or don't believe at this moment. I have no idea what your spies have told you, but I daresay you might be in for a surprise or two yourself. In a moment, I will invite you into my main office, but first I must check to see whether that is going to be now or whether you will have to wait a short while."

Corrivan opened his mouth to speak, but Myrella hissed at him, "Don't even think of saying one thing. My patience is paper thin and about to tear apart. I do not like you, councillor, and I am not sure I like what is happening here. Until I say, you will wait here and when I say, you will enter." She turned to Mannert. "You have my permission to knock this blockhead with a chair or a paperweight or whatever comes to hand if he should even think of coming in before I say so." Leaving Corrivan open-mouthed and Mannert trying to hide a smile at her temerity, she entered her inner sanctum.

There they still all were. Eight of them looking, Myrella thought, cleaner and happier than the day before. She didn't know how long they'd been there or whether they had slept there. Doubtless she would find out later. The fact that they were here meant that yesterday had not been her imagination. Unsure whether she was glad or not about that, she took another deep breath to release the tension in her shoulders and tried to see them all only as ordinary people. Four older people and four younger. They did not look strange or exhibit weirdness that she could tell, apart from the neck things and the markings on their faces, that is. But they were dressed in old clothes and none of them had shoes on their feet, and what they had said and done yesterday had shaken her badly. Myrella felt as if nothing she knew was true anymore. It would certainly explain why she had lashed out at Corrivan, releasing years of frustration. Her anger also came out of fear, but it was a fear she could not easily name. Was it the fear of recognizing that she was nothing and nobody and counted for less because of that bloody tree? Was it simply fear of the unknown and that these ragged-looking people both knew more than she did and were able to do more than she ever could? She tried to shake herself free of such thinking. As she fought to understand herself more, the woman who had arrived last, Meldren, stood up.

"I'm sorry if we're causing you any problems by being here. We heard some noises outside but thought it better not to interfere." Myrella had a sudden vision of these ill-clad people opening the doors to the protestors and imagined the uproar that would have followed.

"Thank you," was all she said. "There are others in the government who would, of course, want to meet with you and discuss the role of ambassador." She faltered. "However, I am not so certain that the presence of the rest of you would be easy to explain. I saw you arrive and I still cannot explain it to myself. Having eight of you here might be too much to handle for anyone else."

"We could leave," said Carmeena. "Nobody would have to know. After all," she said, looking around at the others, "we all agreed that we've done what we were called here to do, didn't we? It would be fun to stay a while longer, but there's no real need. So we decided to go, but we thought it would be rude to not say goodbye first."

"However," put in Meldren's companion, name of Javin?, "I hope you don't mind, but we had a look through some of the papers here," Myrella could not hide the wince, "and we found out about these people they're leaving behind with another ship. Because of that, we thought it would be useful if some of us kept in contact with you. Or, at least, kept you informed about what was going on with them. It is easy for us to travel, as you've seen. But we all feel that you don't really trust them. We haven't met them and we haven't felt anything which might make us feel that way, too, but," he shrugged, "there's no harm in keeping an eye on them, is there?"

Myrella hadn't expected this. "Why would you do that?"

She thought it was Isselta who answered. "It's hard to understand perhaps, but all of us here have a very, very close relationship with Haven. We are just as anxious to know what is going to happen as you are, but probably for different reasons. Think of it as us doing what we feel is the right thing. You can choose to accept what we say or decide not to have any more contact with any of us. Whatever you decide, we're all still going to watch these people to make sure they bring no harm to Haven."

"What do you say?" asked Javin.

Myrella felt her command of the situation slipping away again, if indeed she had ever had it. "If it can be done discreetly, then, of course, I will welcome any and all information about these people. But how... ?" she trailed off.

"Oh, that's easy. When you want us to arrive, just go and tell the big tree. We'll know and we'll come to this room again."

Isselta's smile made the instruction seem so normal. *'Mannert? I'm just going to talk to a tree for a moment. Yes, madam, of course.'* Myrella returned the smile but doubted that it had the same simple sincerity of Isselta's. "I'll certainly do that." Mention of the tree stirred the earlier fear. Again she pushed it away.

Meldren nodded decisively. "Good. That's agreed then. Let's say our goodbyes and hope to see each other again soon." With that, they all began to hug and smile and look sad and happy at the same time, leaving Myrella feeling, once more, distinctly like an outsider. All her earlier anger, based, she was sure, on fear of the strangeness of it all, had evaporated. Now she felt like a schoolchild, watching friends plot out their vacation with her not knowing what she was to do with herself. It made her very sad.

When everyone had finished and the original six were in a circle, the youngest, Pol, skipped out and held hands with Javin and Meldren. Looking hard into their eyes, she said, "I need to tell you both this. Whatever happens, you must always hear the Sun. No matter where you are, the Sun will hear you. It's a different song to listen to, but you must find it. Always. And don't worry. You'll be safe." And with that, she returned to the circle. The six of them waved to Myrella and then they began to hum. The sound grew in a way which did not seem possible for human throats. As it did so, a mist formed around them and began to thicken until they could no longer be seen. At that point, the music faded away into nothingness and then there was only Javin, Meldren and herself in the room.

She looked toward the two, standing hand-in-hand, her raised brows a sign of her amazement.

Meldren smiled at her and said, "It does look a little strange from the outside, doesn't it?"

Myrella agreed. She dragged her focus back to the political present and the reason (or was it an excuse?) for her original anger. "If you agree, I have someone outside who would like to meet you and then, perhaps, we can talk about what being an ambassador involves?"

"Of course," said Meldren.

"I should warn you that this person is not a friend to people who choose to live a simple life such as yourselves or your friends. In fact, he is my political opponent and will probably be rude to you. I would appreciate it if you would at least tolerate him? His name is Corrivan."

"Of course we'll meet with him," repeated Meldren, taking a seat.

Just as Myrella turned to call him in, a sudden thought occurred to her. "Have you eaten since last night? I should have thought of this before. I apologize. I can get Mannert to have some food sent in if you'd like?"

Javin, smiling, held his hand up to stop her. "We had a very good breakfast, thank you. And, before you ask, we also slept well. We're used to sleeping on the floor and this soft floor-covering was a nice addition for us."

"Oh. Good. That's good," said Myrella vaguely, feeling as if she had been found wanting as a hostess. "I'll go and get him then." She halted and turned back to her desk. With a small, embarrassed smile, she tidied up the papers she had left and locked them away, trying to not feel totally incompetent.

She pressed a button and called for Mannert to escort Corrivan in, settling herself behind her desk. After a moment, Corrivan walked in, his pale blue eyes narrowed suspiciously. Without rising, she beckoned him to a chair to one side of Javin and Meldren who, she noted, were also examining him with tilted heads and narrowed eyes, as if trying to see or hear something beyond her senses. There was a notable tension as Corrivan took his seat and stared back at the two off-worlders, unable or unwilling to hide his distaste.

"Javin and Meldren, may I introduce you to Councillor Corrivan? Councillor Corrivan, may I introduce to you Javin and Meldren... ," a delicate pause, "who are to be our new ambassadors?" Saying it out loud for the first time brought home to her how much had happened in one day and how she had never really questioned it after the tree and the first six visitors. Realizing that of herself, she sat back and watched Corrivan's reactions.

There was a look of utter shock followed by anger. "You simply cannot be serious about this." He turned to Myrella. "These... these... *ragamuffins* are hardly the type of people to represent us! If I ever wanted infallible proof of your incompetence, Myrella," his use of her first name was extremely rare and showed the depths of his anger, "these two persons are undoubtedly it. How can we, as a government, as a people, possibly condone these two beggars as being representative of our planet? No! It is not possible. I absolutely forbid it. We will be a laughing stock, seen as incompetent and irresponsible. And what are those horrible things around their necks? It's all too ridiculous."

He would have said more had Meldren not leaned forward and tapped him on his knee. "Why are you so angry? We certainly didn't want to be ambassadors, but we've accepted and we'll do the best we can. But I don't think there's any reason to be angry about it, is there?"

He looked at her as if she were a diseased beggar on the street, disbelief matched with horror. "Madam, I have no idea where you came from, but you can go back there right now." He turned back to Myrella, "And you, you can say goodbye to being President. I am going to tell everyone what is going on here."

He started to stand up, but Javin said, "You are absolutely right. You have no idea where we have come from. Nor do you know what we do. Perhaps we should show you."

The way he spoke, or something in his voice, made Corrivan pause and resume his seat. Javin continued, "What you don't understand is that neither ourselves nor this lady here had anything to do with us being here, being your ambassadors. There was someone else involved." He let the sentence dangle.

Finally, Corrivan could not but help ask, "Who was it that arranged this farce then?"

"Perhaps we should go and meet?" said Meldren sweetly. She stood up and indicated that Corrivan should accompany them. Myrella, being an observer so far, knew where it was going and she began to relish what she thought was going to happen.

"Where are we going?" Corrivan demanded.

"To give you your answer," said Meldren, still in that same, sweetly innocent voice. "But," she added, "the answer might bring more questions. So, why not be quiet and let us show you?"

The corridor was now empty of Corrivan's supporters and they quickly entered the chamber. Leading the way down to Myrella's desk, Meldren stopped.

Corrivan looked around with unconcealed disgust. "There's nobody here. The Assembly is not in session. You are wasting my time."

Meldren tapped his shoulder and pointed ahead to the tree. "There is always somebody here, Councillor. Allow me to introduce you to Haven."

Whatever patience Corrivan might have had, and it was obviously very little, evaporated completely at this point. Myrella watched him and could not hide a smile. As she did so, she realized that at some point over the past two days she now accepted that the tree was not purely a ceremonial totem as she and so many others had thought, but was a living, breathing being of immense, and somewhat unknown, powers.

"Do not insult my intelligence, young woman. I demand that you answer the question of how you were chosen to be ambassadors when anyone can see that you can hardly keep yourselves clean or well-dressed."

"Hold your tongue, Councillor," Myrella barked. "Allow your question to be answered."

Corrivan fumed, but silently.

Meldren turned to Javin and said, "I suppose we call Her here and let Her show him? I can't think that anything we say will work, do you?"

"I doubt it," he replied. Addressing Corrivan, Javin said, "I don't really know what will happen next, only that it will be an answer to your question. I strongly advise you to watch and try to understand. What is going to happen next is something very few people will ever get to witness, but I think it is the only way you will know how we were chosen."

Turning back to Meldren, he reached for her hands and together they took a deep breath. Then, starting on a low note, they began to croon or hum, Myrella didn't really know which it was. But, at the same time, the snake-like things around their necks began to unwind from around their necks and slide swiftly to rest around their foreheads, the tiny heads with the sparkling eyes craning upwards and adding their own sounds into the mix. Myrella felt a chill run down her spine as the sound thickened and swirled. She could hardly take her gaze away from them but did see out of the corner of her eye than Corrivan had an uncertain look on his face, somewhere between fear and wonder.

The sound grew around them in some strange way, as though it was creating something, knitting the very air into something solid. Myrella noticed that the same scent and sense of a forest she had felt earlier became obvious, and at the same time, the tree's branches began to move as though a wind was blowing through them. She became aware that the sound began to lessen in intensity and there was a moment when there was only the four of them and the tree and then there was the moment when something or someone, vast and potent, was with them and she felt insignificant and full of wonder.

For a moment, after the sound had tailed away, there was only a massive silence and then all of the branches of the vast tree whipped to point at Corrivan, who shrank back with a cry, warding off the nearest leaves. Myrella also took a step back at the speed of it all. As Corrivan sought to regain his balance, a voice was heard and felt. It was such a voice that Myrella's bones shook to it and her head emptied of everything else. It filled her until there was no space for thought or feeling.

"I am here," it began, and a cascade of sounds formed a background: rain, thunder, wind in the grass and the slow rumble of glaciers and earthquakes were part of it. "I am here, and you are here to witness me. I choose those who respect and know me. I chose these two now and no-one else. I watch and I listen and I see and I know what is said and what is thought. These two are chosen. Do not attempt to stop them. You will not survive me."

Myrella, just as stunned as Corrivan, watched in amazement as the huge tree restored its branches to their original positions and then, she would have sworn it was so, it bowed to Javin and Meldren still holding hands, still looking at each other, still smiling. And then, as if a door shut, the presence was gone and there were just the four of them again. Javin and Meldren's snakes slid back down to their throats and the two of them turned to Corrivan who was breathing heavily and had a distant look in his eyes. Myrella swallowed once, twice and felt a sense of loss and of emptiness in the chamber.

"Well?" asked Meldren looking calm as if nothing had happened. "You have had your answer. Whether you believe it or not is up to you."

Corrivan did not look capable of coherent speech yet, so Myrella took his arm and said, "Let's go back to my office, shall we, and talk about what happened? I've had a little experience of strange things recently, but this is new to me as well. I certainly could do with a drink and I'm sure that's true for you."

After a short while, as they were seated in Myrella's office, Mannert passed around some soft drinks and offered some fruit and cheese before leaving them alone. Corrivan, by this time, had recovered enough to speak.

"What was that?" he asked finally. Myrella cocked her head at Meldren. She, too, was interested in the answer. She thought she knew but she wanted to be certain. Hearing someone else say it out loud would be a relief.

"Haven," said Meldren simply. "The planet. That tree is not really only a tree. In its own way it is the whole of the planet. But that was Haven who spoke to you."

This was too much for Corrivan. He shook his head. "No. No, that cannot be. That is impossible. A planet cannot speak!"

"And yet you heard it and you felt it," said Meldren.

"I certainly felt and heard something that I cannot explain," said Myrella. To Corrivan, she said, "I heard a voice out of nowhere, and I saw the tree move. I felt a presence in there that I have never felt before. Perhaps it's all too much to take in straight away. Perhaps we all need to let that experience sink in before we judge it." She definitely needed some time to herself. The past two days, on top of the previous weeks, had presented her with a variety of experiences that she could never have dreamed of. She was on overload. She wanted time to process it all. She also wondered when that would be.

Corrivan made a dismissive movement with his hand. "What you said happened is impossible." Pointing an accusatory finger at Javin and Meldren he said, "You must have done something, hypnotized us in some fashion. For all I know, those things around your neck are responsible for what happened." He leaned forward as if to grasp Meldren's snake, or whatever it was called. However, as he neared it, it extended and hissed at him. Meldren reached to stroke and reassure it as Corrivan fell back into his chair.

"You saw that! It attacked me. Those things are dangerous and should be destroyed."

Javin, silent until now, said in a menacing voice, "Try to interfere again and I will make sure it bites you. There are unpleasant aftereffects. You are a foolish little man," he continued, now full of scorn. "What you witnessed just now was meant only for you. It was something incredibly special, something which no more than a handful of people will ever witness. It was an honor. But it was something you cannot explain and so you automatically reject it and attack those who showed it to you. You heard what was said. Do not interfere. What do you think that tree was doing in there in the first place? Did you think at any time that it was more than a decoration? Are you really that stupid?" Javin shook his head in exasperation. "You asked us a question. If we had told you without showing you, you would have thought we lied. Instead, we showed you as best we could, and you were graced with an answer directly from Herself. And still you cannot accept it. You have been nothing but rude and ill-mannered to us and we have done nothing to deserve it. I think you should go away. Now."

Corrivan balled his fists, his mouth a taut line and his eyes cold. "I shall see to it that these people here are exposed as charlatans and enemies of the people of Haven. What happened must have been some trickery, something easily explained that you wished me to believe was something else." To Myrella he added, "And I shall certainly see to it that you are removed from your post for gross incompetence or even treason."

Myrella was taken aback at the venom she felt from him but before she could respond, Javin said, "You will do no such thing, Councillor. If you do, please be assured that we will provide Myrella here with all the information she needs about you and your attacks on defenseless communities all over the planet. Names, times and who was in charge. I think that people will not believe what you say after that. Be quiet and all will be well. Speak out against what you had the privilege to witness and all will definitely not be well. It's not just us two saying this, it's Haven as well. Please remember those last words you heard: '*You will not survive me*'." He looked carefully at him. "Do we understand each other now?"

Corrivan's breathing was loud in the silence which followed. He blinked rapidly a few times and clenched and unclenched his jaw. He appeared to be wrestling with his emotions, but finally managed to nod his agreement. With a slight tilt of her head, Meldren indicated he should leave. There was a collective intake of breath as the door shut behind him.

Myrella poured herself a large drink, offering the same to Meldren and Javin, who refused with a smile. Slumping down in the chair vacated by Corrivan, she took a long swallow. Letting out a long sigh releasing the tension she had been holding she asked, "What I don't understand is where did you get that information about him attacking places? How could you possibly know that?"

Javin looked a little sheepish. "I was reading those papers on your desk last night and talking with the others about places being attacked. There were suggestions that Corrivan was involved and I... , well, it's hard to explain this next part, but I listened to him and there was something about him that was not right. I'm sorry I read the papers. But I said what felt like the right words and they must have been, by the way he reacted."

Myrella took another, contemplative sip and thought about what Javin had said and done. Yes, she had been at fault over leaving private government papers out in the open, but the end result more than made up for that. She couldn't find it in herself to chide Javin. And there was an upside to it all.

"Don't apologize for reading them. That's my fault for leaving them out. But, there is one thing which has become clear indeed about you two. You can negotiate like a politician, like an ambassador in fact. I don't understand even half of what you are capable of, but what I do understand, I like." She raised her glass in a toast. Putting it down, she stretched the remaining tension out of her shoulders and wiggled her head. "What I really want to do is sleep for a week. However, that is not going to be possible. Instead, shall we come to an understanding of what is going to be expected of you and what we would like you to remember when negotiating? Good, then I'll call Mannert in here, and he can make notes of it all."

And so they spent the rest of the day.

15

W hen Javin and Meldren were eventually introduced as the chosen ambassadors, initial reactions were of shock and amazement that the two of them had never been heard of before. Corrivan in particular was voluble in his disparaging of them, but did not go so far as to make personal attacks. The warning he had received had obviously remained with him. However, over the days, there was a strange and rapid change to one of general acceptance. Even Corrivan became less talkative and was seen less and less frequently in the media. It happened, as Javin said, because Haven needed everyone to agree.

"Haven is, I am quite certain, changing the way people are reacting to us," he said in a quiet moment to Meldren.

"What makes you say that?, she asked. "I mean, apart from the fact that everyone starts out by being rude to or about us, and then they change their minds... ." Her eyes widened as she realized. "Oh, so Haven's singing new songs for them so that they really do like us." She chuckled.

"It would also explain why my sprite has been buzzing for a while. Very low, so that I can hardly hear it, but it's definitely doing something," said Javin.

Meldren nodded. "Mine, too, now you mention it. I hadn't thought of it as anything other than being around so many people. It is tiring doing this, isn't it?" The 'this' she was referring to was having to meet and talk with so many people, probably more than at any other time in their lives. At the end of every session, they felt drained and needed somewhere to rest quietly. Myrella, thankfully, had noticed how they tended to droop and had been vigorous and effective in restricting the time spent dealing with large groups.

Over a period of days, Javin and Meldren had become familiar faces around the globe, been interviewed countless times (the questions strictly controlled by Myrella), and had meeting after meeting with various officials concerning Haven's perceived needs when trading with the Empire.

The day before their departure, they had had a long conversation with the crew who would be taking them to the Empire's home planet where they would meet its officials and begin the negotiations. By this time, the visitors from space were less newsworthy than the ambassadors. It had been explained to Javin and Meldren how much baggage they could take and where they would be staying. A brief tour of the scout ship which would take them into orbit where they would transfer to the mother ship was arranged and then, finally, they were left alone for their last night before launching the next day.

"What did you make of the captain?" asked Javin that night as he stood and stretched, arching his back and neck.

"I think she is hiding something, but what it is, I have no idea," answered Meldren, running fingers through her hair. "She was too busy making us look at things we had no idea what they were or what they were for. Also, too much talk."

"So it's not just me, then." Javin had his arms out and was turning his body from side to side.

Meldren tossed her hair over her shoulder and chuckled. "No. But whatever it is, I don't feel that it is something that involves us." She cocked her head. "Unless you picked up something I missed?"

Javin, now standing still, shook his head, glad, as ever, that the two of them were so in tune with each other and with the world around them.

"Tell me again," said Meldren. "Why is it that we are doing what we are doing? And I'm not even really sure what it is we are doing, even after all those meetings and all that talking."

"The same answer as always. The same answer for all of the things we've done: it's because a planet wants us to," said Javin.

"Oh. Good. I thought it was because we're really nice people and that this was some sort of reward. But it's nice to know that someone or something thinks well enough of us to give us tasks we don't understand in places we don't want to be amongst people we don't want to be with." Meldren sat on the floor, her back against the bed, her face thoughtful. "Seriously, Javin, how do we get involved in things like this? Are we really supposed to make things right for Haven with this Empire they talk about? We're not the right people. We don't know how to start. I could understand when we helped out the children from here. It made sense."

"Not at the time, it didn't," said Javin. "It was only later that we understood what we were meant to be doing." He shrugged. "Probably going to be the same thing here."

"Good point," nodded Meldren, patting the floor beside her. "I tend to forget how it was at first." She waited until Javin was settled, his legs stretched out, before reaching for his hand. "So this is just the part where we have no idea what we're getting ourselves into, but when we look back, it will all make sense. Is that what you're saying?"

"Yes, it is. At least, that's what I think this is. I know we haven't had much time to ourselves since arriving, but in some odd moments, I've tried to catch a feeling about what's ahead of us." He paused.

"Well?" prompted Meldren.

"Nothing. More accurately, nothing bad that I can sense. If you want to know, the only way I can picture the feeling I got was that it wasn't something like us helping the children. That was small, if you like. Small and sort of all in one place. They were either with us on Harmony or we were with them on Haven." He cupped his hands. "It was all in one place. It was something we could see the beginning and end of. But this... ? This is something different. It's not in one place. It feels like it's much wider or bigger in some fashion. Or maybe it covers a bigger area." He shrugged again. "I don't know."

Meldren considered his words. "Makes some sense though, doesn't it?

There's definitely going to be a bigger area this time. We're going to a new place, the Empire. But we're dealing with the people here as well. So those two things alone make it much bigger."

He shook his head slowly. "Maybe. But it feels like a different sort of bigger than that. I don't know how to say it, but, when you get the chance, check in yourself and see if you can feel the same sort of thing. All I know is that it's something new." He puffed his cheeks out at his inability to adequately express what he felt.

Meldren leaned back against the bed, arching her neck and closing her eyes. After a while, she opened them again and nodded at Javin who had been watching her. "Definitely spread out. But it's to do with us. Not that we're spread out. At least, I don't think that's how it felt. But something bigger than just us." It was her turn to shrug. "Whatever it is, we'll find out. But, before we have all the crowds of people staring at us tomorrow, is there anything we've forgotten to provide? Anything we need to sing to have ready for tomorrow? I'm good for clothes, no matter what the women here think of them. I don't need all that fancy stuff draped around me. Unless, that is, you'd like me to look like them?" She turned her head to Javin with an impish grin on her face. "It can be done."

Javin knew she was teasing, but he also knew that she disliked being talked about by people who were critical of the way the both of them were dressed. They had politely but firmly refused many offers of clothing and other apparel in order to keep wearing what they were comfortable in, which was loose-fitting shirts and tunics. Meldren wore skirts sometimes and leggings at other times, occasionally a shift which she cinched at her waist. Sometimes Javin preferred leggings, and sometimes he preferred what could only be called a kilt. Both went barefoot at all times. The clothes had been the only point of outright disagreement with Myrella. She had pleaded with them to dress differently and, in the face of their implacable opposition, had finally shouted and accused them of dishonoring the entire planet, her brown eyes, normally warm, becoming hard. It had made no difference. All they had done to appease her was to make sure that there were no holes or stains in any of their clothing, singing new items as necessary. Of course, Myrella's anger had quickly dissipated and been transformed into gentle acquiescence under the spell of Haven and the sprites. So Meldren's question had been nothing more than a simple tease.

He smiled at her and said, "Well, maybe having one of those fancy hats would be nice. You know the ones I mean? The big, wide, floppy things that are shiny and have stuff hanging down all around the edge. They might suit you."

"And why would that be?"

"Oh, you know, they hide so much, but in such a nice way." He had a huge grin on his face and ducked his head down as Meldren swatted at him.

"You want me to hide my face? Because I'm so ugly? Is that it?" She continued swiping at him, but was too close to do much.

He lunged closer, grabbing her around the waist and hugged her to him. With his nose nestling in her neck near her ear, he whispered, "I don't want everyone else seeing how beautiful you are."

She stopped trying to hit him and pushed herself back in order to look at him better. "That was close. Very close. But I admire the way you saved yourself." She looked around the room with some distaste. "I suppose it's all very comfortable and everything, but I don't like these beds at all, do you?"

"Not at all. I'm comfortable on the ground. Not something I thought I'd hear myself say on Haven in one of the most expensive hotels on the planet, but it's true. I like the floor. I like it even more because you're next to me." And he reached for her as he lay down. "Anywhere you are is the right place for me."

"Mmmhmm," she murmured. "Keep saying the right words like that and we'll be fine."

16

Later the next day, after the endless ceremonies and speeches, they were all in the landing craft with the two crew who would return to Haven, trying to hold on wherever they could.

Stobbant kept an eye on Javin and Meldren, who were trying to see as much as they could of the planet as well as take in as much of the ship as they could. Having been given a quick tour of it previously, they had a rough knowledge of what was where. But, in flight, with lots of tiny lights, some of them flashing on and off, and various screens being active, she thought, not kindly, they were like little children in their interest.

Then there was the weightless moments as they docked with the deep space vessel. Weightlessness was a cause of much hilarity to both of them, with Meldren in particular giggling irrepressibly as she twirled round and round upside down compared to Javin. Finally, to Stobbant's relief, they managed to get themselves and their small amount of baggage on board *Lightning*.

Stobbant returned to the lander once she was sure that her two passengers were busy being shown around the ship. She looked hard at Lessterenman and Parra-Hopshan. "Don't let us down. Go back down there and be perfect little people. But, get as much hard data as you can and send it back via the beacon. I want to be seeing a string of good results from you when I get these two back to The Prime. Remember, you're not just the representatives of the Emperor, more importantly, you're representing us. You're going to make sure that this entire crew gets paid enough to retire and then some. Clear?"

The two of them nodded in unison.

"You can rely on us, Captain," said Parra-Hopshan.

"I have no choice, do I? So see to it I don't come back and strip you of any family ties and send you down as clone material."

Again, two swift nods.

"Be nice, be efficient, but above all, remember the rewards." It was Stobbant's turn to nod. "See you when we get back."

Returning to the main craft, she found that both Javin and Meldren were in their quarters, and that Evan and Norall-Severent were busily working at the pre-flight checks. She tapped once on the door to the newly named guest quarters and opened it to find both of them sitting on the bed looking, if not unhappy, then certainly a little lost.

"How are things?" she asked. "I know there's not a lot of room here, but I think you'll get the hang of it soon enough. We'll be launching very soon, but you won't feel as much as you did when lifting from Haven, so it should be comfortable for you. You've probably been told when and where meals are served, but don't worry, we won't let you starve. Now, is there anything else I can help you with before I go back and get ready for launch?"

Meldren raised a tentative hand. "Are there any windows? I'd like to see where we're going."

"Sorry, but no. The only viewports are the small ones you'll have noticed on the flight deck. You're welcome to come up and look out of them whenever you like, but, sadly, the design of this ship didn't include any more than those. Is there anything else for now? No? In that case, please excuse me while the crew and I get ready to leave Haven for the Empire." And with that, she withdrew.

Entering the flight deck she made an '*I can't believe it*' face at Evan sitting in co-pilot's seat. "They want windows to see where we're going! Are they really the best ambassadors that could be found?"

"What about those things around their necks?" asked Evan.

"When we were introduced and we talked for a while, I asked them about those animals, because that's what they are I found out, and whether they would be a threat on the voyage or need some special treatment. Their answer, and trust me when I say that they sounded completely honest, was that the things didn't need any special attention at all and that they stayed around their necks all the time. Myrella agreed and said she hadn't noticed anything else odd about them. Animals around your neck and they don't need anything." She shook her head in disbelief. "I'm sure I'd feel just great with some sort of snake at my throat. It just makes me feel more than ever that those two are going to be so out of their depth on The Prime that they won't last two days without doing something so stupid as to make Haven a penal colony. But that's not my concern."

She ran her eyes over the board in front of her. "Course in and checked? Fuel checked? Enough food? Real food, that is? Anything I should be aware of?" Lights turned green and she nodded as they did so. "Good, let's get out of here and to The Prime and back as soon as we can negotiate our share." She sat back and let Evan take over while she ran through several pleasing scenarios in her mind about what she would do with her share of the money.

17

When the captain had left them, Meldren looked at Javin and said, "I don't think she likes us very much and I'm not sure I trust her, either. I haven't had much time to really see what her colors are, but I'm guessing that by the end of this trip I'll know her a lot better than I want to."

Javin looked a little dejected. "I can't hear her very well, either. But worse than that is that I can't hear much at all." In answer to Meldren's questioning look, he added, "On Haven and Harmony it's easy to hear the songs of everything because whatever is there is part of the planet. But this?" he said, tapping on the wall behind him, "this is not natural and I don't know where it came from. I can't hear anything about it. Maybe it's this amount of metal which is blocking me. I can hear you perfectly fine. I wish I could hear other things better."

Meldren stilled her mind and let her attention fall away from herself and into her surroundings. She tried to hear the songs which made up the ship and could only make out a jumble of sounds but nothing coherent, nothing strong enough to have created this ship. "Maybe," she said, "we can't hear it because we don't know the songs of the planet it was made on, or because it wasn't made by one person. Or maybe it's something else that's blocking us. I have no clue what it is."

"One thing I do know," said Javin, "is that I really don't like traveling like this. Wrapped around with so much metal. No sky to look at. No breezes." He gave a little shudder of distaste. "I don't want to have to do a lot of this. Even the bed is uncomfortable and the floor is much harder than the ground would be." He sighed, looking quite dispirited.

Meldren felt the same way but hated seeing him like this and wanted desperately to cheer him up. "It's not natural to travel like this. That's the way I feel about it." She nudged him gently, a small smile on her face. "I like the way we travel much better, don't you?"

He gave a grudging nod.

And then a thought occurred to her. "If this isn't natural and we can't hear anything inside of here, what about if we listen outside instead?"

"What do you mean?"

"Remember what Pol said, just as she was leaving?"

"Not really. Something about the Sun, wasn't it?"

"Yes, she said to listen for the Sun, no matter where we are and that the Sun will always hear us. If not those words, then something pretty close to them."

"So you want us to listen to the Sun from in here?" asked Javin.

Meldren shrugged. "Why not? We've got nothing better to do, have we?"

Javin was cautious. "I'm not so sure about this. I know Pol has these insights, but she's never heard the Sun. You and I both know it's not something that you actually want to listen to. It's so... so big! I feel like it could suck me into it and I'd disappear."

Meldren knew he was telling the truth. It was the same way she felt. But something about the way Pol had spoken made it seem different somehow. She tried to think how to explain that it was different this time. "When we heard the Sun before," she began, "it was always after we'd heard Harmony. It was like Harmony was introducing us to Her father. But it hasn't always been like that, Javin. Think about it. When we had to travel to Haven, we both heard another, bigger song come in and carry us across. That song had to be the Sun, didn't it? Nothing else could have done that, could have sounded that big. Then there was the last time, just recently, when we got lifted from Harmony suddenly. I hadn't given any thought until now, but that couldn't have happened without the Sun being involved. And it wasn't scary. It was helpful. Why can't it be like that now? Why can't we hear it now, but safely? And Pol did say we'd be safe. We're not asking for anything. We're not wanting anything from it. All we want to do is to hear it. Surely we'll be safe, won't we?"

Javin thought about it a moment and then a smile spread slowly across his face. "I can't hear anything wrong in what you're saying. And what you said did make sense. So why not? As you say, we'll only be listening for it, not trying to make anything with the song."

"That is a scary thought," said Meldren. "I don't really even want to think about using the Sun's songs for anything. It would be like making a planet appear." She shook her head sharply, as a shiver ran down her spine. "No. That's not even a dream I want to have."

"Good, because neither do I," said Javin. "Let's try it, shall we?"

With that, the two of them sat on the floor side by side and held hands. Both took deep breaths and let them out slowly as they relaxed. Closing their eyes, they sought the song of the Sun. For Meldren it was difficult at first to ignore or block out the sounds of where they were as well as the song that was Javin. She could pick up the tiny songs of their baggage but forced her attention to move beyond the room. The first new song she heard was hard to pinpoint, but she became aware that it was the engines creating it. Although she knew nothing about how they worked, the song she heard meant that she understood that they were creating something new as they operated. The song of the engines was the song of creation of new matter. That was all she could say.

For a moment, she was happy simply to listen to it, but she again forced her attention further away, to where the ship and the tiny sounds within it were almost lost. As she felt herself moving away, so she felt rather than heard a new sound. It was something which seemed to reverberate in her mind, so deep and pervasive was it. Therefore, to begin with, it was not a sound, but a pulsation which seemed to come from nowhere and everywhere. It permeated everything, was everything. As she felt the immense depth and reach of it, she found that she could begin to hear it. At least, she could hear some of it, for she knew instinctively that it was impossible for her to understand or to hear the true range of the song. It was the origin and destination of everything. As such, there could be no beginning to it, nor could there be an end. The sound she heard was all that she could sustain and survive with. Any more and she would have been subsumed within it.

Fascinated by it, she let herself drift beside it until she felt the time to leave had arrived. Reluctant to withdraw and lose contact with the vast complexity, well beyond anything she had ever heard or imagined, she nevertheless found herself listening for the small song of the ship; first the engines and then the room. She slid down the rope of sounds and felt herself sitting on the floor and Javin's hand holding hers still.

She took another deep, slow breath and opened her eyes to find Javin watching her with an amused smile on his face.

"Well?" he asked.

Eyes wide, she let out a quickly suppressed laugh as she gave a slow, disbelieving shake of her head. "That was... it was... I have never, ever known anything like that."

"Me, too," he said. He kissed her on her forehead. "Me, too. I'm so glad you suggested it. The sound of it! I knew it was big. I knew that before. But I never knew it was that big and that wonderful."

Meldren patted his hand, as if to reassure herself that she wasn't dreaming despite her elation. "It's thanks to Pol for telling us. Without her we'd never have thought of it."

"Of course," said Javin, "this now means that we're not ever going to be bored on this journey."

"True. But," said Meldren with a certain reluctance, "I think we ought to limit ourselves. It would be too easy to get lost out there and never come back. At least, that's true for me."

"Maybe so," he agreed, also reluctantly. "But I'm feeling better about what we're doing."

"So am I," she said, before kissing him carefully and completely on his lips.

18

After the small craft had touched back down again, Lessterenman switched everything off and sat in silence a moment listening to the clicks and hisses as it cooled. Sitting next to him, Parra-Hopshan stared at the bulkhead, smoothing her clothing and biting her lip. Neither of them wanted to move. She wanted to stay right here on this ship and keep the door locked. The very last thing she wanted to do was to open it and smile at people. Because once she did that, there would always be people. When would she be on her own again?

Both of them had spent plenty of time with various officials and there was a timetable of sorts prepared to ensure that they would have been seen in every major city on the planet by the time they thought the mother ship should have returned. Somehow, in all of that, they had to undertake some serious prospecting and ensure the details were relayed back via the beacon they had set up on entry into this system.

Parra-Hopshan cleared her throat. Then again. "I don't think I can do this," she began, but Lessterenman put his hand up to stop her.

"You're right. We're not trained for this. We joined up because we wanted to get away from people, not spend time with them. I know all that. We've said it enough times to not need saying it again. But we have a job to do. And the better the details we send back, the bigger the reward will be. Big enough, with any luck, to never have to talk to anyone ever again."

Parra-Hopshan was still smoothing her clothing down, her hands on automatic as her brain fixated on other things. "You heard what the captain said. About us failing? Do you think she really meant it?"

"Yes. Definitely. But you've less to worry about. I'm the one without useful alliances, so I'm the one for clone material, not you."

Parra-Hopshan finally left off smoothing down non-existent creases. She turned to look directly at her fellow crew member. "I don't want to be in charge."

"And yet you are," he said with as little emotion as possible. "You outrank me. That's your right. And I do not wish to take that away from you." He was thankful now that his lack of family alliances made him junior. "Once we get started, it will probably get much easier."

They both sat still.

Finally, in something like a spasm, he hit the button to open the door. Looking at Parra-Hopshan, he said, "After you."

She gave him a murderous look but unbuckled and headed to meet the inevitable crowd.

The first few days were difficult for both of them. But after many interviews for various media outlets, interest in them began to show signs of subsiding. They could walk down major streets, now dressed in Haven style clothing, and only a few people would point them out or shout out greetings. Even that grew less as time passed until, one day, sitting in a restaurant, Lessterenman said, "I think we're becoming invisible. Nobody has bothered us since we arrived."

Parra-Hopshan nodded and finished her drink. "That will make our job a little easier, at least." She looked around at the other customers and nodded again. "Perhaps that Myrella woman was right after all. Keep us in plain sight for long enough and people will get tired of seeing us."

"I have to say that I quite like some of the food here," said Lessterenman pushing his plate away. "It's all quite rural and quaint as well. Old buildings, bad streets and poor lighting. I could almost be back on my home planet in terms of amenities." He shuddered. "The thought of that is depressing. Give me civilization!"

This planet was also, in some ways, similar to her home, but she wasn't like Lessterenman. She didn't have to have all the trappings of civilization to be happy. She was used to it, of course, but that didn't mean she couldn't live without it. She didn't want to admit it but, deep down, there was a sense that she could probably survive here, if she could find somewhere nice and quiet. There was a small, swift smile which softened her eyes as she looked out.

"Maybe it's helping me to see my home in a new light," she said. "You know, compare it with this and see that it wasn't quite so bad as I once thought." In return, all she got was a raised eyebrow.

Forcing herself back to the present, she said, "Do you think we could hide away from everyone and start on our surveying? By ourselves?"

The look on his face was enough of an answer. "No hope. We're probably being followed by someone from the government right now. At least, that's what I would do in their place."

She wrinkled her nose at the idea of being tailed. "Well, we'll stick to the schedule and go to meet with our -- what's the word they used? -- guides. We're to meet the first in two days' time."

"I wish it was sooner. I want to get started sending data back, so we can be seen to be doing our jobs." He gazed out of the window. "It seems that we've already wasted so much time doing nothing here."

"But there's a lot of time to waste."

That soon changed for them both. Two mornings later, there was a discreet tap on their hotel rooms' doors and they were whisked away to a meeting where they were introduced to their guides. These were mainly academics who would be helping the two strangers as they went around the country. There had been a considerable tussle, Parra-Hopshan discovered, for these positions. Each university had representatives, and even to her naive experience it was clear that these guides would be after as much information as they could get in their allotted time. At the end of the day, both she and Lessterenman had left with bulky folders full of names, photos, times and places, but she couldn't help feeling that, despite the pressure from their captain, she would have preferred to have stayed anonymous in the city.

The next day, they were driven to their ship. It was under close guard to prevent anyone tampering with it or trying to take bits of it as souvenirs. Lessterenman ran multiple checks to see whether there had been any interference and to ensure that communication with the beacon was both open and secure. He was finally satisfied on all counts and it was only then that Parra-Hopshan invited the first two of their guides aboard.

The first, a tubby, balding man with laughter lines and bright blue, inquisitive eyes, was named Hannol. He was a professor of mechatronics and made no attempt to conceal his excitement at being on board. He was followed by a tall, grey-haired woman of a sour disposition. Her name was Olfran and she was from a different university apparently, with her specialism being semiotics. The signs and symbols in this craft, as well as the way the two space visitors spoke were what she was going to be focusing on, she had told them.

While Parra-Hopshan was engaged in the pre-flight sequence, Lessterenman explained the procedures necessary to make the craft go, as well as making sure the two professors were comfortable in their seats after storing their baggage. Thankfully, they would not be sleeping aboard, but in a simple building which would be set up and taken down at every location. Normally, it would have been used by the crew during their explorations so it was capable of withstanding an oxygen-free environment, as well as a wide range of temperatures. Here it would easily cope with whatever weather it had to deal with. It was simple but could be heated or cooled and had beds and chairs and a table as well as a place to heat meals. It offered basic comfort but not much else.

The two guides bombarded them both with questions. Parra-Hopshan groaned inwardly at the banality of them and then berated herself equally silently because the level of the questions indicated that there would be little to no appreciation of what she and her companion were actually engaged in. Simple misdirections, leaving out parts of the answers or even outright lies when necessary were easy to do.

"Are you ready?" she asked finally. "The flight will be short, but it should prove interesting for you. Please remain in your seats until we have landed and the engines are shut down, but feel free to keep asking questions." She turned to Lessterenman, rolling her eyes when she couldn't be seen by them.

Lessterenman, with a straight face, said, "Ready when you are. Give the order."

Parra-Hopshan bit her lip to stop smiling and nodded. "Take her up."

The flight was short, but it obviously impressed the professors by the sounds they made. Their first stop, on a long list of agreed stops, was near to a canyon, far away from any large city or town. Lessterenman set up the temporary building and then his surveying instruments. Ignoring the professors's questions, Parra-Hopshan focused on small tasks; resetting controls, doing unnecessary checks, taking food to the shelter. Leaving Lessterenman to answer the questions, she went inside and ensured that the uplink to the beacon was functioning. By the time she had rejoined them, the conversation had turned to Olfran enquiring as to how she and Lessterenman conceived of their own worlds in general and how that might alter how they perceived of this world. She shook her head and set about preparing some food instead.

It was going to be a long, long time before she saw her crew-mates again.

19

After the ship had lifted off and swiftly headed away from them on a blast of sound, Endel looked at Hanna and said, "We should be following them, shouldn't we?"

"Yes, but how? We don't know where they're going," said Hanna.

The two of them, plus Carmeena and Farran, had spent the days since meeting with Myrella waiting near the ship. They had decided, during that time, that they would be the ones to keep an eye on the visitors from space, leaving Pol and Isselta to travel in and out of the city and see if there was any information they could provide. The six of them had spent many hours listening in to each other's songs so that any one of them could zero in on any of the others instantly. Then, it was a simple matter of using that song as a sort of anchor to attach themselves to and use it as a beacon which would then allow them to shift between locations and so transfer information swiftly. In some ways, it was similar to how they had traveled between Harmony and Haven. Then there had been a road of sound along which they had slid, the ends of which had been anchored on each planet. Then, that road had been created by the Sun, but the principle they were using now was the same.

Now, the four of them were sitting under some trees on a slight rise which gave them a view over the whole of the large flat area which had been allocated to the space visitors' craft well away from the city, the tallest buildings of which could be made out as faded grey shapes on the horizon. The entire area was fenced and patrolled and roads into it had barricades in an effort to provide both privacy and security for the special visitors. Hanna and the others had made their way to the present vantage point on foot. The crowds, which had been almost a permanent fixture after the ship's arrival, had thinned day by day. Very few people were to be seen in the area, everyone preferring to stay at home and get a closer view on their sets. Consequently, the four watchers had the plain more or less to themselves.

Carmeena said, "We should have thought about this some more. I thought it would be like the other planes they have: specific destinations and we'd go to the next city and find them there. But after what Pol told us yesterday about how they're not always going to cities, that makes it harder. Now what are we going to do?"

In his normal, rumbling voice, Farran said, "It shouldn't be too difficult, surely? After all, we're following something which did not come from Haven. So, I suppose that if we listen for a song that doesn't have Haven's base in it, then that has to be it, doesn't it?"

Carmeena was not so easily satisfied. "But one song, and it's who knows how far away, and how do we even know where to start listening?" She shook her head. "I can't believe we didn't think this thing through better. I mean, we have been staring at the ship, knowing it would move at some time. Did we think that we'd jump on board and hide or something?"

Reaching out to rest his hand on her arm in an attempt to calm her, Farran said. "Don't take the responsibility for something we all overlooked. I simply assumed we'd know where to go, like we did when we met up with Pol and Isselta. It didn't happen." He pointed upwards. "But right now, there's a big trail of something In the air as well as the sound that ship left in the sky. Why not start by listening to that first and then follow it? At the end of it, that's the ship. Then, once we know what it sounds like, we should be able to find it more easily. Or, if not, we trace the sound in the sky again." He looked at Endel and Hanna. "It's better than nothing, isn't it?"

Hanna nodded enthusiastically, half-annoyed she hadn't thought of that simple a solution. "You're right. It should be easy. But the only thing we have to be careful about is singing ourselves too close to the ship. We don't want to be seen, especially not if we keep turning up at every place they are."

"Listen to the ship first, then listen to where it is -- the song of the land -- and then find a place close in the song," said Endel, as if it was the most obvious thing.

"Can we tell if it's still moving or not?" asked Carmeena. "After all, we're only listening to the ship itself, and that isn't going to tell us if it's in the sky or on the ground, is it?"

"Easy," said Endel. "If we can't hear anything but sky, which is a fairly uniform song, then we know it's still on it way. If we can hear other, smaller songs around it, like animals, and there is the song of the earth itself, then it's landed."

"But," persisted Carmeena, "birds are small songs. We might be hearing them and get it wrong."

Farran took her hand and patted it gently. "We have to trust in what we're doing, Carmeena. Nothing is definite. This is all new. For all we know, we'll find it to be the easiest thing of all. We can't cover every possibility, but we can try our best. If Haven wants us to succeed, then we will. She will help us as best She can. Now, are you ready, do you think, to give this a try? I think it would be best if everyone joined in the listening at first, but afterwards, we can take it in turns to find out whether they are moving or not." He looked at the others and raised his brows in a question. "Shall we?"

Carmeena smiled gratefully at him and shook her head at her own silliness. "Of course, of course. Let's see what we can hear."

The four of them bowed their heads as they turned their focus and attention inwards to where they could hear the songs which made up the world and everything in it. Reaching upwards to the sky, they heard the soft flowing songs of clouds and wind, listened to the short, rattling songs of a flock of birds before a strange roiling noise, barely a song at all, indicated they had found the ship's trail. Once they had it, they locked on and followed it, hearing it gather strength gradually as they approached the source.

Together they followed the harsh song until they could begin to discern other sounds surrounding it. These were more familiar; the sounds of trees and bushes, of rock and soil. Each of the four concentrated on the specific pattern of those songs which would identify a unique place on the planet. None of them had any idea where the ship was; all they knew was that they could identify the place.

Breaking out of her concentration, Hanna said, "I've got the place memorized. I don't think it's too far away as the ship hasn't been gone long. Can anyone spot where we should arrive?"

There was a silence as they each sought to hear some sort of cover not too far away and not too close. Finally, Farran said, "I think so. Listen to where there is a break on the song of the land. There is some sort of gap in it and the songs continues but deeper down. Just before that break, if you follow it along one way, there's a richer song with lots of repetitions which sounds like it might be some trees or at least some thick bushes. Whichever, it should be far enough away from the ship so that if we're wrong, we should still be safe."

The others listened and Hanna said, " I've got it."

Farran turned his attention to her. "Agreed, you have. And Carmeena? Endel? Do you hear it?"

In a moment he heard their songs echoing his as they homed in on the same place Hanna and himself were hearing.

"Then let's sing ourselves there." And to anyone who might have been watching, they would have noticed the air beneath a stand of trees suddenly become thicker looking at the same time as an almost hummable sound made up of complex chords sprang up. After a moment, it faded away and the air returned to normal, and where people might have been, there was only the shade of the trees on the ground.

20

As the days passed, Lessterenman and Parra-Hopshan became more used to the questioning of their helpers, who changed regularly, every ten days or so, each one with a different area of specialism and each one a new personality. From ill-mannered historians to aloof mathematicians to extremely likable astronomers, they had dealt with them all equally. At the same time, they had been surveying different areas of the planet and finding more interesting results.

"I think," Lessterenman said one morning when their helpers were still sleeping in the building outside, "that this planet has a great deal more mineral wealth than we had originally thought or hoped. Here," he said, pointing his companion at a readout, "look at the amount of gold alone we have found since we started. These results are going to make us very rich indeed."

Parra-Hopshan read the readout and gestured for him to silently follow her away from the sleeping professors. When she was sure they were far enough away not to be overheard, she said, "Agreed. Those results are very, very good. But you and I both know what's going to happen when the miners arrive." She paused and raised her eyebrows. "This planet and everything on it will be torn apart. You've seen them at work. It's not subtle. Here, for instance," and she indicated the river to one side and the mountains beyond, "those mountains get leveled and the river goes dry. Nothing grows."

"I know that," he said. "What's your point?"

"Does it have to come to that? Isn't there a better way of accessing that gold?"

He shook his head. "No. With the amounts here, they would have to process a lot of earth for optimum extraction. Anyway, that would only be done after negotiating with the government. It's the usual way of doing things. And besides none of that's up to us. We'll be long gone before that happens. Is that really what's bothering you?"

Parra-Hopshan tried to find a way of expressing what she had been feeling for some time without appearing to lose face or be thought of as being disloyal to her distant crew-mates. She had been struggling with this for the past several days. It had started, she now realized, in the days just before they had embarked on this exploration. She could recall sitting in that restaurant and looking out at all the people with Lessterenman and not hating the planet.

"Well... look at it. This will all be excavated, mined, crushed and discarded. But, it's... it's... not going to be pretty," she ended lamely, wishing she could find the right words. Lessterenman remained in front of her, his face giving nothing away. If only he would blink or smile or do something other than look at her, she thought. She needed courage from somewhere and realized she had been hoping she could get it from him. She was trying to wrestle duty and honesty to where they would blend.

"You said this planet reminded you of your home," he said. "It's nothing like mine, but I could see in your face when you said it how it made you feel."

"Yes; glad I wasn't there any more."

He raised his brows. "No. That's not true. I saw how you looked when you compared it to your home. You like the memory. Tell me truly, do you like this place, this planet? Do you like the people?"

She cursed herself for revealing too much. "I don't have to like it," she said finally, deciding not to reveal any more of herself. "It would be a shame to have some of these things disappear, because beautiful things

are beautiful. But, as you said, we won't be here to see what happens."
She forced a smile. "There will still be other places to see."

He shook his head and the shadow of a smile appeared briefly. "I
want what I want, and this planet will help me get it. Think about it for a
moment. We visit system after system. We look at planet after planet,
asteroid after asteroid. Most are useless: too cold, too hot, not enough
minerals to make it worthwhile, poisonous or corrosive atmosphere. You
know as well as I do that finding a planet like this, a perfect one making
extraction easy, is what we've always dreamed of finding. I don't care
what happens here because I know we'll never find another one like it
again. Make the most of it, I say. And I intend to."

She watched him walk back to the professors and wondered if he had
truly understood her, had pretended not to or was completely oblivious.
Whatever the truth of it, she would have a long time to spend in his
company. And now she had begun to put into words how she felt, albeit
shading the truth, it had suddenly acquired a presence in her mind,
whereas before it had lurked in the background.

With a sigh, half frustration, half irritation, she sat down on a handy
boulder and looked out over the river and toward the mountains. Her
mind reran what she had said and how he might have interpreted it but
could not come to a definite conclusion one way or the other.

After a while, she let herself drift in the peace and the soothing
sounds of the river. This was something she had come to enjoy and
appreciate: silence, but the silence which is filled with wonderful little
sounds. Over the preceding days she had spent a little more time on her
own, time in which she had gradually come to see the planet for what it
was and notice what she had missed seeing before. She'd never had to do
this before, wait on a planet with virtually nothing to do except look
around. And she had discovered something. It was beautiful. Quite,
quite beautiful. Nothing like the mechanized and heavily terraformed
mess her home world had become, and nothing like the artificiality of
The Prime, which always unsettled her in every visit. And she also
realized that the people were becoming less irritating. Or, perhaps, she
was finding them easier to get along with. Even recently at the
university, where they had been answering questions and giving lectures
over three whole days, she had felt some of her normal tension from

being around strangers begin to drain from her. She had even smiled and joked and caught herself in surprise at doing so. Yes, this planet was beginning to feel like somewhere special. As Lessterenman had said, it really was perfect in many ways. But not in the way he saw it as perfect.

She relaxed more completely, becoming still and letting her worries dissolve for the moment into the sounds and sights around her. If those mountains were going to disappear, then she would remember them. She would keep them and their memory, their existence, safe. She looked at and studied them until she felt as if they were becoming a part of her. As she did so, the boundary between what she was looking at and who she was thinned a little. The gentle, ever-changing river sounds grew into something which invited her to let herself sink down into the riffles and rills and burblings. The breeze picked up a little and brushed through the reeds nearby and that susurrus added to her relaxation, so she felt as though she were floating on the sounds, floating in the world.

She let her head move with the rhythm, eyes half-closed as she swayed a little on the boulder. As she did so, she thought she noted some sudden movement a way down the bank to her left, unusual in color. At first, she thought it must be an animal. Still feeling loose and relaxed, soothed by the flowing air and water, she allowed her head and eyes to turn just enough to see more. It was not an animal but, without a doubt, a person. Someone was doing something that looked like washing in the river. She had been assured that this site was far away from anywhere and anyone. It had been offered as a reward for appearing at the university: solitude and silence for crowds and noise.

She watched the person -- a woman, perhaps? -- washing and noticed, with a start, that from this distance it looked like she had one of the strange creatures around her neck. It was hard to be absolutely certain, but there surely couldn't be that many people with that thickness around their necks, could there? It was the exact same thing, or so it appeared, as those ambassadors had. Even from this distance there could be no doubt about it. But, as far as she knew, there were no other people like that. She had asked the guides several times but had been met with shrugs of ignorance. Yet, here was one. Most strange.

She felt like calling out, but stopped herself, or maybe it was the lethargy which held her back. Better to observe, she thought. As the thought entered, so the woman started up, looked directly at her before swiftly disappearing into the bank-side trees.

By the time she returned to the campsite, Lessterenman and the two professors had everything set for breakfast. Sitting at the table was the tall botanist named Henler, who whistled tunelessly whenever he could, and the chatty art historian named Elish, with happy eyes and long, elegant fingers which she used to embellish whatever she was talking about.

After exchanging greetings, Parra-Hopshan sat down. "Do either of you know if anyone is living in this area?"

Elish wafted her fingers in the air. "Absolutely no one should be here. This is a natural reserve, protected from any interference from humans. The nearest settlement would be, oh now let me think, it would be at least 40 kilometers away. Well outside of the borders." She poked a piece of fruit into her mouth, chewed and said, "What makes you ask?"

"I thought I saw someone. Someone washing in the river downstream from where I was sitting."

Henler shook his head. "As Elish said, this is a protected area. Of course, that doesn't mean that nobody is allowed in. After all, we're here. But someone living here, which I assume was what you implied, that would be definitely illegal."

Parra-Hopshan nodded in understanding, but didn't feel like providing any more details. It didn't feel like something she should be sharing, but she had absolutely no idea why. Instead she realized she was determined to find out about the person she saw, if she possibly could. It didn't make much sense logically, but it felt right. "Maybe I mistook whatever it was for a human. It might have been an animal. After all, it was quite some way away, and it was quick."

Henler nodded. "That would be more likely. Although the next question would be what animal it could have been."

That led to a long and detailed discussion roaming over the various possibilities which, of course, led nowhere.

And so the day began. She and Lessterenman monitored their equipment, sharing some of what they discovered with Henler and Elish. Lessterenman assured Parra-Hopshan that all the data was being interrogated and compressed correctly on their ship before being uploaded to the beacon, to be relayed onwards to where their captain could collect it and, if necessary, use it for establishing the claim.

As the time passed, she kept looking out of the corner of her eyes to see whether she could detect any movement at all which might be the person she saw. There were a couple of times when she thought she saw something, but she could never be sure enough. It was probably just the wind ruffling the leaves, she told herself. Nevertheless, she could not shake off the feeling that they were being watched. But whether by humans or animals, she could not tell. It was frustrating.

To take her mind off it, she turned to Henler and asked him about the various plants around them and what they were used for, if any of them had uses. That unleashed a long, detailed and not entirely uninteresting stream of information, as Henler was only too pleased to be able to show off his knowledge.

The day had been pleasantly warm. That night, as they were settling down to sleep with the door open wide, Parra-Hopshan could not get the sight of the woman out of her head. She listened to the sounds outside, wondering whether any of them were being made by the stranger. Unable to sleep in the pitch-dark night, she wasn't, she realized, afraid. If anything, she was intrigued, wanting to know more. That thing around the neck was unmistakeable. But to have another person like the two ambassadors who had recently left was too much of a coincidence.

She folded her arms behind her head, staring up, thinking about what it could mean. She doubted she could have been overheard when she was talking to Lessterenman; the distance was too great. So the secret of the mining operation was still secure. And it wasn't as if they could have been followed. Any other craft in the vicinity would have been noticed almost immediately. Alarms would have sounded. Therefore, she concluded, this must have been a coincidence, however much it didn't feel like it.

21

"What happened?" Farran asked as Carmeena burst into the clearing where they had made their camp.

"I think she saw me!"

"Quiet now, settle down," said Farran, guiding her to a log. "Tell us what happened."

Carmeena tried to gather her composure and took a deep breath before speaking. "I was listening to the songs to find out where they were because I wanted to freshen up a little. So I was crouching down by the bank and I heard two of them getting louder. I peeked through some reeds and there, a good distance away, were the two space people. They were talking about something which made one of the songs get scratchy. If I had to guess from the sound of it, I'd say irritable. That went on for a bit, so I sat down and waited for them to go. Finally, one left, the male, and I waited for her to go as well.

"Anyway, I was watching the river and trying to get comfortable and the other song began to fade away. Nothing very much. I assumed she was leaving and so I paddled out into the river, sure that the plants and things would be enough to hide me. But, when I got out there and was gently washing myself with water, no splashing, I looked up and she was still sitting on the rock and I swear she was looking at me although her head wasn't turned my way."

"What did you do?" asked Hanna.

"I backed up to the bank as quickly as I could and got back here."

"Do you think she'll follow you?" asked Farran.

Carmeena shook her head. "I don't know. I don't think so, but I can't be sure." She was still too upset to think or hear clearly. Above all, she felt she had let everyone down by being so lax in her observation of the woman. What should have been just a simple refreshing morning wash had turned into something almost threatening.

Endel closed his eyes and tilted his head a little as he listened. After a moment he opened them and gave a dismissive shake of his head. "No. She's not coming here. Nobody's coming this way. I can hear four songs clearly together and also that annoying little sound that's always there in the background with them. They're all in the one place from what I can tell. I'm pretty sure we're safe."

"You're sure she saw you?" asked Hanna.

"As sure as I can be." In fact, she was bone certain she had been seen.

"So, the question is," said Hanna, "how did it happen? I'm not blaming you at all, Carmeena," she said reaching out to her. "You're far too experienced to miss something like a person you want to avoid still being there. Something must have happened. Can you remember anything unusual while you were waiting for the woman to leave?"

Carmeena's brow wrinkled as she thought back over the recent events, trying to clear her mind. "There were the two songs and, like I said, it sounded as if something was going unevenly. That's just my imagination perhaps. Then he left and she sat there. And I was sitting still, listening." She stopped and frowned. "That's strange. Now I think about it, her song began to fade away. It sounded like it was her going away, but it wasn't. Obviously! But it faded. It faded to almost nothing. That's what fooled me. I should have realized that her song would still be there no matter where she was, but because it faded, I took that for her leaving." She looked around at the other three. "I'm sorry for missing that. I'm sorry I put us in danger."

Farran pooh-poohed the idea. "Pah! We're not in any danger. If someone were to come, you know as well as I do that we'd just sing ourselves out of here, back to the last place. No, don't worry yourself about that. Of more importance is why that woman's song faded. That's a new thing. That's something worth thinking about." He looked around. "Any ideas?"

"I know how we each sound," said Endel. "And I know that we can find each other because of how we sound." He paused.

"Go on," said Farran.

"Well, I know those things, but I don't know how we sound if one of us is listening to Haven."

"What do you mean?" asked Hanna.

"Carmeena said that the woman was sitting and doing nothing. And then her song faded. Couldn't that mean that she was listening to Haven, and that her song got sort of swallowed up, like it was being faded into Haven, a part of Haven?"

"Hmmm," rumbled Farran. "That's an interesting idea. And one that's easy to prove one way or the other." He pointed at Hanna. "Could you please listen in on Haven? Try to hear Her basic song, the one all the others rest on. While you're doing that, the rest of us will listen to you. Is that fine with you?"

Hanna nodded and settled down into a relaxed slump against a log and closed her eyes. As she did so, the other three also closed theirs and tuned into the girl's song. Carmeena heard Hanna's strong, clear song easily. But, as she continued listening, so she heard that same sinking away she had heard from the woman. It sounded as if the song was receding, becoming less clear. When she was quite convinced, Carmeena opened up her eyes, saying, "That's it! That's what happened. It sounded exactly like that. The song sort of faded away."

Endel agreed. "It sounded like that to me as well."

"And me," said Farran.

Hanna, alert once more, said, "That's good to know, but what does it mean?"

"It means, I think, that the woman was listening to Haven," said Farran.

"Really? She was listening to what Hanna was listening to just now?" asked Endel.

Farran made the 'maybe' gesture with his hand. "That we don't know.

But if Carmeena said it sounded the same, then the woman must have been listening to something and listening to it clearly enough to have started losing herself in the sounds. I can't think of anything else to explain it."

"But does that mean," said Hanna, "that she can hear like we do? Or does it mean that Haven has also chosen her for something?"

Farran rubbed his neck as he thought about it. "I don't know. Maybe. Maybe Haven has chosen her. Or maybe she has the talent to hear Haven. But as to how well she can hear Haven, that I don't know."

Carmeena said, "But it's obviously something worth thinking about. This woman can hear Haven, whether she understands that or not. I don't feel as stupid about being seen now we've found this out. But I think we should keep a closer eye on her from now on." She felt lighter in spirit now.

"Agreed," said Farran.

"What I want to know," said Endel, "is what is that annoying little sound that's in the background when we listen to their songs. It's only there when they are outside. It doesn't happen when they're traveling around, only when they're stopped in one place like today."

"I've heard it as well," said Hanna. "I think it's coming from those things they set up when they stop. But I have no idea what it is. It doesn't seem to have any meaning, just a continual stream of sound. I wouldn't even call it a song."

"Well, maybe we'll find out what it is and maybe we won't," said Farran. "But it's another thing to look out for and pass on to Pol and Isselta."

Later that day, as the sun was setting, they set out to see if they could get close enough to understand what was going on. This was the first time they had done anything but watch, but the day's earlier events had made them more curious than usual. What, for example, was the importance of the woman? Could she really hear Haven and, if so, what did that make her? How important was she? There was also the annoying issue of the sound which was not a proper song. What was it about? What was it a song of? There was so much they didn't know about these people.

As a result of this lack of knowledge, Carmeena and Hanna had decided to get as close as they could to where the four travelers were sleeping in the hope that such proximity would allow them to hear the woman's song more precisely, giving them an opportunity to hear any tiny nuances which might otherwise have been drowned out by being further away. Farran and Endel meanwhile would be trying to discover more about the stream of sound that came from the equipment. It might mean nothing, or it might mean a lot. Of course, as Farran had said, "We might not even understand anything at all about it."

The dark night was no hindrance to them, as they had previously listened to the land they were to cross and there was nothing really to concern them. No hollows, no protruding rocks, no thick vegetation, just smooth, rolling grassland.

Carmeena used the woman's song as a beacon and followed it as she and Hanna stepped as silently as they could. When she felt they were close enough, Carmeena touched Hanna's arm and they sank down to their haunches to begin listening.

"We're going to try to understand her song, what might make her seem valuable to Haven," Carmeena had said prior to starting out. "We need to listen to her, hear her story if we can. You remember how Javin and Meldren listened to us back on Haven? They followed our songs back. So we're going to try something like that ourselves. Not that I'm sure we're as good as those two are, but we'll try. Hanna, you listen for anything which might link her to Haven, any rhythm or small song at all. I'll be listening for what she's like underneath. You know, angry, afraid, in love; those sorts of things. If we can find out anything at all it will be helpful."

"What about the man? Shouldn't we listen in on him as well?" Hanna had asked. "After all, you said that what you heard between them sounded like something was not even or in tune. Maybe they're lovers and it was an argument. Wouldn't it help to know that?"

"You're right, of course," had said Carmeena. "It's just that... well, I don't really like listening in on people like this. It's not right. They have a right to privacy. But the woman obviously has some link to Haven, that's why I think we need to hear her. But, as you say, listening to the man as well makes sense." She had wagged a finger at Hanna. "But I'm not making a habit out of this, my girl. And you shouldn't either."

Hanna had smiled and reassured her, and together they had agreed to pay most attention to the woman and then, if they had any time, to listen to the man.

So it was that the two of them were side by side giving all of their attention to the song of the woman behind the wall about ten meters away. Carmeena sank inside herself, letting her attention flow from within her stillness and reach toward the song she recognized. She knew how she herself felt inside when she was sad or angry, and she tried to listen for those sorts of feelings in the song. What she found was confusing. Elements of the song felt like loneliness. She recognized it because she had been lonely herself for so long. It was easy for her to hear. She could understand it. This woman was very, very far from home and far from her other friends. Loneliness made sense. But then Carmeena listened at a deeper level. The song she heard was almost as strong as the loneliness but entirely different in tone. There weren't the somber, deep rolling notes of sadness and separation. Instead there were upbeat little rills and glissandos of notes over a continuously changing chord sequence which itself felt uplifting. Curious, she tried to follow it back, doing what Meldren had said she had done once, using the first notes to see where they had come from. Although Carmeena didn't feel that competent, she was reasonably sure that this new, happier song was relatively recent. But what it meant was not obvious.

She moved her limbs cautiously to ease them and turned her attention next to the man. His song was much simpler to understand. The loneliness was there, but in bigger and bolder notes, swelling up and over. Beneath that, however, there was a small song of... Carmeena tried to think how to describe it to herself. It felt and sounded like anger, or maybe hatred. No. Jealousy? Envy? She could never understand the difference between the two. Whatever it was was a secret. Or it felt like one. And, as she thought that, so she heard another, minor, quiet, suppressed song. This one really was secretive. As she listened to it, she realized that it underlay everything she was hearing, supporting and contributing to the others but never showing itself. 'This man is hiding something,' is what she felt. 'But doesn't everyone?', her reasonable voice answered. 'Maybe, but not as deep as this', came the reply.

Having heard enough, she turned her attention to Hanna's song to see if the girl was close to being finished. She heard a change of tone, a change in the sharpness of the song which indicated that Hanna was also withdrawing, becoming unentangled in any other songs. Carmeena gently shook herself into being alert to her surroundings again before reaching gently and touching Hanna's arm, the signal for them to leave.

When all four had reassembled back at their campsite, they shared what they had discovered.

"That stream of sound in the background?" began Endel, "that's something coming from those things they set up. The sound goes from there into the ship where it stops."

"But not completely," added Farran. "We heard an occasional spurt of sound, definitely not a song, which went from the ship to somewhere else. We followed it when it happened, but it went a very long way away."

"Away from the planet," said Endel. "We don't know where, but we do know that it didn't seem to be heading to any other place on this planet. At least, not from what we could hear."

"I'm not sure what we found out," said Farran, "except that the noise is something to do with the equipment and it maybe has something to do with the sound going into space."

"What did you two discover?" asked Endel. "I hope it made more sense than our information."

Carmeena could barely make out the shapes of the others in the darkness of the night. But her hearing provided her with more detail than her eyes as to where each of the other three were sitting, as well as how they were feeling. She said, "I'll tell you what I think I learned and then Hanna can tell you that she thinks. Firstly, and really not a surprise considering she's more or less alone on this planet, I felt that she was feeling lonely. But, underneath that there was something new. That newness, to me, anyway, felt more like being happy. And it sounded quite recent, as though she had become happier, but at a really deep level. Something that had real meaning for her."

She sighed. "I wish I was as good at this as Meldren and Javin. They can hear so much more detail than I can." She shook off the feeling of inadequacy, knowing that the others were probably picking up on them in the dark but were too polite to say anything, and marshaled her thoughts about the man. "Now, the man was different. There was something about his song I simply didn't like. There is something big he is hiding. At least, that's what it sounded like to me. He is not happy, not deep down. There are all sorts of emotions going on in there, but overall it amounts to the fact that he's not happy. What were his songs saying to you, Hanna?"

"I agree with you about the woman. She felt happy. Lonely but happy. I couldn't hear anything much else that seemed important. I'm not sure if she was asleep or not. I think she wasn't, because the songs were even, not changing very much, whereas with dreams, the songs can change really rapidly. So, I think she was awake and she was not unhappy, put it that way. But the man was different, as Carmeena said. I didn't like listening to his song. It felt... I don't know, angry and deep down upset with everything. If we had to talk with either of them, have any dealings with them face to face, I'd trust the woman more than the man."

"Should we pass all this on to Isselta and Pol, do you think?" asked Carmeena. "It's not much, but it might be of use later on somehow."

"Can't hurt," said Farran, his voice rumbling in out of the dark. "I could meet with them tomorrow and let them know."

Carmeena felt better for having done something more than simply following the visitors from space. But she was also aware that none of them had really answered the question of how important the woman was to Haven and whether she should be considered as a possible friend with maybe a talent, or as an enemy.

22

M eldren had looked at Javin and sucked in a deep breath to release the tension which had been building up over the past several days. They were about to leave the landing ship and begin their duties as ambassadors. The voyage had been, in Meldren's words, 'boring but interesting at the same time.' This was because they had learned to listen to the song of the Sun without being damaged by it. That was the interesting part, even though the song faded away into nothing as they left it further and further behind. The boring part was the rest of the voyage.

"I'm not used to being in a small space with nothing to look at," Meldren had complained. "I like the wind on my face and the sun on my back and things to do. I don't like having nothing to do."

Javin had agreed. "The last time I was in one of these things I was drugged and didn't even know about it. I can't help thinking that that's a better way of traveling, knowing nothing about it and waking up only when we arrive."

"Maybe, but you also didn't have any memories. Not real ones, anyway."

The crew had been busy making sure everything was as clean as possible, making it very clear that their two passengers were very much in the way. Then they had transferred to another ship because, the captain had said, the ship they had traveled on was not designed to be on a planet with gravity holding it down. It was a space ship. And that's where it was now; in space somewhere. They had left it some time ago and now, this new ship had landed after seemingly interminable stops and starts and slowdowns and hurry-ups. The final checks had been made, the crew were looking smart in their uniforms and were standing tall and straight.

Neither Javin nor Meldren had learned much about the crew; the conversations had always been polite but distant. They could have listened in on them, but they had both agreed there had been no need to do something so impolite. Only if they had felt threatened would they have done something like that. In the end, the two of them had decided to take their meals in their cabin and leave the rest of the ship to the crew. They slept much, listened to the Sun and were generally very bored. Now all that was about to change. The captain had invited them to look at some screens to show them the size of the crowd waiting to welcome them. To Meldren's way of thinking, seeing all of those strangely dressed people waiting just for them was not helpful or settling at all. Hence the deep breath.

The doors had begun to unseal with hissings and clickings. The last door irised open and the wind of this new world brushed against them. Extending from the door was a gentle ramp, a few paces back from the end of which stood an imposing group of people in what Meldren guessed were respectful poses.

Not knowing what to do or how to do it in such a way that would be ambassadorial, Meldren and Javin had stood for a moment, unable to move. "I don't like this at all," hissed Meldren. "I like arriving when I want to arrive and where I want to arrive at." In answer, Javin reached for and held her hand, giving it a slow squeeze.

The moment had been broken by the captain stepping up close behind them both and saying, in a taut voice which Meldren thought indicated a lot of stress, "Just start walking. I'll be right behind you and I'll help you." Meldren couldn't help but hear what she really meant, *'Why can't you just behave like normal people and this wouldn't have to be embarrassing for me?'*.

Together, smiling nervously, the two new ambassadors of Haven had walked down onto a new planet to meet and greet many new people and listen to many speeches and be invited to make many of their own, which they did, but in a very brief fashion which obviously bemused their listeners who had been expecting something more elaborate than a variation of, *'Thank you. You're nice. We're here. This looks a nice place. Thank you'*.

Meldren noticed that the captain and her crew hurried away to another vehicle, casting a dark look at her as they did so. She was almost certain she had overheard the captain saying something about getting their claims in for the bounty. But she might have misheard in all the movement around her.

In fact, the welcome extended over several days and the rush and flow of people around them had more than made up for their earlier solitude. Now, they actively looked forward to being on their own, which happened every day, but late at night after having eaten another meal or having seen some sort of exhibition.

Tonight, as the doors to their new home closed behind them, Meldren turned to Javin and said, "How long does this go on before we can go home?"

He said, "I get the feeling that this hasn't even really started yet. We have to talk to people about Haven first, and all the talking we've done has been about nothing at all from what I can recall of it. It seems that it's been people being nice and nothing else."

Meldren harrumphed. "I don't want people being nice, I want people to listen to what we came here to say and then we can go back." She felt sulky and didn't mind showing it. There was a discreet tap on the door. Still feeling annoyed, she called out, "Come in!"

The doors opened a crack and a head peered round it. It was Edwallan-Sipcort, the person who had been delegated to look after them and be their go-between with all the media and interviewers and anyone else who wanted to interact with these new and somewhat strange-looking ambassadors. Javin and Meldren had learned of this view of them by overhearing what others had been saying.

"I'm so sorry to disturb you, Your Notabilities," he said in his usual, low, ingratiating tone, using the honorific which neither Javin nor

Meldren liked or really understood, yet which was said in such a way as to emphasize the capital letters. Was it because they weren't nobles or was it the normal way of addressing someone notable who had been sent from another planet? Whatever the truth of it, Meldren gritted her teeth upon hearing it.

"But you have," she said far too sweetly, trying to let her frustrations not be too obvious.

He bobbed his apologies. "Nevertheless, I am here to inform you of a meeting tomorrow at the Emperor's palace. It will be before lunch, which you will be seated at." He looked quite excited. He bobbed again. "The information just this moment arrived and I thought it best to pass it along to Your Notabilities directly. I apologize for disturbing you at this late hour, but it is an honor and you should be prepared for it." Bobbing again, he disappeared, closing the door with hardly a click.

"Perhaps they heard us," said Javin. "Maybe they're listening in on us here."

Meldren raised her brows. "Really? They do that?" If it was true, she could feel herself deep-down angry about it. But, until she knew for certain, she'd leave it there and only drag the anger out and up into her head if she needed to.

Javin shrugged. "Who knows how these people think? Maybe they are and maybe they aren't listening. Doesn't really matter, does it? After all, we're not hiding anything, are we? We just want to talk to somebody in charge and go home again."

Meldren was silent a moment, thinking what they had to be prepared for. "Why do we have to stay for lunch? Why can't we just talk and go? Why does it always have to be so difficult to do the simple things here?" She flung an arm out to indicate their surroundings. "I mean, look at this place. It's big enough to have several families living here without getting in each other's way. How many rooms are there? Six? What do we need six rooms for? And everything is too soft or too fancy or both. If I thought that place we stayed in back on Haven just before setting out was big and fancy, then this place must be the fanciest place anywhere at all."

"It probably is," said Javin. "I would think that ambassadors would be given the best places to stay."

Nothing was going to mollify Meldren, and she needed to take out her frustration on something. "Well, I don't like it. It's too big, and half of the things here I don't know what they're for or how they work, and I don't want to know." She turned to Javin, a pleading look on her face. "I only want something simple and out in nature. We've been away from nature, from the true songs of the world, for so long I've forgotten what the wind feels like anymore and what the earth sounds like. How do people stand it here? There's nothing natural about any of it. Even back on Haven, in Pannedon, there was always the feeling that open spaces were close by. But not here. Not at all."

Later, to show she meant what she said, she dragged a few probably very expensive covers on to the floor and threw down what looked like cushions then laid down on them to sleep, Javin holding her as she drifted off into dreams of trees and flowers growing in the hallways and the roads, covering the towering buildings in living tapestries.

The next morning, they were eating breakfast in their rooms. The food had arrived via some unknown process, showing up on a table which hadn't been there the previous night. Presumably their movements had triggered something. However it worked, they sat and tried the various dishes, having by now recognized some familiar-looking shapes and colors. As they finished, there was another quiet tapping and Edwallan-Sipcort entered smiling and bobbing.

"You're looking very fancy in those clothes," said Meldren. They were indeed much more garish and flamboyant than anything they had previously seen him in.

He bowed his head but slanted it to one side as if afraid the compliment would stick to him. "Thank you, Your Notability. And how soon will you both be ready?"

Meldren stood and swept her hands down, taking in her blouse and long skirt. "This is it. We are ready now." Both she and Javin had put on simple leather slippers but apart from that, they were dressed as usual.

Edwallan-Sipcort (he had insisted on their using his full name) blanched visibly and lifted his hand to his mouth. "But surely, Your Notabilities, you will not be taking the necklaces as well?"

Meldren had woken up in a much better mood and was determined today was going to be a good day, a day of progress. But she was also determined that she would only be able to enjoy such a day if she was to truly be herself and that meant familiar, comfortable clothing and freshly washed hair. The simple truth was neither she nor Javin had anything other than simple, comfortable clothing, but it was her determination to revel in wearing it which was to the fore this morning. She knew their sprites were the cause of much speculation and interest here. It was not possible for either herself or Javin to even to think about going anywhere without them. They both had tried to give some basic explanation as to what they were but had given up in the face of general incomprehension when they began using terms like 'songs of nature' and 'hearing the planet'. To everyone they met, the sprites were simply living necklaces which had been proven to be free of any threatening diseases and that the two of them would be emotionally damaged if separated from them. That last part was Javin's idea and had made the sprite's acceptance much easier.

"We most certainly will be taking them with us," she said.

"Oh... Very well. Of course. That is your prerogative, Notability." To Meldren's eye he was battling with himself about something, but she could not say what, until one side obviously was the victor. "Might I suggest, purely for the sake of being more at ease in such illustrious surroundings, that Your Notabilities might find yourselves dressed in something which might be considered indicative of the nature and culture of your planet so that all might be better able to admire and understand more of whom you represent?"

Meldren listened to what he said, trying to follow the twists and turns of it all. Javin was smiling. Seeing that, she understood a great deal more very swiftly.

"Tell me something, Edwallan," watching him wince at his foreshortened name, knowing he was adding 'Sipcort' silently, "are you suggesting that we are not dressed well enough to meet people, despite the fact that we've been dressed the same as this and met everyone there is to meet?"

"Everyone but those at the palace."

"And we should dress differently for those people, should we?"

Without actually saying anything, Edwallan-Sipcort managed to convey by twists and bobs and grimaces that such an idea was one to be fervently embraced.

Meldren was starting to enjoy herself and knew from the glint in Javin's eye that he was in the same mood she was. "Well, Edwallan," -- wince -- "we could change into our other clothes." She watched his eyes light up at the idea. "That would be my short dress with a small hole near the shoulder and it is held together by the leather I sometimes use to hold my hair back, and Javin would be wearing a kilt and a sleeveless top, also with a leather belt that he sometimes uses to tie things up with. There's only a couple of tears in the top, but I think he looks good in it." Their clothes had no such flaws in them but she was not about to say that. Plus, she was not going to say anything about being able to sing whatever clothes they wanted. She was more interested in making it plain that she and Javin wanted to be themselves. She smiled as Edwallan-Sipcort processed the images in his mind and broke into a nervous smile.

"I'm sure Your Notabilities are more than adequately dressed to represent your homeworld here. It was presumptuous of me to have suggested anything else."

"I've not heard that word before," said Meldren, "but I know what you are saying and I accept your apology. Now, shall we get going?"

The journey was the longest they had made so far. Meldren did not feel comfortable traveling in something which moved so swiftly and so silently. She gazed out on the view of the city. Towering, thin buildings, glittering in the sun with strange ribbons of materials linking them. Travelways was how Edwallan-Sipcort had called them, assuming that would be sufficient. Other vehicles, some bulbous and others, like the one they were in, long and sleek-looking, whizzed or trundled in a variety of bright colors at various heights above the ground and heading in different directions. She wondered how they managed to avoid colliding. Craning her neck up at an angle, she could see the sky. But it wasn't the clear blue as she was used to; there seemed to be a haze or something which gave it a silvery cast, almost as if there was a translucent covering across the whole arc of the sky.

As they traveled, so the towering buildings thinned out and large, open spaces appeared surrounded by lower, thicker buildings.

Meldren nudged Javin. "Look. I think I can see some trees at last."

"The ornamental parks are the beginning of the Emperor's Palace," said Edwallan-Sipcort from the opposite seat. His eyes were closed and his fingers were laced over his belly as if he were simply too bored with the view. "The buildings are for some of the household officers as well as for governmental departments. It's all part of the Palace and is really the hub of the Empire."

"So this is all the Emperor's palace? But I thought a palace was a building," said Meldren.

"It is. But if you think of a very large building, a very, very large building, one which has many different rooms and many different people doing many different tasks and there are places to sleep and to work and to play, then why cannot this whole area be a palace? However large a building you were thinking of, think of it as much, much larger."

"But, there are other buildings here. You don't have buildings inside buildings."

"This is nevertheless the Palace." A deep, long-suffering sigh came from the opposite seat. "Very well. If you insist." He cracked one eye enough to glance outside. "The Palace as you are thinking of it is coming up soon."

Sure enough, the vehicle slowed down and halted. Meldren and Javin made to get out, but Edwallan-Sipcort put out a restraining hand. "Not yet. Not yet at all. This is merely a security checkpoint." They sat back down.

As they sat and waited, another vehicle passed by. Meldren nudged Javin, pointing it out. "That's the captain in there. I'd swear it was her. I'd recognize her nose up in the air anywhere." They watched as the vehicle headed toward a low-slung building half-hidden behind some sort of large, yellow plant.

"What building is that?" asked Meldren.

Edwallan-Sipcort leaned forward. "That? Oh, that's where claims are registered."

"And... ?" nudged Meldren.

He wafted his hands around as if that would make it clearer. "Claims! People who have found things of value to the Empire. They make their claims there and the results are evaluated. If successful, some people can become very wealthy. It can take a long time in some cases. Some claims never amount to anything." He shrugged. "For owners of large, validated claims, it's a way of rising up through society. Money and power here, as everywhere, are important social tools."

Meldren felt there was something she as missing, but shrugged it aside. The vehicle had disappeared and they were still waiting. "How much longer are we going to be?" she asked.

"It depends," came the reply.

"Is this the only place we stop?"

"There will be others."

And there were. Each time they were inspected, the vehicle was inspected and small disks were passed back and forth before resuming their journey. Five times this happened, with Meldren getting increasingly annoyed.

"Why doesn't anyone trust anyone here?"

"Because where we are going is a place of power. And power attracts many people. Some of those people handle power responsibly and others find it... difficult. Having access to this amount of power is too exciting for some irresponsible people to resist. Hence the checks, because nobody in their right mind would trust anyone's word for wanting to come here." Edwallan-Sipcort's voice was still toneless and bored-sounding, although Meldren could spot the underlying excitement in the way he fidgeted as well as the flashing of various colors around him, as if he was finding it impossible to keep his thoughts an any one thing. He merely wanted to look as if this was boringly familiar, whereas he was just as excited as he had been the previous night when he had told them. "Patience. We will arrive, and I will inform Your Notabilities of what is expected and where you will go and when you will go there. As ambassadors you will always be escorted so as not to lose your way or be late. After I have briefed you, I will see you back at the hotel again."

Meldren knew he really wanted to get inside the Palace, but all he was allowed to do was barely enter it before having to leave. Of course, he wanted to seem as if he was so used to it all that he was bored with it, when in reality he was desperate to experience what they would be seeing.

Finally they disembarked and Edwallan-Sipcort directed them down a wide colonnade to where he introduced them formally to several people who were obviously expecting them. He took his leave and they were escorted through various large doors, crossing spacious rooms with expensive-looking furniture into other spacious rooms, along corridors and through smaller rooms until, at last, they were swept graciously into what seemed like a very large, well-lit, comfortable suite of offices filled with many different people, all seemingly very busy.

They made themselves comfortable in two of three large chairs which seemed to mould themselves to their shapes. As they were getting used to this form of seating, a figure appeared beside them, dressed in flowing robes which they had by now gathered indicated a level of formality. The man in them was completely bald and had piercing grey eyes above a thin, humorless mouth.

"I am Emessor-Patkillin-Thren at your service, Your Notabilities," he said in a rich, mellifluous voice, bowing as he did so.

Meldren struggled to sit up in the chair which seemed reluctant to let her go. The man indicated that she should remain seated and sat in the third chair.

"You're not the Emperor, are you?" asked Meldren.

"Hardly, Your Notability. Merely a lowly servant." His eyes never seemed to blink, she thought.

"But we have to see him and tell him what we are here for."

"Do we speak with you instead?" asked Javin. "We don't really mind who we talk to, but it would be nice to get it out of the way, and then we can get on with our lives."

Meldren saw a quickly stifled expression which she could only guess was surprise. But she wasn't sure why. She had a sudden thought to check his colors and berated herself for not thinking of doing such a thing long before now. However, she was distracted again by the man speaking to Javin.

"Your Notability, we are certainly going to make sure that you will be able to deliver your messages to the appropriate persons as swiftly as we can. However, I'm sure you'll appreciate that there are many formalities which have to be observed in their correct sequence so that the process of who you represent and how they may become a mutually advantageous part of the Benevolence can be carried out to the complete satisfaction of all concerned." He gave a thin smile as if that would make everything more clear.

"The Benevolence? What's that?" asked Meldren. "I thought I'd heard it before, but... ."

"The Benevolence is merely the theme of the Empire under the guidance of His Majesty Hemellikon-Prastor the Third. Each Emperor chooses a theme to be the guiding light for all his servants and officers during his reign. Our Emperor has chosen the theme of Benevolence."

Meldren was still confused. "Why do you have three names but the Emperor has two, the same as the one who brought us here?"

"Your Notability is very quick indeed. My full title contains the three major family alliances I am entitled to use. Our Emperor, for the sake of efficiency and with great humility has decreed that only the first two of his seventeen major alliance names are to be used in day-to-day affairs. He specifically ordered that those of more than two names, such as myself, should keep them and not engage in trying to emulate his enlightened manner. As I was already known and addressed by these three names, it was easy for me to comply." He leaned back as if asking for any questions before continuing.

"My office here is engaged in the registration of all ambassadors. Therefore, with your gracious permission, I should like to begin the process?" With that, he pressed a button on the side of his chair which eased him into a standing position. He showed Meldren and Javin where to achieve the same effect and then ushered them in to another room where the process began.

They were photographed and recorded and their speech patterns analyzed and the phrases they used were noted so that common terms could be translated better and they could then be helped to more clearly understand elements of the culture here and vice versa. Questions were asked about their beliefs, which caused great confusion, which were only amplified when it became clear that they were not actually from the planet they were representing and that their surnames, Harnatta and Sarnum, didn't really seem to mean much to them. They were a convenience only. That appeared to cause the bureaucracy to screech to a halt with nobody seemingly able to continue.

Emessor-Patkillin-Thren entered and dismissed the clerks with a flourish. "My apologies for the inconvenience. We are not presently geared toward a secondary planet's persons acting as ambassadors. The planet you are from has not, so it seems, made a request to join the empire, yet you are from it and are also representing a different planet entirely. It is... unusual. Please forgive us our laxity in this, but rest assured that it will be dealt with as quickly as possible. We should have liked to have completed much more in this visit, but I do assure you that it will be continued at a later date. In the meantime, I am pleased to announce that it is time to make your way to your meal with the Emperor Himself." He bowed them out of the office and into the arms of a guard of honor consisting of five armed soldiers in rather fancy uniforms and with attitudes of bored indifference, who surrounded them as they were seated in a floating vehicle of some kind and which whisked them effortlessly away.

Comfortably strapped in, with the soldiers around them, Meldren and Javin stared in disbelief at the number of rooms and courtyards they crossed, each one seemingly more ornate and larger than the previous one. Pedestrians scurried away at the sound of the warning chimes emitted by the vehicle. Finally, after a longer ride than they would have imagined, they were helped down to the ground by the officer in charge, who bowed formally, still without showing any interest, and who then led the way to the imposing doors in front of them. These opened at his command and he bowed them in to where they were taken in hand by another three uniformed people who guided and led them toward a vast table at which a large number of people were talking, some of whom were seated. The chatter ceased and all eyes seemed to be looking at the two new arrivals.

Taken to their seats, they gratefully sat down and nodded at anyone who looked at them, whilst feeling embarrassed at the sudden mass attention, before the talking recommenced.

"I feel very strange being here," whispered Meldren to Javin.

"I'm not really liking it, either," he whispered back.

"I thought we'd be eating with the Emperor. Just the three of us. Not like this," she added.

"Maybe it's some sort of honor," suggested Javin.

"Nothing of the sort," boomed a voice. It came from the person sitting next to Meldren, a rotund man, red of face and cheerful of disposition.

"Do excuse me for overhearing. I'm Yorg Bennon, by the way. No extra names or anything like that. Just Yorg Bennon, first and last. At your service, or however you want to say it where you come from."

After Meldren and Javin had introduced themselves, Bennon continued with a quickly dismissive glance at those opposite and leaning in closer so as to be able to speak more quietly. "This is not some sort of honor, although everyone thinks it is. It's more just a way of keeping people like you and me occupied." He waved his pudgy hand taking in the room and everyone in it. "Look at them all. Acting like it was something hugely important. But, tell me, can you actually see the Emperor? Hmm? No. Of course not, because when he arrives he'll be a tiny dot at the far end of the room, and everyone here will think they've been blessed by his presence."

He sucked at his lower lip. "I should give you more details, shouldn't I?" He pointed at his chest. "Yorg Bennon, like I said. I'm the ambassador for a backward little planet in the middle of large amounts of nothing which had the good fortune of having a lot of some precious metals which are highly prized and a lot of land we didn't need. We're too small to be of any interest to others, so I am quite free to be as I am. I've been to countless of these things. But this looks like your first. So, share what you want about yourselves and we'll see if we are going to be friends or not." He grinned hugely and beckoned to Meldren. "Here. Swap seats so I can sit between you. That way we won't get interrupted by any other idiots here." Meldren noticed a few raised brows, but nobody said anything, so they swapped seats despite one uniformed person who had been standing against the wall making as if to move toward them and stop them. Yorg pointed a finger at him and shook his head slowly with a stern look on his face. The attendant stopped and thought better of it, returning to his post.

"Now," said Bennon. "Where are you from, and what have you been getting up to since you got here? I'm starved of good conversation and you look like you want to talk. So... ?" And he laced his fingers and rested them on his belly, looking at first Meldren, then Javin.

"We're new ambassadors for Haven, a planet. But we're actually from a different one," said Javin. "And that caused a bit of confusion."

Bennon's eyes twinkled. "I bet it did. Were you with that old idiot, Emessor? Too oily for his own good. Yes, I can see you were. Oh, I would have loved to have seen his face. Does not like having his routine messed up, does Emessor." He cackled. "That alone has made you my firm friends. Anyone who can upset Emessor is someone I like." He patted Meldren's arm. "But tell me about yourselves and those delightful things around your necks." He peered closer and then squealed in delight. "They're alive aren't they? Oh, this is fabulous. I can only imagine how much these have been an irritation to everyone. I am liking you both more and more by the moment."

"One thing you can help us with," said Javin.

"Anything at all. Anything."

"How long will it take to negotiate a treaty and for us to be able to go back home?"

Bennon's face registered shock. "Go back home? But you're ambassadors! You can't just wander home any time you like. No, no, no, no, no. That is not how it works at all. You stay here, and everyone pretends they like you while keeping you busy doing very little and, over time, you get to put all the things you want to say and have done on record which gets to the right people, and they take their time getting back to you with all the changes they want to make. And so it goes, back and forth, to and fro with hardly anything getting done at all and everyone very happy about that as long as they get to eat as often as they want." He stopped and turned to each of them, a sad look on his face.

"My dears, I had not realized how new you were to all this. I must think of ways I can make your time here be something you can enjoy. I shall make it my responsibility to ensure that everything is moved as quickly as possible for you both, but even that, I fear, will be too long."

Meldren was shocked at the news and could see in Javin's face the same reaction. "But... we didn't know. We can't stay here. This is not our home. This is not how we want to live."

Bennon patted her arm. "This must be a huge shock. To you both, I imagine. Let us get through this meal first, and then we can begin to think of ways to help you. Ah, here comes the Emperor. Perhaps we can get served soon."

Looking up from the table, Meldren saw a small figure, whose features at this distance were indistinguishable, being escorted to a slightly elevated seat by several other people. The room became suddenly quiet and Meldren was startled by a voice, apparently emanating from the air above her, welcoming them all and announcing the start of the meal. Servers appeared soundlessly and food was place in front of her, but she felt empty of hunger.

This was not how it was meant to be. Why would the Tree require them to leave their home forever and live amongst these people? It was not fair. After everything they had been through. They had done everything asked of them, and this was their reward. She felt tears welling up and she sought to hold them back but could not. Bowing her head, she bit her lip to try to control herself but it was impossible. With a barely stifled cry, she pushed her chair back and ran for the door they had entered by, aware at some level of two things. First, the shock of all the other diners at her actions, and secondly, that Javin was right with her. That was all that mattered.

Bursting through the doors, Javin shouted out, "We need assistance. We do not wish to upset the Emperor, but fear that we need to leave now. It is imperative that we get to our hotel immediately. Help us!"

That set off a swarm of people, all buzzing to help. Meldren was so grateful for Javin's quick thinking, and she leaned on his shoulder and let her tears flow. She was only aware of him holding her and gently reassuring her that everything would be fine. Finally, one of the vehicles used to bring them here arrived and they were on it with a hastily arranged escort and at the main entrance before too long.

Slumped in her seat as they sped through the city back to their hotel, Meldren looked up with bloodshot eyes. "What are we going to do, Javin? What are we going to do?"

23

"I think we should do something," said Hanna. She was sitting on a log, chewing on some bread and cheese she had sung, watching the ship's passengers in the distance at the foot of some hills. She was watching them from behind a stand of bushes which hid her and the others from sight.

"But what?" asked Farran. "We're following them still, and we can't find anything wrong, and we've told Pol and Isselta and they've told Myrella what we're doing and I don't know what else we should be doing."

"For one thing," put in Endel, "I think we should stop that scratchy sound that links the equipment with whatever it's linked to."

"But why?" asked Carmeena. "We don't even know what it is."

"That's a good enough reason for me," said Endel. "If it was something that made sense, I'd leave it alone. But that, together with whatever secret that man is hiding, makes me think that we should stop it."

"And another thing," added Hanna. "We still don't really know what it is they are doing with that equipment. Every time they stop somewhere, they set it up and turn it on. But what for?"

"Pol said that Myrella told her that they were surveying the land," said Farran, "and that it had been agreed that they would do that."

Endel was still not satisfied. "But what about the scratch sound? Is that part of it as well?"

"And there's another, very short scratch sound coming back," said Carmeena. "I've heard it occasionally."

Hanna ignored that. "But what are they surveying for?"

Farran shrugged. "I don't know."

"Well, can we find out at least?" asked Endel. He was beginning to become annoyed at the way this conversation was going round and getting nowhere. "It seems that the more we follow them, the less we know what they are doing. This is not their planet. It's ours. And we should know what they are doing."

"I suppose I could ask Pol to ask Myrella... ," began Farran, but Endel interrupted.

"I don't think we should be waiting around any longer. I think we should get involved more. After all, shouldn't we at least get to know more about the woman and find out if she is a talent or something like that? We found that out because we decided to investigate. But here we are still just sitting around and doing nothing."

Carmeena tried to smooth things over. "I know how you feel, Endel. I'd like to know more myself, but I can't think how that would work or what we could do."

"Actually," said Hanna, "I'd like to know why you feel so strongly about this. Is it something you have a feeling about, something you sense happening? We've been doing this, following them, for a long time, so why now?"

As soon as he heard her speak, Endel knew that she was right. It was something which had been growing inside him of which he had been unaware until she mentioned it. He had thought it was because he wanted to know more about what they were doing or why they were doing it, but instead it was really that he felt something was wrong about the situation, wrong about what they were doing, even if he didn't know what it was.

He smiled at her, grateful for her insight. "You're right, Hanna, exactly right. I feel there is something going on that we can't see or don't know about somehow, and it's important. And it should be stopped. Or, at least, we should be interfering more." He closed his eyes and ran his hands through his hair trying to let the knowledge which had been locked away come to where he could see it and to feel the right way to speak about it. Opening his eyes and taking a deep breath, he said, "I think that both of them are doing something that they don't want to admit and that it is going to be very bad for us all, the whole planet even, if we remain seated here. And maybe that's what you were feeling too, Hanna, when you said we should be doing something."

As was so often the case, once something had been said, it became real for the others as well. Hanna gave a nod of acknowledgement and he noticed, and enjoyed, the small smile she gave him. "Do you have a sense of what we should be doing?"

"Stop that noise! That's the very first thing we should do," he said emphatically. "We have to go and stop it ourselves."

"Yes, but how?" asked Carmeena. "It was hard enough getting close to them the first time. Are you suggesting we actually go inside the ship somehow?"

"Why not? We can sing ourselves anywhere, can't we?"

Farran was not so sure. "Maybe we can. But we've only sung ourselves to places we know about or, which is more important, are part of Haven. That ship isn't natural. It doesn't come from Haven and I have no idea how to even think about understanding any of the songs there."

"So you're saying we have to get ourselves inside it somehow without singing?" asked Carmeena.

"Would you want to sing yourself into the inside of it? I wouldn't," he replied. "If Endel is right, and I feel he is, then we have to do something else to get there and change things."

"Shouldn't we at least let Pol or Isselta know what we're doing?" asked Carmeena.

"And what could they do? It's better if we can tell them about something we've found," replied Endel. "The problem is, how do we do it?"

Silently, they each thought about this challenge. Carmeena shrugged. "I can't think of anything."

"I may have an idea," said Hanna. "But it relies on a couple of things.

One of them is you, Carmeena and the other one is how close we can sing ourselves to the ship."

"How am I involved?"

"You were the one seen by the woman. At least, you were reasonably certain she saw you. What I was thinking was that you get seen again. Only this time, it's deliberate."

"Why?"

"Because you can keep them occupied while we, or whoever, gets inside to have a look around and stop that noise that Endel's worried about."

"I'll be the one who goes," said Endel. "It was my idea. I should be the one to do it." Nobody objected.

"But how do I keep them occupied? Are you saying I just walk up to them?" Carmeena pointed at the distant ship out in the open with no shelter or shade nearby. The small building they always put up and took down was the only other thing there. "I can't walk across all that way. And how would you be able to do anything if I did?"

Hanna nodded. "I agree. Where they are right now is not going to work. But anywhere they stop where there is somewhere better to hide or be hidden from them would work. Like when they were at the river."

"But what do I say to them?"

"Anything at all," said Endel, taken with the idea. "My guess is they will be asking you lots of questions, you just have to find a way to answer them without telling them what you are really doing."

"Like what?" asked Carmeena, far from committed to this course of action.

"I don't know," said Endel, feeling frustrated again. "But I'm sure telling them about your sprite would interest them. You could say you were lost, or had decided to have a long walk from somewhere to somewhere else and you saw them and decided to say hello. The point is, just keep them occupied a while."

"For how long?"

"For as long as you can," said Hanna. "Don't worry. You're not going to be hurt or anything. It's perfectly safe."

"Not perfectly. Possibly. Possibly safe is what you mean. That and plain embarrassing," said Carmeena.

Three days later, the next stop for the ship and its personnel matched their requirements. The ship rested near the bank of a deep but narrow stream with some rolling hills behind and plenty of forested areas all around on both sides of the water to provide cover.

Carmeena and Hanna decided what to do.

"It's perfect," said Hanna, pointing out her suggested route as she spoke. "If you come out of those trees over the other side you can cross over where two of them have fallen and made a bridge. It'll look like you're just out for a walk. Plus it's nowhere near where we are now."

" A walk? Where from?"

"Say you've been camping or something."

"Why would I be camping?"

"You like being in nature?" suggested Hanna. "Or you wanted some time on your own to think about your life." She shrugged. "Say anything. It won't matter, not when you start talking about your sprite."

"And that's another thing. What if they ask where I got it? Things like that? I'm really not very good at telling lies, Hanna. I don't feel good about this."

Hanna sat back on her haunches and looked at her friend. "I know, and I'm sorry for making it seem so easy. Look, how about you mentioning that you saw or heard the ship and that you wanted to say hello and find out what it was making the noise? That is easier to say, isn't it? It means they have to do more of the talking as well."

Carmen considered this a moment. With a wry smile and a tilt of her head, she sighed and said, "All right. I'll try. But I can't promise to keep them interested for very long. I'll do what I can, and that's all I can say."

The other three watched as Carmeena heard the songs of the land to help pinpoint the place in the distant trees she would arrive at and then saw her disappear. They turned their attention to where she would be appearing from, checking occasionally on the four people by the craft. As usual, the equipment was set up and the scratchy sound was happening again.

Carmeena appeared and walked deliberately to the log bridge, crossing it and continuing along the bank until she was seen by one of the people.

At that point, Endel began to hear his way across the land to the place where he could arrive without being seen. At least, that was his hope. Farran and Hanna would keep watch and, if anything looked like going wrong, they had promised to act as some sort of diversion. What that might consist of, however, they had no idea.

Farran tapped Endel's shoulder. "They're talking. Go as soon as you can."

Endel took a deep breath, sang the song he needed and vanished. He opened his eyes to see that he had arrived as planned, the ship's body between himself and the others. He could hear Carmeena's voice and could make out that she was urging them to look toward the hills and even move off in that direction. From what he could hear, it seemed to be working. He tried listening to the songs of the people but realized that it would not help, because he could not tell which way they were facing. He slowly peered around the ship to see that all five were facing away. Hoping they would remain that way, he moved as quickly and as silently as he could up the short ramp and into the ship itself.

Keeping away from the door, he sidled around the interior, shutting his eyes every now and then to locate the place where the irritating noise was coming in from the outside equipment. Through trial and error, he ended up facing a panel of flickering lights and dials which meant nothing. All he knew was that he had to make it not work. The trick was finding a way of doing that.

Briefly, he checked in on the voices outside and was relieved to hear that they seemed just as far away. He focused his intention on the panel before him, listening to it. It was a strange song, unlike anything he had ever heard before. There was no underlying rhythm which he could find. It felt... wrong, but it also felt -- what was the word? -- efficient. Realizing that, he also realized that all he had to do was make it inefficient. He could do that by introducing some new notes into the repeating sounds he was hearing. It would take some time, because it was something different to anything he had experienced before, but he was sure he could do it.

One last check on the sounds outside, and he crouched down, resting his hand on the panel to come into as close a contact as he could. He heard where the repetition occurred and, waiting for it to come around again, he imagined which notes he could place there so that the next repetition would not be exact. If he was right, all he had to do was listen for the sounds which were projecting up into space. If they faltered and stopped, he had achieved what he had come to do.

The moment approached and he put everything else out of his mind, hearing only what he needed. As the tiny break in sound arrived, signifying the beginning of the cycle, he hummed the notes he heard and felt the ribbon on his face twist and move to his forehead, something he had never felt before. Normally, he only knew it had moved because others told him. But this time he felt it. It was as though his skin was moving and changing his face as it did so. It was, almost, unnerving. As he focused, the voices outside sounded as if they were coming closer. But he waited until the start and end point came round again and this time he heard the new sound which was still embedded. The voices were definitely getting louder now. Then he sought for the sounds which reached up to the stars and it was gone.

He turned around now and saw the shadow of someone and heard a voice saying, "I'm sure you'll be interested in all of this. We'd be delighted to show you, if, in return, we could take a look at that wonderful creature you have around your neck."

Knowing he could not now escape without being seen, he moved back to where chairs were fixed to the floor and hid as best he could behind one of them. He hoped that they would stop before they entered the ship and that Carmeena would find a way to draw them back out again. Listening to them, he quickly realized that was not going to happen. Desperate to escape, he shut his eyes and listened for Hanna's song. It was the one he knew so well. He caught the soft strains of her song instantly. It was soft and gentle, like her. He zeroed in on her, hearing her song swell in his head as he did so, blotting out the voices on the ramp which were now dangerously close, meaning he could not sing, but only follow. With a supreme effort, he let her song engulf his mind and surrendered to it, letting it take him to her.

He heard her stifled shriek as he felt her squirm beneath him. It was a wonderful feeling that he had no interest in ending. A huge sense of relief washed over him along with the physical thrill he felt. But she obviously did not share the same feelings. Shoving him off, she sat up and glared at him. She was furious, because she was scared.

"What do you think you were doing? You could have killed me! You can't just jump in someone's song. You could have ended up... we could have become... ," she locked her fingers together in explanation. "We could have died. Don't ever get inside my song like that again."

He felt ashamed and embarrassed in equal measure; his previous feelings washed away. He tried to explain. "I'm... I'm sorry! I didn't think. I was trapped in there and they were coming up the ramp. I had to get out quickly. I couldn't think of another way. I could only think of you, your song. I'm sorry. Truly, I am."

Hanna was still very unhappy. "I could feel something was happening but I didn't realize what it was until it was too late. You have to promise me that you will never do anything like that ever again. If you have to, then leave my song to arrive beside me. But nothing like that again." She shuddered. "You have no idea what that felt like. It was as though someone was actually inside me, tearing at me somehow."

Farran laid a hand on her shoulder. "He didn't mean it, Hanna," he rumbled. "And he said he was sorry. He was trapped and had to find a way out. He said that his first thought was of you. Which was a compliment. He's learned from it, haven't you?" Endel nodded enthusiastically, still looking at Hanna. "In fact, we all should learn from it. But let's now think about what we can do about Carmeena, shall we?"

Hanna looked at Endel, and he was sure he noticed a warmth in her eyes and the beginnings of what could become a smile on the edge of her lips. "I'm sorry and I accept your apology. It must have been frightening. But," here she took a decisive breath, forcing herself to deal with other issues, "did you hear anything of what Carmeena was saying? Anything that might help us help her?"

Endel shook his head, reluctant to let the moment end. "Nothing that I can think of. They were coming close, too close for me to have the time to listen. I suppose we had better give her some time to let her get herself out of there."

"I propose that we listen in on her song," said Farran. "That might give us a clue as to what's happening with her."

"Just a moment," said Hanna, peering through the bushes. "I think she's leaving. Or, at least, they're further away from the ship than the last time I looked." She paused. "No, I really think she's leaving. They're waving goodbye and she's heading off to the hills."

"Probably when she gets there she'll sing herself back here and we can find out how she got on," said Farran.

They waited and watched as Carmeena hiked up one of the gentle hills and disappeared over the brow. A short while later, she appeared to one side of the clearing.

"Well?" demanded Hanna. "How did you get on? What happened? Tell us everything. Endel stopped the noise and gave me a scare," here she gave him a quick smile of reassurance, "but what happened with you?"

24

The moment she saw the woman walking towards them, she felt a shiver of surprise and, strangely, anticipation. "Eslennet Parra-Hopshan", she said to herself, using her quiet name, "that is the woman you saw. You were right. She does exist!" She felt excited at the prospect of meeting her.

The woman eventually arrived, introductions were made and everyone was welcoming and intrigued in equal measures. Although the woman was dressed in a simple and somewhat dirty dress and walked barefoot, she seemed perfectly at ease and her hair looked clean and brushed.

"I'm Carmeena," she said. "I've been camping with friends back there a way," pointing to the trees beyond the stream, "and I decided to go for a walk. I've not been in this part of the country before. What are you doing here? I thought nobody else was about."

"We thought the same as you," said one of the new guides, Garran, a professor of medicine. "We were assured the place was empty of people."

"Oh, it was. That's why we chose to come here for a time and just relax in nature. It is beautiful here, isn't it?" Carmeena looked around, smiling at the view.

"May I ask what it is you have round your neck?" asked Parra-Hopshan. "It looks most interesting."

"Oh, this?" said Carmeena reaching up and stroking the strange necklace. "This is a sprite. At least, that's what I call it."

"And I've never heard of one of those, or seen one either," said the other guide. This was a woman named Fesha, a professor of clinical psychiatry, whatever that was. Parra-Hopshan noticed that Lessterenman was saying nothing, just watching.

"Well, it might have a different name for all I know," said Carmeena. "I didn't find it here, but a long way away."

"But is it alive?" asked Parra-Hopshan. "I thought I saw a movement." She felt herself very much drawn to this creature which looked more like a twist of wood than anything else. It felt important to her, but she had no idea why.

"Yes, it is alive. But it doesn't do very much. It stays round my neck and eats occasionally, but I don't think it does anything else."

"Fascinating," said Fesha, moving in for a closer look. "I wonder what exactly it is." As she leaned in, Parra-Hopshan got a sudden clenching feeling of fear in her belly. At the same time, the creature unwound a little and lunged it's head at the professor, hissing and making a burbling noise.

This obviously took Carmeena by surprise as she flushed red and apologized. "It's never done that before. I didn't even know it could. I am so sorry. Are you all right?"

Fesha assured her that she was, although there was a considerable dent in her dignity, Parra-Hopshan thought. But she also wondered to herself how had she known that something was going to happen? Something was not quite right. Yet she could not identify what it was, only that it had something to do with this woman.

"This might sound strange," she said, "but I think I saw you some days ago. At least, it might have been you. I'm almost positive that whoever it was had the same thing, the sprite, around her neck then as well. Could it have been you?"

Carmeena shook her head. "No, I'm sure I would have remembered meeting you."

"We didn't actually meet. I caught a glance of someone, and I thought it looked like you, that's all."

"Sorry," laughed Carmeena. "There's only the one of me and I don't recall anything like that."

Trying to pin down that feeling of 'something', that 'not smooth' feeling she now felt in her life, Parra-Hopshan continued. "But do you know of anyone else who has a sprite like yours? I'm positive I saw one around the neck of whoever it was."

Again Carmeena shook her head. "I was lucky to find mine, so I suppose whoever you saw had the same luck as me. But I don't know of anyone else with one. Sorry."

Parra-Hopshan smiled politely and let the others take over the conversation as she tried to make sense of how she was feeling. This meeting now felt as though she was on the verge of something both large and intimate at the same time. But what it was or what had caused it, she was none the wiser.

Lessterenman offered to show Carmeena around the ship, but she was, thought Parra-Hopshan, strangely reluctant to take a look inside. Everyone else they had met had been so eager that they had rushed to look around. Eventually, Carmeena was persuaded to take a look and she did so, but still walked very slowly up the ramp. Parra-Hopshan walked behind her, studying the sprite as if that would give her the answers she wanted. She was focused so closely on it that she didn't hear Fesha and Garran talking until Garran asked her, "Are you sure you saw another of those creatures? They would be most interesting to study. Would you please keep us informed if you do come across one later on in your journeys?"

She shrugged in reply. "Of course." But this gave her an idea. "I'll ask her more about it if you like," she said. "I'll speak to her myself, and, as I'm not from here, it might be easier to get some details from her. At least, I hope it will."

That seemed to satisfy the two guides and she dropped back a little, waiting for an opportunity to speak with Carmeena alone. She didn't have long to wait.

"You weren't in the ship for very long."

Carmeena smiled. "I'm not that interested in all that technology and the little lights and things if I'm being honest. I do like the open spaces more."

"I can see that they do have a certain attraction." She smiled back at the woman and turned to face the hills. "There is nothing quite like this where I come from. This is all very new for me."

When she turned back, she saw that Carmeena was looking at her very intently but quickly switched on a warm smile. "I'm glad you like it here so much," she said. "I wasn't born here either, and I find it very... relaxing."

"Where were you born, then?"

Carmeena shook her head. "Oh, it's a long way from here and you wouldn't have heard of it probably. I like to sit and let myself sink into the scenery." She gave a little laugh. "I know that's not a very good way of saying it, but it's how I feel at times. How about you?"

Parra-Hopshan considered. "Yes," she said. "That sounds about right. The scenery, the country, it sort of fills me up inside." She shared a smile with Carmeena. "I can seen why you like walking so much." For a moment, Parra-Hopshan felt as if she heard a sound so deep, so wonderful, that it made her almost stop breathing. She could have sworn that the sprite had opened its mouth, but it could not possibly have made such a sound, so sonorous as to be felt as well as heard.

"Are you feeling well?" asked Carmeena with a look more of interest than concern on her face.

"Perfectly fine, thank you." Parra-Hopshan smiled as she sought to find her emotional balance. To take attention away from herself, she said, "Actually, the main reason for this conversation is that I promised our two guides here that I would ask you more about the sprite, as they are both very interested in learning more about it. I think they would like to find one or two themselves and study them."

Carmeena turned to look at the the two guides who were standing near to the stream's edge and talking quietly with Lessterenman. When she turned back to face her, Parra-Hopshan thought she was being judged in some fashion. "The truth about these sprites... ," began Carmeena, and Parra-Hopshan's chest tightened as if some immense secret was about to be revealed that would break into her world and overturn it. "The truth is, they don't come from around here. And I also think that you have some sort of ability which you're not really certain about. I think you do really like this planet, but you have no idea what that can mean." She gestured at the other three. "You can tell them that sprites are very rare and they'll be very lucky indeed to find one, let alone two. But the real reason you are here talking to me is that, somehow, you already know this but don't know how you know it or even why you know it."

Here Carmeena laid a hand on Parra-Hopshan's arm. "When you're ready, there will always be someone you can turn to." She held Parra-Hopshan's gaze a long time, her eyes half-lidded as if listening to something she herself could not hear. Finally, she withdrew her hand and her face broke into a smile. "Now, I think it's time I should be going. You have lots to think about and you don't want me around making that more difficult. Come, let's go to the others and I'll say my goodbyes and leave you all to get on with whatever it is you are doing."

Parra-Hopshan at first could only watch as Carmeena walked away to join the others. She swallowed once, twice and blinked rapidly as if waking up. She had heard every word but they did not make sense. And yet... there was a truth in there somewhere, if only she could bring it to the surface. Reluctant to dispel the fragile web of awareness she felt settling on her, she pushed herself to follow Carmeena and join in the conversation, forcing a smile on her face as she did so.

As she watched the strange woman walk away from them, up the slope of the hill, she knew that she had reached a watershed in her life. Continuing as always would bring known and understandable results. It was a future she could already tell. But that woman, Carmeena, had made her be able to think that there was another path she could follow. What it was, what it looked like, what it would ask of her, where it would take her: all those things were unknowns. But at least she now knew that a different path existed.

And far away, at the edge of the solar system, the beacon waited for the next data stream.

25

When the shock of the discovery of what their appointment meant for them both, Javin and Meldren took to going out, anywhere, on their own. Edwallan-Sipcort had been astounded by their early return and kept asking and asking for details, probably, thought Javin, to make sure he wasn't going to be held responsible in some way.

When they refused to give him any information and announced their intention to go wherever they wanted whenever they wanted, it was another hammer blow to his pride.

"I simply cannot perform my duties to Your Notabilities if I am not privy to where you go, who you see and what you engage in. You surely must see that?" he implored.

"I do see that," said Meldren, "and I don't care. We have decided this is what we are going to be doing from now on, and that is final." Looking dumbstruck, making gestures of conciliation and forgiveness, he was firmly ushered from the room, Meldren watching as the door locked behind him.

Javin had been as devastated as Meldren upon hearing what Yorg Bennon had told them. But he had been wounded far more by seeing how badly it had affected her. She had bounced back from every previous setback they had faced together, but, somehow, this one had been harder than anything else.

"I don't know what I'm going to do, Javin. How are we meant to live on a planet like this where nobody is honest or trusting, and you can't see the sky properly? Everything here is so artificial. It breaks my heart to be here, knowing we can't go back." She was sitting on the edge of what they had assumed was a bed.

"I honestly don't know, my love. All I know is that we wouldn't have been sent here, been picked to go here, if there was no way back for us. Either that or we would have found out before we left Haven."

"Yes, but how? That's the question." Her face was puffy from crying and her hair, which she normally took pride in braiding, was hanging loosely around her face. It cut at him to see her like this.

"That's why we're going to go out and we're also going to talk with Yorg Bennon again." He sat cross-legged at her feet, looking up at her. "We also need to go out to be in touch with nature again. No matter how it looks to us, nature, the planet, is out there and we need to get in touch with it again. And we need to talk more with Yorg to find out all we can about what we can and can't do." He reached out to her, stroking her leg. "And that idiot in charge of our ambassador things or whatever it is he is in charge of, can talk to the walls and the floors and the strange chairs all he likes, because we're not going back there again. Going back would be admitting we're following their rules. And we're not going to do that at all. Not any more. So, goodbye Sipcort and everyone else who keeps trying to get us to do the correct things. We're in charge of our lives from now on. Agreed?"

She nodded, still sniffling a little.

"This isn't the end of anything," he said, sounding more certain than he felt. "You know, deep down, there's a way out of this, something we can do to change things. We wouldn't have been chosen to be sent here otherwise. All we have to do is take the time to find out what it is we are really here for, because I guarantee you that we're not here to be normal ambassadors." He smiled up at her, holding her gaze. "You do realize that we're not anything like normal and never have been? This is a situation which is perfect for us then, isn't it?"

She smiled weakly back at him. "That's very true. Normal is something we do not do very well."

Feeling heartened by her attempt to cheer up, Javin continued. "I think the first thing we should do is go outside and feel the wind on our faces and maybe find some earth to dig our toes into. What do you say?"

So it was that a little while later, the two of them were sitting on some grass in what appeared to be a large park. They had walked there, hand in hand. They had been the only people walking although the path was wide and just soft enough to make walking comfortable and easy. They had passed what they now called the park several times in vehicles arranged for by Edwallan-Sipcort but had never stopped to look at it. It was a broad space set between large, low buildings. Like everything else they had seen, it was carefully manicured and arranged with a variety of different plants in clumps of colors. There were small hillocks and a few little streams to make the place visually appealing. But neither of them could sense much more than the surface effects. There were no 'deep-down songs' to be heard. It looked pretty, but it felt artificial. There were people using the park, but presumably they had all arrived in various types of vehicles, although none of those vehicles were presently visible. Some people were wandering to and fro, others were standing and talking or occupied in what might have been some sort of game involving colors and something hovering and weaving amongst them. Sitting on one of the rises, Javin and Meldren watched them all, a never-ending stream in various colors and types of clothing and strange hairstyles. There were distant sounds which meant nothing to either of them. It was simply a backdrop of noise.

"How are you feeling now?" asked Javin

"A little better. Less afraid, I think. But still upset. It's probably not really sunk in. How about you?"

"Something like that for me as well," he said. He gazed around them at the carefully planted and landscaped grounds. "This is nice, but it's not what I think of when I think of nature. It's like it's all been tamed and nothing is allowed to be out of place." He sighed. "But one thing I have realized."

"What's that?" asked Meldren, changing position to laying prone on the ground, eyes closed against the bright sky.

"We haven't once tried to feel out what this is about. Not once, and we have always done that."

"Probably because we've never traveled this far before," said Meldren looking at him, shading her eyes with one hand.

"So why not try it now?" said Javin.

"Let me sit up," said Meldren, "and let's do it." She rested on her arms behind her and flexed her neck as she took a deep breath. Javin, sitting beside her, hugged his knees to his chest and dropped his head down on them as he shut his eyes.

He let himself block out all the strangeness around him, became aware only of his breathing, and then sunk his attention down into himself and let whatever was there come to be recognized and acknowledged. After a moment, he opened his eyes and waited for Meldren to become alert.

"What did you get?" she asked.

"Something not that easy to say," he began. "At first it was like there was very, very long distance, but it was also short at the same time." He made vague sketching movements as he sought to put his feelings into words. "Then I felt like there was something really good at the end of all this, because I definitely felt that there was an end to it, and not that far off. But what it was or how it will be an end or even what it might be like, I have no idea." He shrugged a little and made a face. "Sorry I can't be much clearer. Did any of that match anything you got?"

Meldren was on her back again, eyes closed. She reached out a hand and Javin took hold of it. "I think I sort of know what you mean about the distance, or maybe it was a journey. It couldn't have been about how we got here, because I was feeling the future, not the past." She paused a moment. "And, about the ending, I suppose that would be a good way of describing what I felt. Bright. Very bright. That's the best way I can describe it. But not scary bright, just that that's how I saw or felt how it would be." She smiled, still with her eyes closed. And it was the first time for so long that she had smiled a genuine smile that Javin's heart skipped a beat in happiness. "Of course," she continued, "it's not a lot of help in details. As usual."

Javin squeezed her hand. "But it is really good at telling us that there is an end to all this and not that long. That's something worth knowing."

He lay down beside her on his side, propping his head on his arm to look at her. He gently stroked her face with his other hand. "And that makes me think that we should find that Yorg person and find out everything he knows that might be useful to us. If he was even half true in what he said and how he acted, I think he's going to be feeling very guilty about letting the news slip at the meal. He, at least, seemed to be honest, even if it was for his own amusement."

"Where do we find him, do you think?" asked Meldren.

"I know someone who'll be happy to tell us," replied Javin.

"You mean Sippy Sipcort."

"No. I mean Edwallan-Sipcort. The whole name."

"Hmmm," mused Meldren. "The way people are named here is confusing. All these extra names. That's something I'm definitely going to ask Yorg about."

They both lay on their backs, eyes closed, holding hands for a few moments more. Javin was able to feel complete again. Here they were, side by side, holding hands again and together. He was no longer a person apart, on his own. He was with Meldren and she... she was with him and that was what made his life so wonderful. If Meldren was upset and unhappy, it unbalanced him. He knew he would do anything to make her happy, because then he was himself more than he could be alone. Life was good.

"You know what I think?" asked Meldren.

"Nope."

"I think we won't have to go and find Sippy. I think he's going to be somewhere close enough to keep an eye on us. He's desperate to be close to us, or work for us or however he sees it. I'm positive he won't have taken no for an answer when we kicked him out. I'm certain he's here and close by. All we have to do is spot him when we sit up. He'll be the one looking out of place."

"First one to spot him gets to choose where to go on this planet," said Javin.

"Really? The whole planet?"

"Certainly. We are, after all, Our Notabilities, and that must mean something to someone." The fact that Meldren was interested in playing this game showed just how much she was getting back to her normal, vivacious self. Javin smiled at the thought.

"All right," agreed Meldren. "On the count of three, we both sit up and start looking. Ready? One, two, three."

They sat up, scanning the few passing people without luck.

"He's not going to be walking past us all the time, is he?" said Meldren. "He must be lurking somewhere."

"Agreed, said Javin." "But where? There's not much here to hide behind."

They both scanned the parkland for anything big enough. There were some large flowering plants with strange, sticky-looking purplish leaves growing in a stand not too far away. They both looked at it and then at each other.

"Has to be, doesn't it?" said Meldren with a twinkle in her eye.

"Again, agreed."

Meldren stood up and hauled Javin up beside her. Waving her arms, she called out, "Edwallan-Sipcort. Can we have a word with you please? We'd like to ask you something."

Nothing happened for a moment. Finally, there was a brisk movement of several fronds and the small familiar figure of their guide issued forth, trying to look as though he was naturally interested in the plant and just happened to be walking in their direction. He was fooling no-one.

"That means we both get to choose," said Javin quietly.

"I like it when we both win," said Meldren still smiling.

26

"I simply cannot emphasize how deeply, deeply sorry I am for giving you such news. I assumed, wrongly, that everyone here knew what was involved." Yorg Bennon appeared almost heartbroken as he looked at his two visitors.

"Tell me how can I repair, in some fashion, the damage I have done to you both?" He leaned forward, hands clasped beseechingly.

Meldren, who was seated in a large, form-fitting chair, had been watching Yorg closely as he had welcomed them in and called for some light refreshment. "Tell me a lie, if you please, Yorg."

This obviously took him by surprise. "A lie? I am not sure what you mean?"

"Something that you will tell me and which is not true, that's all."

Javin tried to explain. "Meldren has an ability to see someone and, if they are telling a lie, she will know it. She is asking you because, once she knows what a lie from you looks like, she will then know what the truth will look like as well."

From the way Yorg looked, this was not as helpful as Javin might have liked. However, Yorg tried his best to be accommodating. He gave a small confused smile. "Do recall that you are asking an ambassador to lie. It is what we do a lot of. Small or large, depending on the situation."

"Then," persisted Meldren, "it will be easy for you, won't it? Better yet, tell me two things in succession. One of them the truth and one of them a lie and I'll see if I can tell which is which."

Yorg's eyebrows raised. "Very well," he said, after a moment, stroking the arm of his chair with his fingertips as if in thought. "Here they are. First, I like the life of an ambassador here. It is easy, lavish and requires little effort on my behalf." He paused, but Meldren's nod encouraged him to continue. "And, secondly, my little planet is wealthier and safer than it has ever been now it is a part of the Earth Nations Alliance." He folded his hands in his lap and sat back a little. "There. Will that do?"

Javin looked at Meldren, recalling how she had asked him the same thing. But then, his statements which he believed to be true hadn't been quite as simple as he had thought. He waited.

"Hmmm," began Meldren. "I can see why you're an ambassador. Nothing is really as straightforward as it appears, is it? The first thing you said, about liking being an ambassador here is not quite true. A lot of it is true; the easy life part, for example. But you don't like it here. And, as for the second, that is mostly true as well, but I get the feeling that you don't like what has happened to your planet, even though it is richer than before. So, Yorg Bennon, I think you tell lies wrapped up in truths. Is that what an ambassador does?"

Yorg had been listening closely, giving nothing away. He laced his fingers and tapped his two thumbs together. Finally, he lowered his head in acknowledgement. "My dear lady... Meldren. You do indeed have a rare talent. I am almost ashamed at how you have seen through me so clearly. I do indeed like the life here but not the role I have to play. And I do wish that my people back home were less in debt to the Empire. But such things are not usually said aloud, and if they are, they are not welcomed. Hence the need to block any outside ears." Here he indicated the arm of his chair, revealing a series of controls. "It jumbles things up. Sometimes it's gibberish, apparently. Sometimes it's not. It keeps them interested in the wrong things. It is a precaution all ambassadors take in one form or another to ensure a little privacy." He smiled. "Every ambassador is listened to, even when they don't want to be heard."

He shrugged at the expressions on his guests' faces. "Don't let it concern you. What is of greater importance is that you, Meldren, were exactly correct in what you said. Sadly, I do wrap truth and lies together. It has become a habit. And that is not an excuse, merely an explanation. I am, I confess, deeply intrigued as to how you do what you just did, but I suspect that I would either not understand the explanation or find myself severely limited in any abilities I might have in that direction." He sat forward again. "But, now you can tell the difference --and that, I must admit is a somewhat nerve-wracking realization -- how does that knowledge help you, or help me to help you?"

Javin looked to Meldren, who nodded for him to go on and share what they had discussed. "We want to know what else we can do here, instead of sitting around and doing nothing for day after day. Specifically, we are extremely tired of where we live presently and would like to explore more of the planet, even finding some more wild, natural part of it. You see, we come from a very natural planet. A place where there is little machinery and where it is easy to feel the planet. We feel lost here. Not just lost in the sense of not knowing where anything is, but of not being able to feel the true planet. Not the carefully landscaped one with the clever arrangements of trees and bushes and all the rest, but the real planet, the one that is underneath all this man-made stuff."

Yorg helped himself to a small cake of shifting colors from the table floating beside his chair, indicating that his guests should do likewise. Swallowing the last of it and inspecting his fingers for any errant crumbs, he finally answered. "My dears, I had no idea how hard this is for you. You may be able to tell a lie from a truth, but I have the ability to hear what is painful. And both of you are in pain. A pain of separation. That's the way I would say it.

"However, the simple answer to your question is that, being ambassadors, you can go where you wish, within reason. This whole planet should be thought of as one vast building. Which it very nearly is, what with all the government departments and so many, many people working here. This is the very center of the Empire. Everything about any planet comes here and is filed away or ignored, sometimes both at the same time. You can go wherever you wish, as long as you tell someone what you intend to do. But, as for finding the true, underlying planet, I'm not at all sure that is even possible anymore. Everything has been built on or over, dug into or re-made into something else such that I would be surprised if anything original exists. Not that I'm saying it doesn't, but that there might not be much left if there is." He spread his hands to show his helplessness.

"That is useful to know," acknowledged Javin. "But, from what you said earlier about being overheard, I think it's about time we had our own place to live, instead of a hotel room, don't you? And, how would we go about that now?"

"Ah, now that is much easier. As accredited ambassadors you have a right to your own consulate." Seeing the question forming in Meldren's face he hurried on. "What that is is a building or a place, any place at all, which you claim as your own and in which you are free to do as you please... with the exception that you now know you will be listened in on. The only thing you have to be aware of is that the place you choose should not be someone else's consulate. Not as silly as it sounds, as there are a large number of ambassadors here, some with many, many staff, and not all of them are always here but carrying out other duties elsewhere on this planet. That means that some buildings will look empty or unused but they're not really. To claim yours, you simply go to the appropriate department -- to which I will accompany you both -- and give the address and other details." He spread his hands. "That's it!"

"Are you sure we're accredited?" asked Javin. "After all, that man got confused over our names and the fact we're from a different planet. It certainly didn't feel like it was finished back then, and we haven't been called back since"

Yorg waved the notion aside. "He likes being difficult. It's what makes him happiest. But, you were invited to a meal with the Emperor. That alone is enough. All the rest are details."

There followed some discussion about what sort of place would be most suitable for Javin and Meldren, but the three of them could not come to an agreement. Yorg urged them to be nearer to him, which meant being in the midst of many, many buildings, while they felt themselves being called to somewhere further away with more space around them.

Just as they were taking their leave, Meldren stopped and turned to ask Yorg, "I've been wanting to ask you about peoples' names here. Do you mind?"

"Of course not. Let's sit again and you can ask away."

"Our... helper?... guide?... the one who calls himself Edwallan-Sipcort, gets very offended when I call him just Edwallan or just Sipcort. And that man who got confused with us at the palace had three names and seemed very proud of them. What is it all about?"

Yorg smiled and steepled his fingers as if preparing to give a lecture. "What you must understand about this place, the whole planet probably, is that it is all incredibly formal. People here are known by their alliance names. Alliance names are the names of important families they or their ancestors married into. Families are only important if they are wealthy. They are especially important if they are both wealthy and in control of many other people. To leave out one family name, as you did, is considered an insult, as if the family left out was unimportant."

Javin puzzled over this a moment. "But surely there are plenty of people with the same alliance names? How do you tell one from another?"

"Ah," said Yorg. "That is through the hearth name, as it is called. The hearth name is the name given to the child. Mine is Yorg. Yours, presumably, is Javin. If there are others with the same hearth name then the province or district of birth is added. And nobody at all ever uses another's quiet name without personal, formal permission. Assuming, of course, that you know what it is."

"Quiet name?" asked Meldren.

"The name the person calls themselves. It is known as the quiet name because nobody else usually hears it. It is often, so I'm told, the name of someone they look up to or it has a special meaning to that person. It would be used, for example, between lovers, sometimes with close family members. But never address someone by the quiet name in public. If it were used in such a way, it would be to humiliate the person completely: a total and irreversible breach of trust, something almost like declaring war on the person."

Meldren pondered. "That's certainly more complicated than I thought it would be."

Yorg nodded. "Remember. This is the central planet of a very large Empire. Everyone here -- everyone except for me, that is -- wants to have as much power and influence as they can. The use of names is just one way of showing that struggle for power."

"Why don't you want to have power?"

Yorg waved a finger at Javin. "Good question. And my answer is that if I had a lot of power, I would be required to do a lot of things I wouldn't want to do. Here, as I am, I have only a couple of staff and nobody bothers me. I can go where I want, eat what I want, when I want and still have people opening doors for me and generally making my life comfortable. Why would I want that to stop simply because of some sort of power? No, the thought is ridiculous."

"I can see that would make some sort of sense," agreed Javin.

"Well," said Meldren, getting back to the point of the conversation, "I'll still be calling him Edwallan every now and then, because he won't stop calling us Notabilities. But at least now I'll know why he gets upset about it. Thank you, Yorg. You have been of great help today. And, please, don't feel sorry for having told us something we didn't know. We needed to hear it."

"Thank you," he bowed. "You are very kind."

That night, as they sat on the floor in their hotel apartment and Javin was experimenting with changing the colors and textures of the floor-covering, they talked it over.

"We can sort out where we live later, but I want to see more of the countryside," said Meldren firmly. "I've no idea where, but I suppose we keep traveling until we find it."

"I agree," said Javin, choosing a soft green with long threads, something like grass. "I would like to do that too. But there's something else we need to talk about first."

Meldren raised a quizzical eyebrow and gestured around the room as if to ask if what he was going to say would be something they didn't want to be heard. Javin dismissed the concern with a shake of his head. "It was something that really only became clear to me today. And that is that we haven't been using our talents much at all since we've been here. Except for today. That was something we should have been doing before now."

"Well, we did get a feel for the future which wasn't that helpful," said Meldren. "What else are you suggesting?"

"It was what Pol said, before we left. You remember? About listening to the Sun?"

"But we did. On the journey here we listened to it as it got fainter." She sighed happily in reminiscence. "It was wonderful, wasn't it. Even if the journey itself was so dull."

"Yes," agreed Javin. "But what if we were only half right about it? What if Pol meant for us to listen to the Sun here as well?"

"Maybe," said Meldren cautiously. "But I'm fairly sure that half of the time Pol herself doesn't know what's coming out of her mouth. I only know that it sounded or felt right. And why would we want to be listening to this Sun anyway?"

"I'm not sure, to be honest. We haven't even tried to hear the planet yet but, to me, for some reason I can't describe, it feels more important to hear the Sun."

"But if we started off by listening to the planet first, wouldn't we get a better idea of the Sun's song because it would be the background?"

Javin tried to find a way to give voice to what he felt instinctively. Then he remembered. "Do you recall when we sat down and tried to feel what was going to happen? We wanted to find out what was ahead of us?" Meldren nodded. "And what was it we both agreed on? Do you remember?"

"It was something very bright," she said. "Bright but not scary. Is that what you mean? So you're saying that what we saw as bright was really about us and the Sun?"

"Exactly! At least, I think so. I think we have to listen to it for something; some reason I don't yet know or understand. There has to be a reason for what we saw and what Pol said. They have to be related somehow, and the only thing I can think of which makes sense is listening to the Sun."

Meldren looked thoughtful.

"So," prodded Javin, "how does what I've just said sound or look to you?"

Meldren half-closed her eyes a moment. ""Yes," she said, when she opened them. "It feels right. I think we should be listening to this Sun as well."

Javin cocked his head. "Now's as good a time as any, isn't it?"

"Why not," said Meldren. "Just let me get comfortable first." She placed some cushions behind her back and rested against a piece of furniture which looked vaguely like a sofa. Javin also made himself comfortable in a similar fashion against the other sofa-like object, after making adjustments to make sure it wouldn't move off and find a different place. He also dimmed the ceiling.

"Let's do it like before," he said. "Start off gradually and see if we can block everything else out. But be safe. No dipping into the song. Just listen to it."

He took a few deep, calming breaths and closed his eyes as he let his attention move to what was outside of his body. He knew the room from the strange new sounds around him. He was intrigued by them and let himself wander mentally around hearing these new small songs. Then he shifted his attention away to sense the building, letting the stronger songs which formed it swell up around him. From there, he expanded to a wider perspective. From the cacophony, he guessed he was hearing the city. From there he reached upwards with his mind, letting the expanse of air songs surround him. Far beneath, the city still throbbed, but he blanked it out as he went up and up.

Finally, he felt the songs of the planet dwindle away and he knew he was at the limit of the atmosphere and he tried to relax even more so that the whole planet was only a backdrop to him. Cautiously, little by little, he allowed his attention to move outward into space, ready to hear the Sun.

And then, it was on and in him. A vast swelling array of sound and song so deep, so complex that it was breathtaking, soul wrenching. Once he felt it, he felt incapable of doing anything else except bear witness to it. He hung in space, cradled within the vastness, fulfilled simply by being there.

As he drifted on the edges of the song, never dipping into it too deeply, an awareness of a presence began to build within him. The song of the Sun was simply that, the vast outpouring of an immense being. It was not the being itself, just as a person singing a song is not the song. But, here, almost as if tiptoeing into his sense, if such a word could be used of something as huge as the Sun, Javin felt a tendril, a mere wisp of something finding its way toward him. The movement was so gentle yet it contained so much power that it was as if a giant wanted to touch an insect without crushing it. One slip of attention and Javin would have vanished, taken up within the immense song.

But, instead, the tiniest sliver of awareness touched him and a question was formed. As it happened, so a bubble of silence formed around him, holding him secure and apart from the maelstrom of noise beyond it. He was not strong enough, he realized, to make any sound which could have been heard over it. Here, in this bubble, he could be attended to, listened to, heard.

In response to the question, Javin, released from the overwhelm of sound and song, tried to formulate an answer. There was nothing he could think of which would make who he was known in any meaningful way.

Again, the sliding touch of a question.

Javin's mind slid to the song of Harmony's Sun. He tried to bring Harmony's song into the forefront of his mind. As he did so, he couldn't help but think of the Sun they had listened to on their journey. And then Haven came into his awareness as well. The three, somehow, became entwined in his mind. He was incapable of holding such intricate and powerful songs directly, but he could make it clear about the relation between the three of them. There was a balance of which he only became aware when recalling the three songs. He had never heard it before nor had he conceived of such a thing, and yet there it was inside him.

With the dawning awareness, the touch upon him inside the peaceful bubble became stronger and seemed to be listening. The harmony of the three songs Javin had grasped was there to be heard by this Sun. After an indeterminate period of time, this Sun poured another song into the bubble where it swirled around and within Javin. Hearing it, he began to realize that this was not a song of the Sun, it was a song of existence, a song which told a story rather than maintaining a creation. Letting the repeating song fill him, Javin found the start of it. It was this Sun. It was this world. But the song spun out from there and it showed him a pathway, a strong thread leading away. Far away. Following the thread of the song which was being shown to him, it wound its way across other such threads but always it headed away. Finally, the thread arrived and it touched and joined another Sun. From there, other, finer threads sprouted out and they each terminated in a planet, for he could see them spinning beneath them, each with their own songs.

Following the thread again, but this time, in reverse, the journey was much quicker and he found himself back listening to this Sun's muted song again. Gradually, little bit little, the song withdrew and left him in the silent bubble a moment before that, too, dissolved as he drifted back down to the song of the planet. From there, he quickly followed the trail he had listened to at the beginning and, with his usual reluctance to leave the songs behind, he once more became aware of the tiny songs around him. Specifically, he listened to the familiar song of Meldren beside him. With a final deep breath he opened his eyes and watched her carefully for signs that she was also returning to this present moment. He saw her swallow, take a deep breath and then her eyes opened. She found him and broke into a wide smile, eyes bright and shaking her head as she did so.

"Amazing. Absolutely amazing. I didn't want to come back."

"Neither did I," admitted Javin. "I suppose that's one of the dangers of doing this, being so wrapped up in it all that you never come back."

They sat in companionable silence for a while, holding hands.

"What happened for you?" asked Meldren finally. "For me, it was just so big, but so gentle. I don't understand how something that big can be like that."

"Did He surround you with silence?" inquired Javin.

"Yes. Like a bubble. And then He came and he asked me who I was."

"That's exactly what happened to me!"

"So, what did you do?" asked Meldren.

"I didn't know what to do because I thought He wouldn't know anything about me anyway, but then I put the songs of Harmony and Haven and the Sun in my head for him to hear."

"I wish I'd thought of that," said Meldren. "I just tried to hold different things for him to see, like us on the island, and when I met you, and things like that. Memories."

"That's good though," said Javin. "It shows that you have the ability to hear songs."

"So what happened after you sang Him those songs?"

Javin began to describe what had happened. But, as he was telling it, he realized something. He had just told Meldren of the threads connecting everything when he said, "I've just realized what it was. The Sun at the other end of the thread was Harmony's Sun. There were Harmony and Haven and the other, smaller planets." He became excited. "Do you realize what this means? Everything is linked with songs. Everything! It's not that songs create everything, but that they also link everything together. All those threads I was shown were the links, the lines of songs between Suns. Because I had sung Him our Sun's song, as best as I could anyway, He had identified it, together with the planets, and so this Sun has shown us that He knows where we are from!"

Meldren had been listening, eyes growing wider. "That is amazing. And it makes sense of what we felt about going to something bright."

""It must mean that all the suns are connected, and that they all talk to one another," said Javin, still excited.

"Do you remember, very early on when we were just getting used to hearing Harmony?" said Meldren. "I'm sure I recall something we heard, or maybe it was just me that heard it, about singing to other suns. We had enough to worry about then, but now it makes sense."

"That's what Pol must have meant about listening to the Sun," said Javin.

Meldren shook her head as she smiled. "As I said, I'm not sure that girl knows half of what she says. I think maybe something else tells her what to say at times. Just like it happened to me, remember? The first time we met. That was... strange."

It was Javin's turn to laugh. "And this isn't?"

"And what about the you-know?" asked Meldren indicating the room and who was listening.

Javin was in too good a mood to be concerned by anyone outside of the room and what they might think. "I hope they are enjoying listening to this because, no matter what they do with it, it will make absolutely no sense at all."

After another silence, filled with smiles and holding hands, Meldren asked, "But what do we do with this? We can hear Him, but... so what? There has to be something else to it, surely? I mean, it was very pleasant and everything, but is that all we are going to be doing? Listening to

Him so that we forget what's bothering us here? I can't believe that's all it is."

Javin knew she was right. It had been bubbling up in his mind. It was fascinating, but beyond that? He didn't know. "All I can say is, that whenever we've had some sort of experience like this, there's always been a reason behind it. It's never been just an accident. Maybe we'll get to find out soon enough. Perhaps setting off to see something natural will make us see something or understand something we wouldn't normally do. Beyond that, I don't know."

Meldren snuggled up to him. "If you're right, and you probably are, then it's going to be a scary thing at first but then it will be fun." She buried her head in his chest as she hugged him. "At least, I hope that it will be fun."

27

Over the next few days, Javin and Meldren tried to find someone in charge who would listen to what they had come to say, about how Haven wanted to be treated and to negotiate any problems that caused. But, time after time, in office after office, they were directed elsewhere, explained themselves over and over again to different people who asked them the same questions and essentially got nowhere. They had thought it would have been fairly easy to do this before setting off to find somewhere 'less civilized', as Meldren had termed it.

After another dispiriting day, they found themselves back at Yorg's residence. Meldren had said that she wanted to be with someone who liked them and there was only the one person on the planet who that could be. She felt dejected and dirty from the city air, and she knew Javin was feeling the same despite the small smile he flashed at her as she announced their presence. They were ushered in to find the rotund man smiling and waving to them to come join him at a table full of food hovering nearby. The room looked entirely different from last time, mainly due to the walls having been rearranged differently, presumably to accommodate the now missing guests.

"I am so glad you are here! What a piece of fortune. This was meant to impress someone who was supposed to be worth impressing for some reason I have forgotten, but instead he and his entire staff decided not to be impressed and so here we are with food enough for ten people." He poured drinks for them. "Eat up! It will all go to waste otherwise. I can only do so much myself."

"This will be thrown away?" asked Meldren, horrified at the thought as she scanned the various dishes.

Yorg threw up his hands in resignation at the fact. "My dears, there is nothing to be done. There are laws and regulations about this sort of thing. I shall give my staff free pick of anything they can carry home, but other than that... ," he shrugged. "The caterers will return this evening and away it goes with them."

All three were soon happily eating, seated at a side table.

Meldren mopped at her mouth and swallowed a morsel of something curly and shiny and multi-colored she had never seen before, but which tasted wonderful. "Yorg, you always make me feel better. Thank you for this."

"Absolutely no need for thanks. This was going to be eaten by someone else. But I'd far rather it was you two who would benefit."

"Why is it that you like us so?" asked Javin. "We both like you because you have helped us so much and because you appear to enjoy yourself, which is not how most people seem to live. I'm not asking for praise, but I am interested. We are hardly efficient ambassadors after all. We don't even know the basics of the job, yet you have looked after us when we can do nothing in return."

Yorg released his plate with a contented sigh and watched as it floated back to the table. He dabbed at his lips, taking a sip of wine before answering. "I like you both because you are without pretension, without artifice."

"I'm not sure what that means," said Meldren.

Yorg beamed. "That's a perfect example of it. You say exactly what you are thinking and have no care for others. That is sooo unlike any other ambassador or civil servant here." He laid a gentle hand on Meldren's wrist. "Please take this as a compliment, my dear, for it is meant as such and nothing else, but the two of you should be role models for every one of us officials here. You show emotion, you speak plainly, you know exactly what you are after and you are rude to no-one," he bowed his head, "Edwallan-Sipcort aside, that is." He looked up again, the familiar wide, easy smile once more in place.

Meldren smiled back at him, finding it very easy to like him. "It's very sweet of you, Yorg," she said, "but the truth of it is we are awful at what we do. We've had another wasted day trying to find someone who will listen to us and allow us to set out what the people we represent want us to say." She sighed heavily, feeling tired and a little angry. "I just wish we could have our say and go home. I don't care about having to stay here. We could go back and find someone better than us to replace us."

"But I would miss you," said Yorg, looking sad before brightening again. "But tell me, if you will, what have you been up to today which has made you feel like this? Perhaps I might be able to help?"

Meldren looked at Javin with raised brows, not knowing where to start. "We've been trying to find the right person to arrange for us to speak to and who will pass on our message to whoever else needs to hear it. Today was the fourth different office we went to, and they said, like all the others, that we were at the wrong one and would need to see someone else." She sighed heavily at the memory of the wasted hours while everyone seemed to be too busy to speak to them.

"First," said Yorg, "there is no correct place to go." He raised his hand to block the questions. "When they are ready for you, they will call you. And the timing of that is entirely up to them. They may be dealing with a crisis on a planet or planets elsewhere, or they might be busy on other internal business, or they might simply not want to start anything at all until they feel they have time. At that point, they will contact you, and the process will begin. As you are new, they will probably speed it up a little, but I wouldn't expect anything for at least another ten, twenty, even thirty days. And that's just the beginning. Saying what you want to say is only one part of it. After hearing it, they will go away and discuss it and read reports and do who knows what else before they give you an answer. And that answer, I guarantee you, will not be an agreement to everything you wanted. Instead, you will have to read what they say and then the negotiations begin. How long those will last will depend on how far apart you both are from agreeing at the start." He paused, looking sadly at them. "This is not the news you wanted and, yet again, here I am giving it to you. Please forgive me."

Meldren, picking at her thumb and feeling like hitting something, said, "Not your fault, Yorg. Not your fault. But, can you suggest something or anything we can do to hurry things along, even a little bit?"

Yorg slowly shook his head. "Neither of you really have much which would be valued by the officials here. And, yes, my dear innocent Meldren, officials can be bribed, and often are. That is, if they want anything which you have. And, by your own admission, you have very little." He looked from face to face, seeing the sadness and resignation there. "The only thing which comes to mind is an old saying from where I come from. Roughly translated it is, 'If you have to dig a big hole, don't do it quietly', which means, if you're going to be doing something, make sure that someone knows you're doing it. In the case of hole digging, make some noise. In your case, I'm not quite sure how it would translate into actions for you, but in essence, make it obvious that you are here and mean business."

Javin nodded thoughtfully and Meldren looked around vaguely, trying to make it all make sense. She felt confused and the anger which had been swirling around inside her since leaving the last office and heading here was trying to find a way out. Determined not to let it out in front of Yorg, who had been so kind to them, she thought back to the time she and Javin had spent listening to and being understood by the Sun. The memory of it swept away the darkness and made room for a smile. The sight of it acted on Yorg as well.

"Ah! That's better. It's good to see you smiling."

"Yes," said Meldren, keeping the reason for the smile to herself. "We've decided, before we came to see you, that we were going to visit the country. Our going to see officials was in hope that we could get that out of the way first. But, from what you have just told us, I think we need to get away first."

Yorg nodded earnestly in agreement.

"Which means," said Javin, "that we probably won't be seeing you again for a while at least."

Meldren added, "The one good thing about all this wasted time is that we've learned a lot about how to get around. And Edwallan-Sipcort, " she grinned at giving his full name, "has been helpful in adding to that knowledge. Apparently, we have a vehicle which we can use to go quite far. But you know about such things, don't you?"

Yorg responded with an apologetic incline of his head.

"Whether it will go far enough, we'll have to see. But it will be fun exploring."

"I shall, of course, miss both of you, my ambassadorial role models. Everything will be much less fun without you. But I do insist that you come to me first when you return and tell me everything you found." He gestured flamboyantly at his girth. "You will remark that I am too sedentary to have the adventures awaiting you. But that does not mean I cannot enjoy them second hand." His smile when he finished was full and genuine.

"Of course we will come and tell you everything," said Javin. "But I'm not so sure we'll have that much to tell you which will be news. I think you know a great deal more about this planet than you say."

Yorg made a 'maybe' face, and his smile broadened. "And," he said, "what about speaking to people here? About you being ambassadors?"

"If it really is as you say it is, Yorg," said Meldren, "then I suspect that when they are ready for us, they will definitely find a way of letting us know, because they will know where we are all the time. Won't they?"

Another wide, easy smile. "My dears, you are becoming wiser and wiser every day."

28

It was some days after Carmen and Endel's adventure that Farran thought of a possible problem with what they had done to the equipment on the ship. They were lounging in a grove of trees in yet another stretch of countryside, empty but for the ship and its four passengers. It was a familiar routine. The four followers didn't know what else they could be looking for and had settled into a kind of sluggish boredom, rotating the watch and trying occasionally to listen in on one person or another to see if it could help them understand what the strangers from space were doing.

"I've just thought of something which we should have considered before this. It's been rubbing at the edges of my head ever since Endel came back, but I didn't really know what it was until just now. What if they find out that scratchy song has been stopped?" he said. "Shouldn't we try to make something like the original so that it seems to be working?"

"But I didn't remove it," said Endel. "All I did was stop it going up into the stars. It shouldn't need replacing."

"But what if they can find out if it goes to the stars or not?" persisted Farran. "That would tell them that something had been done to it. And who knows what would happen after that?"

"Wouldn't it depend on what the song was for?" asked Hanna. "It had to have been going to some place in the stars, surely? Which would mean that it had to be a type of message. But, if Endel stopped the song, stopped the message that is, does that have to be a bad thing? After all, there's no message coming back from the stars, only that strange burst of a tune, too short to be a song, which happens once every two or three days."

"Three days," said Carmeena in a very definite tone of voice. "I've heard it regularly. It comes late in the afternoon." She looked around at the others staring at her. "Well, there's nothing else to do, is there? I might as well listen to what's going on. It's plain boring following them around."

"I agree about the boring part," said Endel, " but I don't see how they can find out if it's not going to the stars, it's just a noise."

"But it's going somewhere," said Farran, refusing to give up.

"Wherever's happening to it, it's not doing what they want it to, and that's the most important thing of all," said Hanna. "They were doing something behind everyone's backs. And it's our planet after all. You've told Pol about it, haven't you?" Farran nodded. "And she will have told Myrella, who will be able to come to some sort of conclusion. We've done the best we can, haven't we? Well then, there's not much else to be done, is there?"

Farran did not feel content with that answer but could find no argument against it.

INSIDE THE SHIP, LESSTERENMAN WAS TAKING SOME TIME AWAY FROM THE others. The two latest guides were mathematicians and had been engaged in an argument about which particular member of their respective faculties was the least productive. It had been rolling on and on ever since their arrival two days previously, and both he and Parra-Hopshan took whatever opportunity presented itself to escape their presence. She was more likely to walk off by herself and sit staring out at the view, not saying or doing anything. He, on the other hand, had to find something to occupy himself with. He was not built for sitting and staring at nothing. Therefore, on the pretext of checking the equipment, he left them arguing, ignored Parr-Hopshan's glare and stomped up the ramp.

Once inside, he slumped into a seat in front of the controls and wished, again, that this would soon be over and that he could get back to being only a communications officer, but with a large fortune at his disposal. He looked forward to two days' time when the arguers would be leaving.

Looking around for something to do, he checked fuel levels and the pressures of various liquids. He checked the navigation system and wanted to tear it down to rebuild it, usually a calming activity. Instead, he turned away and checked the readouts coming in from the surveying equipment. Everything looked fine. He decided to look closer and see what was being uploaded, to make sure that there was no signal corruption. The data was compressed before being uploaded after various checks were run. Instead of looking at the summary, he decided to look at the uplink data stream itself and compare it with the actual data as well as the check back, which the beacon sent out to ensure the data had not been corrupted. Normally, he would do this once only every several days, making it a formality rather than a necessity. But today, he was going to dig deeper in order to keep from murdering one or both of the mathematicians.

With one last look outside to make sure he wasn't going to be disturbed, he settled down and called up the reports and began comparing them with the actual data. Losing himself in the numbers was pleasant. File after file appeared and, after evaluation and comparison, was dismissed. He was more interested in wasting time in the ship alone and figured that having all these files on the screen was a perfect excuse should Parra-Hopshan come and find him to try to drag him outside.

As he made his way through the backlog of files since his last, cursory examination, he found himself humming, the first time he had done that in a very long time. However, something caught his attention. He had to scroll back and forth several times to locate what exactly it was that his mind had registered before his eyes could lock on to it. No longer humming now, he zeroed in on the area and, after re-reading and checking again and again, he swore.

It could not possibly happen! There were so many safeguards and check and alarms which should have been triggered. But the evidence was right there on the screen. No matter how much he didn't want it to be true, the ready signal from the beacon at the edge of the system hadn't been answered in over five standard days.

He swore quietly and vehemently for several seconds. Then he left the screen on and pushed away from it hurriedly to bring Parra-Hopshan in to see it. She was sitting with a fixed smile on her face far enough away from the still-arguing academics as to not be obviously separate from them. He walked swiftly and bent down to whisper in her ear.

"There's been a problem with the beacon. You need to come and see this. Now," he hissed.

The smile vanished and a look of alarm replaced it. "What sort of problem?" She, too, spoke quietly to avoid being overheard.

"Come see," he said, backing away and beckoning her to follow. The academics ignored them.

She sat and looked at the screens and the data, and he pointed out the anomaly and her jaw dropped. "And this started five standards ago?"

"Far as I can tell."

She rubbed her forehead with one hand, looking distraught. "You know what this means, don't you?"

"Yes. I do unfortunately. Is there anything we can do about it?"

She stopped rubbing and looked off into the distance. "I don't think so," she said finally. "That's something we'd have to fix on the beacon. Even if we sent a signal now, it would be too late. Far too late." She took another look at the data and then suddenly slammed her fist down on the arm of the chair. "No! This cannot have happened!" Taking a deep breath, she said, "I know it's too late, but get that signal back on line right now. When they arrive, they will at least know that we are alive. It might make some difference. But I doubt it. And right after that, you and I are going to go over all the equipment, everything, tear it apart and check it for any faults, anything at all. If that can go wrong, who knows what else might have happened."

"I can't start right away, because we're meant to be leaving tomorrow morning. If we stay, we'll have those two idiots still here and we'll probably set off some sort of search party or be accused of something by someone who doesn't want us here. It will take at least a day to strip this down and then, I suppose, we could take one piece of equipment at a time and strip, test and rebuild." He huffed at the thought. "We can't let anyone know that something's gone wrong with anything here. There would be too many questions to answer. And we both can't be working on this at the same time. Again, too many questions."

"You're right," she said, looking drawn and tired suddenly. "We'll take it in turns and tell them that it is part of the regular overhaul schedule. We can even let them look. They're not going to notice anything, because all this is strange equipment, strange technology. Best guess? They'll get bored in a day and leave us be." She shook her head. "But we have to find out how it happened. Make that your priority. Can you get that done before we leave tomorrow?"

He shrugged. "Maybe. If I work late, I can probably find out what's caused it and, with any luck, re-establish that signal link again. No promises though. If there's something broken, it's going to stay broken. We've no spares. This is as advanced and reliable as it gets, otherwise it wouldn't be on this ship."

"I know. Let's hope we aren't the first ship to break down."

He felt genuinely sorry for her. But only for a moment. She would be the one to be found responsible for losing the claim. It was on her head. He felt angry enough about what that meant, but at least the two of them were alive and could call for a wrongful claim investigation. But that would be against the Emperor. They wouldn't, couldn't win. But they might get some compensation. Nowhere near enough for an alliance of any value for him. But something would be better than nothing. One thing was clear to him; he would never crew with her again. Nobody would. She was bad luck.

And he had been so close to being so wealthy!

OVER THE FOLLOWING DAYS, AS BOTH OF THEM WORKED TO CHECK AND RE-check the equipment, Parra-Hopshan found herself looking up at the sky every now and then, even though she knew it was much too soon to expect to see anything.

They found nothing else wrong with any of it. Lessterenman was able to re-establish the checking signal, their signature if you like, which told the beacon they were still alive. Not that it would do any good. If two such signatures were missing, the beacon waited for a programmed amount of time, three standard days, before it blasted its emergency help signal back to base where its co-ordinates would be known. After that, any and all data from that beacon would have been analyzed and, the assumption would then be made that no crew were left alive or able to communicate, all prior claims would be terminated and a fleet of mining ships bearing the Emperor's claim would be dispatched. Their task would be to strip the planet cleanly and efficiently of any and all minerals or other valued metals. Parra-Hopshan knew, from stories passed among the survey crews, that the fleet would take no account of who else might or might not be on the surface. They would radio ahead and expect anyone else to leave before they settled and stripped the carcass bare. And if they didn't or couldn't leave, well, that would be collateral damage.

She had taken a long walk to where the ship was a small slim shape in the distance. Now she was sitting on the grass trying to come to terms with how she felt. As the days had passed since Lessterenman's discovery, she had found her emotional response had not been exactly as she would have expected. Lessterenman had made his dislike for her very clear. That was only to be expected. She was in charge down here and things had gone badly wrong. She would take the blame and it would be hard to find anyone else who would want to be part of her crew in the future. A lone surveyor wasn't a viable idea, so she would probably have to go back to her home planet in disgrace. Her alliance would want it broken as well. She would be starting from the very beginning again, but this time she would be incredibly lucky to leave her planet.

The pain of that thought hurt deeply. It's sharpness surprised her. She had loved traveling, seeing new planets, whole new systems. It was always a wonderful thing. Like this system.

And then the thought of what would happen here caused a hitch in her breathing and she felt tears welling. Hearing the stories of other planets and what had happened to them was so different to actually sitting on a planet it was going to happen to. She turned her face to the breeze to let it dry her tears. She remained hugging her knees trying to remember every tiny part of the view before her. The thought came that she might be the only person in the universe who would recall this particular view. Everyone else would be dead. To remember it completely felt like a burden, a heavy responsibility.

"You can't go on like this," she said aloud to herself, an echo of when she had been a little girl. It had been a way of dealing with the loneliness of an only child of busy and preoccupied parents having to deal with issues larger than herself by herself. She only reverted to it now in times of high stress. She was aware of that as she spoke harshly to herself. "You are feeling sorry for yourself. Which is fine as long as it does not continue too long. And this is becoming too long. Eslennet, you must not do this to yourself!" So saying, she smacked her hand against her thigh hard enough to make the fingers sting. "Get up and walk," she ordered herself. "Walking will do you good. It will help you think. Get up and walk."

But she remained seated a while longer, staring at the landscape. Finally, reluctantly, she rose to her feet. She turned her back to the ship and decided instead to walk in a long, sweeping arc taking her past the distant trees and around a grouping of rocks which seemed to be bursting upwards before returning to the ship. And the time it would take would be her chance to let herself feel and think and plan. She brushed her hair back. It was now long enough to cover her face, an unthinkable length aboard ship in space, but another detail which seemed to bring her closer to this planet. Her length of hair was the length of her stay. The two were part of each other.

She set off, and began to give herself a thorough talking to.

29

"She's coming over here!" Carmeena hissed, beckoning at the others. "What are we going to do?" asked Hanna. "She's going to see us here. We can't hide and we can't just leap up in front of her either, can we?"

The four of them had set up their camp behind the boulders which they had originally thought would be more than far enough away, based on what they knew about the people they were watching. Nobody had ever wandered that far from the campsite and the ship. At the most they had watched as the woman, who seemed to want to put more distance between herself and the ship than any of the others, had gone about a kilometer. Yet she was clearly heading their way. There was no place else to go. The boulders were well over a kilometer away, but they were also the nearest place they could access easily without being seen. There was a space barely large enough to contain all of them in the middle of the jumble of rocks. There were gaps between the rocks large enough to walk through, except on the side facing the ship. The arrangement had made Carmeena think of a large, stone flower with the tall stones being the petals, and they were at the very center of it. The only other place which might have been considered was a large grove of trees, but that was more than double the distance of the boulders, too far for observation.

"Perhaps they spotted us?" asked Farran.

"She'd have come directly here then, wouldn't she?" reasoned Hanna. "So, it's not deliberate. That's for sure."

"Maybe it has to do with that scratchy song I stopped," said Endel. "Because it's back on again just like before." The others looked at him. "I heard it a few days ago. It started up again. What if they knew it was us that stopped it and are trying to find us?"

Hanna was dismissive. "As I said, if they were coming to get us they would have come together and come directly. She's on her own and she's wandering, not walking hard. Look at her!" She herself peered cautiously around a rock.

"Why didn't you tell us it was back on again?" asked Farran. "I didn't think to check, but you obviously did."

Endel shook his head. "I didn't tell you, because there has been no other opportunity like there was before. And now... ?" he gestured in the direction of the approaching woman.

"We have to do something," said Carmeena. "She's already seen me, so it's not like I can pretend we've never met. She'll suspect all sorts of things. We could sing ourselves back to the last place"

"How close is she?" asked Endel

"Not enough time for that, she'll be here too quickly. She'd hear us and probably hurry and get here before we've finished. And it looks like she's talking."

"She must be talking to the others by the ship. That means she <u>does</u> know we're here," said Carmeena.

"Not necessarily," said Hanna, ducking back. "She's waving her arms around and I can't see her holding anything to talk in to."

"Maybe it's strapped to her head or really small," argued Carmeena.

"For goodness' sake," said Endel, "For all we know she's talking to herself. And in a few minutes we'll find out anyway. There's no need to get so upset by it." Carmeena gave him a definite 'look'.

"Can we listen to her?" Hanna said. "I mean listen to her song? Maybe we can hear something which might help us? After all, she does have that strangeness about her."

"It's worth a try," rumbled Farran. "Quickly. Let's each work as fast as we can."

So saying, they all closed their eyes, tried to banish thoughts of what might happen and focused instead on the song of the woman approaching their camp.

"Sounds incredibly jangled and jumble," said Carmeena after a moment.

"Not happy is how I'd say it," said Endel.

"Definitely unhappy," agreed Farran.

"Why don't we ask her what the matter is?" said Hanna. When the others turned to stare, she added, "Look, she's nearly here, so something's got to happen. Yes, I agree. She's not in a good mood. Unhappy and something else is going on. That's probably why she's talking to herself. So why don't we take the initiative and be the first to speak rather than wait here and be found out and then act all embarrassed?" When there was no response she said, "Well, can you think of anything better? After all, we're far enough away from the ship that we can still be behind these rocks and talk with her without being seen. And by the time she gets back, we can be far away from here, so nobody would ever believe her anyway. It's worth trying at least, isn't it?"

Farran nodded. "You're right. I can't think of anything else, so why not try it? Carmeena? You should be the one to speak first. As you said, she knows you. Just say hello or something and the rest of us will show ourselves after a moment or two." Seeing the look on Carmeena's face, he made shooing motions, "Ask her why she is taking a long walk or something. Go on."

Squaring her shoulders and with a nervous smile at her three friends, Carmeena stepped out of the encircling ring of boulders and stood squarely in the path of the approaching woman. "Hello there," she said. "Nice to see you again. But why are you feeling so upset?" Then she winced as she realized she'd said how the woman was feeling, not how she looked or what she was doing. She wished she could have remembered the woman's name. Something with two names. One of them sounded like hopping or something. Too late for that now.

The woman was completely taken by surprise, her jaw dropping and eyes widening. She came to a halt and then recognition dawned. "You!

What are you doing here?" It sounded more like an accusation to Carmeena.

"I've come to say hello," she said, offering a smile to the woman in the hope that it would help release some tension. But the reply suggested that it didn't work.

"Are you following us? Is that what you're doing?" The woman looked around. "But how can you do that? How do you travel? And why are you following us?"

Carmeena made calming gestures with her hands but stayed where she was, so as not to leave the shelter of the rocks. "There's nothing here to be afraid of, please. I can see you're upset... "

"I have a perfect right to be when you jump out on me."

"But that's not the upset I was referring to. I mean, you were upset before you saw me, weren't you?"

The woman glowered at her and then advanced toward where Carmeena stood. Carmeena took a step back. Pointing a finger accusingly, the woman said, "You have no right to follow us. And you certainly have no right to listen in on me." Glancing behind her, she added, "And just how did you overhear me? I was too far away for you to know what I was saying." Narrowing her eyes, she said, "Are you playing tricks on me in some fashion? Are you even real? Is this some sort of vid projection? Is there someone else doing this?" She moved as if to lunge at Carmeena, but as she did so, the other three stepped out.

"What is going on here? Who are you all?" She looked as if she were about to turn and run away, but Hanna moved swiftly to reach out for her arm, hoping that nobody from the ship was looking in her direction.

"We're not here to hurt anyone. Especially you! You're important. We simply want to talk and see if we can help in any way. That's all." She let her hand drop but didn't move back.

The woman was obviously conflicted as to what to do. She looked from one to the other. They waited silently for her to come to a decision. At some point, something must have caused her to either trust them or to at least listen to them, for they saw her shoulders sag as she relaxed a little and took a step or two towards them. "You want to help me and you say I am important but why should I trust you? You appear out of nowhere and have obviously been following me, following us, that is. What is it you want?"

In answer, Farran indicated the space in the middle of the rocks and said, "Why can't we just sit down a moment, and I promise we'll answer your questions as well as we can?" And he indicated that the other three should go through while he waited with the woman. She watched them carefully as they sat down and then turned to stare at Farran, who responded with a gentle inclination of his head and small movement of his hand as if inviting her to join them.

Slowly and with some reluctance, she stepped into the center and checked that there were other ways of leaving. Reassured, she leaned back against the nearest tall rock, looking down on the others, now that Farran had also sat. "You owe me an explanation, as well as an apology for scaring me. Who wants to start?"

Endel spoke first. "We wanted to follow you to see what you were doing. We didn't know if you had any other reason for traveling around, and you came from another place far away, so it seemed to us to make sense to see if you were to be trusted. That's it, really."

"But how do you follow us? We have equipment which would show if there was another ship nearby. How do you travel?"

Farran sighed. "That's one question where, even if we told you, I really doubt you could believe us. We don't have a ship. That's a fact. We travel... differently. And before you ask, yes, we could show you but unless you actually traveled with us I very much doubt you'd believe what you saw. I'm sorry it sounds like we are hiding something from you, and in a way we are, but not for the reasons you might think. It's just too hard to explain, that's all."

"Try me," she said, her voice harsh and impatient.

"All right," said Hanna. "We travel because we can hear the songs of everything and, by listening to the song of your ship, we can follow it wherever it goes and then we listen for the sounds of somewhere we can arrive without being seen. Groves of trees are favorite obviously, lots of bushes or places like this. That's how we travel." She looked up at the woman with innocent eyes.

"Songs? You expect me to believe that? Really?"

"Actually, yes we do," said Carmeena who was feeling sorry for the woman. She had no doubt she would not have acted as well if she had been faced with something similar. She tried to find a way of making her feel less threatened. "When you and I met, I knew there was something special about you. It's like you can almost hear them yourself. You are drawn to this planet, the scenery, the land. It tugs at you in such a way that you have never felt before. It brings you peace, doesn't it? And," She held up her thumb and finger close together. "And that is this close to hearing the songs Hanna here spoke of. Everyone can look at the scenery, but not everyone loses themselves in it."

"Don't be silly. I don't lose myself in it."

"Yes, you do," Carmeena said gently. "I've heard you. You were there, and then you weren't. Only someone who is close to the planet can do that. You are so close to it that it embraces you. All that's missing is you hearing the songs."

"There you go about songs again. It makes no sense! And what do you mean about me not being there? Are you sure you are all not mentally unbalanced or something? You act like stalkers. For all I know you could be assassins sent by the government to kill us."

"If we were," said Endel with a hint of exasperation, "don't you think you'd be dead by now?" He looked to Farran for help.

"What if we could prove what we said?" he rumbled. "Prove about the songs? Would that help?"

There was a cautious nod.

"In that case, please sit down. I'm too old to chase you, and if anyone else did, you'd be seen by those at the ship pretty quickly, especially if you called out." He sighed once more. "You're safe here. But the only way you'll know that is to trust us. Please?"

Slowly, the woman slid down the stone until she was seated but clasped her knees to her chest protectively. She gave a tight nod and said, "Go ahead and prove it then."

Carmeena leaned toward her, encouraging her to relax. She said, "This might sound very strange to you, but everything, and I do mean everything, is made up of songs. And before you say how wrong we are, give us a moment. What that means is that if you can hear the songs, know what they sound like, you can, with some help," and here she touched the sprite at her neck, "create the things you hear." She looked around at the others. "What shall we sing for her?" She caught herself. "Oh, I am sorry, I have forgotten your name again. Mine is Carmeena and yours is... ?"

"Parra-Hopshan. That's what you may call me. Parra-Hopshan."

Carmeena inclined her head in acknowledgement and repeated her question. "What shall we sing for Parra-Hopshan?"

Hanna immediately replied, "Warm bread! I'd love to eat something warm."

"Would that be acceptable as proof, Parra-Hopshan, if we could sing some warm bread here on this stone in front of us?" Farran asked.

Again a cautious nod.

"You can see we don't have any such thing here, and if it was warm, you would doubtless smell it. Do you agree?" he continued.

Another nod.

"Very well then," he addressed the others, "who wants to sing, say, two large loaves for us?"

"I'll do that," volunteered Carmeena. "I owe Parra-Hopshan here both an apology and a demonstration." She then sunk down on herself, relaxing her spine and closing her eyes. She began to sing a strange, multi-tonal song, rising and falling and following no known cadence. As she did so, the sprite at her neck began to extend outward a little and added its own strange voice. The sounds it made were definitely not human, but added to and interwove between the notes being sung.

Parra-Hopshan was watching very carefully and then, with a gasp, pointed at the stone where two steaming loaves had appeared. As the sprite resumed its position, Hanna reached forward and tore a piece from one of the loaves, juggling it in her hands, blowing on it before stuffing it in her mouth making sounds of evident enjoyment. Farran wrapped his hand in a fold of his robe, grasped the other loaf and held it out to Parra-Hopshan. She placed a finger on it and prodded gently before leaning in and smelling it.

"Go ahead and eat, if you want," said Farran, indicating Hanna. "It's obviously not poisoned." Endel was flapping at the other loaf to cool it a little.

"But it just appeared! Out of nowhere. How?" Parra-Hopshan

demanded of Carmeena. But she did cautiously tear a small piece of the crust off and hold it in her hand.

"Songs. I sang the song of bread and my sprite helped me. Without the sprite I doubt that I could make anything happen. Everything is made of songs. Endel here, and Hanna and Farran and myself and you. We are all made of songs. That's what I meant when I said that I heard you. I heard your song."

"But you just said that you heard me and then you didn't. Make up your mind."

"I heard your song, that's true," said Carmeena, trying to explain it as simply as possible. "I was listening to it so that I would know when you had left so that I could go to the river and wash without being seen. You remember where it was you first thought you saw me? You did see me then. Well, we were all hiding and I was listening to your song. But then the song faded away and I, not thinking, assumed you had gone back to the ship. Except, when I walked out from where I was sheltering, there you were. But your song had faded away. Tell me, if you can remember, what were you doing there? I think you told me that the scenery filled you up when you looked at it. But what was really going through your mind then? I think it was very important. Can you recall?"

Parra-Hopshan was silent for a while as she thought. Finally, in a quiet voice, she said, "I had been looking out at the scenery. That's what I remember. I felt it was very peaceful. Very quiet. It made me feel good. It was like I stopped thinking about anything much. It doesn't often happen to me, so I can remember when it happened." She looked down at the bread in her hand. "That's what I remember."

Farran nodded. "That makes so much sense." He held his hands apart, slowly drawing them together. "You and the scenery sort of mingled together. Except, it wasn't the scenery as such, but the planet. The planet here, Haven, is singing the songs of everything and I think it heard how your song was fitting into the land. I think," he said carefully, "that Haven knows you and how much you like Her."

Parra-Hopshan didn't speak for a while, but put the piece of bread in her mouth and chewed it. "I don't know how to believe you and what you say, but I've just eaten something which shouldn't be here. And you," she said, pointing at Carmeena, "talked about me being upset. And what you've just told me, even if it's entirely stupid, makes me feel even more upset." She then told them of the stopped signal and the resulting mining fleet and what would happen. By the time she had finished, her four listeners looked grey and drawn, and Endel was trying to hold back his tears.

By the time he had finished explaining what he had done, Parra-Hopshan looked shocked. "You shut off the signal? And you got in and out without being seen?"

"That's why I was there," said Carmeena. "To distract you. Plus, I wanted to see if there was anything about you which could have explained why I stopped hearing you that first time."

Parra-Hopshan shook her head. "I hear what you're saying, but it makes no sense. But the real issue here is the mining fleet. I've told you we can't stop it. Any signal we send will be ignored on the assumption that we are either killed or captured and being told or forced what to do. As far as I know, nothing will get it to stop once it's set out."

Endel, having recovered some of his composure, said, "Well, the very least we can do is inform the government here. That's the right thing to do. They should at least know what is going to happen. Perhaps they can think of something. I can't believe I've put the whole planet in danger. Most of the people here will die? Is that what you're saying?" He put his hand to his mouth and choked back a sob as he heard his own words and what they meant. Hanna had moved to be beside him and had draped her arm around his shoulder, pulling him into her to give him some comfort and reassurance. She looked as if she were close to tears herself.

"Look, I'm not happy about any of this. I only know what has happened in the past and what is likely to happen here, given the data about the amount of gold for extraction. They will come in, assuming that this planet and everyone on it is hostile, and they will land and fight off any approaches and begin strip mining and blasting and all the other destructive activities. With luck and a lot of persistence, they might be persuaded that it was a mistake, but they will already have done a lot of damage. I'm sorry." She looked at the glum faces. "If you like I'm willing to cancel what was planned and go back myself with the news."

Farran waved aside the offer. "No need. I'll go right now and speak to the President." He saw her look of bemusement. "Songs, remember? Songs."

30

P ol and Isselta were already in Myrella's office when Farran
appeared. Myrella was, by now, more used to witnessing the
strange comings and goings of the two girls, so was quite composed as
Farran arrived. He looked around him as he got his bearings. This was
the first time he had been here since meeting with Javin and Meldren. He
took in Myrella's presence and gave her a slow nod of acknowledgment.

"Well, well," said Pol. "Perfect timing, Farran. We just arrived
ourselves. Myrella called for us." She turned to the President. "Is there a
problem?"

Myrella got the three of them seated before she answered. "Actually,
I'm not sure." She paused a moment. Finally, "You know how the off-
worlders are escorted everywhere by people from the various
universities and other learning institutes? What you might not know is
that we've been asking them to watch the two off-worlders for us and
notify us of anything they felt or saw or heard which we needed to know
about. Most of the time, there's been little to report: the same routines,
the same topics, their questions about whichever place they arrive at.
Nothing really amiss." She looked down and shuffled some papers
aimlessly on her desk.

"Except... ," prodded Isselta.

"Yes. Except for recently. The woman who is nominally in charge, she's called -- let me find it, I know it's here somewhere…,"

"Parra-Hopshan," said Farran.

"Indeed. Parra-Hopshan." She gave Farran a quizzical look before continuing. Apparently she has been acting a little differently of late. More moody, less talkative, and there seems to be some sort of tension between her and the other crew member. Lessterman. No. Lessterenman. None of the professors can work out why, but that hasn't stopped them from offering a myriad of reasons. But the overall concern is that these professors are thinking that she might be involved in something, plotting or planning something, which will have a direct bearing on our entry into the Empire. And that's why I asked the two of you," she said, directly addressing Pol and Isselta, "to come in order to see if there was anything you could add to this, bearing in mind your special skills."

"No need," said Farran speaking to Myrella. "Normally, I come to speak with these two here, but this time I needed to speak with you. So it's rather lucky that this is where I ended up. What I have to tell you will explain everything you've just said." Myrella noted how somber he looked and it gave her a bad feeling. "There's a large mining fleet on its way here. It thinks that we are hostile and have captured, killed or are holding the crew members as prisoners. As a result of this, it will arrive and set about stripping as much as it can from the planet, with especial regard for gold. And, having had Parra-Hopshan explain very precisely what that means, I can tell you that the population will be attacked, the land destroyed and there will be little regard for us at all. The size of the machines which are coming will allow them to do untold amounts of damage very speedily."

"What? How do you know all this and why are they coming anyway? What about our entry into the Empire? Our ambassadors! What can they do?" Myrella was staggered by Farran's words and the questions bubbled up and out. Pol and Isselta shared shocked looks.

"I know because I've recently spoken with her and I have to say that our meddling with their equipment was the reason for an alarm signal to be sent initiating the fleet's launch." He then explained what Endel had done and how they had eventually had a conversation with Parra-Hopshan.

Myrella felt sick to her stomach. "I do not doubt you for one moment, Farran. I can understand why Endel thought it had to be done, but it really would have been better to have discussed it first, wouldn't it?" She clenched her fists as she tried to control herself. What good would it do to punish Endel? The act had been done. What was needed now was to focus on the effects of the act. Endel would have to wait. "But that's in the past. Too late for that now. Let's focus on the present. Everyone needs to hear this, and they need to hear it from the two crew members themselves. Everyone needs to know what is going to happen and then... then we need to find a way to stop or at least minimize the damage. First though, we need that ship back here and we need to have her say what she told you." She felt on the verge of tears. Her thoughts turned to Corrivan and what he would say when confronted with this news. His beloved technology-driven Empire turning against him. She shook herself free of that. This was no time for personal vendettas. If he had some useful ideas, he would be welcomed, as would anyone who could help at this time.

She turned to Pol and Isselta, who had both remained silent, in shock at the news. "Is there anything either of you can do to help in this situation? Anything at all? Is there some power you have which you have kept secret until now? If so, this is the time to use it. Is there anything at all?"

Isselta shook her head. "No. I can't think of anything we can do which would help in this situation. But that doesn't mean we will do nothing. We will try everything we can think of and more, I promise."

"I don't think this is going to happen." Pol sounded very sure of herself to Myrella's ears. "I don't think it will because Javin and Meldren are the ones to make this stop or to change it in some fashion."

"But they've gone! They're not here. They're who knows how far away? How can they possibly help us?" demanded Myrella, knowing she was sounding petulant.

"Because they were chosen to go." The girl's assurance seemed both strangely out of place and comforting at the same time. She was standing with a faraway look on her face as if seeing something hidden from anyone else. "And they were chosen by the planet, not by any of us. It was taken out of our hands." She shook herself free of whatever vision she had seen and looked around at the other three. "Think about it. Whenever there has been something which threatened the planet, it was eventually down to them to fix it. They had help, of course, but the point is they fixed it. Wherever they are, they are in the perfect position to do whatever they have to do. They're back at the center of this Empire. Where else would be the right place to resolve this? It has to be there, surely, doesn't it? I am certain that they know about this, or they will know about it, and they will know what to do, or they will find the right help they need. Why else would this planet allow them to go if there was any danger to it?" Her eyes unfocused a moment again before she shook her head as if to discount any other possibility. Or was it to shake herself free of whatever had held her as she spoke, Myrella wondered? "It just doesn't make any sense any other way. Javin and Meldren will do something. I know it and I feel it."

Myrella looked long and hard at Pol: a slim young woman with calm grey eyes looking out from under long, dirty blonde hair caught at her shoulder with a braided piece of leather. Farran's story had twisted her inside, wrenched her and made her want to cry. Yet here was another voice telling her that this nightmare would not be allowed to happen, because a planet, her planet, would not permit it. If she had not known these people and what they could do, she would have dismissed it out of hand and had them thrown out for being maniacs. But she had witnessed them as she had witnessed the tree, and that gave her pause for thought. Maybe Pol was right, yet nobody else would trust the words of one so young and so unknown and secretive. Neither the people nor the politicians knew her. She was not dressed like them and did not act like them. She looked an outsider and nobody trusted outsiders. Especially ones with a message of hope based on how a planet might or might not be feeling.

In the end, however, it didn't really matter whether she trusted Pol's words or not. She was President and, as such, she had to make sure that plans for every eventuality were laid as carefully as possible. She could not sit back and wait for help. She had work to do.

"When will this fleet arrive?" asked Myrella.

Farran shrugged. "Apparently, it's not that easy to know. There was some talk using science which none of us understood but which translates as probably long enough for us to have enough time to get used to being very afraid."

"Lots of fear. That's what I was afraid of," said Myrella.

"Shall I get the space people here?"

Myrella suddenly felt an immense tiredness settle upon her. "No. There's no need to. She was honest with you. It's real and I don't need anyone else to tell me that. Keep them on their schedule. Anything else would be raising an alarm." She didn't even notice when Farran disappeared.

31

"Well that was different," said Meldren, unpacking her satchel. "And this also is different," she added, looking around her at their new home. Prior to leaving to try to find some uncultivated and underpopulated countryside, they had asked Edwallan-Sipcort to find them a place away from the busy center but avoiding having tall buildings around them, also with some private gardens, but not too big. He had done very well, and both Javin and Meldren were standing in the main room, looking out at a very carefully crafted landscape with several large trees and even a small waterfall.

"Thank you, Edwallan-Sipcort," said Javin. "This is very well chosen. We appreciate it."

Edwallan-Sipcort bowed and simpered. "I trust you both had a wonderfully refreshing time in... wherever it was you went to. I am glad to welcome you back to your new consulate."

"Now that you mention it," said Meldren slumping down onto a large and comfortable sofa which shifted its shape to accommodate her, " the countryside was... well, as I said, it was different. Not what we were used to by any stretch of the imagination."

"Even the so-called natural parks didn't feel natural in any way. I doubt there's anything natural left of this planet. Everything has been changed so much."

"Change is always good," beamed their liaison, and Meldren knew then he either wasn't listening or was incapable of hearing. She couldn't decide which and couldn't be bothered to find out.

"Speaking of which," said Javin, "what change is there on the progress of reaching someone who will listen to our proposals?"

"Things are moving along. Oh, most certainly they are."

"And that means what?" asked Meldren.

"That progress is being made."

"But the progress is not yet complete, obviously, otherwise we would have appointments, wouldn't we?" she said.

"That is the case, Your Notability."

"If you promise not to call either of us that again, I promise always to use your full name," said Meldren with a sweet smile.

That appeared to cause confusion. "But... there are formalities, niceties... there are certain ways of doing things, of giving due honor and the like..." He tailed off.

"None of which are of any interest to either of us," she said. He said nothing in return but stood there awkwardly. She could almost see inside him, watch him wanting to wring his hands in consternation "Good. That's decided then," she continued. "So tomorrow we would like to go and see whoever is the latest person who doesn't want to see us, so that we can discover just how much they don't want to see us, and we can then find out who is the next disinterested person to go visit. You can do that for us, please, Edwallan-Sipcort?" The name was said slowly and with emphasis.

With a melodramatic sigh; all lifted shoulders and downcast face, he nodded. "Certainly." He appeared to bite his lip for a moment. "That can be arranged. I shall escort you in the morning." Looking from one to the other, he said, "If there is nothing else I may do?"

"Only to arrange for us to meet with Yorg Bennon afterwards," said Meldren. "We did promise to visit him when we got back."

"Of course. And anything else I can do for Your... for you both?"

"Nothing else, thank you," said Javin, trying hard not to smile at the man's discomfort.

When they were alone, Javin asked, "Do you think the entire planet is like this? There's nothing wild left?" He gestured out of the window to their private garden. It had rocks and plants of various colors and sizes, as well as the waterfall and trees and none of it felt real. The view, he was certain, wasn't real, because it showed a distant parkland with a large body of water, and he knew for a fact that fairly close behind was another large building, not a park. "Look at what they can do. There's probably nothing original left on the surface. I assume there are still rocks and things like that underground."

"I know," said Meldren, feeling glum. She had hoped to have seen at least some place which had real rocks or a proper lake or even a forest with some wildness in the heart of it. Some wildlife would have been nice. Something roaming free and unconfined and uncontrolled. But, in every place they had stopped, it was the same thing: a land which had long since been tamed and where everything was constructed and manipulated to a frightening degree. Even the sky was a uniform color with no clouds as such, just that same sheen as if sunlight had to be filtered so that it was the same anywhere at anytime. Rain only happened according to a schedule, and then only gently enough to keep the ground moist without washing away any earth. There were no storms, no lightning, nothing which would indicate that it was out of control. They had tried listening to the songs around them, but they all felt strangely muted and distant somehow, as if buried beneath the surface, suppressed and repressed.

The only lighter parts of it were when they sat and listened to the Sun. Each time they did it, they ended feeling refreshed and happier. All they did was listen to as much of the song as they could without damaging themselves. The Sun seemed to recognize them each time, enclosing them in its bubble and feeding them songs of other places, other Suns. The impression they both had from these contacts was that the Sun was happy that somebody was able to hear it truly. Perhaps, Javin had suggested, it had become dispirited with the way one of his planets had been so completely artificially landscaped that its soul or song had been buried and could barely be heard, and that anyone who could hear the true songs was to be welcomed.

Other than that, it had been a dispiriting journey in many ways.

Hiking had been out of the question, and they were not about to try singing their way across the land, so they had been allocated a vehicle, and they simply chose where to go by looking at a map. The map, incidentally, was the first Meldren had seen. She had known of the word from Javin, but had not been able to see the use for them. Now, in this context, she could see that such things might have their place in something as built up and large as this planet. But beyond that, she hadn't changed her overall opinion. As she had said, "If you know the places, you can sing yourself to them. Distance doesn't matter."

"But not everyone does know the places," Javin had replied. "Us, for instance."

"I still think they're not much use," she had said and had refused to look at it from then on, as if that made her point of view more valid. Not that Javin seemed to mind, she thought. He enjoyed picking out places. She had been happy simply to arrive at whatever point had caught his eye. Food arrived from somewhere each day. Javin thought it was because having an ambassador starve to death would have looked bad. Someone would have been blamed. Meldren thought it was that Edwallan-Sipcort (she let herself call him 'Wally' when they were traveling) had made sure they were being followed by some caterers. Whatever, food was delivered by some sort of flying robot every morning and evening without fail. And that, in itself, had added to the artificiality of it all.

It had been a break, however, for them both to get away from the formalities of the palace. Meldren hadn't been sure what she had hoped to have gained from it, but it had given them some new insights, if nothing else. And now they were back from their travels, and she was trying to feel at home. Not just in this building, but more generally. Despite having been here for much longer than she had wanted, planned or dreamed, she knew for certain that this was not somewhere she could live. And that was true, she knew, for Javin as well. That was one definite result of their journeying.

"It doesn't feel right," said Meldren, looking out at the garden as she curled her toes into the rug, which responded by lengthening its fibers and curling back loosely over her toes in return and sending some warmth through them. "This whole planet. It doesn't feel like it is natural. We should do something about it."

"Like what?" asked Javin.

"I don't know. What is missing from all of this?"

Javin thought a moment. "Mud? Mountains?"

She wrinkled her nose at the suggestions. "Something else. Something we take for granted."

"What? Like the wind, you mean? Storms which come and go when they want to?"

"Yes," she nodded. "Something like that. But easier to do." She suddenly snapped her fingers as she realized what she had been thinking about. "I've got it! It's insects. Flying and crawling things that make a noise in the background and are always busy. That's what's missing."

Javin was unsure. "Insects? Really?"

"Why not? Some pretty ones, for example. They would look nice out in the garden, wouldn't they? It's the one thing which would mean that this wasn't all so... so *clean*."

"Sure, I guess. Insects wouldn't have been my first choice, but I understand what you mean. But, Meldren, do we have the right to do that, make things appear if they don't already exist here now?" He shook his head. "I don't think that's right. We'd have to get permission from the planet Herself, wouldn't we?"

Meldren felt her enthusiasm draining away, knowing Javin was right. "It's a nice idea though, isn't it?" It would be fun to see something natural flashing around. I'd even put up with being bitten every now and then. It would at least prove that whatever bit me was wild, untamed." She got up and wandered into the garden feeling sorry for herself and wishing, yet again, that she and Javin were back home on Harmony. She reached toward a long, slender, startlingly blue, leaf-like plant which responded by splitting into two halves, each of which tried to fold itself gently around her hand, as if to say hello. She shook her head and stroked her sprite. That, at least, was natural even though it was strange, and she still wasn't sure what it could do. But it reminded her of Harmony.

The next morning, as promised, Edwallan-Sipcort arrived with a different vehicle from the type they had used for their travels, and took them to a building with similarly furnished offices and the same busy people scurrying past doing, presumably, the same sort of things. Finally, someone arrived and, after a brief conversation, with a swift perusal of the documents they carried, they were so sadly directed to another office at another time, after which they left with the clerk's best wishes ringing in their ears.

They headed off again. But this time Meldren thought she recognized the buildings from their first visit when they had ended up meeting Yorg at the meal with the Emperor. Instead of heading onwards to the palace as before, they turned down one wide avenue and drifted silently to a halt before an imposing entrance. As they got out of the car, Meldren was surprised to see a familiar face, that of the captain, Kellerman-Stobbant, walking toward them, obviously leaving.

"Hello, captain," said Meldren with a wave.

Kellerman-Stobbant came to a halt. The look she gave Meldren and Javin was murderous. Meldren didn't need to look at the colors around the captain, for she could feel the emotions pouring from her, aimed at them both.

"You!" the captain shouted accusingly. "I ought to kill you both, and I would be justified in doing it." Marching swiftly to Javin, being the nearest, she took him by the shoulders and shook him. "What happened to my crew? My ship? Have they been murdered? Was that the plan all along? As soon as we left, you would kill them to keep your gold?"

Javin, taken aback by the swiftness and force of her attack, tried to back away as he sought to loosen her grip, all the time saying, "I don't know what you're talking about! Let me go!" His sprite partially uncoiled and opened its mouth to hiss at the captain.

Meldren, amazed at what was taking place, leapt at the captain, adding her weight and anger to prying Javin free, her sprite acting the same as Javin's. "I swear, if you don't let go, I'm going to do something you're going to regret!" Something about Meldren's tone of voice, plus the fact she was outnumbered, gave Kellerman-Stobbant pause, and she slackened her grip. Javin brushed her hands from his shirt.

Meldren continued, "What are you talking about? We came with you. How could we know anything that is happening back there? What has happened to make you so angry?"

Kellerman-Stobbant was obviously fighting to keep herself from erupting in anger. In a tight voice, with shoulders hunched and head lowered as if to butt Meldren, she said, "The emergency beacon has been activated. And that can only happen if something has happened to the ship and, therefore, to the crew. For that beacon to be set off, there has to have been an attack. Those things do not go wrong by themselves." She pointed a finger at Meldren. "I hold you and your people responsible for the murder of my crew and I will see to it that you both are held accountable."

Meldren was genuinely confused. "I don't see how you can be so definite about it all. For all we know there was a problem on the ship or it had some bad weather -- ,"

The captain cut her short. "Those ships are designed for the worst that can happen. The worst! And still they function. This was no accident!" she shouted, her fists balled as if wanting to strike out.

"But how come you know so much about what's happened? Neither of us has had any contact with our planet since we arrived. We didn't even know it was possible, did we?" she said, aiming the last at Edwallan-Sipcort, who had moved back to the vehicle, holding the door open ready to make an escape. In response, he merely held his hands up as he shrugged, as if to say, 'I'm not responsible for any of this, and don't blame me for anything which might have happened'.

Kellerman-Stobbant continued as if she hadn't heard Meldren. "My crew are dead and my ship is destroyed and now, because it has been declared an emergency, my shares, my bonus for finding your stinking planet, has been revoked. My claim is no longer valid, as it now belongs to the Emperor. My crew relied on me! I've been in this building for days, fighting for them, for what is theirs. Fighting for their futures as well as mine. You haven't just killed two of my crew, you've crippled the future of the rest." She turned away and took a pace before facing them again. "The only good thing to come out of this is that your dear little planet will be stripped bare of everything it contains as punishment for what you have done. And you will never again see it the way you left it. It will be bare and full of the dead and dying. If you ever return to it, if someone takes pity on you and takes you back, it will be nothing more than a graveyard." And she spat at their feet before walking away for good.

Meldren watched her leave, feeling herself shaking from the adrenaline. Tears welled up with anger at the attack on them both, at what she had been told, and what her imagination conjured up for the future of Haven. She found herself holding Javin's hand so hard that he winced and put his other hand on hers. Looking down, she saw a trickle of blood where her thumbnail had penetrated the flesh. With a gasp of apology, she let go, grabbing his elbow instead.

Javin licked and rubbed at his wound and gave her a wry smile. "I'm as confused and as scared as you are." He stared around a moment as if lost. Finally, seeing Edwallan-Sipcort still holding on to the door, he nudged Meldren. "I think we should go and see Yorg. He might be able to tell us what is happening. The captain was angry, but she might have said things because she was angry, not because they were true. Yorg will know." To Edwallan-Sipcort he said, "Take us to Yorg Bennon."

Yorg, when they arrived, was as shocked as they were at the news. He activated the counter-surveillance equipment, called for strong drinks for them and insisted on being told precisely what Kellerman-Stobbant had said as he listened closely. Finally, he sat back, a serious look on his face.

"If what she said was true, and I have no reason to suppose she was lying, then your planet is, indeed, in for a very unpleasant visit."

"But how did she find out anything at all?" asked Meldren. "We have no way of communicating with Haven, but she seems to know everything that's going on back there. How can that be?"

Yorg made placating motions with his hands. "Please, hear me out first before you say anything. The fact that she has been in contact is only partly true. I would imagine that she has been receiving data from the crew she left behind via some sort of direct channel. The fact that you do not have such a channel of communication is due to the delay in your being processed and accepted as ambassadors. And, yes, I know I said that eating with the Emperor was enough proof. It was true as far as it went. That alone, sadly, does not give you the accepted and undeniable status of full ambassadors for your planet. Once that is established -- which is what is taking so long -- you will be given access to such direct communication. For example, I had to wait one whole season to be fully accredited before I was able to communicate with my planet. And that was after I had arrived and formally taken over the duties of my fully accredited predecessor."

He gave them both a kindly look, but it was one which was full of sorrowful understanding. "It seems I am always giving you news you do not want to hear. I know that this must be difficult for you both to comprehend. It must seem so very unfair. But this planet and virtually everyone on it is dedicated to organizing, controlling, and dealing with many, many differing aspects of a large number of planets and their populations. Different demands, different problems, different customs and so on and on. It is always busy, not always busy with doing the right things, but always working."

"But what did she mean about the shares we had deprived her of?" asked Meldren, still shaking a little from what had happened.

"Survey ships' crews get paid very little. They rely on finding precious minerals, and then they negotiate a share of what that market value might be if and when it reaches market. It's not an exact science and often crews find very little of value, or a bigger find elsewhere will knock down the value of their find. From what your captain said, it sounds like your planet has very valuable minerals in large quantities. That being the case, if an alarm and rescue beacon was indeed activated, then it would be considered a threat to the Empire and, as a result, the Emperor would assume all title to whatever might be found there, because it would be interpreted as a direct attack on him. If he felt in a generous mood, then he might offer minor shares to the crew or some other compensation. That doesn't sound like it happened. Alarms are not a regular occurrence, from what I hear. Rare, in fact. But if one goes off, then an action against whoever caused the alarm to go off is a reasonable reaction, as it assumes that subjects of the Empire have been attacked."

"But that's not fair!" said Meldren. "Nobody was going to attack the crew! There were lots of people who welcomed them. Sure, there were a few who didn't like the idea, but they weren't the sort of people to go around attacking and killing others. I know it. I just know it."

Yorg looked genuinely distressed. "I am sure you are right. But this is something which has been started, even if by accident, and which is impossible to halt. I have known of two such incidents, both by hearsay, and neither ended well for the planets in question. I do not know what I can say or do for you at this time, but please, if there is something, anything, I will be only too swift to accomplish it for you if it is within my power so to do."

Meldren looked at Javin with a heavy heart. Her head seemed full of fog, and she could not grasp any thought long enough to hold on to it. Everything was swirling around so much inside that she felt dizzy. There was nothing to say and nothing to do, and for the first time in her life she felt utterly and completely useless. No songs could deal with this. No sprite would be powerful enough to help. She felt empty of will and devoid of anything except sorrow and bitter, bitter tears.

32

That night in their new home, Javin and Meldren sat silently, as if in a daze. The reality of what they had been told, the implications to Haven and all the people on it, had barely sunk in. All that was spinning around in Javin's mind was that something immense and wrong was going to happen to Haven and they were unable to do anything about it. The inability to communicate gave him a deep sense of guilt. He felt that since they had arrived here they had let everyone on Haven down. They had achieved nothing, done nothing which might have -- somehow -- helped diminish or even precluded this catastrophe.

Neither he nor Meldren felt like eating and neither was capable of sleep. Instead, they alternated between sitting and shaking their heads at the enormity of what was unfolding, or walking around and around to try and relieve the nervousness coursing through them in a futile effort to attain some sort of calm in the midst of the emotional storm.

Time passed and Javin was feeling more and more exhausted from running the same thoughts over and over again in his mind.

"What if there is something we're missing in all of this? Something we haven't thought of?"

"We've said that before and same as before I ask, like what?" Meldren's voice was low and toneless.

"If I knew, I'd say," he replied, trying to keep irritation out of his voice. "But what if there is something?"

Meldren just shook her head.

He scrubbed hard at his face, willing himself to think. "Remember when we decided to listen to the Sun when we were coming here because of what Pol had said? And then we thought of listening to the Sun here, but much later. We hadn't connected the two ideas together. But when we did, we found out that this Sun knew our Sun and where we came from. Do you recall that?"

"Of course," came the tired reply.

"So what if we are missing something like that now? After all, we both agreed that there had to be a reason for being here, and that neither of us really felt that anything bad was going to happen, did we? Did we?" he prompted.

Another shake of her head.

He began to allow himself to follow where his words were taking him. "So... if we didn't feel anything bad was going to happen, do you think we would have been so useless as to have missed out this moment now? I know it looks bad. I know that. We've talked about it over and over, and it still looks bad. But, and it's a big but, we did not feel that this was coming up. And, Meldren, if we didn't feel it, it must mean that it is looking bad, but not that it is going to end up as being bad." Warming to his theme, he went on, "Come on, Meldren! How often have we been wrong when we have felt out the way ahead for us? Eh? How often?"

Meldren looked up at him with a face puffy from crying. "Never."

"Exactly! Never!" He was becoming excited now, although he could not see where this was leading; he knew it felt good. "There's something we can do, or something we haven't yet seen which will change things. That has to be the truth, doesn't it? We've been feeling sorry for ourselves and for what will happen to Haven but we haven't really spent any time on thinking of what to do about it."

"Because there isn't anything *to* do." Meldren sounded exasperated.

"I believe you're wrong. I believe we've both been wrong. I believe we're looking at it the wrong way. What is it we would ideally want to be able to do? What's the first thing we would need to do in order to go about stopping this thing from happening?"

"I don't know. Maybe find out what's happening on Haven. See for ourselves what the truth is? Or maybe we need to talk to the Emperor and persuade him to stop what's happening. Either is impossible."

"Maybe. Maybe." Javin found his brain was beginning to work again. "What do those two things have in common?"

"Going somewhere?" Meldren hazarded, still morose.

He snapped his fingers. "That's it, Meldren. You're right! That's exactly what it is. Traveling. Going to different places. You complained that maps were useless because we could sing ourselves wherever we wanted to go, you remember? Well, what's the one thing we've found we're good at? Better than anyone else at? It's going to different places."

"Yes, but we knew the sounds, the songs to listen for when we traveled." Meldren looked as though she were becoming engaged with this line of thinking despite herself.

"I know. I know. Let me think for a minute." Javin struggled to sort through his thoughts and find what he knew was hiding. He took to pacing back and forth as if that would force his mind to work better. "There's something I'm missing. I know it. I just don't know what it is."

"The Emperor is nearer, but with everything being so artificial, I have no idea how we'd get to find him. And we can't hear the song of Haven. We can't even hear the song of our Sun from here," said Meldren. "There's no way we can sing ourselves there from this far away."

Suddenly it all fell together for Javin. He stopped suddenly and turned to face Meldren, pointing a finger at her as if pinning her in place with his sudden awareness. "You've got it! That's absolutely right! That's what we need to do." He knelt down beside her, pushed her hair back and planted kisses on her confused face.

"What are you talking about?" she asked.

"You're right in that we can't hear the songs we need to hear. But this Sun can hear them. He showed that to us when we listened to Him. All we have to do is ask Him to let us sing ourselves back to Haven, back to our home. Then we can find out what's going on. And afterwards, we can sing ourselves back again here. After that, it should be easy to sing us into where the Emperor lives, shouldn't it? And then... well, we get things sorted out. We're only in this position because we don't know what's going on. Once we do know, we can do something about it, can't we?"

Meldren heard this and became quiet and thoughtful, the sadness slowly disappearing as she worked it through, although the occasional gulp of breath showed her underlying disturbance. "Are you sure that He could or even would do such a thing? We never asked our Sun to do anything like that."

"But He did though," said Javin excitedly. "Remember when we went to Haven from Harmony? Don't you recall that, as soon as we were wrapped in the song, another, bigger one, came along and was with us all the way, fading out at the end when we arrived? That had to be our Sun doing that. So, if one of the Suns can do it, why not this one as well?"

Meldren gave a cautious nod of agreement. "What about these, though," she said, waving her hands around to indicate the eavesdropping.

"Don't know and don't care. If we are meant to do something, I think we'll get it done, don't you? And besides, this is our culture," he said with a broad wink, "and we have a right to pursue our cultural heritage, don't we? So what if they hear us? What could they do? Come with us?"

Meldren nodded slowly, thoughtfully, finally getting her breathing under control. "I think you're right. I think that it's possible, and I think it's something we should do. And soon." She finished with a loud sniff and by looking at Javin and standing straighter then before, her decision now evident in her posture.

He held her hands, wiped at the dampness on her face and planted a firm kiss on her lips. "This is why I love you; you're willing to try something like this. I love you!" She smiled at last, and he felt so much better for seeing it, as if a weight had been lifted. The darkness inside was dispersing, and only she could do that.

"So you should," she said quietly, giving him a return kiss. "So you should." She took a deep, controlled breath and smiled again. "So, my love, the theory sounds good, but how do we do this? I mean, it's not exactly like we can have a conversation, is it?"

"Well, maybe it is," said Javin cautiously. "When we listened to Him, He recognized us and showed us places, didn't He? Well, why can't we show Him the place we want to go to and make it so that He knows we want to go there ourselves?"

"I'm not sure I can do that," said Meldren. "It sounds too difficult. How do we let Him know we want to travel and that we want Him to sing us there?"

There was silence for a while until Javin snapped his fingers again. "That's it! We can show Him how our Sun helped us travel from Harmony to Haven and back. We can show Him that and then show Him Haven."

"I suppose so," said Meldren slowly. "But the last part, getting Him to understand that we want to go to Haven, that might be tricky."

"Couldn't we show Him ourselves on Haven? Or show him over and over again us going there from Harmony? I mean, we're talking of a Sun here. A Sun who does amazing things every moment of every day and who has to have an amazing mind to do that. It's not like we're asking Him to show us how to be Suns, is it? I have to believe that, for Him, it is something really easy to do. If He knows our Sun, then it's not even as if He has to find out where to go. He already knows. All we're doing is asking Him to take us along instead of showing us. Sing us there instead of giving us the songs of the places to listen to." He paused. "Then we'll have to do the same thing with our Sun to get us back here. But, hopefully, that shouldn't be too hard... ."

Meldren tilted her head, half-closing her eyes as she looked at him, and Javin knew she was gauging what he had said from the colors she could see around him. "It looks right," she said. "Very strong colors. And it feels right as well. It sounds like the right thing to do as well. Why not go ahead and do it? After all, what's the worst that could happen? Apart from being violently sick upon arrival or drifting somewhere in empty space, that is."

"Not something I'd considered," said Javin with a grimace. "So thanks for bringing that to my attention and making me feel completely at ease about it all."

Meldren grinned, the earlier sadness now completely vanished. "My pleasure." Then, holding out her hand to him she said, "Shall we, then?"

They made themselves as comfortable as they could, loosening clothing, pulling pillows and cushions around them from where they were piled against one wall. Just as they were getting ready to drop into that meditative state which would allow them access to the songs around them, Meldren said, "No. I don't like it here. We should be out there, outside. At least it's nearer to being natural, even if it has been shaped and made into something else."

So they took themselves outside, the pillows following along, and repeated the process of becoming comfortable. Even the ground conformed to them, holding them comfortably. When they were ready, they held hands and shared a long, lingering smile before Javin gave Meldren's hand a final squeeze. "See you on Haven. Let's aim for the President's offices shall we? We know that place from before." And with that, they both shut their eyes and sought out the songs of the place which they could follow up and into the clouds and beyond, just as they had done on their trip.

Very soon they found themselves hanging at the fringe where the stars became evident and the song of the Sun began to swell in their ears. They sang their songs of who they were and listened for the response. It came swiftly as they were recognized. As before, they found themselves surrounded by a bubble of silence. As soon as that happened, Javin began to focus as hard as he could on their journey from Harmony to Haven. His sprite sprang upwards, coiling around the top of his head and added its own strange notes to everything he sang. Time after time they repeated the song of that memory. Then he changed it slightly so that coming to Haven ended up in Myrella's office. He sang the Tree in the chamber and the offices close by. Again and again, he and the sprite sang the song of their trip, and then he changed Haven to this planet beneath them. He sang the song of the two planets and ended with what he hoped could be understood as a request, a hope, a plea.

Throughout it all, he heard the roaring song of the Sun, muted as if it was the thunder of a thousand storms in distant mountains. Then the tone of the thunder changed from a thousand storms to only one, and that one was coming closer, as if to examine this new, tiny song emanating from these minute beings. The thunder moved around them and Javin felt or at least knew on some level of being that it was examining the songs, seeing them and playing with them.

Again, he tried to sing what they wanted to have happen, the journey from here to Haven to Myrella's office. He sang the song of their planets, and their Sun's song as best he could, knowing that Meldren was doing the same thing. He and the sprite repeated and repeated it until he could no longer hold the song in his mind for weariness. He remained, cocooned and exhausted. Even his sprite slumped down around his neck, instead of moving with the fluidity he had always associated with it.

There was silence. The bubble seemed to have thickened or something else had happened to have shut out everything. It was such a deep silence that the blood flowing in his ears sounded like an ocean. He did not know how long this lasted, but suddenly, sound poured back into his awareness. It was a song which showed him the journey from here to Haven. It was a song which was a question, not a statement. It repeated back to him everything he had sung originally. Then there was another brief silence before the song repeated but, this time, halted near Haven. It was as if the song was waiting to be finished. In its way, it was a question. Javin summoned his strength to sing, feeling the sprite move into place as he did so. As clearly as he could, with as much detail as he could, he sang the office of Myrella on Haven and sang the vision of himself and Meldren there, not as they had been, not in the past, but he sang of the near future. He held that song as long as he could before mentally caving in once more.

The silence surrounded him again, but only for a short time. The bubble opened up slightly and he saw he was suspended above the planet again, watching it turn slowly beneath him. Then the vision of both he and Meldren sitting holding hands down there was shown to him. It appeared and disappeared. Once, Twice. Three times it came and was shown. And then Myrella's office was shown, with the two of them standing there. For the space of a breath, if he had known he was breathing, he was shown this.

He sung whatever he could as a thank you, not knowing if it would even make sense. It was small, but he put as much emotion into it as he could.

Abruptly he felt himself falling. Not gently, not evenly, but a mad hurtling fall as a boulder from a mountaintop. He crashed back downwards, flashing through the clouds, the air and toward where his and Meldren's bodies were. If he could have screamed he would have, but there was no time, no breath for that. Suddenly he was back in his body, he was himself again, aware of the world and, for a short stabbing moment, he thought they had failed and that they had been rejected. Before that thought could take a grip on him, the world around him blurred and a song to end all songs rushed around them both. Immense, gigantic, titanic; none of those words felt right to him for what he heard and sensed around him. One moment he had been sitting and holding hands with Meldren, and then he was cocooned in something which was beyond sound, beyond anything he had ever heard or thought of. It was, if anything, the negative of sound. It was the sound made by something which was too big to be heard and all that remained of it in his head was the force and breadth of it, a shape of sound.

He didn't know if he was still holding her hand, or whether he was breathing, or if his eyes were working. There was only this colossal wall of something which he assumed was the Sun's song and which permeated everything so that there was no Javin and nothing which was not Javin. It was all one, and he felt as if he was himself a giant such that he could touch the stars and not be harmed.

How long it lasted, he had no idea. But then into this cataclysm of non-sound, another source began to make its presence known. It grew and grew until there was a stasis, a balance between the two and he was cupped in that middle ground. The new presence gained in strength as the first faded slowly until it was a background. Again, with no sense of time, he had no idea how long this second phase lasted. All he knew was that at some point, this other vastness began to slide down in scale and scope until there was a familiar, lower song, easier to hear and understand: the song of Haven. Down this he felt himself gliding and slipping until the solid cocoon began to unravel from around him as mist will lift under the morning sun.

He was not sure his eyes were working until he saw something beyond, outside, not Meldren and, at the same time, he felt something beneath his body, something he was sitting on.

As the last of the songs left him, he first looked to see that he was indeed still holding Meldren's hand, and then he looked up in wonder at the faces staring down at them both.

He coughed a few times, before he could trust himself to speak. "I'd love something to drink. Preferably very, very strong indeed." And then he was suddenly too tired for anything else and fell back gently and closed his eyes.

33

Myrella had reacted to their presence by calling for assistance and for food and drink to be brought. She had been in the middle of a meeting with Pol and Isselta about Corrivan's continued attacks, both physically and in the media, against Revivalist supporters, as well as trying to decide what, if anything, they could do about the imminent arrival of the mining fleet. Corrivan had not attacked the idea of the Tree, had not mentioned it and had been careful to avoid outright condemnation of what it represented. The obvious conclusion was that he had recalled the double threat of both the Tree and Javin. But that had not stopped him encouraging a campaign against the Revivalists. Myrella was as concerned about Corrivan as she was about the fleet. Was it the right time to release the news when, as far as they could know, nothing could be done to stop it from happening, and nothing could be done to help the people? Millions could die and there seemed to be little to be done to save any of them. The mood was somber.

Myrella had just concluded the meeting by saying, "We have to assume that there is something we can do. Without that hope, we might as well lie down and wait to die. For me, I'm not willing to watch Corrivan go on attacking people, for the simple reason that it's against the law. And, until we are certain that there is nothing to be done, I shall keep looking for a solution and I shall keep holding the law, and you two, please, will keep me informed of everything about the space travelers and their ship. Everything. I want to know everything. There might be something we would otherwise overlook." With a determined glare at the two women, challenging them to disagree, she indicated the meeting was over. Then, as they were about to leave, Javin and Meldren had appeared as if in a multi-colored whirlwind of sound, and both had fainted or fallen asleep when the sound and color had vanished.

"How is this possible?" she asked.

Pol and Isselta both shrugged. "I have no idea," said Isselta, looking as surprised as Myrella felt.

"But I suppose it's similar to how we traveled here from Harmony," added Pol. "Songs. Sounds. But... ," she shook her head as she looked down on her two friends, "this is something much bigger. Much more powerful." She squatted down next to Meldren's inert figure. "The real question is why they are here."

Myrella, as ever, was impressed by this young woman's ability to not be distracted by events, but instead look to the heart of them for meaning. It was something she had prided herself on during her political rise to power. "Well," she said, "we'll soon find out, I suppose."

In a short space of time, there were refreshments, and two of the office chairs were reclined and into which the now awake but groggy visitors were helped. Myrella tried to contain her impatience but waited until both had eaten and drunk, smiling encouragingly and making small talk. Pol and Isselta were just as encouraging and, from the look on their faces, just as eager to know what this was all about.

Finally, Javin wiped his hands clean on a towel and looked toward Meldren, as if to ask if she was ready. When she gave a brief nod, he turned to Myrella. His face was serious. "We came because we heard that something had happened here which might cause a problem and we wanted to know if it was true." He was obviously choosing his words carefully.

"If you're referring to a mining fleet coming here, we know about it already," said Myrella. "It happened because one of the people following the crew who were left behind switched off an emergency beacon, or something like that. And that caused the fleet to be sent. At least, that's how it was reported to us." She sat back and watched for a reaction. Javin exchanged glances with Meldren and then looked to the other two women for confirmation.

"We only recently found this out ourselves and wanted to see if we were being lied to," said Javin.

"We have got nowhere ever since we arrived on that planet," said Meldren. "Nobody wants to talk to us or help us, but everyone seems to know more about everything than we do. When we heard the news, we decided that we had to do something, so we... we found out we could travel here directly."

"How did you do it?" asked Isselta, unable to contain her question any longer. "Is it the Sun? I would think it is. Is it?"

Meldren smiled at her and then at Pol. "Yes. It's the Sun. Actually, it's the Sun here and the Sun there. Thanks to Pol for reminding us to listen. Otherwise I doubt we'd have thought of it."

Myrella wasn't interested in this at all. "But what is it that you can do? Can you stop this fleet from arriving? Is that possible, and how long will it take? The entire population of this planet is under threat, and I need some answers, some help. I cannot sit here much longer and pretend to people that everything is fine. At some point, it will leak out, and they will know and they will die soon after that. So, with the greatest respect for your travels here, I am looking to you for help. What can you provide?"

"Truthfully? I don't know," said Javin. "We had hoped that what we had heard was a rumor and that coming here would allow us to find out the truth. But now we're here, I'm not sure what we can do. Someone we respect greatly back there told us that this was a rare occurrence and impossible to stop once it had started. Frankly, both of us were scared once we heard about it. But," and here he gave a sad sigh, "now you know about it, I'm not sure what there is to be done."

Myrella wanted to scream in frustration. Here were two people able to travel vast distances across space without any apparent equipment and at a moment's notice, and they were saying there was nothing they could do. "That's not good enough! If there is something you can think of, no matter how outrageous, I want to hear it. No, actually, I *need* to hear it."

Meldren frowned in thought, seemingly oblivious of Myrella's frustration. "We did say that we might travel to where the Emperor lives and talk directly to him after we found out what was going on here. We haven't been able to get close in all the time we've been there."

Myrella dismissed this thought quickly. "That won't work at all. You cannot simply appear in front of him as you have appeared here, because he will see it as a threat. He is an Emperor. He is probably surrounded by hundreds of people and probably has some power. Does he? Have power, that is? Or is he just some sort of figurehead, a person with a title but nothing to go with it?"

"From what we've seen and heard, he does have power. Yes," said Javin.

"In that case, you most definitely can't appear in front of him. You'll probably be killed or imprisoned or something else." She shook her head. "No. That won't work. He won't listen, although he'll pretend to if he has any sense, and then you'll be exiled or killed. We need another idea." Turning to Pol and Isselta, she said, "Don't just sit there! This is vital. Start thinking of what these two can do." She felt as if there was an answer to the problem, but she couldn't see what it was. She had been carrying the strain of the knowledge of what was going to happen to her planet for long enough that it was a blackness in the pit of her stomach which consumed her a little more each day.

"I really want to apologize," said Meldren, shaking her head. "I feel that we've been less than useless since we left Haven. And now, coming back here, it seems like we have only been playing and ignoring the catastrophe which is happening." She reached out for Javin's hand. "I just want you to know we're very, very sorry for being so useless, and that we're going to do everything we can to prove you were right to trust us and stop this from happening."

Myrella didn't know how to respond for a moment. Something in the tone of Meldren's voice, or maybe it was a truth in the words, made her think for a moment that everything could turn out well. She tried to keep her anger and tiredness out of her voice. It took a great effort. "Don't feel bad. We're all going to work to solve this. We all have our parts to play. I don't think any of us really understood what could happen, how things could change, after the Empire found us."

She was about to say more when Pol said, "I know this isn't directly involved, but what are Farran and the others doing now? Are they still following the ship?"

Myrella nodded.

"But they don't need to do that anymore, do they? Why don't we bring them back here."

"To do what?" asked Myrella crossly. She realized that she was the only one in the room who didn't have the ability to leave Haven and go to Harmony. It intensified the vulnerability she was feeling.

"Two things, I think," said Pol as if she, too, had not noticed Myrella's anger. "First, they can visit all the Communities, or as many as they can get to, to see if they are able to produce more food, or offer other help in any way, because I'm assuming that the heavily populated areas are going to get hit hardest. And also, we need them to find whatever the fleet will be looking for."

"Why?" asked Myrella, now a little more interested and a little less angry.

"Because if we know what they are after, we can find the most attractive areas and begin to get the people out of harm's way." Pol frowned a moment. "I suppose it might even be possible to sing all the various things into one place, but that might take too long and it might not stop them looking elsewhere anyway."

Myrella was, once more, brought face to face with the difference with which these people viewed the world. To even conceive of such a plan, to bring various types of minerals into one place, was the result of such a view. Again, she felt like the outsider in the room. However, she could also see that it could help, even if only a little. "Good idea. We need to ask them what it is the fleet would be mining, in order of importance. Can we get them here or ask Farran to find out?"

Isselta said, "I'll go and tell them. We'll know very shortly." And with that, she focused her attention inward as her sprite uncoiled a little. The room filled with the background noise which sounded almost familiar to Myrella, but she could never place what it reminded her of. As the sound grew, so Isselta became wrapped in mist which solidified, and then it vanished and she along with it. Myrella had seen this happen many times before when Pol and Isselta had arrived for meetings, but familiarity did not make it any less amazing to see.

She turned back to Javin and Meldren, who were talking quickly in low tones. "Any more ideas about what can be done?"

Javin looked up. "If we can't speak to the Emperor, then perhaps what we need to do is something which will either get his attention without putting ourselves in danger or, and this is what we're leaning to more, we try and stop the fleet."

That caught Myrella's attention. Her heart skipped a beat at the thought. It would mean she would be free of this responsibility and this pressure. Could the planet really be saved? "Stop it! How?"

Meldren scratched at her neck, as if she had no confidence in what she was about to say. "We were thinking that if we could find the fleet somehow, then we could, possibly, get on board and force the captain to stop or shut the engines down somehow. That's as far as we've got," she finished lamely.

If, possibly and maybe didn't sound so fine to Myrella's ears. But it was an idea. Pol voiced her concerns. "And how can you find them? You don't know their song. You have no idea, even if you could hear it, that you could follow it closely enough to get on the right ship and I doubt you can sing the engines off. And then what would you do? Come back here or back to the Empire? You can't just leave a fleet hanging in space. What do they do? It sounds good, I'll say that, but it's far too difficult and has too many problems, even for you two, to seriously consider attempting."

"But there must be something we can do to change things!" Javin banged his fist against his thigh in frustration.

Myrella tried to think, the surge of optimism falling away, and the familiar heaviness replacing it. "It seems that our options are first, try to negotiate with them when they arrive and hope we can save as much of the planet and its resources as possible. Second," she ticked off the points on her fingers, "we persuade the Emperor or whoever to recall or at least stop the fleet, but that seems unlikely given the time and distances involved, let alone the slow bureaucracy you have encountered. And third, the fleet is, somehow, halted or prevented from arriving in some fashion." She made a wry grimace. "And that seems the least likely. So it would seem that we have to focus our efforts on this planet now and the people here. Once we have some idea of what these miners are after, we will be in a better position to make concrete plans. But, until then, I suggest that we think of anything that can be done in whatever fashion, using whatever methods, to lessen the impact of their arrival and subsequent actions. And we do not let this information go beyond this room until we are certain that this is something which will happen."

"Isselta will be back soon," said Pol," so we might have something to start with. But I think we need to think about the least likely option, and don't ask me why. I only know that one sounds -- no, it *feels* -- like the right one to go after." Turning to speak to Meldren directly, she added, "You need to think back over everything you've done so far to get here. The answer is in there somewhere, I'm certain of it."

Meldren looked at her and raised her eyebrows as if to ask her what to do. Pol just waved that look away and repeated. "You have to find a way to stop that fleet or get it turned around. That's why you were made ambassadors. Use what you know." As she finished speaking, so Isselta returned in a fog on a pathway of sound, and Myrella turned her attention to find out what information she had brought back.

34

The next two days were exhausting for everyone, but for Meldren and Javin they seemed particularly difficult to get through. They were in a hotel room near the parliament building but were able to communicate directly with Myrella and the others. She had told them not to leave the room until they had good news for her, but that they had to report twice a day directly to her. Myrella, when they spoke to her, sounded and looked more and more tired and frustrated, and when they told her that they could not think of any way to achieve what Pol had said, they could hear the fear behind the exhaustion, but there was also a fierce resolve in evidence.

"I don't know why, but I trust what that youngster Pol has to say. If she says that you are the ones to stop this, then that is what you are going to do. So stay there and think or whatever it is you do, but find me that answer!" There had been no brooking her.

Just as Meldren was about to call Myrella at the end of the second day to report that neither she nor Javin had made any real progress, Myrella's face appeared, looking more angry than fearful.

"Stay in your room, both of you, and do not leave for any reason. I'm sending some guards over there now and they will be outside shortly.

They have orders not to enter but they are to prevent anyone else from entering. Do you understand me?"

"Why? What's happened?" asked Meldren.

"What's happened is that somehow Corrivan has found out that something is going on and has been making threats. He intends to let the world know that we have been hiding the truth from everyone in order to make private deals with the Empire. He doesn't know all the details, of that I'm certain. But he is sure enough that something is happening without him knowing about it that he is willing to commit to this course of action." She closed her eyes and took a breath to steady herself before continuing.

"He has also decided that all of you who can do the things you do, all of you, are now a threat to the state and must be rounded up and imprisoned, exiled or, probably, executed. He certainly has sufficient followers to make the threat viable, and the last thing I need now is a civil war. That's why I'm sending guards to protect you both. Don't let anyone in without me knowing. Corrivan has decided now is the right time to take over in the name of the people." These last words were said with heavy irony. "He has threatened to destroy each and every one of the Revivalist communities. I'm doing what I can, but I don't have an army on standby here. It will take time to mobilize. In the meantime, I need you both to find that solution. We're doing what we can to minimize the damage and destruction, given what the female pilot of the craft has told us, but it's not going to be enough. We need a miracle, and we need it now." She rubbed a hand across her face and shook her head, her eyes dull and full of pain. "I don't know if there is any way of avoiding total disaster, but having a power-hungry idiot with too many ignorant supporters is not the answer." She looked at someone in her office and appeared to listen for a moment before turning back. "I have to go. Remember, nobody enters without my knowing, and we need that miracle now." The image flickered and faded away.

There was silence in the room for a while before Meldren said, "That sounds really bad... and we have nothing to offer to help."

Javin got up and quietly palmed the door to lock it and then pressed his ear to it for a moment. He returned to Meldren. "It does sound bad. If this Corrivan does what he says he wants to do, then no-one on this planet has any hope at all of surviving. It'll be war. And then the fleet arrives. And that will be it."

"Unless we find an answer," said Meldren.

Javin scrubbed his face in an attempt to feel more alert. "Are we even sure that Pol was right? I know she sometimes says things that later on turn out to be right. But we've spent two whole days trying to figure out we can do. Everything we've thought of is either impossible, way too difficult or complicated, or would take too long."

Meldren felt despair tugging at her and tried to shrug it off by speaking of what she felt was true. "Even Myrella said she believed Pol was right. I've never found anything she has said like this to be wrong. Sure, she's young and impulsive, and maybe she doesn't have the right words for what she senses, but I really do believe that she's right and that the answer to how to stop the fleet is something we know already."

"But what is it?" Javin got up to pace back and forth in the middle of the room. "We've tried to think of ways to speak to the Emperor or to the fleet itself. We've tried to think of ways we can confuse the fleet, even thought of getting the planet to hide, like Harmony did. But when we tried that, tried speaking to Her, She didn't want to listen, and it was too difficult to explain what was happening. That took up nearly one whole day on its own and got us nowhere. So what have we missed?" And he turned to face Meldren. "What have we overlooked? I can't think of a single thing we've missed out on. Going to and from the Empire on the Suns' songs doesn't make any sense unless we are able to actually do something at one end or the other. And we've already decided that there's nothing to be done." He let his body collapse gradually down until he was on his back on the floor, staring at the ceiling's swirling colors, supposedly set to be soothing.

"Whether Pol was right or not when she said about thinking back over anything we've done, it all comes down to the same fact that the fleet has to be stopped. Whether she was right isn't important." Meldren felt tired. Deep down tired. She wouldn't admit to the fear which was also there, lurking in the background, the fear that she and Javin would let everyone down, let the planet down and allow it to be attacked and severely wounded. How could she go back to living on Harmony knowing that she could not prevent such a thing?

Ever since they had left Haven, she had felt useless. All that time wasted in traveling to the Empire and then more time wasted doing nothing, achieving nothing and now here they both were locked in a room while everyone waited for them to have an answer to prevent a catastrophe. Tired and useless and worthless. They were letting everyone down, and they had been doing that from the time they became ambassadors. Even if they could leave and go to Harmony when the fleet arrived, she knew they could never do it. It would have been an admission of guilt and of cowardice to leave a world they had been chosen to represent be destroyed. Whatever fate the people here might face was the same one she and Javin would face.

She stretched out on the floor next to Javin and held his hand. "It's not about letting them down, it's about letting ourselves down. There is something we can do. All we have to do is find out what it is."

Javin let out a snort of frustration.

They both stared up as if the answer lay in the softly moving patterns in the ceiling above their heads. She knew that it was too easy to give in to despair. Doing that would ensure their surrender to fate. But, if there was to be no despair, then what?

"This has got to change," said Meldren finally in a firm voice.

"What do you mean?"

"I mean we have to stop this feeling sorry for ourselves. Ever since we've come back we've been saying how sorry we are for being failures, for not doing what we were meant to do. Although, I'm still not sure what it was that we *were* meant to do in the first place. We have been thinking that we are letting everyone down, putting all the guilt on us, so we can feel terrible."

She pushed herself into a sitting position and looked down at Javin. "And that is what has got to stop. All we are doing is letting ourselves down." She looked away and shook her head disbelievingly. "I mean to say, what have we been doing ever since we got sent here? We have sat and sulked about not being able to find an answer. We have thought how awful we must be, how useless we must seem, if we can't find an answer. And now, when Myrella is facing a rebellion and trying to protect us at the same time, what do we do? We lie on the floor and we get sad because we can't give her a miracle. Well, I say it's time to change that.

It's time to think we can find the miracle. That's what we do. We make miracles happen. At least, that's what it looks like to other people."

She stood up and then offered her hands to help haul Javin to his feet. "So what do you say to us stopping feeling sorry for ourselves and actually doing something about the situation? And, no, I don't know what that is, but I am quite sure we will find a way. We did last time. You found the idea when I was feeling bad. Maybe it's my turn today. All we have to do is let it come to us. Without all the drama about how awful we are. Let that go and we can do anything!" She finished her speech, which left her feeling a lot better, by kissing the tip of Javin's nose and hugging him.

Javin returned the kiss and then said, "You're right. As usual. But how do we deliver the miracle? That's the question. We may have been wallowing in our feelings, but we've also spent a lot of time and effort in trying to think what we can do. So, yes, I agree with you, but no, I don't know what to do. It's the details we need."

Meldren began to pace from the door to the opposite wall. She felt caged, trapped in the room and in her head, and the movement helped to give her some sense of freedom. "I keep going back to Pol and what she said. It's something we know already. Forget schemes and plans and ideas for a moment. Let's talk about what we know already. Perhaps that'll be the way to the solution."

Javin had pulled a chair to him. "Not that we haven't been doing that for ages, but perhaps we can find a different way of looking at things. Where do we start?" He paused briefly. "Let's start at the beginning. How about we know how to listen to songs?"

"Good. And we know how to make things with songs."

"We know that Harmony listens to us, or we can hear Her, which is much the same thing at times. And the same with Haven."

"But Haven doesn't want to do what we ask. Also, we know that the Sun back at the Empire listens to us, or hears us at least." Meldren felt a tingling in the small of her back, a feeling that something important was about to happen. She continued, "And we can locate certain people." The tingling eased a little. Must be the wrong thing. What else was there?

Javin's forehead was wrinkled in thought. "Do we know if this Sun can hear us? Have we spoken with Him, shown Him our songs?"

The tingling turned into a buzzing. "Not directly, but He helped us travel to Haven and the Empire's Sun obviously spoke with Him so, in a way, we have had communication with Him." The buzzing intensified to where Meldren rubbed at her back and wriggled as she did so.

"What is it?" asked Javin.

"Something to do with this Sun here. I keep getting this buzzing sensation in my back as we're talking about Him, so it has to be something to do with Him."

Javin stood suddenly, the light of realization in his eyes. "That's it! That's the answer! It has to be! We've been thinking it's all about us. It isn't."

"We should tell Myrella right away and you can explain it to both of us at the same time," said Meldren turning to the comms unit to contact the President. She waited but there was no answer.

"She's got a lot of problems right now so maybe it's not surprising she is busy," said Javin, putting a hand to stay Meldren. "And, actually, I've got a better idea," he said.

35

P rior to Javin and Meldren's arrival from the Empire, Myrella had called for the mobilization of however many troops she could call upon, citing extreme emergency and using the attacks on Revivalist communities which had been happening with increasing regularity as proof. She knew it would take time, however, and hoped to avoid having to meet and explain her true reasons to the Assembly, as that would allow Corrivan the opportunity to launch a coup or a personal attack on her. She was relying on using her executive powers to rush things through.

At the same time, she had also recalled the space visitors and requested an immediate conference with both the captain and the singers (her private term for Isselta, Pol and the others) to see if there was anything new which might help her. In the interim she had been trying to locate Corrivan, gain as much new information as she could and generally trying to avoid saying anything of the crisis which was unfolding, but which she believed -- or was it that she hoped? -- would be avoided.

Now she was waiting for the first of them to arrive after having dealt with too many curious representatives and news people. She noticed she had missed a call from Meldren and Javin, and was just about to call them back, when Farran, Hanna, Endel and Carmeena arrived in their usual fashion, which was that strange combination of song and chaos and fog. Hanna and Endel, she noticed, arrived holding hands. It was Endel, she recalled, who had precipitated this crisis, albeit with the best of intentions. It was obvious that Hanna was not going to let him suffer alone. The look and the smile she gave him upon their arrival made that very clear, as did the steady look, almost a challenge, she turned upon Myrella.

She stood to welcome them but others shimmered into view, strangers she had not seen before. One was a bulky man with sad brown eyes and he was swiftly followed by a younger man, dark complexioned and bright, alert eyes. Then came a still younger man, but one whose broad shoulders made him seem bigger and somehow older. Yet his eyes were happy, and he looked as though he rarely stopped smiling.

Myrella was taken aback by these new arrivals, but whatever she was about to say was interrupted by the arrival of an older woman, thin with grey hair and startlingly pale green eyes. In contrast to the boy who had arrived before her, it looked as though she rarely smiled. Upon her heels a young woman, no more than a girl really, who had bright blonde hair which contrasted with her dark eyes. Just as Myrella thought the room could hold no more, two others arrived. One of them a man with light blond hair and the look of someone who had suffered a lot and the other was a woman with long black hair who also had an air of past pain about her. They all were dressed very simply and most had bare feet. That they knew each other was obvious from the gasps of delight and hugging which took place.

"Well," began Myrella. "Who are you all?" But before she could get an answer, the last two, Pol and Isselta, arrived and interrupted her.

"We're really sorry, but these are the rest of those who can do what we can do. We rounded them up from all over Haven because we thought, well..." Isselta shrugged, "the more the merrier. We've tried to give them the basic facts but having them here might give us other options. They might see things differently or have other ideas."

Myrella was aware of all the new faces watching her. Actually, it wasn't a bad idea to have them all here, and she nodded greetings to them. She hadn't thought that there might be other singers. But why shouldn't there be? "I'll put names to faces later, if you don't mind. There's two others who are due to arrive shortly, the crew of the space ship. I'm hoping that one of them might have some other thoughts about what we're facing and, now that you're all here..." she took a deep breath and tried to project optimism, "well, it might be the breakthrough we need."

Isselta spoke to the group. "And don't forget we've got Meldren and Javin working on this as well. And there's something we should share with you, Myrella," she added looking, Myrella thought, somewhat evasive.

"Which reminds me," said Myrella, "I noticed they called recently but no-one was here." She reached to make the connection when the door opened and Mannert entered followed by Parra-Hopshan and Lessterenman. Rising to greet them, she noticed that the man looked very uncomfortable, glancing around him and hunching his shoulders, whereas the woman looked far more at ease, nodding at the others and striding purposefully to shake Myrella's hand before taking a seat in the chair indicated by the President. The singers remained standing, filling the room.

"I'm glad you are here, captain, and you, sir," began Myrella, taking her seat behind the desk and indicating to the others to sit wherever they could. Her office really wasn't meant to accommodate this number of people comfortably. "You have both obviously been introduced to some of the abilities these people have. Some you know, and these others present have similar talents and we were hoping that either of you might have thought of something to help avert the crisis we are facing or have some other helpful material for us."

The captain leaned forward as if eager to help but was shaking her head. "I am truly sorry, Madam President, that I can think of no other information which might be of use to you. I have been searching our operations manuals for any possible loophole, however small, which might provide some small glimmer of hope. I am sorry to report that I have found nothing. All I can tell you is that I estimate the arrival of the fleet in this system as being no more than a day or two at most. I could be wrong, but if so, it won't be by more than a day or so either side. They could already be at the outer reaches of this system and have not yet been picked up by your people. No matter when they arrive, as I said before, they will be under strict orders to ignore all your attempts to communicate with them. They will be acting under the assumption that they will be facing a hostile and dangerous enemy." She looked down at her hands clasped on her lap. "And I know that is not true, but it is what they will believe. I am sorry."

Myrella placed her elbows on the desk and rested her chin on her fists. She felt bleak but managed to nod her thanks. "It was as I feared, captain. But thank you for your honesty and for your attempts to help us. We appreciate it."

As she sat wondering how to phrase her next words, she realized that, although everything was looking terrible, there was some part of her which could not fully engage in that feeling. There was a part of her which remained, if not optimistic, then certainly defiant. She wondered where that had come from. Had it happened because she had been spending time with these people who had strange tattoos or weird creatures around their necks? Or was it because she had come to accept as fact that she could walk into the Assembly, stand in front of that huge tree and say to it that she needed to speak with Isselta and Pol and that she knew it heard her and that it somehow responded? Even so, to admit to herself that the tree was, in some strange way the whole planet was a step too far. But perhaps just being in its presence, talking to it, was enough to change her perceptions about everything else, including this imminent threat?

She looked around at the faces in the room, noting that the crewman had found his way to the rear and was still looking ill at ease, casting what seemed to be fearful glances at everyone around him. "Well, everyone, it seems that it is going to be down to us to come up with some sort of plan to minimize the damage. Releasing the news would give two or three days of unprecedented panic and chaos to break out, but not telling anyone will mean that when it arrives, there will still be panic, but it will have a focus rather than a vague fear. The question now becomes, it seems, do we tell the world now or later? Corrivan, my political opponent, has somehow acquired this knowledge and has given me an ultimatum about telling the world at large about the arrival of the fleet. If I don't say something, he will. And, knowing him, he might well not keep his word about the timing. Either way, there will be many deaths, and that is before the fleet sets to work. Or, and this is still my hope, is there something else we can do?"

Their grim faces and heads being shaken told her everything she needed to know. The silence seemed to her to have a distinct aspect to it, a stickiness almost, clinging to each person, weighing down their spirits. To speak felt like an enormous effort.

The crewman at the back of the room finally broke the atmosphere, his voice bitter. "It's not our fault that this planet is going to be wiped out. It's you who should take the responsibility. If you hadn't tampered with our equipment, we'd have left here and gone home to our fortunes." He stood up as his anger took hold. "You all deserve to die. You've robbed us of our futures, and the only good thing about it is I won't have to watch you all weeping and wailing over this horrible, backward little planet." He made a scything gesture at the room and then marched stiff-legged to the door.

As he did so, Parra-Hopshan rose, white-faced in horror at his outburst. "Crewman! You will remain here and you will apologize for your words!"

"No Parra, I will not. We have been prisoners here for too long, and you still side with these uncivilized people. You are the one who should apologize to our real captain and to the Emperor for your loss of face here." And he left.

"Madam President, please, I apologize profusely for the words my crewman used against you. I do not know why he is as he is, but I am most --"

"Please do not trouble yourself, captain," said Myrella, waving away the apologies and embarrassment. "We are all under a great deal of stress here, and we all will react differently to it."

"I should go after him, Madam President. If you will excuse me?" Parra-Hopshan turned to the door, but was beaten to it by Mannert opening it from the outside and who coughed quietly and remained in the doorway, looking directly at Myrella, said, "Unfortunate news, Madam, but I have confirmation that Corrivan has pre-empted this meeting and is even now in the process of making a planet-wide statement to the effect that a mining fleet is expected imminently."

"What?" Myrella had half expected something she didn't want to happen, and this met that feeling perfectly.

"There is more, Madam," continued Mannert imperturbably as Parra-Hopshan returned to her seat having taken the hint from Mannert's look that she should stay. "He is saying that this fleet is evidence of the good intentions of the Empire, and that it will be helping us all to gain a favorable trading position with regard to the Empire."

Myrella was confused. "How on earth did he find out about all this and where did he get the notion that it was a good thing for us all?"

Isselta gave an embarrassed cough. "We," she said, indicating Pol beside her, "thought that it would be helpful if we let Corrivan know of the fleet and that you were going to be hiding just how wonderful it was for everyone so that he would... I don't know how to say it well enough..."

"He would make a fool of himself in front of everyone, which would make it much easier to get him away from you." Pol took up her friend's explanation. "Of course, we are assuming that we are going to survive all this first. But having him say these things, we thought, would also help to calm people and make them less afraid. And then when everyone finds out he lied to them, well, it would make him less powerful." She puffed her cheeks out and reached for Isselta's hand for courage. "We're sorry if we did wrong, but we thought it might make things a little easier for everyone. We hadn't expected him to react quite so quickly."

Myrella watched them in amazement at their words. At first she wanted to smack both their faces for being so presumptuous, and then she wanted to tell them to mind their own business before finally realizing that they had made a very clever decision. She took a moment to choose her words carefully, aware that they were expecting some sort of reprimand. This was not, she realized, a time for anger but for recognizing that help came in many forms. "I think what you have done is remarkable, and more than that, it shows so much hope for the future and that we can come through this somehow." Then a thought struck her. "I have no idea where he is, but I do know that he has taken a dislike to the tree in the Assembly and, despite what he was both told and shown, I think it might be a good idea..."

"Don't worry about that," said Endel standing up. "I'll make sure it remains safe." He looked around and held his hand out to Hanna. "Shall we go and stand guard over the Tree? I'm looking forward to him trying to get rid of it."

Hanna blushed slightly, smiled and held her hands out for Endel to help her to her feet. "I would like to meet this Corrivan person myself. Thank you for asking."

Myrella watched them leave and felt the room shift into a new feeling which had the beginnings of what she thought could be called optimism.

"Are there any other surprises I should know about? Good surprises, that is?"

As if in answer, everyone except Myrella, the captain, and Mannert, suddenly jolted as if shocked and the sprites reached upwards and made a keening note which filled the room. The tattoos on the others whirled and formed a dense black circle on their owners' foreheads which seemed to pulse larger and smaller for as long as the sprites made their calls.

"I think," said Pol when everyone had recovered, "I think that was the answer. I think there has been a solution." She looked around at her compatriots for confirmation and there was a general nodding of heads and murmurs of agreement.

"Well? What is it? What is the solution?" demanded Myrella.

"That I don't know," said Isselta.

It was hardly the answer Myrella was expecting. "So how do you know it was the answer then?"

Pol frowned, trying to get the words right. "Because all of us here felt it at the same time. Because it was a powerful feeling, a feeling of... of success, of achievement. I don't know how to convince you if you didn't have that same feeling."

"We're going to have to wait to find out," added Isselta. "But I am positive that Javin and Meldren are behind it."

"I should have returned their call," said Myrella, her memory jogged by hearing those names. "Earlier, they contacted here, but didn't leave a message. It could have been about what they were going to do to make what just happened happen."

She reached out to initiate the call when Meldren's voice could be clearly heard outside. "There's no need. We're here and we thought we should tell you what we've done."

Everyone made to rush for the door, but Mannert managed to hold a space for Myrella to be first through into the larger outer room where Javin and Meldren stood holding hands and wearing face-splitting smiles. It contained two desks for her assistants which were placed so that, between them, they could see who entered the room and who was leaving Myrella's office. In addition, there were two sofas and several other chairs scattered about for people waiting to speak with Myrella or for quick conversations. Unlike her office, this was also much lighter, with less wood-paneling and more bright pictures. Javin and Meldren were in the middle of the room standing behind two of the chairs.

After everyone had arrived and more hugging had occurred and people were talking excitedly, Myrella clapped her hands to get their attention. "I can see that something important has happened and everyone else here has apparently sensed something important has happened, but what we all want to know is what exactly *has* happened. Please put us out of our misery. Have you found a way of stopping the fleet from arriving?"

"Well," began Javin, "the fleet has been stopped--," there was a collective gasp and shared looks of joy and wonder, "but we really can't take credit for it. We had an idea which we thought might work, but --," and here he was interrupted by Meldren.

"Don't make them wait! I'll tell you what we did. We contacted the Sun, this one here, and we told Him, as best we could, what was going to happen to His daughter, Haven. And, like any good parent, He was enraged at the thought of Her being harmed by these people but had the good manners not to wipe the fleet out." She beamed around the room. "You'll never guess what He did."

"Oh, for goodness' sake," said Javin, taking his turn to interrupt, "He somehow stopped the fleet at the edge of the system. Neither of us knows how, but, apparently, it just stopped moving forward. He showed us, as best He could. If anyone here has had any news about it, witnessed it, recorded it or seen it with some of your instruments, I'd love to have confirmation." Hearing that, Myrella snapped her fingers at Mannert and nodded at him. He hurried out.

"How did y0u do it?" Myrella thought it was one of the newer arrivals who had asked, possibly the thin-looking woman with black hair.

"You do realize that we're going to have tell it all again to Endel and Hanna?" This was from Isselta.

"Why? Where are they?" asked Javin.

"Gone to guard the Tree. The idiot, Corrivan, had been heard to make threats to cut it down."

Javin and Meldren's eyes widened at that. "He does know that's a bad idea after what It told him?" asked Meldren. "I don't think it's the Tree in need of guarding, but this Corrivan instead. We met him, didn't we? I thought he was an idiot then, but this confirms it. Surely, after what he saw, he can recognize It's not an ordinary tree. It can and does command the power of the entire planet of Haven. It would be like having a thunderstorm chasing and attacking you if you decided to attack the Tree. Or something much larger and more powerful, like a... ," she moved her hands as if demonstrating an explosion and looked to Javin for help.

"A volcano?"

"That's the thing, a volcano. Only he'd be sitting in it. He's in for a nasty shock if that's what he intends to do."

"In that case," said Myrella, "if there's no danger to it, why don't we bring those two in here as well? It will save repeating ourselves, I'm sure." Isselta rushed out and Myrella pulled out a chair from behind one of the desks and placed it to one side from where she could see most of the people. She noticed that the captain had come through and remained with the group instead of going in search of her crew-member. That spoke much of the tensions in that relationship, she thought, as well as how the captain viewed the people here. She was sitting slightly apart, as a stranger at a party. The captain was, Myrella then realized, hiding a smile at the thought that a powerful fleet from her Empire had been brought to an abrupt halt. That was most interesting.

Isselta arrived back with Endel and Hanna in tow. There was another round of greeting and hugs and excitement, and even the captain got a few hearty slaps on her back, at which she beamed her thanks.

There were too many people here now for comfort, but Myrella was happy to keep them in this one place instead of any more delay in hearing the full extent of the news. "Now that we're all here, can we please have the whole story? This might never go beyond these rooms -- imagine what politicians would do with this news -- but for my own peace of mind, I would dearly like to know the whole of it. If you please?" and Myrella made a sweeping motion of her hand to indicate that Javin and Meldren had the floor. "Oh, before you start -- sorry -- Mannert will hopefully be returning with the confirmation you requested. Carry on."

Javin looked around and saw one unfamiliar face: the captain. He tilted his head as if examining her for a moment before nodding and smiling to himself. He walked over to her and held out his hand. "I'm Javin and that is Meldren and you are someone I've never met, but I think I heard you somewhere." They shook hands but the captain had a very confused look on her face.

"You heard *of* me, did you mean?"

"No. I am sure I heard you, heard your song, that is." Seeing that hadn't helped he looked around as if for assistance. "You know we here can hear songs. Yes?"

A cautious nod.

"And that songs are really real?"

Another cautious nod. "I've heard that said."

"Everyone is made up of songs. They *are* songs in a way. I can tune in to hear people, what they are like, what their song sounds like. And I'm sure I've heard your song before."

"But what does that mean?" she asked finally.

"Truthfully? I'm not sure. But it was you, or your song, that I heard." He turned to Meldren. "Did you hear her as well? When the Sun was showing us what he'd done?"

Meldren screwed up her face as she concentrated. "Maybe. But you're much better than I am at this. I trust you."

Javin smiled at the captain and returned to Meldren's side. "The beginning, then."

"First, though," said Meldren, "we decided to leave the hotel room, because we thought if there were guards around and Corrivan saw them, he'd know something was worth guarding, so we left and went to a park somewhere. It was quiet. That was the main thing. It sounded lovely, so that's where we ended up, in the middle of some bushes so we couldn't be seen."

Myrella silently acknowledged their actions and caught herself once more underestimating these people because of their simple dress and strange habits. It was as though she denied them a more cunning intelligence. Something, she knew, she was going to have to overcome.

Javin and Meldren then told of the way they had come to realize that they had to convince the Sun that His planet, His daughter, was in serious danger and what that danger would look like.

"Excuse me," said Myrella, "but are you saying that you knew what to do based on how Meldren's back was feeling? Really?"

Meldren nodded but looked puzzled. "Of course. Why wouldn't we? There's no such thing as a coincidence. It all has meaning. And the more that Javin went on about the Sun, the more my back became painful or uncomfortable. And when he said that we had to talk to Him, the Sun, that is, all the discomfort vanished." She spread her hands as if it was an obvious fact she was stating. "That was confirmation. Everything was going to go smoothly if we did that."

Myrella noted that there were several heads nodding in agreement as Meldren spoke, as if it was as obvious to them as well. She felt, once more, the odd one out here, not being able to appreciate something that everyone else thought was incredibly simple. She had her own gut feelings, but nothing as strong as what Meldren had described. It was an uncomfortable moment. "I'm sorry," she said. "It's not that obvious to me, but I think I will be more aware of how I feel in the future if it can be so helpful. Please, do carry on."

Javin and Meldren continued explaining that they had to first let the Sun know they could hear Him, and used their experience back at the Empire to help them. Then they had to explain what was going to happen to Haven.

"It's not that simple," said Javin, "trying to persuade something that big that we knew something it didn't. We tried all sorts of things, but the same problem kept coming up; how do we sing a song about something we don't know or haven't experienced? In the end, we showed Him what we thought the ships might look like or how they would be moving and then sang sadness and terror and put them together, or tried to, in how we were singing about Haven. It took a while, but very soon He showed us what He understood and it matched pretty closely with what we had been trying to say.

"Then He showed us the ships. And these had to be the real ones, because they weren't anything like the ones we had tried to sing. And He showed us them being stopped." Here Javin looked toward the captain again. "Just after, that is, when I heard your song. He was singing or showing us what Haven was like now and there were lots of different songs going on, happiness and so on, but there was a brief moment when your song was there."

"Oh, I remember that now," said Meldren, nodding. "Yes. That was definitely you He was singing. Sounds like you are someone rather special to Him in some way. I wonder why?" Then she grinned and shrugged. "Doesn't matter in the end. We've found out that if you are wanted by Him or by a planet, you get to find out, and you don't have much choice about it either." She shrugged, but her eyes echoed her wide smile. "Welcome to the songs and to this group of wonderful people as well!"

Myrella watched the captain trying to understand what she was being told. Myrella was having a hard time coming to grips with it all herself. Songs that could show things? A sun that could hear and understand them? Something as small as humans could speak with the sun? It all seemed incredible, and yet nobody else seemed to be having any problems. But she kept her eyes on the captain and watched her smile shyly as Meldren welcomed her to be part of the group. It made Myrella wonder whether she would ever be in such a position herself or would she even welcome it? What must it be like, she wondered, to speak with a star or listen to a planet? How could you possibly remain normal after such an experience, and yet these people apparently had no difficulty with it. They were seemingly without malice or pretension and laughed and smiled and were sad like anyone else. They showed no superiority, no condescension. And yet they were different in such huge ways as to make them seem alien by comparison. Or was it she who was the alien here?

A question from Hanna brought Myrella's attention back to the moment. It was, as was becoming more and more clear with these singers, that it was not any sort of question she would have even considered asking.

"How did you not die from hearing the Sun? I remember back on Harmony you warned us not to listen to Him because His song was too strong? Is that not true?"

Javin answered. "I think it's still true if you were to open yourself to His songs. But we sang at Him first, showed Him we were there. And, like when we listened to the Sun back at the Empire, when He heard us and recognized us, he sang a bubble around us to protect us from the sounds out there." He half-closed his eyes as he recalled the experience. "Those songs: His, the other Suns, and the space between them, they are... they are vast. They carry all of our songs, everything, the planets, the people, everything inside them." He shook his head, a look of wonder still in his eyes. "It is something too big for words. Too big."

There was a silence following this, where everyone was absorbing what had been said. Looks were exchanged, quiet comments murmured and a sense of peace spread around the room. Myrella caught the captain's eye, and they shared the look of people out of their depth. Myrella doubted that either of them had really grasped half of what they had listened to, but they both felt they had shared something important.

The peace was broken by Mannert knocking and entering. The changed atmosphere in the room was acknowledged by his discreet double-take as he glanced around. He approached Myrella, but she stopped him.

"Whatever the news is, Mannert, everyone here can hear it. I hope it's good."

Mannert inclined his head slightly. Not quite a nod, more of an acknowledgment. "Indeed, Madam, there is very good news. I discovered from a disappointingly long communication with our astronomers that there would be a good deal of time required to direct their instruments in the right direction before they could even begin to take note of what might or might not be there. However, their help was no longer an urgent necessity after I had sent someone out to find the other visitor who had left earlier." He emphasized the word 'visitor' and looked at the captain as he did so, who colored slightly in return. "It did not take long," he continued, now addressing Myrella, "because he was looking for me. Rather it was you, Madam, he was looking for. He was very angry indeed, speaking about some sort of revenge, carrying what I took to be a weapon of some kind, a bludgeon or so I assumed, and I required some help in restraining him. He was calling you what I suppose were some unpleasant names amongst other things. Anyway, the gist of his complaint was that he had at that very moment received a high-speed communication from the captain of the approaching fleet, apparently relayed from the ship to his personal receiver, in which he was informed that every single vessel had lost power and had come to some sort of standstill. 'As if they had hit a wall' was how he phrased it. He, of course, blamed us all for this, but I am quite convinced that his anger was real and the message as he relayed it was also true. It would therefore appear, Madam, that, as of this moment, we are safe from mining depredations." He finished with a slight bow and everyone began to clap and cheer.

Up until that moment, Myrella had not realized she had been holding her emotions in check. But now, suddenly, she felt such a sense of relief, of a release of pressure, that her eyes filled with tears and she found herself sobbing and laughing at the same time as she stood and hugged Mannert. Mannert was obviously not accustomed to such behavior from his employer and reached round to pat the President of Haven gently and very awkwardly on her back a few times before extracting himself and standing by the outer door.

As everyone began to regain a sense of calm, Myrella addressed them all. "This has been a day to remember. Frightening, exhilarating and, sadly, never to be shared with any other person. Thank you all, because all of us here in this room today have shared something unique. We have had experiences we cannot explain to others and knowledge which is ours alone. I am grateful to have had you all as companions in this. Thank you again."

That brought another round of clapping and calling out, but everyone felt, deep down, that the crisis had passed and they were able to breathe freely again.

36

After Javin and Meldren's news had been confirmed by astronomers, Myrella set about planning for what she hoped would be the next phase in Haven's history. Corrivan and those who supported his views were so obviously unaware of the role the planet and the sun had in shaping society. But to expect everyone to change their views overnight was unrealistic. Certainly, having the singers show their talents would have some impact, but it would probably be nothing more than a magic show. Somehow, she realized, she had to bring people to a place where they could at least begin to accept that there was another way of looking at the world. She had had trouble herself believing what she had seen and accepting what she had been told. She could expect the same thing from others. Nevertheless, it was something she felt she had to do. It was no longer feasible to allow Haven to go on in the same fashion and have the divide grow larger between those who opposed the Revivalists and their desire to be closer with and work with nature and those who supported them. She had to begin to bridge that gap.

She could not possibly discuss her ideas with anyone who had not had her experiences. She had felt a presence, she had experienced something she could not describe, and she knew it was both real and incredibly potent. She had witnessed just how different the singers' views were because of what they could do. And they had told her that others could do what they did. It was not as though they were some strange sect, set apart from everyone. They really wanted everyone to see the world as they saw it, as a place of natural wonder and incredible complexity yet with an underlying... she wanted to avoid the word 'soul' but was having trouble thinking of an alternative phrase. Her gut feeling, even if it was so weak compared to Meldren's, for example, told her that she was doing the right thing, not just to make herself more powerful. After all, how could she be as powerful as a planet? That alone put limits on what any realistic politician would reach for from now on. She had felt things and witnessed things she could not explain, and so it was down to herself and Mannert, who had shared the same experiences, to go over possible ways to bring people together more, to begin the process of a shift in perspective.

The first thing to do was to discredit Corrivan and what he stood for. Then she had to expose the singers to the world in a way which would encourage others to emulate them. The question was, how swiftly could that be done? Corrivan, having been fed lies by Pol and Isselta, was not going to waste time. He would be gathering a show of force. That would take a little while. But she was expecting him to march in at any time full of fury and indignation. Speed was of the essence if she was to take that anger and turn it against him. His beliefs had to be shown to be wrong. Not in some quiet way, but publicly. And it had to be done without her seeming to be orchestrating it. It had to be natural and as a result of his own actions.

Knowing that she had little time, she called in a media crew, saying that she had an important announcement to make and that it might need some editing before release, but not much. Once that was done, she let the news of such an announcement be known, certain that it would entice Corrivan. The only real concern she had was whether or not she could get the singers back here in a reasonable space of time. They had left her office, some having gone back to the communities they had been working in, while others, Meldren and Javin in particular, had stayed close by in hotels and parks in case they were required. She had deliberately not shared any of her ideas with them, wanting their reactions to be genuine. As an afterthought, she placed a call to the observatory and asked that the director and his assistant make themselves available as soon as possible. She had not slept, and she felt gritty and untidy. She took some stimulants, adjusted her makeup and hoped that she would not look as tired as she felt.

Running over the plan again in her mind, she nodded gratefully at Mannert as the media crew announced their presence. "Please let them in, Mannert."

"Certainly, Madam. And, if I may say so, I wish you the very best of luck. You said yesterday that it had been historic. I would suggest that today is of even greater importance." Then he bowed once more and ushered the crew in.

There were three of them, each with various pieces of equipment. Two of them began setting up while the third, a man named Ackman, tall, with red hair and an intricately manicured beard, approached Myrella.

"We shall be ready very shortly. You said to record, rather than make live?"

Myrella nodded. "I'm not entirely sure how this will go, so I might need to stop and re-think. This is not a carefully scripted moment, and I think you'll see the reason for that as it unfolds. I can tell you that what is going to happen is going to make history, and I want it to be live and unscripted, nothing formal about it." She could see that had got his attention. "But, if I do change my mind, is it possible to go to direct streaming? Across the whole planet?"

Ackman nodded. "It is possible, but I will have to make certain that we can break into the various channels without too much delay. Give me one moment while I set that up, Madam President." And he pressed a bud to his mouth and began speaking quietly and urgently at the same time as directing the other two to make some sort of alterations to what they were doing. It seemed that the arrangements had been finalized, Ackman nodding vigorously in affirmation at her, when Myrella heard a minor commotion in the outer office. She allowed herself a slight smile and beckoned Ackman over and said, "I've made up my mind. I think we'll do this live. And, whatever happens, do not stop the stream unless or until I say so." He looked surprised but nodded and murmured to his crew a moment before giving the thumbs up. It was at that moment that Corrivan barged past one of her protesting secretaries and marched into her office.

"I know exactly what's going on, Myrella," he said, his face red with anger and pointing a finger at her. "You have come to some sort of arrangement with the Empire behind our backs and have stopped the fleet from bringing equipment vital to the expansion of our resources and weakening our trading position. You have gone too far this time and I will see you hounded out of office for it. You are a disgrace to this planet and to the position you hold."

"Ah, Assemblyman Corrivan, what a pleasant surprise," said Myrella with a broad smile. "And what precisely have you been hearing?"

Corrivan glared at the media people. "I would prefer to have this discussion in private," he huffed.

"But that is not possible because you forced your way in here," she said in a sweet tone. "I was about to broadcast an important message here, as you can see. With an appointment made in the usual way, it would certainly have been the case. However," and here she shrugged eloquently, "we must make do with what we have. So, again, I will ask what is it that you have heard which has so incensed you?"

Corrivan strove to limit his temper, obviously taking the time to choose his words. "I know that there is a fleet at the outer edges of our solar system which has been sent from the Empire, but which you have refused to allow to enter. I wish to know -- no, I demand to know -- why you have done this and what damage it has done to our relations with the Empire?"

"On that last point at least, I can reassure you that it has done absolutely no damage at all. Definitely not. As for the rest, even if I told you the truth, you would not accept it."

Corrivan stared at her a moment in amazement. "And that is all you are going to say about this? Really? Well, I am going to do something about it, even if you are clearly incapable."

"Before you do, my dear Corrivan, please do tell me what it is you were saying about this fleet before anyone else seemed to know anything about it? This was supposed to be the central point of the broadcast," she indicated the media. "I wonder how exactly you got such information to begin with and how certain you are as to the truth of it."

"I am in contact with those who think like me and who are able to access information which should be public knowledge but which isn't. How much else are you hiding?" Myrella allowed herself a small hint of a smile when she imagined what Pol and Isselta would have thought about being considered like Corrivan. "And, quite obviously, the Empire sent such a fleet as a show of support for those like us who are more forward thinking and eager to embrace the new technology it offers. That's all I have said on the matter. It is public knowledge concerning my stance vis-a-vis the Empire, new technology and the need to become less misty-eyed about nature."

Myrella rocked back in her chair, aware of Ackman's growing comprehension of the nature of what he was seeing. She doubted he could bring himself to stop recording even if she begged him. Her first thought was how arrogant Corrivan was, but that was followed swiftly by his dismissal of 'nature'. It was this which spurred her to make a decision she had toyed with in her planning with Mannert. She wasn't sure if she would regret it later or not. What might happen as a result was not necessarily certain. But, trusting her gut feeling, she went with it anyway.

"Your hard-eyed attitude toward this 'nature' you are so quick to dismiss: is that the reason behind the attacks on the communities known as Revivalists?"

"Are you accusing me of such attacks? You know perfectly well I believe those communities to be outdated and unproductive, as well as inciting of a dismissive attitude toward efficient and effective governance. I shed no tears over them, but you cannot connect me with any attacks. I believe the rot in our society began after the fall of the military rule," and here he turned to the media, attempting to use it for his benefit, "and you can easily look up my past speeches which have said the same thing." Turning back to Myrella, he continued, "And that stupid, idiotic tree in the middle of the space where we as a people come to discuss, formulate and oversee reasonable and judicious laws," he was becoming pompous, Myrella recognized, using this as an opportunity to promote himself as an alternative leader, "is nothing more or less than an abomination and directly undermines our role as an Assembly. I have said it before and I repeat it now, I am more than willing to take an axe to that tree and restore this Assembly to the people and only the people."

She knew he would have got round to the tree at some point but was pleasantly surprised at how quickly he had arrived there. She wondered if he had really forgotten what had happened earlier, or whether this was simply posturing for the public gaze.

Whatever his motivation, this was the moment. She pushed herself up and looked squarely at Corrivan. "Perhaps it would be instructive to go now and, with the help of the media here, we can perhaps share another view of the Tree and to a much wider audience." The way she emphasized the word 'Tree' capitalized it for all her listeners. "I am sorry you have no axe with you, but I think I can assure you that, within the hour, if you can retain your patience for that long, you will not only have the answers to all the issues you have raised here today, but you will also have had an opportunity to have a different perspective on many things. Can you give me one hour of your time if I promise you these things?"

Faced with being recorded, Corrivan had no option but to agree, and that with poor grace.

There was no session today, so Myrella, Corrivan and the three media personnel entered the Assembly where the tree, known and recognized across the planet, stood tall with its branches spreading out over and above all the seats for the representatives. Myrella invited Corrivan to take her usual seat behind the grand desk in the well of the room. He looked at her as if she were offering him some sort of poison, but he accepted and seated himself gingerly. Myrella remained standing. "You promised me an hour of your time, and I ask that you remain seated and please do not interrupt what follows. You will undoubtedly form your own opinions about me, but I ask you to restrain yourself until everything has come to an end. The whole process is being recorded or broadcast, isn't it?" she asked of the crew who obviously could not believe their luck at being here at this time.

Ackman quietly said, "This is live, Madam President. Should we keep it that way?"

"Certainly. I have nothing to hide here, and I would appreciate everyone being able to see for themselves, without any editing."

Despite having done this several times, Myrella still felt a little foolish as she stepped toward the Tree. She had never had an observer before and had to take a deep breath or two to set herself. Aware of the need to be heard clearly by the others in the room, she drew herself erect and lifted her chin. "I wish to see all the helpers, the ones I know as singers, in this room as soon as possible," she said in a clear voice. "Also, please ask that someone bring along the captain of the ship and the recordings she has of communication from the fleet currently at the edge of our system. Thank you." She knew that mention of the fleet would be enough to keep Corrivan quiet, but she nevertheless felt a little embarrassed when she turned to take up her place in front of and to one side of her desk, allowing Corrivan to see the room clearly but remaining slightly in front of him, emphasizing herself as the leader, the initiator despite him being in the seat of the President. His accepting to sit there had been a major mistake.

When she had done this before, the quickest Pol and Isselta had arrived was about an hour after she had spoken to the Tree. She was praying that this time, asking for them to arrive as soon as possible, would speed things up. "You did promise me that hour, didn't you?" she said without turning to Corrivan. "Perhaps you'd like to start the timing now?"

The minutes ticked away and nobody spoke. Corrivan cleared his throat. Myrella checked to see where the media were and to ensure they were able to get a clear view. If she was right, what was going to be recorded would go down as one of the key moments in Haven's history and would be a turning point for all of society. All she had to do was wait and hope that Corrivan wasn't too patient. She remained as still as she could.

Finally, Corrivan asked in a tone which clearly indicated he was becoming irritated at the lack of action, "Remind me again what we are waiting for? And how long until we give up and can go about our business? And who were you talking to? Is this going to be some sort of magic trick?"

Without turning, Myrella said, "I asked for an hour. I did not promise an action-packed hour but I did promise that by the end of it you would have your answers, Corrivan. Has the hour passed?" This was directed at Ackman. He shook his head.

Silence descended again.

"Why are we staring at this tree anyway? Are we expecting it speak to us? This amounts to nature worship not proper governing. We should have removed it from our Assembly as soon as it had appeared. Folklore, stories to scare children, and superstition is what keeps it here, and those are not right or proper attitudes to have in a place of governance. We should be above such things. We are not children. In fact, as soon as this charade is over, I fully intend to get rid of this... this... plant! whether you like it or not."

She forced herself not to turn. He had to be seen as someone who was totally out of touch with what was about to unfold. She must not engage him, but she had to be seen focusing her attention on the Tree and, by extension, what it represented, even if she was unsure herself what that truly was.

Her silence obviously irritated him further. "I demand an explanation now, Myrella. This has gone on long enough." She heard the chair squeak as he stood up, but still she didn't move. But now, the reason for her immobility was due to her feeling something. As he moved from behind the desk, so she was sure she noticed a gentle stirring of the leaves of the Tree. As he approached her she put up a finger to halt him and then pointed at the movement. She dearly hoped that the recordings would capture it.

At the same time she felt the familiar unsettling swirling in the pit of her stomach which indicated that someone was about to arrive. Now she looked at Corrivan and as her eyes met his she inclined her head toward the Tree to drag his attention away from herself.

Then began what came to be known later simply as The Arrival. A haze began to form in the space between her desk and the Tree. It became thicker and thicker, and as it thickened, so a sound began to be heard. This grew proportionally with the solidifying air until it filled the heads and minds of the observers. As Myrella looked and the cameras recorded, the thickening air grew in circumference and, growing larger, began to dissipate as the sound that was almost a song receded until there were three people standing there: an older woman and two younger people. By now, Myrella knew all the names and so could recognize Allegara, Pelle and Bodren. They stepped forward smiling and then took in the other people there.

"Don't be concerned," said Myrella reaching her hand to them. "We're expecting the others as well. I'll explain everything when we're all here." Even now she controlled herself to not look at Corrivan. She suspected she knew what expression was on his face, but she wanted the recording to show her attention on something other than her political opponent.

Again the mist began and the same sequence of events occurred, ending this time with Dennet, Enrick and Timoss. As they stepped away, so Perray, Carmeena, Hanna, Endel and Farran arrived. Behind them were Pol and Isselta. Finally, Javin and Meldren arrived escorting the captain, Parra-Hopshan, holding on to her between them. The captain's face was one of wonder and amazement as she looked around at her new surroundings and she tottered unsteadily toward Myrella clutching a black cylindrical object tightly.

Before she could introduce everyone, Corrivan said, "What are they doing here? These are not Representatives! They have no right to be here. They are an affront to the dignity of this place and I, for one, wish to know how this magic trick was carried out." When Myrella finally turned to him, his face was puce and his eyes bulging with anger. "I demand that these people be placed under arrest immediately while the truth of who and what they are is uncovered."

"You'd arrest your own planet's ambassadors?" The quietly laconic voice of Meldren interrupted Corrivan. "For what reason, I wonder?"

"You wanted answers, Corrivan," said Myrella. "You're about to get them, and part of the answers lie in the people you see here before you."

"But-- ,"

"Sit down!" Myrella's voice was ice, her eyes cold and hard. "You demanded answers, and now you shall have them. You and everyone who watches this. It's about time you knew the truth." Beckoning the captain over, she said, "Please tell everyone, for the record, who you are and what it is that you are carrying."

"My formal name is Ensdottar Craylish Parra-Hopshan. I am the captain of the survey ship left behind when my other crew members left to take your... ambassadors back to the Empire." Interesting pause over the word 'ambassadors' thought Myrella. "Myself and the other crewman, Lessterenman, have been traveling all over this planet. This piece of equipment is the data recorder for all transmissions to and from the ship." And she held it out in front of her as the recorders zoomed in for a closer look.

"Have we heard, any of us here, have we heard what is on this recorder? And is it possible to do that now?"

"Nobody has heard, although I have told some of you about it, and it is possible to hear it. I just need to link this to your system."

As she set up the instrument, Myrella felt the beginning of a soaring sense of joy mixed with a little apprehension. She looked at Corrivan, who was watching the captain very closely, his expression guarded and cautious. When everything was complete, the captain said, as she pointed to the relevant places, "This will switch it on. This will fast forward. This will pause and this will adjust the volume."

"And is this set to play at any particular place? Any particular message, is what I mean."

"Pressing play will play the first of the last three messages my ship has received."

"And who are they from?"

"The captain of the fleet currently at the edge of the system. The first is announcing his arrival and the reasons for it and the other two are as a result of his being held up." The captain did not appear to be apologetic or unnerved by the situation. Indeed, she looked, thought Myrella, more relaxed and open than ever. Perhaps it was also a relief for her to have this situation out in the open.

Myrella noted Corrivan looking up sharply at the mention of the fleet. She felt ready to sink the knife now. "Corrivan, it is your contention that the fleet is ready to bring us many technological goods to upgrade what we currently have. Is that correct?"

Corrivan was now looking wary. He obviously suspected a trap but did not know what shape it would take. "I have been given to believe that that is the case, yes."

"You have in fact stated that publicly in a broadcast made very recently, yes?"

He nodded, unwilling to commit anything else verbally.

"In that case, would you please push that button so that we may hear the captain of the fleet." When he hesitated, Myrella said, "Come, come, Corrivan. Nobody could accuse you of planting any message on this machine and you cannot be responsible for whatever is to be heard. You said you wanted the truth, well, I believe you are about to hear it."

Reluctantly, he started the playback. The quality was surprisingly clear and easy to understand, given the strange emphasis on a few words and the slightly unusual intonation of the speaker.

"This is captain Hostwin-Capchi of PM418, lead vessel of the mining fleet summonsed by the distress beacon. Assuming you are alive, this is to warn you to evacuate the planet as soon as possible and to take up a position at least two solar units from the planet. Have your radio on constant send when in position and we will transfer you aboard this vessel. Assuming you are unable to comply for whatever reason; capture or death, anyone capable of hearing this should be advised that the fleet will touch down as soon as preliminary surveys have confirmed the original data. We will then begin mining immediately. Any resistance will be crushed severely. This is a punishment expedition, and no recognition of civil rights or liberties will be allowed. We intend to strip this planet of all useful minerals and then leave it as a reminder of what happens when any of the Empire's servants are attacked. End message."

Corrivan's face paled as the emotionless message was heard. Myrella felt a shiver of fear herself at the contempt accompanying the message.

The next message played. "Hostwin-Capchi of PM418. What is happening? We were informed that this was a lesser civilization. How can they be reducing our speed? Respond immediately! This is considered to be another attack and will bring forth a much harsher response from the Empire. Respond immediately with an explanation."

Then came the final message. "Hostwin-Capchi of PM418. We are now at a halt. We can neither go forward nor back. We have sent a message back, and the Empire will be responding with severe force. It is assumed you are all dead and that anyone who can hear this message has chosen not to respond. In which case, be prepared to see your planet destroyed as soon as the ships arrive. You have written your own death warrants. This fleet might be halted, but the rest of the Empire's firepower will deliver the final verdict on your planet."

There then followed a hissing followed by a click, and the instrument switched itself off. Despite knowing what had happened, hearing the anger and the threats like this brought a fresh chill to the atmosphere. Everyone looked stunned, except the captain, who had heard the messages several times before.

"These recordings have not been tampered with, captain?" asked Myrella.

Parra-Hopshan shook her head. "As a survey ship we have to keep all messages intact without any editing. Messages with dates and times and locations are what provide evidence for our work. We do not have the facility to alter any such message because of that."

Corrivan cleared his throat a couple of times before being able to speak. "This could of course have been doctored. There is no way of knowing, of proving that this is real." He shook his head. "I am not convinced by this, however theatrical it might be."

Myrella nodded and pressed a button on her desk. "Please have Essarin and Brokka brought here." She explained to the media, "They are the chief and assistant chief of the observatory here."

Two men, one older and balding with a belly and a beard, the other younger and with wild hair and excited eyes, entered and came down to where the others were standing. Myrella shook hands with them briefly before asking, "Tell me gentlemen, have either of you heard of any messages from space aimed at this planet within, say, the last three days?"

Essarin, the older man, nodded. "At least, we think that is what it was. We have been decoding it as best we can, but it seems fragmentary in places. It certainly seems man-made in origin but the encryption is very advanced. We have only bits and pieces so far."

"I see. Would you mind listening to this for a moment and seeing if any of it correlates to anything you have decoded so far?" And she indicated to the captain. "Please can you go back to the first message?"

As it played out, the two astronomers leaned in as if to hear better. Every now and then one of them nodded and the younger man at one point turned to his colleague saying, "That's word for word. We are on the right track!"

When it had finished and the captain had switched it off, Essarin said,

'Yes. Definitely what we received. But this is complete. How did you obtain it?"

Parra-Hopshan said, "This is my ship's recorder. It automatically decodes such messages although, to be honest, this wasn't heavily encrypted, just sent in a formal way, high speed and with low-level encryption only."

Essarin wrinkled his nose at the implication that this simple message was proving so difficult for the technology at his disposal. "I don't suppose we could have a look at your machine, perhaps?"

The captain smiled warmly at him. "Of course. Here you are." And she handed it over without a fuss, which Myrella thought was somewhat too easy. Essarin and Brokka immediately lost all interest in other things and bent their heads over the instrument as they examined it.

"I think you should go back now and begin to examine this more carefully," said Myrella, gesturing them to the doors. Turning to Corrivan, she asked, "Are you still convinced this was made up or prepared for you in some way? Or will you accept what you have heard, that the fleet you described as being friendly and helpful was, in fact, sent here to strip this planet of everything without any regard for the lives of anyone here?"

"But I was informed otherwise--," he began,

"But that did not stop you from telling everyone, did it? You never stopped to check facts. You were only interested in stirring up opposition to myself and my government. You would have brought death and destruction down on us for the simple reason that you believe that only good can come from any advanced technology, and that anything natural is automatically condemned to be irrelevant and ridiculous." She felt a relief at finally being able to say what she had known for so long. And the sight of Corrivan finally cowed and backing down and away from her was balm to heal the irritation of the preceding years.

With a sweeping gesture, she encompassed the others who had arrived so spectacularly. "These people here. The ones who arrived in such a strange fashion, these are the ones you need to thank. These are the ones who are continually fighting against your ongoing attacks on Revivalist communities. These are the ones who are showing all of us just what being in touch with nature really means. This Tree behind me, that is also there to remind us never to lose touch with nature. And yet, you want to eradicate everything which is not natural. You even said you wanted to cut down the Tree, truly the act of someone who is no longer in touch with anything resembling humanity or sensitivity." She looked down at Corrivan now slumped in her chair. "For the good of all, Corrivan, you must leave. You cannot remain. Not after hearing what we have all heard. If you don't choose to go of your own free will, I will be forced to arrest you. But before you do leave, there are some loose ends in need of clearing up. I will not have you say later that you were denied the right to hear them explained."

Here she turned to address the media crew directly. "There are some things which need to be explained but which might prove difficult to understand. Trust me when I say that it has been very difficult for me to fully accept everything I have been told. But I have witnessed enough to convince myself of the truth of it all. Now," turning to the others, "I think everyone needs to know what has happened and, if you can, how it happened. Would you," pointing to Isselta, "please, would you start?"

And so began the public unveiling of what Isselta and the others could do, each one of them adding a little more information or background. Although Myrella knew most of it, she was interested in seeing the captain become more and more intent as the information was shared. When Endel spoke, she encouraged him to share what he had accidentally set in motion, even though he was reluctant.

"Don't be concerned, Endel," she said. "This has to be a time of truth." Then to Corrivan, "And if you wish, you could say that the arrival of the fleet to punish us was caused by someone, but I think you also need to hear what the captain has to say before you start accusations." Although he looked beaten and withdrawn, she could not stop herself from saying, "Do not always jump to conclusions, Corrivan. Sometimes it's better to wait before judging."

After they had told their tales, Myrella beckoned to the captain to step forward. "Could you please tell us what would have happened if the fleet had not been sent for, if the emergency beacon had not sent its message?"

"Certainly." She looked directly into one of the cameras she spoke in a confident tone. "I was, as you know, part of a surveying crew. Our job was to locate planets and larger asteroids and evaluate them for their mineral wealth. We entered this system not knowing it was inhabited. We don't like having to deal with people usually. We make our living from the profits of the minerals found, so once we find a likely planet it is important to register our interest in it so that we get payment later. This planet, Haven, is one of the richer ones we've seen, so that we were confident we would be well rewarded. I have to say that because you are out here on your own, with no near neighbors at all, it would have been very likely that you would have had your planet stripped of anything we considered valuable, because it would have been much easier to have done that than to make you part of our Empire. There is little else in this system that is of interest to us, there are no other inhabited systems nearby and you inhabit the only planet we wanted to use. I'm sorry, but the end result would have been as if the fleet had arrived, only it would have taken longer. And my ship would have been very far away when it happened."

She hesitated a moment, glancing at Myrella as she did so. "I... I grew to love this place as we traveled around it. It reminded me of my home planet. When I heard of the fleet, I felt very bad because of what it would do. My other crew-member is now being held in one of your prisons for his threats to individuals here which arose from his attitude toward the people of this planet. I placed him there because it was the right thing to do."

Again she paused and took a deep breath as if plucking up courage. For the first time, her voice betrayed her nervousness. "As we are being open and honest here, I would like to ask you if I might be allowed to remain here on this planet and become one of you. I have skills and knowledge you would find useful. But being with the people we see here, I have learned a great deal about things I never even knew existed before, and I would like the opportunity to learn more of them." She finished with her head bowed.

Myrella had half-expected something like this, but not for it to be made this public. She said, "We are honored that you think so highly of us. But wouldn't this mean you could never go home again?"

The captain nodded. "But I would like this to be my home now."

"This is certainly something we can and will discuss," said Myrella, not wishing to get caught up in a personal story, but wanting instead to keep focus on the main objective, the over-arching theme of how to change everything on this planet.

"All that is left, I think, is how we deal with the Empire from now on. And that is something we cannot do right now, but will take some discussion." To the camera she said, "Thank you for your patience and I hope these events will help us all appreciate what we have here on this, our home, Haven."

37

Meldren looked at all the familiar faces and the one unfamiliar one and wondered how things were going to change for all of them. Now, everyone on Haven knew about the people with sprites and strange tattoos, what they were doing and why they were doing it. She was not sure how she felt about that. She also wasn't sure how she felt after hearing that her role as an ambassador had no real meaning. It was simply a diversion, a wasting of time until the Empire had what it wanted. That was the reason why nobody paid them any attention as ambassadors. On Harmony, nobody took much notice of what she and Javin did. But that was different. Here, on Haven, being somebody who was capable of doing strange things was to be in the public eye. She preferred being anonymous, she realized. But that wasn't going to be possible on Haven. Not anymore. If anyone had not yet seen the events of two days ago, they would surely have been told about them. It had certainly been one of the most important days in Haven's history. The broadcast had been a sensation, and there had been talk of nothing else. The highlights had been on virtually continual replay ever since.

In the immediate aftermath, Myrella had been besieged by calls and demands for interviews. She had been condemned and praised by her governmental colleagues in about equal measure, being variously accused of wanting to become dictator to being Haven's new saint and enlightened leader. Public opinion was also divided, with some accusing Myrella of having set everything up and that it was all faked simply to bring about Corrivan's downfall. Others praised her for her honesty and for showing what was truly important in life in such a dramatic way. The latter group was larger. In amongst these were the reports from amateur and professional astronomers about the fleet still at the edge of the system, as well as the increasingly annoyed and frustrated messages it sent out, none of which were answered, on Myrella's orders.

In amongst these appraisals of her position and actions came an ever-increasing number of reports of people claiming to be able to hear Haven's songs, of being able to transport themselves wherever they wanted and, more interestingly, of people saying that they felt a closer connection to Haven, and that they were sure that they were able to know what their little pieces of land or their gardens wanted of them. Obviously, what they had seen and heard had stirred up a whole new section of the populace to seek to interact with the natural world in a way that they had not either felt free to do before or had not thought of doing until now. How long it would last and how many of the reports were simply to gain attention, time would tell. But, at least it was a change. And that was what was important. The direction of that change could come later.

The meeting room where they had all assembled was much larger than Myrella's office. This room was normally used for larger briefings or committees where the public could be in attendance. It was light and airy with, in this instance, a large table, with gentle curves and adjustable to individual heights. There were plenty of other seats available so that everyone could at least see what was happening. Presently the room contained Myrella, Mannert, Captain Parra-Hopshan and all the singers who had answered Myrella's call to attend. This felt much more comfortable than being crammed into her office. They needed the space to think and discuss without, literally, treading on each others' toes. They were here to formulate a plan, a diplomatic response to the Empire's punitive mining fleet having arrived and been held fast at the edge of the system.

"It's plain," said Myrella, opening the meeting, "that the fleet remaining in stasis at the edge of the system is reliant on the continued singing of the Sun, and there is no reason to assume that it will always be that way. Plus, there can be no doubt that at some point in the future, more vessels with varying capabilities of long-range destruction will certainly arrive. Therefore, it is imperative that some form of a coherent plan needs to be put in place. The delivery of it is to be the role of Meldren and Javin, our ambassadors. I am open to ideas and suggestions. And, please, captain, feel free to offer your view on anything suggested. I think we may take it as fact that you are going to remain here on Haven, so you might as well start acting as if this were your home. And, if I may ask, without being impolite, how would you like us to call you? Parra-Hopshan has always sounded very formal to me and we can't keep calling you captain, but I have no wish to make you uncomfortable. How would you prefer we call you?"

Parra-Hopshan nodded her thanks at Myrella's words and hesitated a moment or two. Meldren noticed that she seemed to be gearing herself up to say something difficult and saw how the colors around her fluctuated, as if thinking of various ways of responding. "Naming is a very formal affair in the Empire, as your ambassadors have probably discovered. It shows alliances and gives rise to ranks and superiority in various forms. Parra-Hopshan is a less formal way of being formal. My rank name is Ensdottar Vannan Craylish Parra-Hopshan, which is made up of my father's name, the place and territory I was born and the two major family alliances. To my family I would be known chiefly as Ensdottar. In highly formal circumstances there would be the names of our other seven alliances added to the end. However, and in addition, each person has their own so-called 'quiet name,' which is the name they call themselves when nobody else is there, or sometimes used by immediate family. It is, if you like, how they think of themselves. If there is a strong attachment between two people, they may choose to share their quiet name with their partner. It is not mandatory, however, but if done, it is a sign of trust and commitment." She paused again a moment, eyes downcast before taking a deep breath and holding her head high she said, "My quiet name is Eslennet. Please use that when you speak to and of me from now on. It means 'country girl' in my local language, because that was where I have always felt most at home."

There was a respectful silence for a moment before Myrella said gently, "Eslennet it will be from now on. And may I say on behalf of us all here, I welcome you to your new home, and we thank you for this trust you have placed in us. We shall not let you down." As she finished, there was a general hum of warmth and welcoming that caused Eslennet's eyes to brim and sparkle. Even the sprites unwound a little and hummed gently.

Eslennet's colors had flared in response, and there was a perceptible shift in the atmosphere in the room, Meldren noted, as everyone relaxed more. She saw the colors of everyone brighten and grow so that, to her eyes at least, there was a wonderfully blended mixture of colors forming a bright cloud enveloping everyone, as if there were no individuals anymore, only one large being. The sight of it made her feel the happiest she had been for some time.

"Now," said Myrella, getting the meeting back to its original purpose. "We need to decide what we can do about the fleet and the Empire. Any thoughts so far?"

Meldren caught Myrella's eye. "I'm not sure how easy or possible it would be to persuade the Sun to keep all such ships at bay as He has done with the fleet, but we can certainly try."

"What about my ship? It's here and it's an Empire ship. Would that be a problem?" asked Eslennet.

"Maybe not," said Meldren. "We made it clear that the mining fleet was here to harm Haven. But your ship has been on Haven and there has been no damage, so I suspect He will not take action against it."

"But I still have to take Lessterenman back to the Empire. He cannot stay here in your prison. I have a responsibility to him. And that means the ship will have to leave."

"Surely not," said Javin. "Is it not possible to take him to the fleet and hand him over? Going back to the Empire would take a long time and how would you return, assuming you would be allowed to, that is?"

"But my ship is property of the Empire. It's very difficult for one person to pilot the ship. The minimum is two, so even if I take him to the fleet, how do I return? The problem is the same. I should, in honor, accompany him and then find a way to return."

"Difficult? But not impossible?" asked Meldren.

Eslennet responded with a grimace. "Difficult. But it can be done. I would not look forward to doing it."

Myrella had been tapping her finger on the table, a distant look in her eye. "I don't think it's a big problem at all, Eslennet. And here's why. I think you should take your crew-member back to the fleet, but I also think that one of these people here could accompany you. And, when all is said and done, these are very resourceful individuals and I would be most surprised if one of them at least couldn't think of a way of using a song or two to help you back here if they can't actually provide the sort of help you are used to. And before you say anything about the ship being property of the Empire, I have an idea about that as well."

Myrella leaned forward a little with a look in her eye which appeared, Meldren realized, when the President was was thinking on her feet to find a way to achieve a goal she had. "What if," said Myrella, "we were able to maintain good relations with the Empire, and that your ship, which I believe you said was incapable of interstellar travel, remained on this planet and was used as a way of trading with the Empire, whose ships would always be barred from entering the system? Could you do that, travel back and forth between the edge of the system and Haven regularly?"

"I think so, but we would need fuel and probably some alterations would need to be made to the interior. You know there is very little space inside, particularly if it is going to be used for trading."

"Perhaps we'll only be trading in small items to begin with. Or we could find ways to drag larger items into orbit." Myrella dismissed the problems with a wave of her hand. "It doesn't matter. What matters is that the ship stays here, and you teach others how to operate it and give us some help in building something bigger, if you would."

"Certainly."

Farran's voice rumbled around the room. "But the problem here is trading, isn't it? How are we going to convince the Empire that trading should happen? After all, we've stopped their punitive expedition. Why should they trust us or want anything to do with us except destroy us? I don't see how we're going to be able to persuade them."

"There's something else to consider," said Eslennet. "If we keep the ship, that's going to be seen as a huge blow to them for the simple reason that it has a complete database onboard which details all the planets they have an interest in, the sizes and types of ships and armaments, customs of various cultures and on and on. We would have much information they would prefer to control access to."

"Are we even certain we want to trade with them?" Carmeena asked. "What do we have that they could want? And do we really want the things they have? It sounds good, but will it really work in practice? I'm not so sure." It was something that Meldren had thought about. But, she said to herself, she knew so little about what people on Haven wanted or were interested in that she was sure she would not be able to recognize what they would value. She reached for and found Javin's hand under the table and gave it a squeeze. All she really wanted to do was to go back to Harmony and get on with living and traveling and simply enjoying life for its own sake. It was so much easier than this. She gave a little sigh at the thought that it would probably be longer than she wanted before she saw Harmony again.

"Good point," agreed Myrella. "Perhaps Eslennet can give us some insights?"

Eslennet appeared to be much more comfortable now that she had shared her name. "Bearing in mind the small space available, at least to begin with, then the obvious things we would want would be instructions, designs, blueprints and so on which we can use for improved instrumentation, industrial processes, spacecraft and so on. In short, data. That's what we would get from them, at least at first. As for what they would want from Haven, well you have a lot of gold here. Admittedly, it needs some specialized mining techniques to get a good quantity, but gold is a high-demand metal. It's the one we were always on the look-out for when we were surveying. So, gold first and then other rare minerals. Those are the most valued items we would offer." Looking at Carmeena, "So, yes, there would be a useful trade, although I suspect they would be trying very hard to make it as much in their favor as possible, what with this ship and everything."

"Do these specialized mining techniques cause a lot of disruption?" asked Carmeena.

Before Eslennet could answer, Pol said, "Doesn't have to cause any disruption. Not if we can sing it for them. And you and I both know we can."

Eslennet looked amazed and Carmeena nodded in agreement.

"Does that answer your question, Carmeena?" asked Myrella. "Now we come to the major problem facing us, which is how to begin negotiations. Javin and Meldren here have reported how slow everything takes and how difficult it is to even meet the right people to speak with. Getting to a negotiating position, following their rules and procedures, is obviously going to take too long. What we need now are suggestions as to how to proceed, so that we may bring this to a swift resolution. Eslennet, do you have any idea how long such things normally take?"

She shook her head. "Sadly, no. I try to avoid going there as much as possible. I really don't know much about that side of things."

Myrella looked around the table. "Well? Anyone with any ideas? And before you ask, we've already dismissed going direct to the Emperor as being too threatening."

Isselta made a suggestion. "Why don't we -- I mean Javin and Meldren -- why don't they hitch a ride with the fleet and use their communication equipment to speak with someone so that by the time they arrive everything's ready? After all, they already know we have the ability to stop them, even if they have no idea how we did it."

Myrella looked at Meldren. "How do you feel about that?"

"Not that happy, to be honest. We'd be on a ship we know nothing about, surrounded by people we don't know and who we've made quite angry, I should imagine. Not something I'd want to do. How about you, Javin?"

"I'm with Meldren on this. We can travel faster than the ship, as we've already proved. That is something I don't think they've realized. I say we should use that ability to our advantage somehow. I'm just not sure how."

Pol asked Eslennet, "Do you think the fleet's messages will have got back to the Empire by now?" When Eslennet nodded, Pol continued, "In that case, they would not expect Javin and Meldren to know about the fleet and what has happened to it. Letting someone know what they know would surely prove of interest? And that might open some doors, mightn't it?"

"Yes, but who do we ask? Who do we speak with?" Meldren was frustrated. "We've spent so long there wasting our time, I don't even know who we should be speaking to anymore. It's just another person and another person and another."

"Make the right person come to you," said Hanna.

"What do you mean?" asked Meldren, noting how closely she was seated next to Endel, and how protective he seemed to be towards her, and how their colors were blending together.

"I think I know," said Myrella.

"What?" said Meldren.

"Ah. A bit like, if you have to dig a hole, make a noise," said Javin. "It's something someone told us. All you have to do is make a big enough nuisance of yourselves so that someone has to take notice. Is that what you meant, Hanna?"

"Yes," nodded Hanna.

"And how do we do that?" asked Meldren.

"Everything you've mentioned about the place seems to be carefully controlled. Nothing natural, I think is how you described it," said Hanna, a little gleam of mischief in her eye. "How about making natural things happen to them instead?"

Meldren still couldn't see what Hanna's idea was.

"If everything is controlled," Hanna explained, "then I suppose they haven't any problems with flies or bugs or weeds. Maybe they haven't had any major storms, or a small earthquake or two might make them want to find out what's going on. All you have to do is tell someone, anyone really, that you're responsible and then sit back and wait to be found. I'm assuming, of course, that you can speak with the planet and use Her songs? And, if not, we know you can speak with the Sun, so if all else fails you could speak with Him and get Him to pass the messages on, couldn't you?"

"I suppose so," said Meldren, thinking back to her wish for insects in their garden after trying to find something natural in the world. And then she had a realization. "Actually, I think there's something else we have that would make it easier for us to negotiate. It's something they don't have, and they would love to have. But there's absolutely no way they can have it for themselves, at least not as they are presently. And I'm also absolutely positive that they would pay whatever we asked of them in order to get it. Plus there would be no need to do any extra mining on Haven."

"What is it?" asked Myrella.

"Oh, I know," said Pol, smiling. "Good idea, Meldren. Yes, you're absolutely right. They'd do anything to have it or at least to have access to those who have it."

"Am I missing something here?" said Myrella, looking a little put out at being excluded. "What is it? What is it we can bargain with?"

Meldren could hardly contain herself, but didn't want Myrella to think she was being laughed at. "It's us! We're the big thing they want. We're the ones who can talk to a Sun and it will do what we ask. We're the one's who can speak with a planet and get it do things for us. Or, we can make things happen ourselves with songs. That's unique! It's what stopped their fleet, and even they must realize that it would have been just as easy to have broken the fleet up or destroyed it as it was to stop it. Once they know that, they'll want to speak with us and deal with us as quickly as possible. I guarantee it."

"How many planets, would you say, are in that database of yours, Eslennet?" asked Javin.

"Planets? Erm... Maybe somewhere in the hundreds of thousands? I'm not sure. Why?"

"And have all those been surveyed by ships like the one you were on?"

"Not all, no."

"And how many more are there, do you think, which have not been located yet? Best guess."

Eslennet scratched at her brow as she tried to estimate. "Maybe somewhere near the same amount. More hundreds of thousands. That's if you count the smaller ones. Why?"

"Bear with me one more time," said Javin. "Out of all those hundreds and hundreds of thousands, how many do you think might have minerals that the Empire would want, even if it's only in small amounts?"

"That's much harder to say. If we're talking really small amounts then probably most of them. Again, why?"

"Because," said Javin with a smile, "what would the Empire think if we offered to speak with the various Suns and ask them if they would be willing to allow one of their planets to be mined for all the minerals that were needed, all in one place?"

"You mean in large enough quantities to make it worthwhile?"

"Absolutely."

"Oh, they'd like that very much."

"And we can do that," said Javin. "Just as Pol said about singing the gold here, we can ask the Sun to sing whatever is needed so that your Empire can take what it needs without disturbing anyone or anything else. Wouldn't that be an interesting thing to do?" He leaned back with a grin and patted Meldren's hand.

Myrella was quick to see the power of that talent. "You mean you could arrange it for whatever was required on condition that they leave us alone except to give us what we need or want? Now that's an offer I would jump at if it was made to me." She shook her head in admiration. "And you really could do that, could you? It would mean we would be in control of the trade. We'd still keep them out of our system, but with something like that, I would think we'd be able to have a larger ship and all the fuel we need in no time. Trade would be so much easier."

"But," said Endel, "that would mean you or maybe one or more of us would have to be on the ships as they approached the Suns in order to sing to them. And who knows even if one of the Suns didn't want to speak with us? What would happen then? It sounds too risky to me."

Meldren had been thinking over what Javin had said and it felt good to her. "Actually, I don't even think anyone would need to go on board a ship at all. I think it could be very easy to do. We found that all Suns talk to other Suns. They are all linked. They know each other. We only need to talk to the one Sun in order to connect to any other. It's simple." She looked around the room. "It's possible and it's safe." To Myrella she said, "If you are happy with what's been suggested, then I think Javin and I need to get started on making someone sit up and take notice of us. The details about the Suns we can discuss later."

Myrella nodded. "I can't think of anything else we need to discuss.

Has anyone any other suggestions or ideas to add?" She looked around but there were only shakes of the head. "In that case," she said, standing up and offering her hand, "I wish you both the very best of success in your negotiations."

This time Meldren did not hesitate to shake it properly.

38

The journey back from Haven was as strange and enthralling as the first time. Javin and Meldren arrived back in their embassy to fend off an alarmed Edwallan-Sipcort. He had been frantic when he had found they had disappeared, as he felt certain that someone would find out and then blame him for their being missing.

"No, we're fine. Honestly we are," said Meldren for the tenth time. He was outside and she was using the embassy's communication system in one of the main rooms to speak with him. "No, there's no need for you to come in because we're absolutely fine. Look," she said, dragging Javin into view. Javin waved. "See? Javin's here and he's got all his legs and arms and so do I. All we want to do is rest for a while. And no, I'm not going to tell you what happened to us or anything else. Just know that everything is fine and we're healthy and you have no need to worry about us anymore." And with that she ended the session and blanked him just as he was about to say something.

"How do we block him from bothering us?" she asked Javin as she scanned the instrument.

He leaned over her and tapped a few buttons and said, "I think that should do it. But we should let him call us again soon. The more we keep him out, the worse he'll get. But that should keep him quiet until tomorrow, I think. Either that, or I've ordered a meal. We'll see." He grinned at her.

They were getting used to the rooms again with their strange liquid walls that they could rearrange and the small garden that appeared so large. Bu the colors of everything seemed 'off' somehow, and the air felt stuffy and full of smells that didn't quite seem right without being unpleasant. The furniture was comfortable but of such a different design as to make sitting down and standing up something you had to give some thought to.

"Well, I don't hear anyone announcing a fresh made meal, so I suppose I pressed the right buttons," said Javin, choosing to sit on the floor where the soft surface sank a little as he did so. He patted the floor beside as an invitation to Meldren. "What we need now is a solid strategy to attract the right people. What Hanna said was a good idea, but I'm not sure what the next step is. Should we announce what we're going to do before we do it, or do it and then announce it? And who do we announce it to?"

Meldren, now settled and comfortable beside him said, "I don't know, but I know someone who does know."

"Good thinking! Yorg's bound to have an idea or two."

"But how do we get in touch with him? If we go out, Edwallan's bound to spot us and make a nuisance of himself, and I don't know how to use that thing to speak with him or how to get a vehicle."

Javin waved his hand in the air a few times using some strange gestures, and the interface opened up before him.

"Oh, very clever. How did you find that out?"

"By accident. I was poking buttons and I must have hit something which triggered the manual. And that's where I saw what to do." He was smiling as he touched a few buttons. "I think all I have to do is get his name right, and it should do the rest by itself. Ah! There it goes. It's doing something." There was a sound which presumably indicated that a connection was being made, and then a face appeared.

"Is Yorg there?" asked Javin.

The person stared back, no emotion showing.

"Yorg Bennon? Is he there? I'd like to speak with him. Please."

"Who is this?"

"It's us, Javin and Meldren," said Javin, getting Meldren to sit a little closer.

"Ah. Javin and Meldren," repeated the person in view. "Yes. Please wait a moment." And his face was replaced by a symbol of some kind.

That quickly vanished, replaced by Yorg's familiar happy face. "Well, well, if it isn't the wanderers? I've had that guide of yours round here trying to find out what happened to you, and here you are. I told my staff here to let me know the moment you made contact. I thought you might want to see a friendly face at some point. Was I right?" He beamed at them.

"Yes, you're quite right, Yorg. As usual," said Meldren. "Actually, we wanted to ask you something, as well as tell you where we've been."

Yorg held a finger up in warning. "It's so nice to see you both again. But it would be so much nicer if we could speak face to face, wouldn't it?" He gave the last words had a slight emphasis. "Shall we say tomorrow? Let's have lunch here, shall we? Do say yes."

"Er, yes. Of course. That would be fine," said Meldren, a little confused.

"Excellent! I'll look forward to it. Goodbye!" And the screen went blank and dead.

"What was that about?" asked Meldren.

"I suppose it was to stop anyone from listening in. I'd forgotten about that." Javin stretched and yawned. "Travel by Sun is all well and good, but it leaves me thirsty and hungry. I wish I had ordered a meal now. Do we have anything to eat?"

"I have no idea," said Meldren. "But I can find out." She left to poke around in various places and returned holding a small box. "I think this is food. At least, it smells like something we've eaten here. But there's not much to it."

Javin took a sniff and sighed. "You know what this means, don't you?"

Meldren nodded. "How do you get that communicator to appear again? And then how do we unblock Edwallan?"

"Edwallan-Sipcort, if you please. Especially if we want him to get us some food."

The next day they arrived at Yorg's embassy, courtesy of Edwallan-Sipcort's organizing a vehicle for them.

"Welcome, welcome!" beamed Yorg as they entered. "Please, do come this way and we'll have a long and detailed accounting of everything that has happened since I last saw you, shall we?" He bustled ahead of them and ushered them into another room where there was comfortable seating and various foods were laid out. Another warning finger was raised before he fiddled with some innocent-seeming controls on the wall.

"There," he said. "That should keep them busy for a while. I'm playing them a recording of a very long and very, very boring meeting I attended some days ago at another embassy. By the time they realize, it will be too late for them to do anything." He rubbed his hands together and grinned as if he were a young boy. "I do so love annoying them when I have the chance."

After they had begun to attack the food, Yorg asked, "So was it four days you were nowhere to be found? Your poor little go-between was quite frantic, I hear."

"To tell you the truth, I'm not that sure of the number of days here," said Javin. "But, yes, however long it was, we weren't here."

"And I suspect that the fact you are here now has something to do with when you weren't?"

"In a way," said Javin.

"So, tell me. Where did you go?"

"I don't think you're going to believe us," said Meldren, after taking a drink of some sort of refreshing juice a bright shade of green. "Before we do tell you, have you heard of anything strange or unusual happening that might have something to do with us?"

"I don't know if it has anything to do with you, but I have heard that there has been a very upset group of people who aren't normally the sort of people to feel upset. Quite high up and something to do with some ships not doing what they were sent to do. All very irregular and annoying for them. I do so hope you had something to do with it."

"If it was a mining fleet that couldn't get where it was meant to go, then, yes, that would be us," said Meldren with a little smile.

"Splendid! Splendid. Well done, whatever it was that you did." Yorg beamed at them both before his expression changed from happiness to thoughtfulness. "But if that was you, then how... ?"

Meldren, still smiling, said, "The how part is going to be very difficult to explain, but we had something to do with it, yes. There is a mining fleet, sent as punishment, which is now stuck at the edge of our system. Can't go forward or back apparently."

"Are you saying that you, both of you, have been in contact with your planet? But how? I know for a fact that you haven't been given the status of having such communications."

"More than that," said Javin, enjoying the look of interest and confusion on Yorg's face. "Both of us have been there."

His jaw dropping, Yorg pushed himself back in his seat as if to create distance from what he had just heard. "No! Impossible!"

"Actually, very possible," said Meldren. "It's a method we have used, in a different way, before this. But essentially it was something we found we could do before coming here. We simply hadn't thought of adapting it, so to speak."

"What method?"

"If we explain the how of it," said Javin, "we'll be here until tomorrow. Please just accept the fact that we have a way of traveling quickly across space. And we're not hiding it from you, and we don't have enough time to teach you the basics, which I think we could to some extent, but please know we are not telling you lies." He sighed a little knowing how inadequate his words must sound.

Yorg leaned forward, narrowed his eyes and held up his hand with thumb and forefinger close together. "If you can't tell me all of the how, can you tell me a small bit of it perhaps?"

Javin finished what he was eating and wiped his mouth before answering. "We had to convince the owner of the system that the ships were a bad thing. After that, He took care of the rest."

Yorg was clearly confused. "The owner of the system? Someone owns an entire system? Your system? What was it? Some sort of secret weapon?"

"You said you wanted just a little bit of it. Well, that is a little bit," Meldren teased.

Yorg wagged his finger at her.

"Oh, very well," she said. "But I think you're going to have a little difficulty believing it." She took a deliberate breath. "We talked to the Sun and persuaded Him that the ships were going to hurt one of His daughters. The planets are His daughters. Once we had convinced him of that, we left it up to Him to decide what to do. And He stopped them before they could do any damage." She shrugged as if to say, *Take it or leave it, but that's what I have to say.*

Yorg was silent for quite a while, studying the faces of the two guests. He slowly shook his head. "I heard every word you said, and little of it made sense. However, because I am lucky to know you, I cannot help but think that what you have told me is something very close to what actually happened. And you are right, it is not something I was expecting to hear. If, however, you were making things up as a form of entertainment for me, then could I please ask for the source of whatever drug it was that allowed you to come up with such a tale? I am sure there would be a large and willing market for it." He shook his head again, a look somewhere between surprise and acceptance on his face.

"I am assuming you didn't come here only to eat my food or to offer me fantastical tales. There has to be something else associated with your visit." He waved his hands in the air as another thought crossed his mind. "Wait a minute! Wait! You can travel from here to there quickly and easily. And nobody here knows you can do that except me? But that's an enormous power. Traveling across space with no ship, no supplies. The Empire is going to want to know more about this and that's an absolute fact."

He became serious again. "You are aware that such a skill would be invaluable and that those in possession of such a skill are in danger of attracting the Empire's interest? Once they find out you can do this, they are going to take both of you apart piece by piece until they have the secret as well. Take my advice. Tell no-one else, and then find somewhere you can live where they will not be looking. Once this comes out, and it will, it is inevitable -- don't look at me, it will come back in some fashion from the captain of the fleet or something that was overheard or inferred -- once this comes out, you will be hunted down. More so when they put together your journeying and the fleet being halted. You two have demonstrated more power than the Empire has. And without technology and without anything at all apparently, except the clothes you stand up in. I don't know whether to be amazed at you or fearful for your lives at this point. You are in danger. Both of you. Believe me on this." He looked from one to the other as if the intensity of his stare would convince them if his words hadn't yet.

Javin had listened to Yorg's song, the sounds which created his words and where they came from and knew that he was telling them the truth as he knew it. But Javin was also aware that Yorg's truth was not his and Meldren's.

"I trust that you believe in what you say, just as you have believed in what we have told you, Yorg," said Javin. "But we have taken a different point of view about it, and please don't get angry at us. The other reason we came here today was to ask you who would be the best person to tell about something we are planning to do here."

Yorg's face took on an even sterner look. "You cannot be serious. You are my only friends on this planet. I do not want to see anything horrible happening to you." Realizing his words were having little to no effect, he sighed heavily and asked, "What is it you intend to do? Knowing that may help me in offering a suggestion, as it is quite plain you are both determined to be targets."

Meldren reached to give Yorg a reassuring pat on his arm. "Yorg, I really want to thank you for wanting to help us be safe. Javin and I do know what we are doing, but we need your help for this next part to work. We need someone who will be placed well enough to make decisions, not pass us on to someone else." She smiled at him. "We are planning to make life a little more interesting for some people here."

"Interesting? That sounds too simple. What is your definition of the word 'interesting'?" Despite his misgivings, Yorg plainly enjoyed anything which would disrupt the careful formality of the place.

"Interesting in the sense of lots of insects, a storm or two and maybe even an earthquake, but just a small one," said Meldren. "We'll try to keep it very localized, but I think it might be more comfortable for you if you were not here when it happened."

"You're telling me, with straight faces, that you can do those things?"

"Put it this way," said Javin. "We know someone who can do those things. They just need to be asked."

Yorg put up his hands in defeat. "I know when I will not understand the answer. So, tell me. What is the end result you are looking for? What's the point of whatever it is you are planning?"

"That's simple," said Meldren. "We want to be able to negotiate with someone powerful enough to make decisions about how things will be between our planet and this Empire. We want someone who has enough power to not only make the decisions, but to enforce them as well."

"My, my, my," said Yorg in an appreciative tone. He puffed out his cheeks and scratched his neck as he looked at her. "Fast track negotiations at the highest level. You are aiming high. And I happen to know the person to contact for such a thing. In fact, you probably know him as well. He's that insufferable idiot in charge of ambassadors. You met him, no doubt. In fact, I know you did, because we first met at the awful lunch with the Emperor, and you had just come from there if memory serves."

"Him?" said Meldren. "I never did like him. But if he's the person we need to contact -- to warn, actually -- then it will serve him right."

"I can give you the details of how to contact him. He's perfect, because he's in charge of all ambassadors to the Empire, so if one set of them, that is your own sweet selves, causes big problems, he is going to find out who he can pass you on to as quickly as possible. And he knows just about all of the truly important people there are to know. If anyone can get you in touch with who you need to speak with, he's the one."

"That would be wonderful," said Javin. "Thank you so much. As soon as we've contacted him we'll get started, so I suggest you leave for somewhere pleasant, say tomorrow or the day after?"

"I will do that, indeed. But, before I give you the details, I have a favor to ask of you."

"Certainly," said Meldren. "Ask away."

"Well," said Yorg, leaning in conspiratorially, "when you get to negotiate with them, can I please accompany you both? As an observer? I so want to see their faces when they see the both of you there. It will be the happiest day of my life since I arrived here."

"Consider it done," said Meldren smiling hugely. "We'll be happy to have you observe."

39

E messor-Patkillin-Thren's main secretary handed him a message, over which he cast an eye and then handed it back. "Is this some sort of joke? What does it mean?"

The secretary held it out again. "They were most insistent that you should be made aware of this."

"So... ? I have been made aware. You have done your job, and you may now go and do some other job. I'm sure there are many waiting for you."

"Indeed, honored sir. But I should point out that the two people who sent this are the same two who seemed to have disappeared for several days and whose planet was the target for the punitive mining fleet."

"Are you saying that these two are responsible for what has happened there?"

"I am merely saying, honored sir, that there is a correlation between these events and that, as such, it might be prudent were you to ask for a closer surveillance."

He snatched the note from his secretary and re-read it. "Are you honestly telling me that they can predict a thunderstorm and an earthquake, neither of which has occurred for more years than I care to think about?"

"With respect, honored sir, they are specifically saying that they are going to bring such things about, not that they are predicting them. It is more that they are saying that they can create them. Given the current status of the mining fleet, it might be prudent to at least consider that they might have some special effects at the ready or, and this is the less likely outcome, that they can indeed bring such things about."

"And insects? Really? Insects? We have long since sanitized this whole planet. Insects are no longer here. There is no... I believe the term is 'ecological niche', for them to fill. Insects cannot arise from nothing. That is ridiculous. They are ridiculous and this note is ridiculous." He was about to walk away when he turned back and asked, "How did we receive this message?"

"It was sent using the correct identification code, with the appropriate clearance codes and using the correct tech."

He was now puzzled rather than irritated. "But that would mean they had access to tech we have not yet given them. They are lacking full accreditation, and therefore lacking full range of tech. They have not been given this office's confidential address. And yet here they are," shaking the message capsule. "Someone must have provided them with the tech and the address. So are you still sure that it is the same two?"

"Absolutely, honored sir. The automatic bio scans show it was these two, and those scans are, as you know, very hard to alter in any way. I am convinced of the truth of who they are."

"And they had help. Well, when this passes, we'll bring in whoever helped them and reduce their role and authority here. Maybe threaten to sever diplomatic ties or have them deported for a period. Because it will not happen, what they have said. And it will not happen because it cannot happen. Is that clear?"

"Certainly, honored sir."

Emessor-Patkillin-Thren had more than enough to occupy himself, and the message or warning was ignored. Other ambassadors to be verified and accredited, embassies to be welcomed and the myriad formalities required of himself and his office took all of his time.

Toward the end of the second day after the arrival of the message, he was enjoying a relaxing drink in his inner office, scanning reports from his agents around the palace, looking for anything which might catch his eye. The door was firmly shut and all his staff knew that he was never to be disturbed, the walls would remain in place and the whole door remained opaque until he himself cleared it.

He looked forward to this time of the day, because it meant that it was nearly over and he could focus his attention on what alliances might be worth pursuing for his second son. The agents' reports were all concerned with who was in negotiations with whom and over what. He was always looking for the small pieces of news, the hints, which might give him leverage in any contacts he might have. He had not arrived at his much envied status by accident!

This oasis of peace and planning was interrupted by a small but irritating noise, something like a tiny electrical arcing sound. It came and went, and the very irregularity of it attracted his attention. He reluctantly placed his drink on the table and spent some time with one ear cocked, trying to identify the direction and possible location of the intrusive noise. He even went so far as to get down on his hands and knees to examine any possible problems around or near the electrical connections that he could see, not knowing enough about them to be able to determine whether it was even possible that they could be the source of the noise, which now seemed to have stopped. He was glad that nobody could see him acting in such an undignified manner. On his hands and knees! The gossip it would have caused. The harm it might have done to his stature with his equals. It did not bear thinking about. He shook himself free of such thoughts.

Finding nothing, he returned to his seat and reached for his drink. He was about to take a sip when something in the ornate glass vessel caught his eye. For a moment he thought that there was some sort of blemish in his drink. But then a closer look showed that it was a small insect floating on the surface. His immediate reaction was to hurl the glass away and he shuddered at the thought of how close he had come to swallowing it. But then he hurried over to where the liquid had spilled on the floor and once again got down on all fours to more closely examine it. Again, he felt gratitude for the opaque office. He felt the protection of some form of providence in keeping such a scandalous site from underling's eyes. It took him more than a moment or two, but he eventually located the tiny body in amongst the shards of the vessel. He snapped some images of it and used them to perform a search after activating the cleanerbot to remove the debris and dry the floor.

The results showed him that the dead creature was indeed a real creature, not a figment of his imagination, and that it should not be there at all because the last time one of them was noted was about twenty years before when the entire insect kingdom was under process of eradication.

"Impossible!" he said to himself. "Preposterous and impossible." And yet there it was. Dead, admittedly. But real and dead.

The experience had left him ill at ease. Something like this was unthinkable, or should be unthinkable. His was a world of control and order and correctness at all times in all things. There was no room in it for something which should not exist. It made everything unbalanced. He knew he was no longer able to focus on field reports, but seeing something normal was necessary to re-establish his equilibrium, he checked his clothing and ran his hands over his hair to ensure it was as it should be before opening his office.

As the walls cleared and the door spun back, his jaw dropped. Instead of the quiet hum of activity, of forms being requested and scanned and all the normal soothing activities of his department, he saw chaos. Everywhere his staff were seen to be running around, slapping at the air or their bodies and screaming or yelling. He was too amazed to order them back to work at first, but then, he heard the same electrical, buzzing sound he had first heard in his office. Insects! In his department! There were hundreds, possibly thousands of them.

Taking a deep breath, he put his head down and sprinted across the room, colliding with a few people, and found his way eventually to the outside. Trusting that nobody had recognized him and also that nobody had noticed his strange appearance outside, he took some moments to regulate his breathing and to try to suppress the fear he now felt gnawing at him. This was wrong. In every sense of the word, it was wrong.

It was then that he recalled his assistant presenting him with that strange message. Hadn't it referenced insects? Something to do with insects appearing. He couldn't recall the details. It was obviously a prank or a misdirected message. And yet, here were insects. Could there really be connection? He shook himself. That was too ridiculous to entertain. Nobody could forecast such a thing, particularly something which should be non-existent. This had to be the result of someone somewhere making a mistake. He would find out who it was. Perhaps some idiot had been showing off to someone important that they could activate old genetic material, and it had got out of hand. He would find them and make sure they knew exactly who they had as an enemy. He would make very sure that they were off-planet and heading to some frontier outworld in as short a space of time as possible.

Planning revenge helped to restore his usual tranquility and he decided to enter the department again as if for the first time and began to organize everyone into getting rid of the creatures.

The following day, his secretary approached him again and handed him a message. It purported to be from the same two imbeciles as before.

He had scanned it before realizing who it was from. Then he hurled it from him and rounded on his assistant. "This is ridiculous! I cannot be expected to believe any of what they say."

The assistant was on his knees collecting the broken parts of the message.

The fact that there was no reply angered him. "What is the point of sending such messages anyway? What is it they expect to achieve? Do they think they are able to threaten me with storms? There have been no storms allowed here ever since we regulated the atmosphere. The Emperor would be most distressed by a storm. It would imply that not everything was under his control. So, I repeat, what is the point of this?"

"Toward the end of the message, honored sir, they did make plain their request." Did he detect a hint of disrespect in that voice?

"What? What did they request?" he said, lacing the last word with heavy irony.

"Discussion of trade relations between their planet and the Empire, honored sir."

"How can they discuss anything? They're not even accredited as ambassadors. They have no standing, no rights, no access to such negotiations. This obviously is someone out to make trouble." He thought a moment. If anyone wanted trouble with him, they would receive it. "Have them brought here as soon as possible. I shall make it my business to find out who is behind this and what role they are playing in this game. Because, quite evidently, they are incapable of having any discourse with anyone for quite some time yet. Not until we have resolved their status at the very least. But they might be being used by someone else. I shall find out who that is." He snapped his fingers at his assistant. "Fetch them here. Now." And then he dismissed him with a wave of his hand.

He channeled his frustration and anger into his work, sending back two potential ambassadors from some ghastly planet with a very long list of requirements they would need to provide quickly before their planet was placed under Imperial interdict, and another pair were summarily stripped of access to various levels of technology for some negligible problem. He felt much better.

It was as Emessor-Patkillin-Thren was preparing what exactly he would do and say to those two annoying individuals about their incredible messages that he noticed a certain darkening taking place. He checked the time and noted that it was not yet night, as he had at first suspected. He faded out the top half of his outer wall to see directly. At that exact moment, as he looked up at the strange darkness of the bulging clouds, a sight only seen in his early youth, a stabbing slash of light made him flinch and put his hands up as a protective reflex. Almost instantly it was followed by the most horrendous rumbling and cracking sound which caused him to let loose a squeal of fright and surprise. The two events had obviously had the same effect on his staff, some of whom flung themselves on the floor whilst others cowered against the nearest wall. As he blinked to clear his vision, there came a growing thrumming sound which, to begin with, he could not understand. But when he saw the torrents of water pouring from the clouds and the rain, yes, actual rain! pounding into the pavements and pathways, and churning the earth into a brown froth, he knew that this was the biggest storm he had ever witnessed. It was probably the first storm witnessed by most people in his office.

Lightning lanced almost continuously as the thunder growled and rumbled, shaking the building. And the water, now as rain, now as hail, whipped by the winds into an angry beast attacking the land, lowered visibility until it seemed he was held within the fist of the storm itself and that it was venting its anger solely at him.

When, finally, it had exhausted itself, he, too, felt emptied and drained of emotion. He felt battered by the sound, and whipped by the winds so that all he wanted to do was hide and not see the world outside with the new pools of water and the washed out trees and uprooted plants neatly stacked against the bottom of his window where the torrents had deposited them.

The following day, the mess of the storm was still being cleared away. He discovered that it had been a very localized incident and that nobody else's offices had been affected to the same degree. Mud marks along the walls and windows still remained, profoundly unsettling in their evidence of disorder. In an angry mood, he stomped into his office and then recalled that he had demanded to see, but had not yet seen, the individuals supposedly involved in this disruption. It did not improve his emotional state. He called for his secretary. "Why did you not bring me those people?"

"Honored sir, they refused to come with me."

Shock! This could not be! "You showed them your badge of office and told them I was expecting them?"

A slow and respectful nod.

"And they refused? Unheard of! What reason did they give?"

"That you were not ready to negotiate or introduce them to those who would, honored sir."

"Did they say they were responsible for the storm?"

Another nod.

"But how can they be?" he exploded. "This is ridiculous. We cannot keep having the work of this department disrupted. They must know that, surely?" To have been shown his badge of office and to have refused to present themselves? It went against every formality. The disrespect for his office, for himself, was unprecedented. This was something he was not used to at all. It was new and very upsetting. Rubbing his hands over his face and breathing out slowly, he decided to give them one last chance.

"Give them this message from me and mark it urgent. They have one day to present themselves to me and to explain who is behind this... this... mess, or they will have cause to regret being here."

Shortly afterwards, the assistant returned, holding another message. "Honored sir, they replied directly. And are asking for a reply."

Emessor-Patkillin-Thren was, for possibly the first time in his life, lost for words. He tried to gather himself and calm his emotions, but it took longer than ever before. "They seriously expect me to pass them on to someone who will negotiate with them now? Or, as they say, 'this department will crack apart'? What does that even mean? I will see that their world is destroyed and that they are exiled to the smallest and loneliest moon in the Empire for this." He took several more deep breaths to try to contain his anger. He made an extra effort to return the message calmly to his assistant. "They will regret this. There is no reply possible. Make that plain."

As his assistant bowed and moved to leave, so Emessor-Patkillin-Thren thought he felt a little dizzy. The sensation grew and then left just as swiftly, but he felt his chair moving beneath him. The walls seemed to sway a little and objects fell to the ground. Desks and equipment appeared to be on wheels and made efforts to roll back and forth. His overwhelming sensation was that he was powerless, unable to sit, unable to stand or walk. The ground was not the fixed and stable thing he knew, but had somehow become a fluid and unreliable creature, almost alive, it seemed.

The shifting increased and his fear with it. From somewhere close by there came a groaning sound, the sound of something large being torn apart. A part of his mind not currently being afraid wondered what it could be, but then the answer revealed itself. It was his office, his whole building, which was being torn apart. Cracks zig-zagged their way up the wall opposite. The window behind him fell apart with one dull snap. The floor began to bulge and parts of the roof began to fall down, some smaller pieces brushing against his shoulder. All he knew was that he had to escape, get outside. He half crawled, half fell out the now gaping hole where his window had been and began to crawl on his hands and knees across the swaying, bucking ground which was still soaking from the previous day's storm. He heard whimpering and realized it was coming from his mouth. He kept crawling and crawling, trying to put as much distance as he could between himself and the building. Once, he glanced behind and saw the building seeming to sag on one side before tipping gently toward the ground as if it was tired.

Finally, the surges beneath him, the unnatural movements, came to an end and he found himself sitting on the wet earth hugging his knees to him as his whole body shook uncontrollably and what had once been his office, his department, his whole life, was now nothing more than a heap of rubble. All around him, his staff were crying, helping each other or wandering in a dazed state. Amongst them, he saw his secretary, seemingly ignorant of blood from a head wound flowing down his face. Emessor-Patkillin-Thren beckoned to the man, but when there was no recognition, he decided to forego his dignity and go to him. He sat with his secretary until there was recognition and awareness in his face. At that point, he said, "Tell them I will make the necessary arrangements."

40

S everal days after Javin and Meldren returned to Haven to report the success of their mission, they were able to persuade the Sun to release the fleet. The Empire's Sun, after Javin and Meldren had spent quite some time trying to convey to It what they had wanted, had sung what had happened and that had persuaded Haven's Sun to release the ships. The fleet had not left, however, as they had been tasked with taking back the other crewman, Lessterenman, and had to wait for the ship to carry him to them. By the time the handover had been made and Eslennet had recorded a formal renunciation of all her family's alliances and properties, the fleet's crew were running dangerously low on food. They would, their captain thought, have only just enough to make it to the nearest base. When Haven's astronomers finally announced the fleet's departure, there were wild celebrations across Haven.

The distant sounds of one of these huge parties formed the background to a meeting in the largest of the committee rooms. Not everyone present could fit at the table, but there were plenty of seats available offering a view of the proceedings. Myrella was chairing it. Javin and Meldren were there, as were all the singers and the main representatives of the various political parties, except for Corrivan, who was nowhere to be seen, his alliance having been torn apart by the events of the past weeks and his support completely evaporated. In his place, however, Myrella was pleased to see several representatives of the Revivalist movement had accepted her offer to attend. They were sitting close together toward one end of the table and looking uneasily around them. She hoped they would become a useful political voice in the near future, adding their insight as to how they saw the world to the considerations of the Assembly.

"We have had final confirmation of the departure of the fleet and that our only little spacecraft, our entire fleet so to speak," she let a smile into her voice, "is due to arrive back here in about three days. Eslennet was confident that she could manage on her own. Thanks to our ambassadors, Javin and Meldren, we now have what is apparently a unique relationship with the Empire. You have probably read some of the details or heard them being debated in one form or another. However, this meeting was called in order to flesh out those details and allow us all to fully understand what this new relationship actually entails. After Javin and Meldren have spoken, any questions you have left will be answered as fully as possible." She tipped her head in inquiry at the two of them, who nodded in agreement. "Good. So, if we are all ready?" and she gestured at them to begin.

Meldren began. "I'm not sure how many of you are aware of how Javin and I are here, how we arrived here, I mean. And some of you may not know what talents we have, talents which are shared by some others in this room. It will make things easier if we start off there and then, when we get to what happened, it might make a little more sense." She looked around, noting the familiar and the unfamiliar faces. "We," she said as she tipped her head to include Javin, "have a way of understanding what this planet wants." That caused a rustle of attention amongst the unfamiliar faces. "More than that, we can also understand what the Sun wants or doesn't want. It's actually more complicated than that, but it comes down to the fact that everything we can see or hear is made from songs. And, if you can hear the songs and can sing them yourself, then... ," she shrugged.

"I've heard about this. I've seen The Arrival but I still don't accept it.

Are you saying that I'm a song?" demanded a man on the far side of the table to Meldren. "Because that's crazy. It makes no sense. How can I be a song?" He looked angry at the notion.

Javin answered before Meldren could begin. "The simple answer is yes, you are a song, just as everyone here is. And that doesn't make you less or strange in any way. All it means is that this planet we're all on decided to sing songs to bring people into existence, and here you are."

"But that doesn't explain our ancestors, does it? They arrived here by chance. The planet didn't sing them into existence."

"I've read about your history," said Javin. "Hasn't it ever occurred to you that it all seemed a little too much of a coincidence? Was it pure luck?" He shook his head. "You arrived in this system with inhabitable planets despite the fact that you were essentially out of control. And you arrived safely without any loss of life. Luck? I don't believe that for one moment. I believe it was the Sun who brought you here. And you came from a place which had another Sun. You can't escape planets and Suns."

The angry man dismissed that with a wave of his hand. "But what of the decisions I make, the things I create with my own hand? They are me, aren't they? They're not a song."

"To the planet, they are the way you sing your own song. The things you do, how you act, they are the ways you express what you are. And what we all are -- every single person -- are little songs. Some of us choose to sing them, or express them, as artists, or farmers or," and here he gestured toward Myrella, "politicians. Some of us love the life we live and others are never satisfied. But we all start out the same, as babies, as songs with the potential to sing them as loud as we want or as quietly as we like. Just like one song can be sung by a choir or by someone who is tone deaf. The song is the same, but the way it is sung is different."

"I still think this is nothing more than gibberish, spouted by people who have no real grasp of science or who have no true understanding of the world." He was not to be satisfied so easily. Myrella knew that and knew also that he represented many, many others. She knew when she convened this meeting that there would have to be some explanation of how Javin and Meldren worked. She reckoned that if the two ambassadors could persuade people in this room, professional skeptics most of them, then those others beyond, the ones partying in the streets, would begin to come round to the idea that there were far stranger and more interesting things going on around them. And the sooner they understood that, the sooner her government would be able to set about creating a world where the needs of the planet itself were given equal consideration. It would not be swift or even easy, but this, she hoped, would be one of the first steps.

Meldren smiled, seemingly undeterred by the antagonism coming across the table. "I know this is hard to believe, and we're not asking you to accept our word for it, but, if nobody objects, we'd like to show you." She glanced at Myrella who nodded her to continue. Leaning forward, Meldren asked, "What if we were to show you how this works?"

That was met with a contemptuous 'humph'.

She looked around the room and asked, "I know you've heard from some of the people here," her gesture embraced the other singers, "about what they can do. But not everyone has witnessed what that actually means. Talk of songs and talents is not the same as seeing it for yourselves. If we are to convince you of what we have helped to bring about, it will make for an easier understanding between us. We're not going to show you something we've prepared, in case you'd suspect we were cheating somehow." She smiled and her gaze took in the room again. "Does anyone here have something they would like to see? Something we could bring into this room? Not too big, obviously, or too active."

One of the Revivalists, a thin-faced, tired looking woman with her hair scraped back into a tight bun, was one of the first to raise a tentative hand. Meldren nodded encouragingly at her and got a nervous smile in return. "I'd like to see a rocking chair." She paused, biting her lip as if unsure of herself now she had started. "We tried to make one, but it doesn't work. They keep breaking. But I'd love to see what a good rocking chair looks like, so I can go back and make one for myself. I've always wanted one." She looked down at her hands clasped in her lap.

Meldren looked to Javin. "A rocking chair?"

"It's like an ordinary wooden chair. Remember the ones we had back on Harmony? Like those but with curved pieces of wood under legs so you can rock back and forth when you sit on it." He swayed back and forth as he spoke.

"Oh, wasn't there one at Newgrange? Or am I thinking of some place on Harmony? Is that the one you have in mind, Javin?" She smiled as he nodded. "We'll certainly do that," said Meldren. To the rest of the people she said, "We'll sing one here for you. Or, rather, with the help of these sprites round our necks we'll sing one for you." She laid a gentle hand on the creature which always accompanied her. Then, grasping Javin's hand, she said, "If you would please just watch, we'll sing it onto this table." Then both of them took a steadying and relaxing breath. Bowing their heads, Myrella thought they looked as though they were listening for something tantalizingly near, yet just out of her reach. Then they began to sing. A strange, lilting sound, almost a tune, fluctuating in rhythm, began to be heard. As it developed, so the sprites unwound a little and reached upwards. As they extended, so they added their voices. The result sounded like a great deal more than four individuals. It also, Myrella noticed, seemed to draw in to the center of the room, not filling the far corners, but almost coagulating into a smaller area above the table. As she noticed that, so a small disturbance appeared, like the air of a mirage, trembling and moving, hiding and revealing shapes. Unlike a mirage, however, the air thickened and seemed to become more solid and, as it did so, a chair began to become evident. The outline seemed shaky at first, but then the details appeared and the structure became more definite until, with a final chorus, a beautiful rocking chair was resting on the table, moving gently back and forth.

There was silence for a beat and then many voices began all at once. Myrella, who never tired of seeing what songs could do, was herself unable to voice what she truly felt, but gathered herself enough after a few seconds to rap loudly on the table and call for quiet.

"I hope that is to your liking," said Meldren to the Revivalist woman, who nodded and nodded and smiled at her with shining eyes, as if unable to speak for pleasure.

To the rest of the room she added, "That is an example. And we're not the only ones who can do this. The others here, they can do the same. You've heard about this, but seeing it is often quite different. We also know that there are many, many of you who can do what you have just seen. It needs practice and guidance. And, if you are able to do it well, and if the planet trusts you, you will know, because you will wake up one day with the same marks on your cheeks as some of the people here have," she said indicating Pol and Endel and the others.

There were a variety of looks shared: amazement, interest, puzzlement, but none, that Myrella could see, which indicated outright rejection. Someone removed the chair from the table and placed it near the Revivalist woman. Myrella raised her voice to get attention and said, "I am sure that, outside of the confines of this room, Meldren and Javin would be delighted to show what else they can do. Or, so would any of the others who share this talent. Now, if we may continue with the main purpose of this meeting?"

Javin and Meldren then shared what had happened and how they had finally gained access to those who had the power to confirm negotiations, and they brought everyone up to date with what had been discussed and confirmed. They showed the authorization of the trading contract, which looked like a black box, but was, they assured everyone, the legitimate object and that, even now, it was transmitting a steady signal which would inform any ship approaching the system that they were an accredited trading partner and that the data stream indicated the exact terms of the contract.

"It doesn't look like very much," said Javin, but it is apparently far more powerful than it's size suggests. "We had a friend check it for us and he said it was transmitting properly. I'm sure when Eslennet returns she will also verify it as well. All I can tell you is that I can listen to it and I can hear something quite powerful coming from it. Apparently it can't be easily broken or taken apart either." He held it up briefly for everyone to see.

"So you're saying that this box, this contract, all this was agreed to because you threatened to cause all sorts of natural disasters if they didn't?" The same man who was dismissive of them earlier was asking the question. "What is to stop them from sending something nasty our way? An asteroid, for example?"

"That's easy," said Javin. "Anything like that, like the fleet that recently left, anything which would threaten us here, it would be stopped by the Sun."

"How?"

"Well, just as we can hear the songs and sing some of the simple ones, the Sun is where all the songs come from." He put up his hand to stop the inevitable question. "The Sun is responsible for the planets and this whole system. The planets are responsible for what happens on them and we are responsible for what we do with what we are given. That's about as simple as I can make it"

"I'll have to accept what you said, although it sounds highly unlikely," said the man, whom Myrella finally identified as one Hassik, a representative of some industrial area way over to the east. Given his power base, it was less than likely that he would be an immediate convert to this new perspective. "And you're saying," he continued, "that they decided to negotiate and keep such agreements because you can threaten them, is that it?"

"Not exactly," said Meldren. "We used those tactics to get their attention, as they had no intention whatever to speak with us. The fleet was evidence of that. When we did finally get to talking, we then offered them something which we knew they would find valuable."

"Ah, that's the offer to get other planets to give up whatever these Empire people wanted. Is that right?"

"Again, not exactly. We offered to find out which planets wanted to help and which didn't. And those who did, we would work with them to make sure they got the minerals they needed. A lot of it has to do with gold, I think. That and platinum, if I remember. That's what they want. And if we can make it easy for them, that's to their advantage."

Hassik was still frowning, not willing to accept what had happened. "And what would happen if one of them decided to capture or kidnap you and force you to agree to a different treaty to the one you say we have at present? They have a lot of weapons, I imagine, and a lot of ways of using them. I mean, there you are, off on some ship or other talking to a planet," here he used his fingers to make quote marks, "and all they have to do is keep you there while they turn on us here."

Javin nodded to show he understood the concerns. "Firstly, it wouldn't be us going anywhere. There needs to be a new set of ambassadors and we'll address that issue in a moment. But, any of us who can do this talking to planets thing is going to be in contact with both that planet and the Sun. You've seen for yourself how we can hear songs. It's just that simple to sing them, to sing a message to a Sun saying we're in trouble. Or even asking for the Sun to keep watch over us. You've already seen what happens when an unwanted fleet appears. And, as we said a little earlier, there are ways of using songs to travel. If we felt in danger for any reason, we could leave a ship and go back without their help. It maybe that it would be just as effective to stay on their planet and make contacts through that Sun. That needs to be looked at in more detail. I appreciate your concerns, but we have thought of the same things and we've proven we don't need any ships to travel." He looked around the room. "Who knows? Maybe that will be the way all of us in the future will travel."

Myrella looked at the faces as they were processing that last piece of information. Giving them the idea that they could travel wherever they wanted? That was temptation. And it would help motivate more and more people to learn what exactly they could achieve. There was a great deal to think about for some of them. "If there are no further major points to discuss, I'd like to move on to ask about what was meant by the new ambassadors just now."

Meldren looked a little sheepish. "Myrella, neither Javin nor I want to keep on doing this. We got chosen, and we did what we could, and we think we did a good job. But, honestly, we don't want to do it anymore." With a gesture she indicated the simple clothes she wore. "We like living a simple life. We like the country and being out where we can hear the natural songs of our home, Harmony. Most of what has happened to us has happened without our seeming to have had very much choice about where we were or where we ended up, or even what we had to do. We'd like to step down and go home and live our lives for ourselves and by ourselves." She looked lovingly at Javin. "We want to be together, on our own."

"I can understand that," said Myrella with a smile. "There are times when I have the same feelings as you. But who will take your place?"

"That's easy," said Meldren, pointing to one side where the others with their markings and their sprites were sitting together. "Any of those could do what we have done. But Javin and I have given it some thought and we think the best people to go would be Endel and Hanna there."

At the mention of their names, Hanna blushed and Endel seemed to squirm in his seat a little. Myrella knew that he was the one who had inadvertently caused the fleet to arrive, and that he still felt guilty about it.

"They're both young and in need of a few adventures, and they like each other. A lot," said Meldren with a huge grin, causing more squirming and blushing. "They're also incredibly talented, and I think seeing someone young like them will make it obvious just how many amazing and talented people there are on this planet. They're also clever enough not to get into trouble."

Myrella had to admit to being surprised at the nominations, but could see what Meldren meant. "So what do you two think of this?"

"I would very much like to go," said Hanna, casting sidelong glances to Endel.

"Same for me," he said, smiling broadly.

"I have no objections that I can think of. Does anyone else have any objections or points to raise about this?"

Hassik, inevitably, raised his hand. "This is not the proper way of dealing with this issue. Surely we should have at the very least a list of suitable candidates with some sort of questioning or interviewing process to enable us to decide who would best represent our interests? Are they even married? Or are we sending people who just want to live together? What sort of impression does that give?"

"I have learned that neither Javin nor Meldren are married in the way we think of it, and I really doubt that should be an issue here." Myrella looked at the couple. "As long as they act with dignity and keep our best interests in mind, I care nothing about how they live privately. As for other candidates, the only suitable ones I know of are sitting here with us. If any of them can do half of what Javin and Meldren have done, then I am happy with them representing us. If you know of any other such candidates, I am sure we would be most interested in interviewing them."

Hassik pursed his lips and glared at Myrella a moment before averting his eyes and shaking his head.

"Very well then, let's assume that this meeting, the major part of it anyway, is over, and anyone who wants to learn more about what you have heard today, about songs and planets and so on, find a place to talk about it. Those of you who are happy with what you have heard, I would suggest joining a party somewhere. There seem to be some still going on not too far away. And as for Javin and Meldren, I would appreciate it if you would come to my office before you leave."

The meeting broke up into small groups, each of which was centered around one or more of those who were coming to be more widely known as Singers (with a capital 'S'). The Revivalist woman -- she really would have to learn names -- ran her fingers over the rocking chair looking very happy before easing herself down onto it and rocking gently. She watched Hassik stand with a frown on his face to one side of the room before moving slowly toward a bunch of people around Pol. She smiled a little and then turned away. It would all work out. It would take time, but it would all work out.

Back in her office, Myrella kicked off her shoes and stretched. She poured herself a large, strong drink and reviewed the recent events. She had shown the people of Haven a new way of looking at the world, she had got rid of her main political opponent, and she had a very favorable trade agreement with a very large Empire, despite only having one tiny ship which only one person, at the moment, could pilot. Not bad. Not bad at all.

She was interrupted in her thoughts by Javin and Meldren entering.

"Ah. Thank you for coming here," she said, offering to pour them each a drink, which they declined with a shake of their heads. "And thank you for all you have done for us." She sank gratefully into a chair and inclined her head to invite them to sit as well. "I don't think we could have survived without you, but I really don't know how to say thank you in a big enough way."

"There really is no need," said Javin, dismissing the thought with a little shrug. He placed the box they had displayed earlier on her desk.

Myrella took a sip of her drink and regarded the two of them from over the rim of the glass a moment. Putting it down on the floor she said, "Are you really certain about those two you nominated to take over? I must admit it caught me by surprise. I wasn't expecting it. But I went along with it because I've come to respect what you say and do. But, I have to say, I still have reservations about them. Put my mind at ease, if you please."

"We're not going to suddenly disappear. Before we do go back, we'll have made sure that they know everything we have learned about dealing with the Empire. I hear they've been learning to read and write, which will probably be of some use." Meldren leaned forward, resting her forearms on her thighs as she spoke. "More than that, we'll take them there and make sure that they can travel by themselves. Don't worry. By the time we go home again, they'll be well prepared."

Myrella chose to ignore the news about their lack of literacy but determined to have them tutored starting right after this meeting. Instead she focused on the other concern she had. "But aren't they rather young for this?"

Meldren said, "Both of them have already had more experiences in their lives than either of us had at their age. They also are really very much in love." Waving a finger to include Javin, she said, "We can see it in them. Their songs, the colors around them; they are going to be the perfect couple. We know it without a doubt. But, more to the point, they, along with the others who we first met when we rescued them, have an amazing talent. In many ways, they are stronger and better than us. Think of Pol and Isselta? You know some details about them and how they think and act. They do the unexpected, and they do it very well indeed. Well, it's just the same for Hanna and Endel. They are the best ones for this. Don't forget also that Endel still feels responsible for the threat from the fleet. He'll be very determined not to make any more mistakes. And, if you are undecided, you could always ask the Tree."

Myrella puffed out her cheeks in a sigh and picked up her drink again. After taking another slow, reflective sip she said, "If I agree to this, then I'll do it with one proviso. You have to be available if we need you. If you are certain about these two, then it shouldn't be an issue. Well? Will you agree to that? For my sake, if for nothing else?"

"Of course we will." Meldren's smile was even wider now. "We'll be ready if you need us. But I don't think you will. And if you do need us... ,"

"I know," said Myrella with a wry smile. "Just go and tell the Tree." She shook her head and smiled at how something which had at first seemed so strange had now become almost second nature. "So what are you two going to do now? You could join in one of the parties going on."

Javin looked at Meldren then at Myrella. "No thanks. Too many people. Sleep sounds good," he said.

"Eventually," said Meldren with an impish grin.

41

"I'll do this if you will."

"But you're the one who hates water. I don't hate it. I'm fine about it."

"I didn't say I hated it. I just don't like it in large quantities. Things like oceans or big rivers. I don't like being in it, and I don't like sailing or floating on it. It's not safe. It never feels safe. Which is why I'll do this if you will."

Meldren looked at Javin and smiled. They were seated on the edge of a wide water-hole formed by a partial dam lower downstream. The water wasn't too deep. Javin knew that because he had listened to it. It was clear and cool and the day was warm. Nevertheless, he was eyeing it as if it was about to snap at him. His toes were barely touching it. She was gently swinging her legs so that she was making small waves which rippled out across the surface. They had found this pool after hearing about it from some of the people in the nearby village of Highcloud. It was the swimming pool for the villagers, hence the dam. In return for some stories as payment for their food and lodgings, Meldren had asked if they could have the pool to themselves for just this one day.

"But this isn't an ocean or river, Javin. It's just a pool. A place to swim and relax."

"See? Right there, that's the problem. Swimming. You go and swim, and I'll do the relaxing."

Meldren's smile widened. It felt good to be alone together again. The Sun was the right size, the colors were as they should be and there were insects flying around. She felt the right weight again and they had nobody to answer to. Nobody was counting on them, and she couldn't feel the pressure of lots of people around them. This was bliss. It was perfect, and the teasing was just the right way to celebrate that they could do whatever they pleased from now on. Assuming nobody on Haven did anything stupid, that is. They only had to please themselves.

"Across the water and back? That's it?" she asked.

"Yes. And together. I'm not doing this on my own so you can smirk at my lack of talent."

"Smirk? Me? I wouldn't know how to. I am above such things. An ambassador never smirks."

"Ex-ambassador."

"Whatever you say, my love."

"Don't try and be nice and distract me. I know you."

She was silent a moment, her eyes still bright with laughter. Then she frowned a little and tapped him on his shoulder, pointing off to one side. "Can you please check out the songs over there? I'm sure I heard something. Maybe it's someone coming."

He turned to listen, and she slipped off her clothes and dived in. He heard the splash, saw the clothes, saw her and wagged a finger at her. Moments later, he was splashing beside her.

There were a few happy squeals and much laughter. They were together. That was all she wanted from life.

And the Sun sang songs to all his brothers, and the songs spoke of the spread of Harmony.

ABOUT THE AUTHOR

Andrew Elgin grew up in England where he studied history and enjoyed philosophy and played with computers. The things about being human which couldn't be as easily explained, such as intuition, began to fascinate him more and more until, in the end, he decided to stop teaching and explored the ideas which attracted him more.

Whether in short stories, novels or nonfiction, Andrew seeks to make this 'other' aspect of being human the foundation of what he writes. He firmly believes that to become fully human is to discover and develop this hidden natural talent for 'knowing.' He seeks to entertain with his writing, but also to present an opportunity for you, the reader, to explore the undiscovered territory within you.

Andrew also writes nonfiction under his real name, Nigel Percy.

www.ingramcontent.com/pod-product-compliance
Lightning Source LLC
Chambersburg PA
CBHW070549260626
47161CB00002B/551